C0-AUG-470

A VERY SPECIAL AGENT

Geoffrey Napier

Funk & Wagnalls
New York

First Printing

Library of Congress Catalog Card Number: 67-25418

Published by Funk & Wagnalls, *A Division of* Reader's Digest Books, Inc.

Printed in the United States of America

[Their] system of spy training is the most thorough and detailed in the world. Nothing is left to chance. It covers a vast variety of subjects, from the techniques of photomicrography to that of physical seduction. It may seem unbelievable that they should go to the lengths of teaching their male spies the most effective methods of satisfying a woman, but there is no doubt about it. An ex-spy named Anatoli Granovsky, who defected to the West, has described the course of instruction in the subject that he underwent in an espionage school near Moscow.

—H. Montgomery Hyde,
The New York Times Magazine

A Very Special Agent

I

SHE AWOKE that morning at half past six with a remarkable sense of well-being. Not since her girlhood could she recall waking like this. She felt warm, she felt as if her skin were glowing from her head to her toes, she felt luxuriously content; she felt, indeed, as if she had been visited during the night by one of those Greek deities who habitually carried on their amours under cover of darkness and in strict anonymity. She had done nothing to encourage the visitation. It had come as an unsolicited gift, a bouquet of sensual pleasure.

And unlike other mornings, when she sprang out of bed as soon as her eyes opened, she lay for a while smiling, still half asleep, amused by this little outburst of sensuality, her knees drawn up, her arms pressed against her bosom, enjoying the delightful sensation of having been loved for hours without end. She was not a lustful woman. But it was such a novel experience to begin the day feeling as if young Eros had flown down to Gramercy Park to have his way with her—inflamed beyond endurance by her mortal beauty—that she was in no hurry to break the spell.

She thought drowsily, I daresay I had some silly dream. Yet, searching the dark regions of her mind, she could not find anything that might have induced her libidinous condition. The dream, if there really had been a dream, had vanished without leaving a trace; the amorous phantom who, unannounced, had invaded her privacy, would remain forever unknown. It was a pity. She mourned his departure. She wished she had caught just a glimpse of him.

Then, following a more pragmatic line of reasoning, she wondered if this unusual physical liveliness might not have a simpler explanation. Could it not be a sort of early warning signal, in anticipation of Burford coming to visit her tonight? She had not seen Burford for six weeks—he had been sick in Cambridge with some unspecified virus infection—and perhaps six weeks was too long for her to exist without him. She had developed a need for his attentions; and she thought, I daresay that's why there's so much excitement down in my subconscious: I am waiting for Burford as others waited for Godot.

Suddenly she was wide awake. She kicked off the blankets and rose, with only the slightest tremor in her limbs to remind her of what she had experienced and what she had not experienced last night.

2.

She took a bath and, wearing a wool robe and slippers, went to the kitchen, feeling her normal self-reliant self again, needing neither god nor man to provide her with sustenance or joy. She made a pot of coffee, carried it on a tray to her study, and shut the door. Nobody would disturb her, now, until she chose to open the door again. She switched on her electric typewriter, poured her first cup of coffee, and sat pondering what to write and to whom.

The study was a big, high-ceilinged room, littered with books and magazines. She sat at a fine old walnut desk which was covered with bric-a-brac, with photographs of her parents and the Southcliffe faculty, and with mementoes of her trips to Europe and South America. There was a black leather armchair for visitors, a black leather sofa for occasional self-analysis or a siesta and, near the window, a smaller desk for her secretary, Giselle Bonney. But nothing could hide the room's chief peculiarity—the impression, which grew slowly and surely in the consciousness of every beholder, that it had originally been an Egyptian tomb. In fact, the entire apartment had this strange Egyptian overlay. Somebody, years ago, must have spent a fortune here expressing his or her intoxication with the splendors and the mysteries of the Old and Middle Kingdoms; and despite the efforts of tenants who came later, despite all the rebuilding, all the renovations, all the repainting, a visitor was apt to feel that the Nile flowed nearby and there were pyramids at the bottom of the garden. It was extraordinary. Sphinx's paws peeped out from under radiators. Fat-bellied columns in the living room supported nothing in particular. Over the coal-burning fireplace there was a splendid bas-relief, copied, possibly, from some Theban temple, that included figures of Horus, the falcon-headed; Anubis, the jackal-headed; Sekhmet, the lioness-headed; Thoth, the dog-faced ape; and sundry vulture-goddesses, snake-goddesses, and cow-goddesses. In the bedroom, one might suddenly become aware of Osiris peering down from the lintel over the door; and Isis haunted the adjoining bathroom. They had been splashed with paint, they had been attacked with hammers and chisels and even baseball bats, several generations of bored children had adorned them with mustaches and beards, but they could not be obliterated. In time they always returned, seeping through the refurbished walls in the mysterious splendor of their whips and sceptres, their lotuses and their scarabs.

3.

She began to type even before she finished her first cup of coffee. These were her morning exercises: letters that would never be mailed—a flexing of muscles, a sharpening of teeth and claws, a limbering-up of her mind for the day to come.

Dear Father Justin:

Greetings. I pray that the sun shines upon you in Widdicomb as it shines upon your spiritual daughter in the park of Grand-Merci.

You ask in your sweet and gentle way how I am, and I must confess to you that I am well, although I stand in sin. I am in the pink, yet I am overflowing with guilt. I bloom, although my name must be a stink and a reproach in Heaven. Name a sin, Father, and five will get you ten that I have committed it. I am culpable on every count: pride, covetousness, lust, anger, gluttony, envy, sloth. Yet I see you smiling, as if you cannot conceive of me committing a sin of ample proportions. Just you wait, Father. I will get there, and you know where.

Dear Father Justin, sweet Father Justin, listen to my plea. I cannot, no, I cannot—at present, anyway—return to the fold. It is out of the question; I cannot even begin to contemplate it; and if I sound distraught and hysterical it is because I *am* distraught and hysterical to be replying to your gentle entreaty with such bluntness, such stubbornness. You may say, raising your eyebrows, that you did not ask me to return when you last communicated with me; and this is true. You did not, in so many words. But, Father, there was not a line you wrote that did not echo with urgency, Katherine, Katherine, Katherine Emory, Katherine love, return, return, come back to us, come back home where you belong. Every phrase of yours wrapped its arms around me and wrestled with me for the custody of my soul; and as a consequence I must stand up now, and say it aloud, and say it very firmly—I cannot, I cannot at present, return to the fold, return to where I yearn to return, return to where I belong, to the true Church of the true Christ. But for God's sake, do not cease to communicate with me, Father, do not cast me out, for I need your affection and your understanding as I need the oxygen in the air.

Father, let me tell you: I am alarmed by your beautiful church, by our beautiful church. I can imagine nothing more utterly blissful than to surrender myself wholly, in toto, lock, stock, and barrel, hook, line, and sinker, to the all-wise, all-compassionate, all-loving, universal Church of our Saviour, freeing myself once and for all of doubt, confusion, folly, and self-reproach; but it is not possible, it becomes less possible with every day that passes. The Church is too gorgeous, Father, too resplendent for me to bear. I think of Rome where—when I last saw it, and as I see it now, sitting in this sunless room—the shining glory knocked my eye out, blinded me with its razzle-dazzle, with its gilt and its marble, with its piazzas and palaces, with masterpieces piled upon masterpieces, loot from the pagan Greeks and Etruscans as well as loot squeezed out of Giotto and Leonardo and Michelangelo. Is this the church for me, Father, for Mrs. Corcoran, for all the little people who go bump in the night?

I hereby invent a new sin, Father: the sin of giantism. And another: the sin of flamboyance. And yet another, a violation of propriety that haunts my dreams: the sin of vestmentism. What, I beg of you, led to the astonishing compulsion to pile garment upon garment —amice, alb, cincture, maniple, stole, chasuble, cope, buskins, gloves, sandals, miter, pallium, mantelletta and rochet, mantellone and cassock, not to mention the succinctorium and fanon? Am I wholly in error to see in these three sins a stupendous form of acquisitiveness; a kind of Baalism, or worship of the Golden Calf; and a fetishism scarcely more sophisticated than that of the African equivalents of our bishops who, dear laughable creatures, adorn themselves with ostrich feathers, bangles, cats' teeth, and some daubs of paint before conducting a service?

Father, I am deathly serious about this. We must return to poverty. I agree with the good Camara: there is no place in our church for apostolic princes. Nor is it enough to give to the poor one tiara, retaining half a dozen. It is our special glory to walk in rags and sleep on beds of ashes. The Cross, so they taught me when I was a girl, was hewn of rough beams of wood, not of silver and gold like the pectorals our princes wear, and it is the symbol of ultimate cruelty, ultimate agony, divine martyrdom, not an elegant piece of costume jewelry. Those who wear it must earn the right to wear it, through tears and through prayer. It is not a thing to be flaunted as an advertisement of piety.

I *must* be wrong in all these things, Father, I *cannot* be right. Clarify my error, please, and pray for me.
Your daughter,

Katherine Millicent

This was an exercise in apostasy, exceedingly important to her but, in a sense, dangerous; and nobody—in particular, her secretary Giselle—could be permitted to see it. She put the typed pages inside a folder labeled *Fish Recipes* and locked it away in the bottom drawer of her desk, where it joined and supplemented *Pressure-Cooker Recipes* and *New England Recipes*—the three aspects of her private life.

The time was nearly nine o'clock. For another hour she worked on the manuscript of her new book, revising pages she had written last night. Then she stood up, yawned, stretched herself, and went out to the living room where Giselle was sitting in an armchair reading *The New York Times.*

"Ah, good morning," Giselle said, her eyes shining.

"Good morning. Is Mrs. Corcoran here?"

"Yes, she is. Crashing around in the kitchen as usual."

"Be an angel and tell her I would like my breakfast now."

"Certainly."

Giselle folded *The New York Times,* scrambled out of the armchair, and murmured, "Oh, bother," as one of her stockings splashed open at the knee. She was a gawky, pink-cheeked Southcliffe girl, with timid brown eyes, a high forehead, straight brown hair, and a large unruly bosom. Her manner of dress, in the best Southcliffe tradition, was generally so subdued that she was almost invisible. This morning she wore a brown tweed suit, a fawn cashmere sweater, pumps, and a single strand of pearls.

She returned from the kitchen after a few moments, her cheeks flushed, and following her, carrying a silver breakfast tray as Judith might have carried the head of Holofernes, came Mrs. Corcoran: tiny, sour-faced, ferocious, clothed entirely in black as if every day of the week were a day of affliction.

"Good morning, Mrs. Corcoran."

"Good morning, Miss Em."

The tray was put down on the marble-topped coffee table in front of the fireplace. Kate said, "Mrs. Corcoran, I have a guest coming for dinner tonight, and I would like you to do some shopping for me."

"A guest?" Mrs. Corcoran asked suspiciously. "It wouldn't be Mr. Griffiths coming down from Cambridge, would it?"

"Yes."

"And about time," Mrs. Corcoran said, with a sniff. "So you'll be wanting a nice thick porterhouse steak. French fries? Brussel sprouts?"

"Just a steak and salad."

"And how about something to wash the steak down with?"

Kate said, "Giselle will have a word with the man at the liquor store—"

"He would drop dead of shock," Mrs. Corcoran said. "*I* will speak to the man at the liquor store, seeing that he happens to be a special friend of mine—"

"He has been taking advantage of your friendship," Kate said firmly. "That is why I want Giselle to look after the wine and liquor from now on. A good burgundy, Giselle. And I believe we may need some more cognac."

"I will check it," Giselle said.

Mrs. Corcoran stormed out of the living room white with rage.

Kate said to Giselle with a sigh, "Mrs. Corcoran can be slightly difficult sometimes, I'm afraid." She glanced at her watch. "Oh, my God, look at the time. I have to be at the beauty parlor at eleven o'clock. Giselle, sit down and talk to me while I have my breakfast."

4.

She had a busy day ahead of her. After the beauty parlor, she had a luncheon date with Mr. Gamage to discuss her trip to the Far East; then a portrait sitting with Marcel Preiss; then, if she could fit it in, there was an opening at the DeLanney Gallery; then a cocktail party, given by her publisher; and finally, at six-thirty, Burford was due to arrive at the apartment.

"I shan't see you again today," Giselle said disconsolately.

"Why do I let myself get so involved?" Kate asked. "But

don't worry, I'm leaving you plenty to do. You'll be too busy to miss me. There are about twenty pages of manuscript to be retyped. And I want you to get me the latest figures on abortions and miscarriages, from the beginning of the century, if possible, year by year and state by state—"

"Are there official figures on abortions?" Giselle asked.

"There must be. If necessary, call Dr. Montagu: he would know. And then—"

On and on went the instructions. They all had to do with Kate's new book, *The Women of America,* which Craven Press hoped to publish early in the new year. But there was still more, related to other projects. "And get from Brentano's," Kate continued, "Edward's new novel, and Wilson's *The Lame and the Halt,* and George Tuckaway's *Prospective Perspectives,* and Sir Charles Sleet's new book, *Enzymes and Society*—"

"Yes," Giselle said, scribbling frantically in her notebook, "Yes. Yes—but you don't want these delivered today, do you?"

"Why not?"

"You won't read them *tonight,*" Giselle said, and suddenly stopped, her hand over her heart.

Kate went on calmly, "And keep an eye on Mrs. Corcoran. Be very firm with her. Don't let her fill the apartment with those monstrous white chrysanthemums she's so crazy about."

"I'll do my best," Giselle said.

Kate said, "Thank you. You really are a great help. I don't know what I would do without you."

Giselle blushed.

5.

At last she was ready to leave, dressed in the black suit she had worn for her other sittings with Marcel, and when she had said good-by to Giselle and Mrs. Corcoran, she stepped out into the October sunshine that poured down on Gramercy Park, and, like a signal from Heaven, she felt a warm flood of joy stream over her body. She felt slim and young and vigorous; she felt beautiful; and even though she was fully aware that in truth she was not particularly slim, and not really young, and by no means beautiful, yet—for once—the truth was of no significance; what alone mattered was the subjective sensation. "But this," she scolded herself, "is sheer Kierkegaardism," and this, too, had no significance; the sense of joy flooding her was paramount. She decided to walk to the beauty parlor, and strode into the golden light as if she were entering a glistening avenue that led directly to Paradise; and she wondered happily, Why am I like this, why am I so elated? Because I woke this morning feeling loved? And why, pray, was that? Was it because some hormone had carried out its task too effectively (a messenger of the gods), because some remote gland was overstimulated? She didn't know, she would never know, and it did not matter.

Romeo himself, of Romeo's Beauty Balcony, wrinkled his perfect aquiline nose at her in welcome. "Ah!" he murmured, "Do my eyes deceive me, or do you look utterly *ravissant* today? *You* do not need *us,* dear Miss Emory. *We* need *you.*" She was pleased by his faëry humor; it confirmed, precisely at the right moment, the reality of the sensations she had been experiencing. "Eric will take you, personally," he said, using an impersonal idiom; and he called out in a high, sweet, birdlike voice, "Eric, Eric, here is Miss Emory. For you, Eric." And moving swiftly, like the gloriously evil hero of a quite incomprehensible Italian movie, Eric pranced forward and received her from Romeo as if she were precious beyond words, a jeweled treasure entrusted to him by his master. "How nice," Eric murmured, "how divine, Miss Emory, I so enjoy—" leaving it to her to complete his greeting in any way she chose. She always felt extraordinarily safe with him. He was tall, young, virile, broad-shouldered, handsome, golden, and he could do nothing wrong—nothing to arouse her, nothing to embarrass her. She sat in a mildly dizzy state as his hands moved deftly over her head, and she could not help wondering why those hands were so sexless, lacking the power to move her in any way. They were such beautiful hands—why did they communicate nothing more than a sort of despairing servility? Burford's hands, which would be touching her hair tonight, were not in any way beautiful; they were heavy and stubby-fingered, and they always carried a trace of iodoform, or formalin, or whatever he had recently been using in his laboratory; but they communicated an inescapable sense of masculinity. She thought, My God, I'm looking forward to seeing him so much, so much, I haven't seen him for so long. And then, to Eric's astonishment, she began to giggle. "What is it?" Eric pleaded. "Tell me the joke, Miss Emory." But she could not possibly tell him the joke. It was far too private. Dear Burford. He was so masculine, so insensitive, so male—all that Eric could never hope to be; and when he made love he behaved just like a dog burying a bone, grunting, snuffling, scratching away like an elderly terrier. *And that,* she thought, *is what I am looking forward so impatiently to tonight, the ceremony of the burying of the bone, that is why I am so elated. Really* (she thought) *it's hilarious, it makes no sense.*

2

MR. GAMAGE, Philip Converse Gamage of the Department of State, was the tallest man Kate had ever known. He was about six feet eight, and he looked like some curious biped that had survived from prehistoric times, unchanged, solitary, and, under its armored hide, exceedingly fragile. He had a small face with a beaky nose, which seemed appropriate at the top of such an elongated body; his shoulders were narrow, his arms were short and crooked, and his legs were thin and disjointed, terminating in large flat feet.

She found, after her first meeting with him about a month ago, that he was a charming and sensible man, and she had developed a liking for him. The gloomy expression, the rather alarming globular eyes, masked a kindly disposition. He was married to a pretty Belgian girl named Frederica who appeared from her photographs to be about half his height; and he had one child, a daughter named Babette who looked as if she might grow to be even taller than papa.

He was waiting at Charlot's, suffering agonies from the compression of his legs under the table. He stood up, smiling, wincing, smiling, wincing, and Kate thought in pity, The waiter ought to bring him a eucalyptus tree to browse on, or something equally delectable, so that he could remain standing throughout lunch. With him were her literary representative, Rushton Wyle, rugged, belligerent, and slightly apoplectic; and a Japanese woman named Miss

Mitsamushi, who wore a gray flannel dress and seemed to have difficulty catching her breath. She was about thirty years old, small, pale, very intense; and whenever she joined in the conversation she spoke rapidly, in a muffled voice, so that Kate sometimes had little or no idea what she was trying to express.

"Drink, Kate?" Rushton asked when she was seated.

"Not at the moment, thank you." She was still elated, still joyous, and she had no desire for liquor.

"Sure?" Rushton said, unable to understand why anybody should pass up a drink.

She nodded.

He eyed her in an amused way and said, "Kate, I have to tell you, you look younger every time I see you. Isn't that right, Mr. Gamage?"

Gamage smiled gravely, and did not comment. Kate said, "That's nice, Rushton," and wondered, as she had frequently wondered in the past, why she had ever allied herself with this man. He was a fearful snob; he worked only with writers of the highest caliber; yet there were times when he gave the impression that he had never learned to read. She suspected that he was bisexual—a woman-chaser when he was sober (although he had never chased her), a chaser of boys when he was drunk. What counted, however, was that drunk or sober he exerted himself on her behalf with great energy; and he protected her, on the whole successfully, from the undesirable pressures of the outside world.

The purpose of this luncheon, as it had been expressed in a memorandum by Mr. Gamage, was to discuss and finalize plans for the trip by Miss Katherine M. Emory to Japan and territories adjacent thereto under the auspices of the State Department. A contract had been drawn up, and what remained was merely the discussion of a few details that needed clarification. But such serious matters could be left until coffee was served, and for half an hour they chatted at random in a pleasant, civilized way. Rushton told anecdotes of the world of publishing and the world of the theater; his pockmarked face became tense as he spoke, his eyes lit up, and Kate disliked him less than usual, valued him a little more, because of his passion for the word, printed, and the word, spoken. Mr. Gamage, a good civil servant, contented himself with telling stories of his daughter Babette. Miss Mitsamushi sat listening intently, giving Kate enigmatic glances, sometimes tearful, sometimes gay.

At last, with the pouring of coffee, Mr. Gamage led cautiously into the subject of Kate's trip. He began, "Miss Emory, may we—?" and paused, favoring her with a sweet primeval smile. She smiled at him in return, and he continued, "Well, now: I am happy to report that there is considerable gratification, both in my department in Washington and in appropriate quarters in Tokyo and elsewhere, about our forthcoming venture. Indeed, I was discussing it only yesterday with the Assistant Secretary, and he, I am glad to say, expressed his wholehearted approval. In fact, he asked me to tell you, Miss Emory, that he would very much like to have the pleasure of meeting you before you set off on your travels in December."

"Thank you," Kate said. "I would consider it a privilege to meet the Assistant Secretary."

"Charming man," Miss Mitsamushi said confidentially.

"Really?"

"Oh, yes. A most cultured person. Oh, oh, oh, I love the State Department. Everyone is so charming and cultured."

Mr. Gamage cleared his throat and resumed his little speech. "I hope, Miss Emory, that you and Mr. Wyle have had an opportunity to read and discuss the contract I sent you? And that you found it satisfactory?"

Kate said, "Yes. I signed the three copies yesterday afternoon."

"Splendid," Mr. Gamage said. "Splendid."

"I," Rushton said, "practically went down on my knees, begging her not to sign them."

Mr. Gamage looked pained. "I'm sorry to hear that."

"I pointed out," Rushton said with deep bitterness, "that she was putting herself totally at your disposal for a period of six months, and for what? A pittance. Literally, a pittance. I'm ready to bet that you pay your coolies more than you are paying Miss Emory."

"I am not sure you are right," Mr. Gamage said. "I can check the current scale for coolies and let you know."

"Very funny," Rushton said. "But just look at her itinerary. First, the University of Tokyo. Then, Yokohama, Kyoto, Hiroshima, Nagasaki; then Taipei, Seoul—"

"Seoul comes before Taipei, I believe," Mr. Gamage said.

Rushton said, "Okay, okay. But I want to go on record as saying that I object strenuously to this itinerary. You are asking too damned much of Miss Emory."

"Do you think so, Miss Emory?" Mr. Gamage asked.

"Let me speak on her behalf," Rushton said. "Six months is too long for Miss Emory to be away from the United States. She has a big book coming out in February, *Tempo* is planning a cover story on her, the television networks and the women's clubs will all be screaming for her, and where will she be? Hiding her light under a bushel in Yokohama, for God's sake. It's ridiculous."

Kate, with unusual placidity, allowed the wrangling to go on. It was Rushton's role in life to start a war at every possible opportunity, galloping into the fray shouting the name of some client, brandishing his two-handed sword lustily in an attempt to gain a few extra dollars, a few extra concessions, from his enemy; and it was Mr. Gamage's role to obtain talent of various kinds at bargain prices and to defend his departmental budget with his last ounce of strength and his last drop of blood. Mr. Gamage would win, of course, for the simple reason that he could not possibly lose; and Rushton would lose for the simple reason that he could not possibly win against such a Herculean opponent. He really didn't mind losing. It was the fight itself that mattered, the blood on his sword, the noise of battle.

The outcome of the argument, in any case, could alter nothing as far as Kate was concerned. She was fully committed to this trip. She could imagine nothing more soothing to her nerves than to be six thousand miles from new York when Craven Press published *The Women of America.* She was thrilled beyond words at the prospect of visiting Japan and various other parts of the Far East under the wing of the State Department. She could hardly wait for this marvelous holiday to begin. She had already made an outline of the lectures she planned to give in Tokyo: she intended to discuss some of the lesser-known American writers. But at the same time, she hoped to gather material for a companion volume to *The Women of America.* It would be an examination in depth of the women of the Far East: the unknown women of Japan who (like Miss Mitsamushi?) were at last emerging from a history of total servitude that (until those bombs fell) must have seemed eternal and unalterable; the women of Korea, of Formosa, of the Philippines, who were—what? She was yearning to find out, to talk to them, to hear the tales they had to tell. In many ways it was a more exciting project than the one she was just completing; it was fresh, it had the attraction of an exotic background, and she would be given an opportunity to acquire a vast store of new knowledge—knowledge of people, of painting and sculpture and music, of books, of ideas, all entirely different from anything she had encountered so far. Glorious, glorious. She could ask in this world for nothing more.

2.

Rushton left at two o'clock. He was due at a conference, he informed Mr. Gamage, with an author who had written a play which was so successful that the unfortunate man was now faced with an almost insurmountable tax problem. "Can I tell him," Rushton asked, "that the money the government is trying to squeeze out of him will help to finance Kate's trip?"

"We already have the money in our budget for Miss Emory's trip," Gamage answered blandly. "But if you think it might cheer him up, by all means assure him that his taxes will be used in some equally worthy cause."

A few minutes later, Miss Mitsamushi rose and breathlessly excused herself. She had an appointment at the Asia Club, she explained to Kate, with a group of dental, or mental, specialists—Kate could not be sure which. But it was more likely (Kate thought) that some arrangement had been made beforehand whereby Miss Mitsamushi would make her exit as a certain point, leaving Kate and Mr. Gamage alone.

"What a nice person she is," Kate said dutifully when Miss Mitsamushi had gone. "Does she work for you in Washington?"

"Not exactly," Gamage answered. "We call on her services whenever necessary." He glanced at Kate with interest. "I'm glad you liked her."

"I liked what I saw of her. Unfortunately, I didn't have a chance to speak to her at any length. Perhaps I'll have an opportunity to meet her again soon."

Gamage said unexpectedly, "She's just finishing a thesis on *hogaku*."

"Really? How exciting! And who, or what, is *hogaku?*"

"I understand it's the folk-music that's played at open-air

festivals in Japan." Gamage paused, and then went on, "She's also a very competent interpreter and translator. She types. She can take dictation in Japanese, English, German. And she knows a great deal about audio-visual devices, films, tape recorders, closed-circuit television, and similar aids to education."

"She's a paragon. You must find her absolutely invaluable."

"We do," Gamage said. "Would you care for more coffee?"

"No, thank you."

"Brandy?"

Kate shook her head.

"A cigarette?" Gamage held out a pack of Kents.

"I don't smoke."

"Of course. Excuse me." Gamage put the pack down on the table and stared at it for a few moments. He seemed uneasy, and Kate wondered what was troubling him. Then, once again to her surprise, he said, "Incidentally, Miss Mitsamushi is a great admirer of your work."

"Oh?"

"She has told me so on several occasions. She was thrilled when I suggested that she join us for lunch. I'm sure she would have expressed all this to you herself but, as you may have noticed, she is rather shy." Gamage paused, and then went on, "What is more, her brother has a great admiration for your work, too."

"I seem to have made a hit with the Mitsamushi family. Do they all live in Washington?"

"No. The brother is in Tokyo. A brilliant young man. Apparently he organizes many of the anti-American student demonstrations at the University."

Kate laughed. "And he admires my work?"

"Very much so. As a matter of fact, Miss Mitsamushi has just returned from visiting her family in Japan, and she told me—confidentially, you know—that her brother is rather disturbed at the present time. He finds himself in an unhappy situation. On the one hand he's a fervent pacifist and, as I just indicated, passionately anti-American because of—among other things—our role in Vietnam. But on the other hand he's fully aware that if American influence wanes in Asia his country will be exposed to a deadly threat not only from its extreme left wing but from the even more dangerous and irresponsible Chinese communists. The same problem is troubling many Japanese today. They are a highly intelligent people." Gamage paused to stub out his cigarette. "Miss Mitsamushi told me that when she saw her brother in Tokyo she happened to mention your forthcoming visit, and he expressed a wish to meet you because of his very high regard for your liberal position. Would you be at all interested in having a chat with the young man?"

Kate stared at Gamage. His face was blank. She said, "I think it might be very interesting indeed." Then, choosing her words with care, she added, "However, I understood that I was going to Japan to give a series of lectures. Aren't you now suggesting something rather different?"

"Not really. We aren't asking you to carry out anything in the nature of a secret mission." He gave a bleak laugh. "That, in any case, would be up to the Central Intelligence Agency, and after the trouble they've had lately I suspect they'd think twice before they approached you."

"Mr. Gamage," Kate said patiently, "precisely *what* are you suggesting?"

"Merely that in the course of your lecture tour you would be doing a very great service to everybody concerned if you were to talk to young people like Jiro Mitsamushi whenever such meetings can be arranged." His voice was low, his eyes gleamed with candor. "It is difficult for us to reach them. Officially, we are their prime enemies. But you could move among them as a friend, as a mediator between our two camps. I am sure this would provide you with all sorts of interesting insights into the oriental mind, and it would be valuable to us, inasmuch as it might enable us to improve our relationship with the Japanese people."

"Does young Mr. Mitsamushi speak English?"

"I am not sure. You see, the Japanese learn to read and write English in school, but not how to converse in it."

"I will be glad to do anything I can to improve our relationship with the Japanese people," Kate said, smiling at him. "There is just one difficulty. I am pretty fluent in Latin; I speak French, German, and Spanish; but my Japanese is nonexistent. Outside a lecture hall I would have a hopeless problem in communication."

Gamage replied, as if he were producing a white rabbit out of an invisible hat, "Ah-hah! You see? That's exactly where Miss Mitsamushi fits in."

"Does she, Mr. Gamage? How?"

"We could arrange for her to accompany you on your tour."

Kate's heart sank. "Miss Mitsamushi? For six months?"

"Why not? She would be delighted to accompany you. Actually, it was suggested by the Assistant Secretary himself. She could open all doors for you." His voice fell almost to a whisper. "I can't guarantee it, I can only hint at it as a remote possibility, but she might even be able to put you in touch with some admirers of yours on the Chinese mainland. Don't ask me *how*. She has her fingers in all sorts of pies."

"You mean, Red Chinese?"

"Exactly. She is a very remarkable young lady. Perhaps in the course of the next day or two, before she returns to Washington, you might find time to have a little chat with her?"

It was a request that Kate could not ignore. She opened

her purse and glanced through the small diary she carried. "Tomorrow? At five o'clock? For cocktails?"

"She doesn't drink anything alcoholic."

"For tea, then."

"Good, good. May I tell her to call you to confirm the arrangements?"

"Yes. She can call me in the morning between ten and twelve."

"Fine. And I believe she has some papers with her that you may find interesting," Gamage said. "They bear on the subjects we've been discussing—anti-American groups, and so on." He gave Kate an apologetic look: "Of course, I can rely on you to treat all this as confidential. I need hardly say—"

"Oh, of course," Kate said. She felt a pang of pity for him. Like all State Department officials he was obsessed by fears of security leaks. *I'm not going to proclaim from the rooftops that Miss Mitsamushi is coming to tea with me tomorrow,* she thought, *so don't worry, my dear dinosaur.* She glanced at her wristwatch. "My God, I'm late for my next appointment, I have to fly. Will you excuse me?"

"I have a car outside," Gamage said. "Double-parked, if I know my driver. We will be happy to take you wherever you wish to go, at the taxpayer's expense."

"It's only to Central Park South," Kate said.

"Nothing could be simpler. Just let me get the check."

3.

She was of two minds as she drove with him to Marcel Preiss' studio. She was dismayed at the prospect of having the not very appealing Miss Mitsamushi, like an albatross, around her neck for six long months; at the same time she was intrigued by the possibilities that Mr. Gamage had hinted at so cautiously. She suspected that he and the Assistant Secretary were planning something rather more significant than merely carrying message of good will to the unruly youth of Tokyo and the other cities on her itinerary. Whether she would ultimately approve of the plans had yet to be seen; and there was always the chance that, in any case, nothing would come of them, they would prove to be a false alarm.

She left him, with a firm and friendly handshake, outside Marcel's apartment house, walked into the building, took the elevator to the top floor, and rang the bell of Marcel's studio. Nothing happened until the moment when her patience ran out and she was about to ring the bell for the second time. Then the peephole in the middle of the broad, faded-green door opened surreptitiously, a monstrous eye peered out at her through the circle of tarnished glass and, at last, the door swung open and Marcel held his arms out to her joyously. "Katterin! I was expecting you! Darling!"

"Were you really expecting me? You were such a long time opening the door."

"To be truthful, I expected you to be somebody else—my best friend, whom I do not wish to see at the moment. Come in, come in, we are making a draft, Andrea will catch cold."

"Who?"

"Andrea. The girl friend of this person I just mentioned to you."

Kate entered, and he closed the door and embraced her carefully, kissing her on both cheeks. "Your odor is delicious, maddening," he said in courteous tones, and led her inside. The studio was vast, littered with furniture, paintings, easels, magazines; and in an area that had been cleared for work, a girl sat nude, holding a red velvet cushion to her bosom. Marcel said, "Katterin, permit me to present to you the lovely Andrea Moscowitz. Andrea, the celebrated Katterin Emory."

"Hi," said Andrea.

"Hello," said Kate.

"Andrea, I have finished with you for today, to my profound regret," Marcel said. He slipped a white silk robe over the girl's shoulders in a gesture that was strangely tender and sentimental, and then, as she stood up, he cried, "Wait! Wait!" He turned and spoke to Kate, his eyes gleaming. "Katterin, will you pose with Andrea for me? We will make a beautiful picture together, The Two Graces, or The Two Muses—you can think up a good title for me later. Quick. Get out of your clothes."

Kate laughed, and shook her head.

"No?" he said. "You are shy? Really? At your age? How charming." He said to the girl, "Go, my dove. Katterin will not cooperate, she is too strait-laced." The girl hurried up a spiral staircase that led to a dressing room, and Marcel said to Kate, "Make yourself comfortable, darling, we will begin in a minute or two, let me just catch my breath and adjust my mood."

He was an elegant man, still lean, still vigorous, wearing under his white smock a beautifully cut gray suit, a silk shirt, and a pearl-gray tie. His socks were of gray silk, his shoes were black patent leather. Kate had known him for many years, long before he had been commissioned to do her portrait, and she could not remember him ever looking different from the way he looked now—lean and vigorous, tanned, distinguished, a trifle arrogant and a trifle overdressed. He must have been sensationally handsome in his younger days, a formidable ladies' man when being a ladies' man was a way of life, and she wished that she had known him then— not to experience the delights he had to offer, but simply to observe him operating at his peak form. The tradition had become passé, like the tradition of stage-door Johnnies and Viennese cavalry officers. It was a pity. She regretted missing that whipped-cream era, just as she regretted missing the Victorian era and, to a lesser extent, the Georgian era.

"May I look?" she said to Marcel as he took the sketch of Andrea off the easel. "Of course," he said, and put it back. He stood staring at it critically, one hand on Kate's shoulder.

It was very good, Kate thought, in its own terms: smooth, clever, highly professional. One could easily identify the influences showing through these two hundred and fifty square inches of sticky paint—Derain, Renoir, Degas, Pissaro, and, like the echo of a distant bell, Botticelli, of all people. They blended satisfactorily. The girl sat there, thickset, healthy, glowing, and she was emphatically a girl, most femalely female.

"The breasts are not right," Marcel said fretfully. "But what do you expect, what could I *do* with her breasts? They are like bricks. Ah, the hell with the women of this new generation. Their breasts are all wrong, something must have happened, they are all mutations." His hand rested a little more heavily on her shoulder. "Except yours, darling. You have splendid old-fashioned breasts. It is a pleasure to have them in the house."

"Thank you, Marcel. You always say the nicest things."

"Have I offended you?"

"Of course not. You wouldn't try to offend me, would you?"

He chuckled. "It is unthinkable." But she had hit the nail on the head. He tried constantly to penetrate her reserve with off-color remarks. She had learned to tolerate it as a game, a form of amusement appropriate to his age, just as when she was in Italy she forced herself to tolerate the imbeciles who occasionally succeeded in pinching her bottom.

The direction of the conversation should be changed, she thought, and she said, indicating the sketch, "Is she really the girl friend of your best friend?"

"Ah," he said, "I did not express myself with absolute accuracy. Yes, she is the girl friend of my best friend, but to do him justice I must add that he has a considerable number of girl friends, among whom she ranks number six, or number seven. But if I had said so she might have overheard me, and been offended."

"Yes," Kate said. "I can understand your delicacy."

"You must meet him. I will arrange a meeting."

"How kind of you. Don't go to too much trouble though. I can wait."

"Nothing I can do for you is too much trouble, darling. Everything is a pleasure."

Andrea came swiftly down the spiral staircase, dressed in a black sweater, a black skirt, black stockings, and black sneakers. There were a few moments of confusion as she departed; she kissed Marcel, smiled brightly at Kate, dropped her handbag, and finally fled, stiff-legged and flat-footed. Marcel said querulously, "Did you observe her? She is a dancer, one of these dancers in the new school of ballet where all the choreography seems to be arranged for a chessboard. That is why her thighs and her breasts are wrong: everything on her is turning into cubes."

"Still, she's very attractive. And you're making a lovely picture of her."

"Another nude. Just another nude." He took the picture off the easel, scowled at it, and said, "Seriously, you must pose for me soon. I am running out of models. The situation is becoming alarming." He carried the canvas across the studio, crouched down and slid it into a wooden rack. Without moving, he called, "Katterin, come here. I want to show you something interesting."

When she joined him he said, "Look." She crouched down beside him, wondering what he was showing her.

"Here," he said, and pulled several canvases halfway out of the rack, all the same size as the one he had put away. Each painting was of a nude, and each was a different girl.

"Well?" he said, challenging her.

"They're beautiful, Marcel."

"Wouldn't you like to join my collection?"

"Oh, Marcel, you're teasing me. I'm much too old for that sort of thing."

"Here," he said, pulling out more and more of the canvases. "Would you be surprised if I told you I have hundreds of them?"

She stood up. "Why should I be surprised?"

She thought she could hear his elegant bones creak as he straightened his body. He said, "Do you know about the lions of the great Japanese artist, Hokusai?"

"No."

"You are undoubtedly aware that there are no lions in China and Japan, so the people of these countries very sensibly invented their own lions, far superior to our lions, which are only a species of overgrown cat. The Chinese lion is a gay and fabulous animal. It is usually colored a glorious turquoise, it has fantastic fur with beautiful curls, all its teeth are curved like fangs, and its eyes—as the Chinese poet says—are like bended bows that flash like lightning."

"When I am in the Far East," Kate said, "I will look out for one."

"They come only in pairs, darling. You see them outside temples and palaces, and they guard the graves of important dignitaries."

"How fascinating!" Kate said. "And they aren't unlike the lions of Greek and Egyptian mythology. The lion, as you pointed out, is chthonian—"

"I did not point out any such thing," he said, affronted.

"He is, though. A pair of lions draw the chariot of the

mother-goddess Cybele. And the goddess Sekhmet is often represented with the head of a lioness—"

"Katterin!"

She said penitently, "Oh, I'm sorry."

"Every morning," Marcel said, "for the last seven years of his life, Hokusai performed what he called an exorcism before he started his work. He drew a magic lion, different each time from the magic lion of the day before. And this lion had the task of driving away all the evil spirits that had been plotting to attack Hokusai on that particular day. With its sharp teeth and claws the magic lion would spring upon Hokusai's enemies and tear them into small pieces."

"Oh," she said, the perfect listener to an aging man's stories, "that's charming."

"So, every day, I paint a new girl. Or, rather, as often as I can find one. They are essentially the same as Hokusai's lions: they are my daily offering to the gods to keep me young, to ward off the evil spirits that are lying in wait for me. But do you know what? I suspect that the gods are trying to drive me mad before they destroy me, because all I can find to pose for me now are these bloody women with square breasts who give me the pip."

4.

This was to be her third and final sitting for the portrait. Generally he required no more than one, when he made impressive passes over the canvas with a large brush and took a number of snapshots from which he could do all his work later, at his leisure. He preferred to work from photographs: they did not change position, they did not smell of gin, they did not have to go to the bathroom at critical moments. But somehow or other the authorities at Southcliffe had learned that the portrait had been commissioned by

Tempo, and they had obtained permission to exhibit the picture, after its publication, in Southcliffe's Great Hall where it would join the gallery of distinguished alumnae who, not so very long ago, had stared down at Kate from their heavy gold frames in singularly grim and graceless disapproval. Southcliffe was proud of the multitude of Southcliffe girls who had achieved renown in Southcliffe's particular tradition—a striking and unique combination of intellectual snobbery, social awareness, and religious fervor. Some had gone on to guide the destinies of other great colleges; some had made their mark in medicine, in law, even in literature; some had traveled to distant jungles, alas, to feed the godless savage; but until now none had been chosen to decorate the cover of *Tempo,* and it was an occasion that Southcliffe could hardly ignore. In turn, Marcel was affected. He was devoting three times more effort to this portrait than usual, and scarcely using photographs at all.

She enjoyed sitting for him. He was not demanding, and once he had settled down to work he did not exhaust her with trivial conversation. She reflected on his nudes, and decided that they were not very different from her early-morning correspondence with Father Justin, Millicent Donothing, and the rest. Gradually she drifted into a long, lazy, highly pleasurable daydream, and Marcel's occasional requests—*Raise your head, darling; tilt your chin*—were just enough to keep her from floating away from him altogether in a hypnotic trance. After she had posed for half an hour he called a few minutes' break, and she then found herself strangely disoriented, as if she had been revolving at high speed in a Baranyi chair which had come to a sudden stop: a medley of thought-fragments continued to spin and tumble through her mind, and she felt decidedly shaky. But when Marcel resumed work, the process of free association became fixed: thoughts and images were all centered on

Burford, her lover and her friend, and she responded to Marcel through some extension of her consciousness that operated by itself and left the major centers of thought at liberty to roam on without interruption.

He must have left Cambridge hours ago, no matter how he was coming, by plane or by train. How nice he looked in a jet plane: sturdy, reliable, intelligent, exactly what he was —unpretentiously masculine. Airline stewardesses were always drawn to him, but then, so were train conductors. How nice he looked in a train reading (and disagreeing with) Jacquetta Hawkes or Carleton S. Coon; how nice he looked at all times, even asleep in bed, snoring gently, his gray hair ruffled.

It's absurd, she laughed to herself, *it's admittedly absurd that I should be so excited about seeing him. But six weeks is a long time to be alone, untouched; my juices need to be renewed, I am drying up. Even more* (she thought), *one needs—one craves—the smiles, the laughter, the sheer sunniness of intimacy, the grotesqueries that are so treasured.* This, more than anything else, was what her marriage had lacked. She preferred not to think of her marriage, which had opened and closed in three fantastically long and terrifying weeks when she was virtually still an infant, twenty-two years old, fresh out of Southcliffe and anybody's prey. In retrospect, the ugliness might have been tolerable if there had only been some accompanying flashes of gaiety; but there was little more than huge, heaving, quarterback's haunches and bitter accusations of frigidity, and pain, intense pain, physical pain and psychic pain, and disgust. Occasionally, in later years, she found herself pitying the wretched youth who had fallen into this appalling misadventure with her; perhaps *he* had expected a few flashes of *his* brand of gaiety, which she was totally unable to provide; perhaps in *his* eyes there was nothing more to the episode than a pale immature bosom and long white skinny legs that were as unwelcoming as a pair of broomsticks.

There had been lovers over the years: an Englishman in Paris, a Norwegian in Rome, an Italian in Dublin. But, over the years. At long intervals. Sex was not a powerful force in her life. She could live happily without men collecting their alleged dues, night after night, from her unappreciative body. A man now and then, every year or two, fitted into her scheme of things, giving her the assurance that she was a normal woman (or normal enough) and providing a few hours of pleasant excitement. That, at least, had been the schedule until she met Burford at an international congress in London, and there, influenced by his solid masculinity and his scholarly discourses on Dart and *Australopithecus,* a new timetable for love was established, based on a hitherto unheard-of weekly schedule. She was deeply alarmed at first. She felt as if she had unexpectedly become addicted to a drug which at no time in the past had exhibited any signs of being habit-forming. But that, she was forced to admit to herself, was the way with drugs; they rarely exhibited signs that they were insinuating themselves into one's system; and she was now hooked on Burford (not really in love with him, just hooked), a fate which she accepted, on the whole, contentedly.

5.

"A thousand devils," Marcel exclaimed, breaking into her reverie and speaking like a character in *The Three Musketeers*: "He has arrived."

Kate, startled by his emphatic manner, cried, "Who, *who* has arrived?"

"Stefan," Marcel said, and hurried out of the studio, leaving her palpitating and bewildered, as if she had been awakened abruptly from a deep sleep. Evidently the doorbell had rung while she was dreaming of Burford, and she had not heard it.

He returned a moment later with a tall, slim, suntanned man wearing a well-cut dark suit, a dazzlingly white shirt, and a black tie with narrow diagonal red stripes. Kate had never seen him in the studio before. "Darling, you must excuse this interruption in our work," Marcel said to her, glancing across at the newcomer with a kind of indulgent affection. "But here is the friend I was mentioning to you earlier. Permit me to present Mr. Stefan Gerhardi. Stefan, I have the honor to introduce Miss Katterin Emory."

Kate's first thought was, *It doesn't surprise me that he has a whole slew of mistresses. A couple of dozen, at the very least.* He was handsome and masculine. His eyes were a lively blue—the color intensified, no doubt, by his suntan. The bones of his face were strong and aristocratic, the muscles of expression around his wide mouth were deeply marked, the flesh of his cheeks hollow, his chin well-proportioned and set off by a not-too-prominent dimple. His hair was thick, but cut short so that it was crisp and curly, and it was flecked with gray at the sides. There was something vaguely military about him: his movements were controlled, precise, graceful, and he was obviously in splendid physical condition.

"How do you do?" Kate said politely.

He bowed, took her hand lightly, and raised it to his lips. "*Madame,*" he murmured, "*enchanté,*" and then stepped back a pace, gazing at her with interest. He had mastered the trick of elevating one eyebrow. "Miss Katherine Emory?" he repeated, and turned to Marcel for confirmation. "The author? Of so many renowned books? Really?"

"Really," Marcel mocked.

"I would be telling an untruth if I told you I had read them all," the handsome man said, turning back to Kate.

"My duties allow me little time for such pleasures. Let me say, however, that it is a tremendous honor to meet you, Madame."

"Thank you," Kate said.

"But no, no," he exclaimed, turning once more to Marcel. "You are putting me on, my dear chap. This lady is too young, too attractive to be *that* Miss Katherine Emory—"

"I assure you," Marcel said, "they are one and the same. The lovely Miss Emory and the brainy Miss Emory. Quite a combination, are they not, Stefan?"

Kate burst out laughing.

"And, as you can observe, she is even prettier when she laughs," Marcel said. "Now, tell me, Stefan: to what do I owe the pleasure of this visit? Why are you not toiling by the sweat of your brow like everyone else, you scoundrel?"

"I am looking for Andrea," Stefan replied. "I had the impression she was here with you." He could hardly take his eyes off Kate.

Marcel said, "Andrea? *Andrea?* You mean, that girl—what is her name?" He snapped his fingers in the air. "Andrea Moscowitz! Is that the Andrea you mean? The ballet dancer, daughter of the rich building contractor?"

"The same."

"Why should she be *here?*" Marcel demanded. "What makes you come *here* looking for this Andrea?"

Stefan said, "It was my impression that she was posing for you today, in the nude."

Marcel cried excitedly, "How can she be posing for me in the nude? Look around you! Do you see any naked girl posing for me? No! Any nitwit can see that only one person is posing for me, the beautiful Katterin Emory, and she, unfortunately, is attired in all her clothes."

Kate was confused by this badinage. It was very European, she supposed, but even so, wasn't it rather childish? She hesitated to make a judgment. They came from societies with which she was not entirely familiar, Marcel from Alsace, Stefan Gerhardi from a country she had not yet identified. Perhaps this was how grown men, in their own surroundings, always comported themselves.

Stefan said, "I should explain that Andrea asked me to pick her up here at—" He raised his forearm to eye level and inspected an impressive gold Rolex watch: "—half past two, to take her for a bite to eat. Unfortunately I was detained, so I am a little late."

"Why did you not tell me this at first?" Marcel demanded.

"I explained to you, old chap, that I was looking for her."

"*Looking*," Marcel said, "is entirely different from *meeting*. When you told me you were *looking* for her I immediately felt bound to defend her against your fiendish rage, the poor child." Marcel inspected his own impressive gold Rolex watch. "But, as you remarked, you are a little late. An hour or so. She has gone."

Stefan shrugged his strong shoulders. "Alas."

"And now that I come to think of it," Marcel said, "she mentioned something about going to see a new boyfriend in Greenwich Village. Yes. She was hurrying down to Washington Square."

"Alas. Alas."

"You are not upset?"

"Frankly, I am rather hungry. I had no lunch. Would you object if I made use of your kitchen to prepare myself a sandwich?"

"Go ahead, go ahead," Marcel grumbled. "Fix a sandwich, fix anything, but stop bothering me, for God's sake, while I am trying to work."

"Thank you," Stefan said, and with a courteous little bow to Kate he strode away to the kitchen.

"A wonderful fellow," Marcel whispered confidentially. "Really, a *remarkable* fellow. Such presence! And what a brain! Almost like yours, Katterin. I have the greatest respect for him. A Hungarian of the best type."

"Did you say he is Hungarian?"

"But of course! It sticks out all over him. Could you not see it?"

"A refugee?" Kate asked. She had observed something in those clear blue eyes, a hint of past agonies, of despair and rage. They were not the eyes of a man who had had an easy life. Her heart overflowed with compassion.

"A refugee?" Marcel repeated after her. "From what?"

"From the uprising of—when was it?—1956?"

Marcel exploded with laughter. "No, no! Absolutely not! On the contrary, he belongs to the bunch that is in power. You do not have to worry about Stefan Gerhardi. He lives like a prince."

"And how does he manage to do that?" Kate asked in a tart voice. She felt cheated.

"He is at the United Nations, doing something fairly unimportant. That, as you know, is the only way to survive in the political snake pit. Remain inconspicuous. Keep out of sight. It has worked well for him." Marcel picked up his brushes. "Now, let us get on with the sitting. Your head a little toward me—the chin raised—ah! Perfect!"

Part of the charm of sitting for Marcel was observing the extraordinary human beings who flowed in and out of the studio in the most casual way, helping themselves to drinks or sandwiches, a cup of tea, a cup of coffee, a bicarbonate of soda or Alka-Seltzer, dropping in to say hello, to chat for a couple of minutes, to gossip or to get information about other members of the group who had dropped in earlier or were expected to drop in later. He seemed to be one of the key figures in a remarkable subterranean culture that she had never encountered before, a tight self-contained society whose existence she had never suspected. Its members seemed to be constantly moving, like paramecia in a pond, constantly visiting each other, forever in the process of going from Dmitri to Eduardo to Marta to the Countess to Petrofski to Juan—shadowy beings whose names Kate had heard repeated again and again, but whom she had never met. Somewhere in the middle of the underground route was Marcel, and failure to drop in to see him in the course of making one's rounds was, apparently, a most serious misdemeanor because the entire machinery of communication might be disrupted as a result. Kate was baffled by these visitors. There was no way, to the uninformed eye, of telling what bound them together, what common factor related them. During her first sitting, a swarm of exceptionally large women had come bouncing in, swathed in furs like gigantic squirrels: they were singers from the Met. A small man with a pockmarked face appeared later and sat glowering in a corner of the studio: he was a driver of racing cars. Then came a stupendous red-haired Polish beauty who was appearing twice nightly at an East Side club, billed as Yasmin, queen of belly dancers, toast of Damascus. She and the racing driver fought bitterly over somebody named Jacques until Marcel led them both firmly out of the studio. At the second sitting there was the same succession of incongruous visitors: a barrel-chested wild-eyed man who had *nearly* won the Nobel Prize in physics, an Albanian lady psychiatrist who ministered to disturbed Albanians in New York and Philadelphia, a nervous Greek girl who pleaded with Marcel to tell her where she could buy a leopard.

The arrival of a Hungarian today, therefore, was not at all remarkable; nor was she unduly surprised when he returned from the kitchen bearing a platter of crackers and cheese. He said to Marcel, "It occurs to me that Miss Emory might care for some refreshment. Is it permitted to offer her a snack? The Camembert is not so good, but the Brie is edible and the Roquefort is delicious."

Marcel said, "My God, we are working! How can I paint a portrait of her when she is eating Roquefort? Don't you understand? The whole character of the face changes." Then he said to Kate with a sigh, "Would you care for some crackers and cheese, darling?"

"And coffee," Stefan said. "I have just prepared a pot of espresso."

Marcel groaned.

Stefan said, "There is really no need for so much temperament. Miss Emory can drink a small cup of coffee while you paint her. Nothing is disturbed."

"Ah, the hell with it," Marcel said. "Katterin, would you care for coffee? Shall we take a few minutes' break?"

She looked at him curiously. His bluster was not real. His voice was false. The expression on his face was sheepish, not at all convincing. Nothing in the scene rang true. She thought, *This is most strange. I could swear it has all been pre-arranged. Did the handsome Hungarian come to the studio for the purpose of meeting me? And if so, why?* There could be, of course, only one explanation: it was Marcel's way of promoting a romance. He may have felt he was doing her a great kindness by injecting this splendid male into her life. She could not really be angry with him. He was undoubtedly acting out of friendship. At the same time, the sense of health and well-being (so clearly related to Burford) was still with her; the mere mention of food was enough to arouse her appetite; and she said with gusto, "Yes, I'd adore cheese and crackers and coffee. Thank you."

"At once," Stefan said, and strode back to the kitchen.

"Between ourselves," Marcel said, "it is just as well if we break now. There is nothing much more to do, I have gone as far as I can go for the present and, anyway, the light is changing." He put aside his brushes and palette, and unbuttoned his white smock. A few moments later Stefan returned, bearing the coffee cups on a round wooden tray, and Marcel called out to him, "Hey, Stefan. I was just trying to explain to Katterin what it is that you do in the United Nations. You are the cultural expert with the Hungarian delegation, are you not?"

"No."

"Then tell us what the hell you are."

Stefan set out the three cups, and as he poured the coffee Kate noticed that his hands were powerful but unusually smooth and well-kept. She was not sure—matching him in her mind against Burford—whether this was a point in his favor or not. It was impossible, really, to pass any judgment; perhaps all Hungarians gave special attention to their hands, perhaps it was a national habit.

He did not attempt to answer Marcel's question until he had handed a cup of coffee to Kate and provided her with a supply of crackers and cheese.

"What is it you do in that big gin palace on the East River?" Marcel insisted.

"Frankly, nothing important."

"But *what?*"

He addressed Kate with a cheery grin. "I am simply a floating body. I am carried by the current into any obscure backwater that is open. For example, I have recently been appointed to the Department of Commemorative Stamps."

"How interesting," Kate said, momentarily surprised. "Are you a philatelist?"

"Not at all. I am only the victim of a system of quotas. So many jobs must be allotted to each member nation, and the question of ability, or suitability, is totally unimportant. Let me give you a little illustration. The head of the department in which I last worked came from one of the smaller of the new African nations. A charming fellow. But before he made any decision he invariably consulted with his witch doctor in Africa by radio-telephone."

Marcel said, "There speaks a true Hungarian. With a forked tongue."

"No, no, I am only using this as an *illustration.* What I found most interesting was that the witch doctor came through, on the whole, with excellent advice. Believe me, I developed a great admiration for the old boy. I began to feel that we should encourage the habit of consulting with witch doctors, and perhaps arrange to have several of them permanently stationed in New York. It is quite possible that they have channels of communication to higher authorities which we know nothing about."

"Is this," Kate asked, amused by his manner, "the official view of the Hungarian delegates?"

He laughed. "Oh, no. As I just explained, I am not really a member of the Hungarian delegation, I am only a floating body kept available for quota purposes."

"Be gentle with him, Katterin," Marcel said. "He is very sensitive to criticism."

"Oh, we can take criticism fairly well," Stefan said. "Particularly when it comes to us from such a charming critic. We do not believe that we are infallible, or that we have been chosen by God to be His voice in the Security Chamber."

She gave him an appreciative smile. In other circumstances it might have been pleasant to continue this popgun duel between East and West, but not today, Burford's day. Her antennae were quivering to pick up the unmistakeable scent, the unmistakeable vibrations of one very special human being, and she could not allow herself to be diverted by this interloper, no matter how attractive he was. She waited a few minutes and then said regretfully, "Marcel, I'm sorry. I have to run along now."

"Run along? Oh, no. You cannot leave so soon."

"A little more coffee first," Stefan said, leaping to his feet and brandishing the coffee pot.

"No, thank you. It was delicious. . . . Marcel, I have a hundred things to do, I really must go."

"But what is your hurry?" Marcel demanded. "Where are you off to at such great speed?"

She replied, "Well, first of all, I promised Martha DeLanney that I'd drop by her gallery. She has an opening of paintings by—oh, I've forgotten his name. A new young Italian."

"Alberto Antonini," Stefan said. "A good painter. Quite good. Very promising."

She turned to him, slightly irritated by his manner. "Antonini, of course. How clever of you to know."

"Not really clever," he replied. "Alberto is a friend of mine. We were in Corfu together." He took some cards out of the left pocket of his jacket, scanned them; took more cards out of the right pocket of his jacket, scanned these; took still more cards out of the inside pocket of his jacket and, at last, found the one he was seeking. He handed it, without a word, to Kate. It was an invitation to the Antonini opening and, as a crowning touch, across the top was scribbled in red ink, *Stefan—Look forward to seeing you—Come early—Martha.*

"What a coincidence," Kate said in a dry voice. She returned the card. "And Martha is a friend of yours, too. How nice."

"We have been friends for many years. We met originally in Tunis."

"You're really a great traveler, Mr. Gerhardi."

"Not really. It is just part of my job." He added courteously, "I trust, now, that I may have the pleasure of escorting you to the DeLanney Gallery?"

She felt trapped. Marcel was watching her, gloating over

her predicament, and she was momentarily furious with him for having connived at such an open attack on her virtue, such an elaborate, *futile* conspiracy to embroil her with this Hungarian. But it was a rage she could not reasonably maintain. Marcel couldn't have anticipated her plans for the rest of the day, and she had to admit that she was the victim of an accident that she could not possibly have foreseen and could not possibly, at this point, evade.

She said, attempting a momentary delaying action, "Marcel, will you come with us?"

"I would be delighted," he answered happily, "but I regret to say I have another appointment. Go with Stefan, Katterin. I give you my word, you will be perfectly safe with him. He is an experienced escort, and he will take good care of you."

Stefan bowed deeply. "Thank you."

"Not at all, my dear friend. I am always ready to give you a testimonial."

Kate sighed.

6.

He behaved very well in the taxi driving over to Madison Avenue. He had with him a black Homburg hat and a tightly furled umbrella, clichés of the diplomatic life; and he held the hat on his lap and rested the umbrella against his leg, between himself and Kate, as a sort of Wagnerian symbol of the purity of his intentions toward her. She was very aware of his masculinity, she was very aware of his attractiveness, and she had to steel herself against him because, quite simply, he was not Burford, he was a stranger.

He said, as the taxi entered Central Park, "Have you seen Marcel's portrait of you? Or not?"

"No, I haven't. We made an agreement that I wouldn't

ask to see the painting until it's finished and he wouldn't ask to read my new book until it's published."

"And when will this happy confluence occur?"

"Not until next February."

"So long? Oh: I understand. Your book is being published then, and that is when *Tempo* will print the portrait on their cover. Am I right?"

"Yes, quite right. But I don't believe for one moment that *Tempo* will print it. Someone much more important is bound to turn up, like a new movie star, or a scientist who's discovered a new kind of atom. I can't imagine why they thought of me at all. I suspect my publisher promoted the whole thing."

"Your publisher is—?"

"Craven."

"Of course. The best, in my opinion. However, I am sure you are wrong in this case, if you will pardon me for saying so. *Tempo* will most definitely print your portrait on their cover for many excellent reasons, the chief one being that they would be extremely foolish if they did not seize this rare opportunity to print a splendid portrait of a very beautiful woman."

She was overcome by embarrassment. She hated herself for her inability to accept a compliment in the same easy way that it was offered. She said uncomfortably, "Thank you. You think it's a good portrait, then?"

"Better than good. Marcel is surpassing himself."

"What a pity. Even if *Tempo* does print it on the cover I won't be here to see it."

"You will be away? Out of the country?"

"Yes. In Japan."

He spoke like a man who is accustomed to sweep aside all obstacles. He said, "But that presents no difficulty. None at all. Copies can be flown out to you. They might even be flown out to you in advance of publication. Or you may find them right there, on the newsstands in Tokyo. You know, the world is shrinking in size every day."

"That hadn't occurred to me. Of course. You're so right."

"You are visiting Japan for a vacation?"

"No. Actually, I'm going there to do a lecture tour."

"Ah, really! How splendid! And how fortunate for the Japanese people! I wonder if they realize how lucky they are! May I ask, do you have an agent who arranges such lecture tours for you?"

"I do have an agent, but he had nothing to do with this. All the arrangements were made by the State Department."

He exclaimed, "The State Department! I should have guessed! Now, do not tell *me*, let me tell *you* who arranged this trip for you. Mr. Edward Smith?"

"No."

"Mr. Victor Williamson?"

"No."

"Then it can be only one other person: Mr. P. Converse Gamage."

"Yes. Do you know Mr. Gamage?"

"Alas, I do not know Mr. P. Converse Gamage personally, although naturally I know *of* him. A very capable person, I hear. Charming. He is the tall man, is he not?"

"Yes," Kate said.

"Extremely tall, married to a pretty little Belgian girl whose name is—let me see, let me see—Frederica. Correct?"

"Yes. But how do you know all this about him?"

He laughed. "There is nothing sinister about it. You see, it was at one time part of my duties to meet with Mr. Edward Smith and Mr. Victor Williamson to explore the possibilities of cultural exchanges between our two countries. I know these gentlemen well, we are good friends, and, naturally, I heard a lot about Mr. Gamage although I never had the privilege of meeting him. The reason is simple: he handles the cultural exchanges with Japan and the Far East, and thus we had no reason to meet." He paused for a few seconds, making an odd musing sound through his closed lips, like a lost and nervous honey bee. "You will be lecturing," he said, "at the University of Tokyo? Then, I suppose, you will go to Yokohama, Kyoto, and without a doubt to Hiroshima and Nagasaki. Then, I presume, to Seoul and Taipei. Correct?"

"You must be clairvoyant!"

"Not at all!" He laughed. "Not a bit!" His furled umbrella slid away from him in his excitement, and he reached for it, picked it up and brandished it like a club. "What I just described is the standard itinerary for Japanese lecture tours. Ask yourself—where else would the State Department send you? Where else *could* it send you? And then ask yourself—is this chap Gerhardi really clairvoyant? Of course he is not!"

"I see what you mean." *He's quite right,* she thought, *there isn't anything special about my itinerary. It's just as ordinary as he says it is. Except for the spice that Mr. Gamage added at lunch today.*

He said in a quiet voice, "My dear Miss Emory, may I at this point say something that might be considered slightly improper?"

She turned her head to him in surprise. "In what way improper, Mr. Gerhardi?"

He replied hastily, "Only improper in the sense of protocol. This suggestion should come from an official source. Nevertheless, let me make it. Miss Emory: have you ever considered a lecture tour in *my* country?"

She was astonished. "In Hungary?"

"Yes. Perhaps the idea had never occurred to you; but I give you my word, you would be welcomed like a queen. You would arouse emotions of interest and excitement in the breasts of thousands. They would *flock* to hear you speak, they would respond in a way that would warm your heart. You would have audiences of young and old hanging on to every word you spoke, capturing—like precious jewels—every thought from your brilliant mind—"

"Oh, come, come," Kate said, laughing.

"But it is true! And besides my country, consider some of our neighboring countries. Have you thought how you would be received, for example, in Poland? Warsaw would go mad for you! The students would hitch themselves to your automobile and pull it through the streets. And what of Rumania? What of Bulgaria? Forget Albania—it is a dreadfully boring little country. Forget Yugoslavia—why would you wish to speak to a horde of Jugs, in any case? No. The progressive countries I mentioned—"

The taxi driver said, "This the place you wanted, the DeLanney Gallery?"

The taxi was pulling in to the curb. "Yes, this is it, my good man," Stefan said, and turned to Kate again, speaking with great urgency. "I beg of you: may we continue this conversation another time?"

She hesitated.

He said, "There is no harm in discussing the possibility I have just suggested. Please let me explain in more detail what it would mean to our people. This evening? Over dinner?"

"I'm sorry, that's impossible."

The cab stopped. He sprang out, and stood like the Black Knight in some old legend of Carpathia: umbrella and Homburg hat were held against his body in one hand, while the other hand reached forward to assist her. He was strikingly gallant in this attitude—too gallant, too handsome, to suit her New England temperament. Burford was not like this. Burford, thank God, was a calm and sensible human being.

"I will telephone you," Stefan murmured. "We must continue the conversation at all costs." She noticed that he had taken on a kind of radiance, a kind of exultation. He joked with the taxi driver as he paid the fare, his eyes sparkled; and Kate understood why. He was a Hungarian. He was conspiring with a woman. He was perfectly in his element. She thought, *Poor man, he is going to be so disillusioned when he learns about Burford. Burford. Ah, Burford.*

3

"I'M *DELIGHTED*," Martha DeLanney said in a voice so choked that it could scarcely be heard. "I *hoped* you could make it. And here you *are*. With *Stefan*. My own darling Stefan *Gerhardi*. How *marvelous*." There was no expression of any kind on her face, not delight and not even curiosity. She was tall, thin, hipless; her skin was pallid, her eyes were light blue, her hair was dirty yellow. She looked about forty, but Kate knew that she was in her sixties. The plastic surgeons had been strikingly successful with her, except that they had taken all the mobility from her face and it seemed to be modeled of wax.

Stefan raised her fragile hand to his lips. She whipered, "I never thought that you and Kate Emory—but why not? She's no different from anyone else, is she? Or is she? A fascinating question." She darted a glance at him (was it a glance of affection? of malice? of amusement? of jealousy?), and her lips twitched in what might have been a smile.

"I have just met Miss Emory for the first time," Stefan explained. "We were at the studio of a mutual friend, and we shared a taxi to come to your exhibition. Nothing more."

"Nothing more," Martha said. "Nothing more, quoth the raven, nevermore, nothing more. So true."

Stefan said, "Allow me to inform you that you look marvelous, Martha. I lose my heart to you each time we meet."

"Marvelous Martha, I *love* that," Martha croaked. "I love it, I love it."

The soft fluorescent light of the gallery obliterated all shadows and, shadowless, Kate felt as if her soul had been sold to the Devil without her knowledge, an odd and quite painless sensation. A few fragmentary phrases passed between her and the specter of a woman, and then she said, "Let me go and look at the paintings now, Martha, because unfortunately I have to rush."

"You're *always* rushing, Kate. Where are you rushing to *this* time?"

"My publisher."

"Tell me what you think of the pictures before you leave."

"Certainly."

Stefan said, "May I go around with you, Miss Emory?"

"I wouldn't dream of dragging you away from Martha. I'll be perfectly happy by myself, don't worry about me one little bit."

He looked as if she had stabbed him to the heart. But she was in no mood to mourn for him. She wanted to be alone, she wanted to look at the paintings of Alberto Antonini with her own eyes, and think her own thoughts about them, without any obligation to listen to long and involved commentaries from a gorgeous Hungarian.

It was still early, and only a handful of people had so far arrived. She knew none of them. The chic and the knowledgeable would come later, at a more fashionable hour. The barman, at a small bar in the center of the room, was still setting up his bottles and making furtive calculations. She could wander from picture to picture, unjostled, unhindered by the greetings of friends and acquaintances. And, as usual, the paintings were a credit to Martha's flair, like the paintings exhibited in a dozen other galleries run by women with flair. They were abstracts, arrangements of blobs and dribbles and splashes of color, strangely like copies (made by an idiot child) of Byzantine devotional panels. She was intrigued by them. They had a decided charm; they would look well on the walls of a doctor's office; and they confirmed, for about the hundredth time this year, her belief that modern painting had an abundance of ingenuity and lacked only genius. This was equally true of music. Some extraordinary disaster had overtaken the human race. After five centuries of creating masterpieces, mankind had lost the ability to paint magnificent pictures and compose magnificent music. The disaster was so conspicuous, and so inexplicable in terms of any known system of aesthetics, that one was tempted to ascribe it to a purely pathological agent similar to others which have afflicted man throughout recorded history—an unidentified microorganism, an aberrant chromosome—that had irreversibly affected clumps of cells in the occipital and temporal lobes of the brain. It was not as catastrophic a disaster as the Black Plague, or the influenza epidemic of 1918-19; it was not, literally, fatal; it had merely inhibited an obscure kind of human activity. One might even regard it as simply an episode in evolution that, in due course, would totally eliminate certain biological sports (like Titian or Rembrandt or Turner, or Vivaldi or Mozart or Schubert) who were outside the mainstream of the human race. We would have more and more Antoninis, painting non-paintings for the waiting rooms of Park Avenue non-physicians, until in due course the ultimate condition of non-existence was achieved.

"What did I tell you?" Stefan said to her triumphantly, appearing out of nowhere. "They are good, eh? Promising, not?"

"Yes," she said, mildly shocked at seeing him again. She

had forgotten the lively blue eyes, the slim tall body, the graceful posture.

He said, "May I get you a sherry? Martha's sherry is always excellent."

"Not at the moment, thank you."

"Then you must give me your expert opinion of Alberto's work. For example, I find that he has an admirable color range, very chromatic, but perhaps a little ambiguous. Do you agree?"

"Too *obviously* ambiguous," she couldn't resist saying.

He pulled at his lower lip, staring at a painting of a green lobster (was it a green lobster?) entitled "Self Portrait." He said, "Yes, I think you are right. You are remarkably perceptive. In fact, I suggested this to Alberto more than once when we were in Corfu. 'You must try to be more subtle,' I told him; '*Suggest.* Do not spell everything out. You are not a schoolteacher.' But, like so many artists and writers, he suffers from a closed mind." He moved nearer to her; and once again she was aware of his physical power. "There is one fact," he said, "one fact that I *must* impress upon you."

"Yes?"

He glanced quickly from side to side. His manner became very earnest. "Miss Emory, many Americans—even those who claim to be friendly toward us—have the idea that we are cultural savages, that we exist in a cultural limbo preoccupied with what is laughably called proletarian art. Miss Emory, this is not true. I want to *assure* you that we are busy searching our souls about our artistic destiny, and it is possible that in the near future you will witness an aesthetic revolution, an aesthetic renaissance, that will positively amaze you." He added, "I am referring, of course, to my own country. I cannot offer an opinion on possible developments in other countries."

She said, "I'm glad you told me. It's most reassuring."

He smiled happily at her. "Ah! You understand!"

She smiled back at him. "The near future. How exciting. Do you mean about three months from now?"

He frowned. Then he smiled again. "One must be reasonable. An aesthetic revolution does not occur in three months."

"Three *years*. Is that more reasonable?"

"Within three years. Yes, I can promise that."

The moment had come to administer the coup de grâce. She regretted, a little, the necessity for a coup de grâce to be administered, particularly to somebody so attractive, but she could not permit this situation to continue. She said, "Mr. Gerhardi, I shall look forward, during the next three years, with the greatest interest to your artistic renaissance. I can hardly wait to see what a wonderful new culture your country will produce." She held her hand out. "Until then, good-by. It was so nice meeting you and having this delightful chat. I found it most enjoyable."

He looked stunned. "You are *leaving!*"

"I'm afraid I must. I'm so sorry."

"But there are still so many things to discuss!"

"What a pity," she said, and repeated mercilessly, "Good-by."

His blue eyes had become frosty. He took her hand, and bowed over it stiffly. He straightened up and gave her a polite smile. "It was an honor to meet you, Miss Emory. Goodby."

She walked away feeling, unaccountably, as if she had behaved toward him in a shabby manner. She had, without a doubt, scored a victory over him; she had administered the coup de grâce with as much skill as usual; but it left a bitter taste in her mouth, as if she had scored a victory over a trusting child.

Martha DeLanney was still standing near the entrance,

dreaming her cataleptic dreams of the world a million years ago.

"Martha," Kate said.

"My dear?"

"I'm leaving now."

The pale eyes were indifferent. "Leaving? So soon? But it was so nice of you to drop in. Have you signed the visitor's book?"

"Yes, I signed it when I arrived."

"People *look*, you know. It's extraordinary how people *look*. They see *Katherine Emory* in the visitor's book, and they tell their friends, 'Guess who was at the DeLanney Gallery! *Katherine Emory*.'" She blinked at Kate. "I was watching you. What a strange, strange woman you are. How could you be so cruel to Stefan Gerhardi?"

Kate forced a smile. "Cruel?"

"Saint Stefan. The arrows are sticking out all over his poor skinny body. He's the total martyr, my dear, and who did it to him? You did it to him."

"Oh, nonsense."

"It isn't nonsense. And you mustn't shoot arrows at men in my gallery, Kate, you aren't even allowed to castrate them here. The rent is frightfully high, scandalously high, and I simply can't have blood and testicles all over the floor."

"Martha, shut up. Do you want my opinion of Antonini?"

"No, I don't think I do. I can tell from your mouth. You're a hard critic, Kate, you're impossible to please, and I guess that's why your public loves you."

"Actually, I'm very easy to please. A pushover."

"You must tell me all about it. Let's get together for a drink soon, oh, about three years from now. Shall we?"

"Let's," Kate said. She walked past Martha to the door.

Martha said, struggling for breath to form her words,

"You're a damn fool, Kate Emory. Passing up Gerhardi at your age. Let me tell you, you're missing something."

"Am I, Martha?"

"He's the hottest thing in pants *you* ever met, baby."

"Good-by," Kate said. "And good luck with the new show." She continued on her way out of the shadowless gallery, into the street. Now she had a shadow again, several shadows, frisking around her feet like little poodles, and she felt lighthearted as she walked the few blocks to Craven Press. This would be her last duty call: then, Burford. *Oh, Burford, dear Burford, my friend and my lover and my friend and my lover. Burford, hurry.* What was Martha's last remark? The hottest thing in pants *you* ever met, baby. Kate said aloud, "Oh, rubbish."

2.

The party was well under way when she arrived at Craven Press. As soon as she entered the outer office, normally occupied only by the receptionist, Miss Hill, she was aware of a loud, shrill, continuous twittering in the offices beyond, as if the party were taking place in a gigantic aviary. An elderly man in a baggy brown tweed suit was perched on Miss Hill's desk, urging her to drink a tumbler of champagne. "Professor Oxham, *please*," Miss Hill giggled as Kate approached. "The bubbles tickle my mucous membrane. Oh, Miss Emory, it's just a madhouse, really it is. Will you go through to the Board Room? Mr. Goodrich is there, expecting you." Professor Oxham swung around and said blearily, "Emory? Emory? Which one of you charming ladies is Miss Emory?"

Kate gave him a friendly smile and walked down the corridor to the Board Room. She could not help laughing. She was confronted by a crowd of men all of whom looked like

Professor Oxham, and a number of women most of whom looked like Mrs. Oxham, or Miss Oxham. They came, for the most part, from centers of learning up and down the Eastern Seaboard, they were all formidably erudite, and they had all contributed something of importance to the book whose publication was being celebrated today. They were etymologists, philologists, phoneticians, geographers, geologists, geometricians, mathematicians, musicologists, minerologists, anthropologists, geneticists, histologists, cytologists, taxonomists, ichthyologists, herpetologists, hoplologists, helminthologists, and so on; and the book, of which Kate had already heard conflicting reports, was the Craven *Universal Senior Dictionary,* Revised Fourth Edition, With Numerous Appendixes, Plates & Illustrations In The Text, Cr.4to., 3,189 pp And Endpapers. A few copies, bound in morocco leather and printed on superfine India paper, were disposed over the great African mahogany conference table; and several disputes, characterized by heat without fire, had already started over various of the entries.

She was remarkably happy as she edged through the crowd in search of Norton Goodrich, her editor. She was at home and at ease with these people; in a way she could claim to be one of them, and she understood their pleasure at being brought together here, like a large pack of beagles assembled for a hunt, wagging their tails and barking joyously. Several Professor Oxhams and Mrs. Oxhams recognized her and greeted her as she passed; a few Miss Oxhams who had been at Southcliffe with her seized her in passionate embraces, claiming her as their own; and when at last she reached Norton she was flushed and slightly breathless. Norton, a tall, sparely built man, appropriately dressed for the occasion in an exceptionally baggy tweed suit, said, "Kate! Kate! Here you are!" and gave her an ardent peck an inch or so from her mouth. "What a bash!" he said: "Come and get some champagne and meet everybody."

"*Everybody?*" she said brightly.

He cried, waving an empty champagne glass in the air, "That's right, the whole blooming world. I want them all to know you've arrived, the Madame de Maintenon of Gramercy Park."

"Oh, Norton!" she laughed.

"It's true, isn't it?" he said. "But first, champagne. Hey, waiter! *Waiter!* Over here, waiter, champagne for Miss Emory."

But he had mistaken a mammalogist for a waiter. The mammalogist merely looked bewildered, and Norton said angrily, "I tell you, Kate, all these damned waiters think the party is for *them.* They won't lift a finger for *us.*" She said, "Norton, as a matter of fact I'm not too crazy about champagne. What I would dearly love to do is look at the dictionary for a few minutes. Could I?" He replied, "Why, that's the easiest thing in the world; there are at least half a dozen copies lying around. Why do it now, though? I'll have a copy sent to you by special messenger first thing in the morning, and you can look through it at your leisure."

She said, "I simply want to look at it for a minute or two." He said, "I can tell you this, Kate: you aren't in the biographical section. I'm sorry, but Dr. Oxham laid down some damn silly rule about not listing any contemporary writers under forty years of age—isn't that crazy?" She said, "Norton, I had no intention *whatever* of checking to see if I was listed in the biographical section. Truly." He said, "Okay," and led her to the enormous mahogany conference table, slid a copy of the dictionary toward her, and said, "Here you are. And I'll be back in a minute with a drink for you." "Thank you," she said.

She slid her hand over the warm morocco leather, opened the huge book to the title page, turned to the contents, saw that the biographical section began at page 2,544; and there, to her great delight, she found the entry she had hoped to see: *Griffiths, Burford Lloyd, Amer. palaeontologist, 1913-* . It was only a single line, but Abraham Lincoln had no more, neither did Darwin or Einstein; and it was a new entry—it had not appeared in the Third Edition —thus signifying the editors' approval of Burford's achievements. She thought, *Oh! I'm so glad!* and a wild but marvelous idea came into her mind. When Norton returned with half a glass of champagne for her—half had spilled out as he struggled through the crowd—she said, "Norton, were you serious when you said you would send me a copy by special messenger in the morning?" He answered, "Certainly. You should know that you can have a copy of any book we publish. All you have to do is ask." She said, "You're a dear, Norton. If I ask nicely, could I take a copy home with me now?" He stared at her as if she were mad, and said, "Kate, you don't want to *carry* that thing. It weighs a *ton*." She said, "Oh, I've carried heavier books in my time. The weight won't bother me, and anyway I'll be going by taxi." He said, with a shrug of his shoulders, "All right. I'll tell Miss Hill to have a copy wrapped and waiting for you at the desk. You can pick it up on your way out." She said, "I'm so grateful, Norton dear. Thank you."

"Hello, Norton," Stefan Gerhardi said almost at the same moment: "You see? I took you at your word to come to your party; and here I am."

"Well, my God!" Norton cried. "Stefan!"

"Yes. Hello, my dear friend."

"This is wonderful!" Norton said. "What a surprise!"

Stefan murmured, "I couldn't pass up the opportunity of meeting so many distinguished scholars. But please forgive me. I am interrupting your conversation with Miss Emory. I will speak to you later, Norton."

"Don't run away," Norton said. "You know Miss Emory?"

"Oh yes, indeed," Stefan said. "It is a special pleasure meeting her again with a mutual friend. And how are you,

Miss Emory? Keeping well, I trust? Having a good time?" He reached confidently for her hand, a small mischievous smile lighting up his face.

She was speechless. She had never encountered such audacity. She shuddered as he touched her hand with his lips. Scarcely able to compose herself, she said, "And how are you, Mr. Gerhardi?"

The fine blue eyes twinkled. "In great fettle."

"Still with the United Nations?" she asked.

"Hard as it is to believe, yes, I am still with them. Perhaps you will be surprised to learn that Norton and I were together in Palermo last year."

"It doesn't surprise me one little bit," she said, and it was true. She wouldn't have been surprised to learn that he had been with Stanley in Darkest Africa, or with Dante in the Inferno.

Norton said (chuckling at an avalanche of uncommunicable memories), "Kate, we had the wildest time—"

"I'm so *glad,*" she said. "I'm sure you *needed* it. Norton, I hate to be a nuisance, but I have to leave—"

"You only just got here!" Norton exclaimed; and Stefan looked down at her in amusement, as if he had expected this move from her, this open admission of defeat.

She said, "I'm terribly sorry, but I have a dinner date, and I have to rush. Could I possibly pick up the dictionary now?"

"You aren't thinking of lugging it out to dinner with you, Kate?"

She said impatiently, "No, of course not: I have to go back to my apartment to change. If it's too much trouble, Norton, we can forget the whole thing."

"Kate, nothing is too much trouble as far as you're concerned. Now, just hold your horses and I'll see if I can get a copy wrapped for you."

"I'll come with you," she said, half in panic.

"There's no need. I'll only be a couple of minutes. Stefan, look after Miss Emory for me, will you? Perhaps she'd like another glass of champagne."

"A pleasure," Stefan said.

"Norton!" Kate cried, but he had plunged into the crowd, he was lost to her.

Stefan said coolly, "Would you care for more champagne?"

"No, thank you."

He produced an elegant silver cigarette case, a relic of old Budapest. "Cigarette?" he said, flicking the case open.

"I don't smoke, Mr. Gerhardi."

"Ah. Forgive me." He closed the case with a click, and put it away.

She said, "What is more, Mr. Gerhardi, I object to being followed, I object to being pursued, I object to being chased. I can assure you that it will not work, Mr. Gerhardi; I guarantee that it will not get you anywhere."

He took some cards out of the left pocket of his jacket, glanced at them, took more cards out of the right pocket of his jacket, glanced at these, took still more cards out of the inside pocket of his jacket, selected one, and held it out to her. It was, she thought as she watched him, a routine he practiced often. There was no need for her to inspect the card because it was unquestionably an invitation to this party with a personal *cri du coeur* scrawled across the top, something like, *Don't fail me. Remember Palermo. Norton.* She reflected bitterly, and also with a certain perplexity, that no matter where she went in New York tonight it was virtually certain that this man would come striding in, an embossed invitation in his hand, the light of lust in his eye. He had apparently won all hearts. He was welcome everywhere. But how had he accomplished this enviable social feat? Was he not a lieutenant, so to speak, in the forces arrayed against us on the other side of the street?

He said, as he carelessly returned the cards to his various pockets, "I must confess that I am a little disappointed in you, Miss Emory. You are renowned for your studies of human behavior. You are famous, in particular, for your research into the female personality. Yet here you encounter a phenomenon that is one of the most common in Nature, the attraction of the male toward the female, and how do you respond to it? With threats. With ominous promises of terrible punishment. You may even have arrived at such a state of panic that you are thinking of calling the police. Miss Emory, I ask you candidly: Is this the behavior of a rational individual? Is it scientific?"

"It's quite scientific, Mr. Gerhardi."

"Oh, really? You are prepared to make a case for it?"

"Yes. I am simply pointing out to you that all your assumptions about me and my behavior are false, that your reasoning will only lead you into a blind alley, and consequently you are doing nothing except wasting your time."

"Perhaps you should permit me to be the best judge of whether I am wasting my time or not."

She said wearily, "Mr. Gerhardi, will you do me a favor?"

"Allow me to say just one thing first."

"No!" she cried.

"How could I ever forgive myself," he said, ignoring her protest, "if I did not make a sincere effort to win your friendship? You are not merely a woman: you are a beautiful woman. You are not merely a beautiful woman: you are a beautiful and intelligent woman. You are not merely a beautiful and intelligent woman: you are a beautiful and intelligent *American* woman. How much longer must this foolish hostility between your country and mine continue?"

She said, "I congratulate you on a most eloquent speech. Now, may I ask you once again to do me a favor?" She did not wait for his reply. She said, "Please tell Norton that I have gone to the reception room. I shall be waiting for him there." She was not angry, nor was she amused. She had, she could truthfully say, other plans for the immediate future which did not include improving diplomatic relations between Hungary and the United States. "Good night," she said, and once again (quite decisively, she thought), she left him.

3.

The dictionary, as Norton had warned her, weighed a ton. She held it on her lap as she rode home in a taxi, childishly pleased at having found such a singular gift for Burford, delighted with the prospect of surprising him and making him happy. He was a modest man. Here, in one line, was the proof, if proof was required, of his accomplishments and the acclamation of his peers. She rehearsed half a dozen ways in which she could casually present him with the huge book and point out the magic entry, but finally she decided that innumerable opportunities were bound to occur in the course of the next eight or nine hours, and she only had to choose the moment that seemed most propitious, either before he made love to her or after he made love to her.

She paid off the taxi and hurried into the house, and as she inserted the key in the lock of her apartment she glanced at her wristwatch. She was overjoyed to find that the time was only a quarter to six. She had three quarters of an hour in which to bathe, and make up her face, and slip into a housecoat, and take the steak out of the icebox, and put a record on the hi-fi. Haydn, she decided. The last complete quartets, opus 77, numbers 1 and 2.

She laughed aloud as she entered the living room. How funny! Mrs. Corcoran had done it once more: huge white chrysanthemums were everywhere. It was possible that Mrs. Cocoran felt they provided an aura of spiritual respectability to Burford's visit tonight, and Kate thought indulgently, *Well, why not?* Burford wouldn't mind.

She hoisted the dictionary onto the baby Steinway, in the middle of the room, and looked around her with pleasure. A glow suffused the apartment, a special warmth, a special sense of comfort and cleanliness. Every piece of furniture was precisely where it should be, every ashtray was polished, every cushion was plumped out, every picture hung perfectly straight.

As always when she had been out all day, a note from Giselle awaited her, in a long white envelope inscribed with the exact time Giselle had sealed it and gone home to Beekman Place. The note listed all the telephone calls that had come in during Kate's absence, and a summary of the work Giselle had done. This evening there was also a note from Mrs. Corcoran, lying beside Giselle's note on the Steinway; and Kate opened this first since it undoubtedly contained information about the dinner she would soon be preparing. She laughed as she read it. Mrs. Corcoran always wrote the most delightful letters:

> Dear Miss M:
>
> The Stake is in the Ic Box. It is a great little Stake just rigt for 2. Hope you think it is a great little Stake.
>
> Also salud. It is in the salud bin in the Ic Box. Dry off in Towl.
>
> Also liquor. It is all There. I will be speaking to you in the morning, that Grizzle of yours, she nearly drove me Nuts.
>
> Kind regards.
>
> Sinserly yrs
>
> P. (Pearly) Corcoran

"The Stake is in the Ic Box," Kate murmured: "How divine." Burford would roar when she showed it to him—he adored Mrs. Corcoran's letters.

She opened Giselle's communication and sighed. Giselle was obsessed by all the trivialities of her work. *Everything* had to be noted, *everything* had to be reported. There were two typed pages: one gave the customary list of telephone calls and an itemized account of work carried out—"Retyped 20 pp of ms, on your desk. . . . Obtained bks, except *Lame & Halt* (Brentano's are ordering for you). They are on yr. bedside table."

The other sheet had been typed before Giselle left for the day.

5:30 P.M.

I tried to reach you at Craven, but the telephone was answered by a man who said he was Dr. Oxham of Harvard. He didn't sound in the least like Dr. Oxham of Harvard, who was a great friend of my father until they quarelled about Pelagian heresy. When I asked if he had seen you, he answered, only in his dreams, and I realized the unfortunate man was drunk, so it was useless leaving a message with him.

The message was to let you know that Mr. Griffiths called from Cambridge, 4:50 P.M., to say he is awfully disappointed he is unable to come to New York as arranged, because a new consignment of specimens has just arrived by air from S. Africa, he will be working on them probably all night, he thinks they are definitely relics of Cro-Mignon man, including a jawbone. He sounded so excited about it, and the way he talked about it sounded so absolutely thrilling, I told him he ought to write a book about it.

Alackaday, I couldn't stop Mrs. Corcoran from buying the chrysanthemums. She seems to go berserk when she sees them.

Your
Giselle

"Cro-Mignon man," Kate said.

She began to walk up and down the big immaculate room, beating her right fist into the palm of her left hand. "Cro-Mignon man," she said in disbelief. "He ought to write a book about it."

She brushed against a vase crammed with white chrysanthemums standing on the floor. "The Stake is in the Ic Box," she said. "It is a great little Stake just rigt for 2."

She heard the vase fall, and turned to stare at the white chrysanthemums spilled over an old Persian rug. "The salud is in the salud bin in the Ic Box," she said. "Also liquor. It is all There."

She resumed her pacing. She laughed aloud. She stopped again, and cried, "What is happening to our country, what is happening to America? Why is it that I am surrounded by such ignorant creatures, why do I pay that illiterate girl eighty-five dollars a week to be my so-called secretary? Burford will be working all night on a jawbone of Cro-Mignon man, Cro-Mignon stake is in the Ic Box, Cro-Mignon chrysanthemums are all over the floor. Oh, my God." She was so overwhelmed that she fell into an armchair and began to weep. She had not wept for years.

4.

She felt terribly old, nearly as old and as shriveled as Martha DeLanney. She wept softly for about five minutes, and it seemed to her that all her grief, all her despair, all this salty outpouring of tears, was due entirely to Giselle writing *Cro-Mignon* for *Cro-Magnon,* and Mrs. Corcoran writing *Ic box* for *ice box.* "Come, come," she murmured to herself at last, "we must be reasonable," and, despite a feeling that all the strength had left her legs and her arms, she forced herself to walk to the marble-topped coffee table in front of the fireplace, and pull a handful of tissues out of a box of Kleenex to dry her eyes. The big living room had lost its glow; everything in it was now hard and bare and unwelcoming. To dispel the coldness, to bring back some of the warmth, she decided to put a record on the hi-fi—music always cured, or tempered, her miseries. But what? Sniffling, she went to the record player and switched it on, and scanned the long crowded shelves over the machine. Not the last quartets of Haydn, nor the quintets of Mozart, nor the two trios of Schubert; not Schnabel playing the last piano sonatas of Beethoven, and not the sextets of Brahms—they were all too poignant, they reached too deep into the spirit. She wanted something loud, lively, a banner of sound; and at last she pulled out the *Lieutenant Kijé* suite of Prokofiev, and let it rip. It was not loud enough when it began. She turned the volume up, louder and still louder, until the trumpets were blaring through her body and the drums were rattling her bones; and over the wild turmoil, suddenly, she became aware of a long, repeated ululation—the ringing of the telephone.

It stood on a small table beside the big settee, and she ran to it in an upsurge of hope, like a schoolgirl, thinking, *It's Burford! It's Burford! He's coming after all, he's calling me from Cambridge to tell me he's on his way to the airport.* She snatched up the receiver and cried, "Hello? Hello?" but she could not identify the voice that answered, the military hullabaloo of Prokofiev was deafening. She said, "Hold on, I have the phonograph playing, let me turn it down, *hold on,*" and she ran to the record player, turned it off, ran back to the telephone, and said, "Hello, I'm so sorry; who is this?"

"The *Lieutenant Kijé* suite of Prokofiev?" a deep masculine voice said. "Really, you surprise me. I would have assumed your musical taste to be much more ethereal." And the voice chuckled at the discovery that her musical taste ran to such vulgar stuff, so raucous and so Russian.

"Who *is* this?" she demanded, her heart beating heavily

and erratically. It certainly wasn't Burford. Burford had once, in her presence, joyously mistaken the opening of Beethoven's Fifth Symphony for the overture to *The Pirates of Penzance*.

"I might have guessed—Chopin?" the resonant voice continued. "No. Chopin is not really your style. Perhaps Schumann, the *Frauenliebe und Leben*, which in a way relates to your work. Or Gregorian chant. But Prokofiev? At his noisiest? I would never have associated this with Miss Katherine Emory. Miss Emory: Gerhardi speaking."

She should have known even before the telephone rang: she should have *known* that only one predator would be tracking her down tonight, disturbing her as a fox disturbs the occupants of a hen roost. She exclaimed in outrage at his animal persistence, "What do you want, Mr. Gerhardi, why are you telephoning me?"

He laughed again, that deep, masculine, maddening laughter. "The reason I am telephoning is simple, dear Miss Emory. It occurred to me that by some remote chance you might be free to dine with me tonight, after all, so that we might continue our conversation—"

She cried, "I'm sorry. I am *not* free to dine with you tonight."

He was undeterred. He said lightly, "Ah. If you are not free for dinner, perhaps you are free later on for what our British friends call 'a spot of supper, what?' They have a remakable penchant, the British, for these expressions that go to the root of the matter, don't you think so? Come now, Miss Emory, say that you will join me for a spot of supper, what. Ten o'clock? Eleven o'clock? It would give me unspeakable pleasure."

"*Unspeakable* is right."

He was taken aback by her violence. "Pardon?"

"It is unspeakable *behavior*, Mr. Gerhardi. How many

times do I have to refuse your invitations before the fact sinks in that I do not wish to see you? Don't you have any feelings, Mr. Gerhardi?"

"On the contrary," he said, defending himself with vigor, "my feelings run very deep. It is precisely because I feel that you are a lady of great intelligence and exceptional beauty that I am telephoning you now."

"Mr. Gerhardi, you are not at all convincing. You use too many adjectives. Kindly stop this nonsense. Good night." And she hung up on him as if she were back at Southcliffe, in her sophomore year, rebuffing some spotty and importunate youth from Yale. "The *nerve* of the man," she cried to the empty living room. "The incredible *nerve!*"

But, for some reason, she had been shaken by the conversation; she was again on the verge of tears, and she knew that *Lieutenant Kijé* was not going to help this time—it had not helped much before Stefan Gerhardi called. Nevertheless, she had to have music to lighten the atmosphere in this Egyptian tomb of an apartment; and for a moment she was tempted to try the *Frauenliebe und Leben*. Then she deliberately decided to ignore his suggestions and chose an album of Schubert lieder, and, as the baritone's splendid voice came rolling out of the loudspeakers, she began to roam into the other rooms. She glanced into the kitchen, where everything had been scrubbed and polished to a state of surgical immaculacy, and she vaguely wondered about eating a scrap of food as a sort of token dinner. Instantly, she felt nauseated. She left the kitchen and prowled through the living room to her bedroom. Mrs. Corcoran's romantic hand was evident here, too. Kate's best embroidered silk coverlet was spread over the bed, requiring only the gentlest tug to slither off and reveal the welcoming petal-pink blankets and the matching petal-pink sheets underneath. Kate shuddered. She could not sleep here. She could not undress, put on a nightgown, brush her teeth, cold-cream her face, crawl between the crisp petal-pink sheets and compose herself for sleep, because sleep would never come. *Oh, damn Burford,* she cried to herself, trying to laugh at her predicament. *Damn Burford and his Cro-Mignon bones, this is a monstrous situation, utterly monstrous and stupid.* There on her bedside table were the books she had asked Giselle to obtain from Brentano's—Edward's new novel of Americans in Rome, *A Feast at the Villa* (she could guess what *that* feast was like), and George Tuckaway's *Prospective Perspectives* (another look at Henry James) and Sir Charles Sleet's *Enzymes and Society*—a perfect banquet of mediocre reading, if she could only insinuate herself into that wide, comfortable bed. But how, how? Her mother, and Dean Gilberta Marchmont of Southcliffe, and Father Justin, and a dozen others, were calling to her from the prompter's box of her mind, bursting to remind her of the many ways she could accomplish this act of innocence and virtue. Unfortunately, she was in no mood for innocence and virtue. She had been conspiring all day to sin, and she was distressed to have purity imposed on her because Satan was simply too lazy to lead her astray. If Satan won't take the trouble to do his job, she thought, we are indeed lost; for if we cannot be saved from evil, what *can* we be saved from?—a theme worthy of Father Justin's attention if it were properly presented.

She returned to the living room, and paused to listen to the baritone. The lovely music tore at her heart. Then, as she stood there, the telephone rang; and this time it *had* to be Burford, sparing a few precious minutes from his work to say, "Hello, my dear Kate," to ask with affection, "How are you," to explain, "I miss you terribly, but these fossils from Witwatersrand must be examined at once—you, more than any other woman in the world, will understand." And she was so stirred by her anticipation of what he would say that her voice failed her as she picked up the telephone. She whispered, "Hello?"

"Miss Emory? Is this *you,* Miss Emory?"

Again! Again! Stefan Gerhardi again! "Yes," she said.

"Miss Emory, you sound strange. Is something wrong?"

She was helpless, frustrated, despairing. "No, nothing is wrong, nothing at all." She did not have the strength to explode at him.

"Are you sure?"

"Perfectly."

"Ah—and what is the music I hear in the background?"

"Schubert."

"As sung by the admirable Mr. Dietrich Fischer-Dieskau?"

"Yes."

"How nice! I am so glad you changed from that boring Prokofiev. Do you know the songs of Hugo Wolf? We must discuss this on another occasion. Can you spare a moment so that I can explain why I have called this time? It is of the utmost importance, I assure you."

She sighed. "Yes. I can spare a moment."

"Good. The reason is, Miss Emory, that I must talk to you confidentially about a possible visit to my country, on the very highest level, in the interests of world peace. I have just been discussing it with a certain person whom, at the present juncture, I cannot name, and he has expressed the greatest interest in the idea and authorized me to approach you about it—are you listening, Miss Emory? Do you hear me? Am I making myself clear?"

"Yes, I can hear you."

"Could we get together for conversations on the matter?"

She waited, indecisively. "I suppose so."

"Some time soon?"

Why not? she asked herself. She was very, very tired, and he was very, very persistent. "Yes, some time soon."

"Would you be kind enough to name such a time?"

"I will have to consult my appointment book. I should say, early next week."

"Oh, come. Sooner, please."

She shrugged her shoulders. "At the end of this week—Friday, perhaps."

"It really should be as soon as possible. You must appreciate that the lives of many, many people might be affected for better or for worse."

"Thursday, then. Thursday afternoon."

"You are so kind," he said. "But I have an even better suggestion. How about tonight? *Now?*"

She thought, *He is a handsome man. He is an attractive man. He is an intelligent man. And he is the only human being in the world at the present moment who cares about me, who desires me, who wants to make love to me, who is aware of the music I listen to, who is concerned about whether I eat or do not eat, who can tell from a single word whether I am happy or sad. How can I go on saying no to him?*

She said, "I am not doing anything wildly important at the present moment, Mr. Gerhardi. If you are free, and feel inclined to do so, by all means come over."

She had managed it tolerably well, she told herself, yielding to him with just the right note of unconcern. And she was pleased when, in return, he behaved in a civilized manner. He had won a significant victory, after an arduous campaign, yet there was no hint of triumph in his voice. He said gravely, "I am delighted, Miss Emory. Shall I come, say, in half an hour? I am only a few blocks from where you live."

"Yes. Half an hour."

"Thank you so much. I shall count the minutes until we meet."

She had time for a quick bath, to put on a green silk housecoat, to fill a bowl with ice cubes, to change the record on the hi-fi from Schubert songs to Hugo Wolf songs. Suddenly she was excited at the prospect of seeing him again; she was glad that he had refused to be deterred by her rebuffs.

He arrived exactly half an hour after she had spoken to him, and he brought her an unexpected gift: an armful of white chrysanthemums. So the affair began, as all affairs should begin, with laughter.

4

THE TELEPHONE beside Kate's bed rang at about ten-thirty. She answered it, and heard Burford's voice. He was calling from Cambridge. She glanced at her Hungarian friend. His eyes were closed, his breathing was subdued, he appeared to be soundly asleep. She murmured, "Just a moment," put the receiver down, slipped into a robe, and tiptoed into the living room. She made herself comfortable on the big settee and picked up the telephone that stood on the end table.

She said, "Hello, Burford."

"Hello, Kate. I'm sorry to be calling so late."

"Oh, Burford, that's perfectly all right. How nice of you to think of calling at all."

"I left a message with your secretary. Did you get it?"

"I did, Burford. Thank you. How thrilling about all these new fossils arriving. You must be having such an exciting time."

She could not have forecast a minute ago how she would respond when she heard his voice again: coldly? remorsefully? indifferently? with a certain agitation? guiltily? Some very ancient area of the brain had the responsibility for making the appropriate choice, a cluster of cells probably located in the thalamus (Dr. Montagu could no doubt tell her more exactly: she must remember to ask him). She was intrigued to find that her brain had decided on simple bitchiness. It was notable because she was rarely bitchy to anybody.

He said in his gruff, direct way, "The consignment arrived unexpectedly, Kate. We had to get right down to unpacking it. Some things can't wait, you know."

"Oh, *indeed* I know. You don't have to explain *that,* Burford."

"Well," he said, "it looks as if I won't be able to get away until the weekend. Perhaps we can have Saturday together. How's your weekend, Kate?"

"I suspect that my weekend is going to be rather busy, my dear. But call me if you get to town, will you?"

He said, "What? Call you if I get to town?"

"Yes. Do that. Good-by, Burford."

"But, Kate—"

"Good-by," she repeated sadly, and put the receiver down. He had stayed away too long, and she was sorry that he was now lost to her.

She returned to the bedroom. Stefan looked at her with bright eyes, devil's eyes, and said, "Where have you been? Come back into bed."

She shook her head, laughing. "No."

"Come back into bed, I say. *At once,* Katherine!"

"No. No. No."

"You look beautiful, you look adorable,you are so desirable, your breasts are like pears. *Come here, Katherine.*"

She inspected herself. "How can you say they're like pears. They're like nothing of the kind."

"Do not argue with me." He reached out for her lazily.

She shook with laughter. "Stefan, be sensible."

He made a sudden lunge, seized her, pulled her onto the bed, tore open her robe, kissed her throat, her shoulders, her breasts, and then, as if he were performing some complicated acrobatic trick, raised her at the hips like a sack of potatoes, flipped her over, and bit into the gluteus maximus. She screamed, and he turned her again, working on her like a wrestler, twisting her hair around his fist so that she was unable to move her head, silencing her scream with a kiss that locked her mouth under his, forcing her legs apart and settling himself expertly between them. It was useless for her to struggle. She lay there, at first as an onlooker, staring up at him incredulously. He had made love to her four times already, and she could not understand how he could go on. He was unbelievably strong. In some extraordinary manner, great reserves of strength seemed to be instantly available to him; suddenly the muscles of his legs and arms, of the inner thigh and belly, could change from human tissue to steel, inhumanly hard and unyielding, so that she was bound to him helplessly, and all the contours of her body were molded into the contours of his body, and all her movements were determined by him. He said hoarsely, "You are my sweetheart, Katherine, love me, love me." *What does he want?* she cried to herself, half laughing, half in anguish. It was like being asked to love a runaway Exercycle. She could not possibly escape, she could scarcely breathe, as those steely ligaments pedaled furiously above her; yet somehow he carried her along with him, his fury was communicated to her, she was joined to him and she became part of his being. All over her body, directly under the skin, there seemed to be a film of fluid that she had never been aware of before tonight: it was a hot, sensitive, uneasy fluid that ran in many directions at once, like quicksilver, sending flashes of piercing heat into the skin above it and the raw tissue below. Very soon, as he gripped her and rocked her and called out to her, the quicksilvery fluid became too hot for her skin and her flesh to tolerate, and she began to plead with him, "Stop, stop, oh stop, please stop," without really wanting him to stop. The heat ran under her skin like thin flaming needles, probing under her breasts and into her pelvis and down her thighs; waves of a sensation she had never before experienced, like pain and equally like the sound of an infinite number of flutes, spread over her, and she was engulfed in the spasms of death, in a huge and indescribably magnificent death rattle. Her brain was spattered with a deluge of color; shapeless blobs, like blue and red and violet amoebas, hurtled through the sky inside her brain; and, most bewildering of all, as Stefan struggled with her, the entire outer surface of her skin seemed to become intensely photosensitive. She saw, with the whole of her body, a quivering curtain of white light, her own aurora borealis. The white light constantly reversed itself, like a photographic negative, and became a quivering curtain of brilliant blackness; then it was a dancing whiteness again, bringing a dazzling pinpoint of pain to every pore. The jumbled complex of sensations grew more and more excruciating; her back was arched in agony, her mouth was open, gasping for air; she was far beyond any recognizable climax; climax had been piled on climax like the flakes of a thousand-layer cake. But it had to end, it *had* to end; and, at last, with a shuddering, uncontrollable death rattle, the universe ran down, the performance clanked ponderously to a stop, there was nothing but a small wave lapping the edge of a golden beach, a kitten's tongue furtively lapping a saucer of milk.

"Forgive me," Stefan murmured. "I could not go on any longer."

She did not answer. She lay there, frail, exhausted, devoid of all humanity. He lay beside her, his head on her shoulder, relaxed, content. After a long time she was able to wriggle free of him. She crawled out of bed, put on her robe again, went to the kitchen, and, like a good American woman, fixed a pot of coffee.

2.

She sat at the kitchen table, both hands supporting her chin, watching the plop-plop of the boiling water splashing against the glass lid of the percolator.

She thought, There has been some terrible mistake in my life. Something vital was withheld from me, and now that I have found it, it is much too late, I cannot make use of it.

She thought, How funny: I believed that I knew everything about this business of sex, of men and women, and now I find that I knew nothing. How can I *pretend* to know any longer, when all I have to offer is my wealth of ignorance, my decades of inexperience?

Then she thought, Come: let us not be so melodramatic. I know *something* about this business—not everything, but who claims to know everything? I have read all the available literature on the subject, I know it all by heart. What occurred tonight was, to state it briefly, an electrochemical overloading of certain nerve fibers derived from ventral branches of the second, third, and fourth sacral nerves, followed by the release into the blood stream of an abnormal number of molecules of various complex proteins, resulting in prolonged peristaltic contractions of the ischiocavernosus and the bulbocavernosus (check with Dr. Montagu). As for the occurrence of what might be termed false or anomalous photosensitivity, this might well have been induced by traces of sulfonamides, or by fractions of some substance like oil of bergamot. It can all be explained, with a little patience. That is one of the vital functions of science, to cast light upon darkness, to make the inexplicable available to the processes of the mind. Why, then, behave as if this episode tonight were so unusual, so horrendous?

The boiling water was splashing excitedly against the glass dome of the percolator, recapitulating *in vitro* (as any good Freudian could have told her) the events of the past two hours. She watched the performance with a kind of disdain. Was it really necessary to go through all this effort just to make a cup of coffee, just to appease the thirst of the flesh? How ridiculous! Then, glancing up, she saw that Stefan had come into the kitchen and was looking at her speculatively; and this, in fact, was her first full-length glimpse of him since he had removed his clothes. He was most impressive: slim, strong, vital, radiating physical well-being. A white towel was draped jauntily around his middle, accentuating his bronzed skin and the powerful ridges of abdominal muscle. There were no signs whatever of middle-age decay.

"Well, well," he said cheerily as she caught his eye, "so here you are, Katherine. And what are you doing, darling?"

"My name is James Watt, and I am just about to invent the steam engine."

"I am afraid, darling, that it has already been invented by a Russian whose name escapes me at the moment, so do not bother too much. Unless, at the same time, you are making coffee?"

"Yes. Will you have a cup?"

"There is nothing I would like more. However, while you are brewing it I would like to take a shower. Do I have your permission to make use of your facilities?"

"Of course."

"Thank you."

He kissed the back of her neck tenderly, and strode out. Fierce little sparks went flashing up and down her spine. His lightest touch, apparently, could still arouse her, she was still sensitized to him. *Am I in love with him?* she wondered: *How can he have this extraordinary effect on me?* The questions were unanswerable, or, as Father Justin might have reminded her, they were not true questions. When the coffee was ready she carried it on her favorite silver tray into the living room, put it on the marble-topped table in front of the fireplace, and sat on the settee waiting for Stefan to reappear.

3.

Now the inevitable reaction of guilt set in. She had not been an ardent Catholic most of her life for nothing. Her lips tightened as she brooded over this evening's events. She could understand some of the reasons for her conduct: she had become overwrought as a result of Burford's neglect, she had turned to Stefan Gerhardi for a few crumbs of comfort, for companionship, for reassurance that she was, within limits, a normal woman. But she could not condone her behavior, surrendering herself shamelessly to a man who was virtually a stranger.

It must stop, she thought. *It must stop, here and now.*

Unexpectedly, her eyes became misty. Why should this relationship stop now, when it had hardly begun? She could not repress a little cry of dismay, recalling the bleakness of the apartment before Stefan telephoned her. After all, he had shown her nothing but kindness (his special form of kindness), and generosity (his special form of generosity). Why destroy this marvelous friendship that had sprung up from nowhere? What could be achieved by slamming the door in his face?

She was not accustomed to such wild fluctuations of emotion. On the one hand, she was profoundly ashamed of herself. Grim and unforgiving, she looked down from the Gothic towers of Southcliffe at the wanton strumpet dancing in the moonlight to the tune of a blue-eyed gypsy fiddler, flinging her skirts up in his handsome face and uttering yowls of sensual ecstasy. A revolting sight.

On the other hand she was ashamed of herself for feeling

ashamed. The acts she had committed with Stefan Gerhardi were not acts of primary sin. In their original form they had been devised by Nature a billion years ago, and they had been practiced widely ever since. What possible reason was there for judging them to be evil? Why should she reproach herself for Nature's lack of taste?

4.

He came bounding back to her, bursting with vigor, wrapped in a large bath towel. "Your shower is splendid!" he cried. "I feel renewed. Move over, my dearest, let us make love again."

She shrank from him. This was too much. She said, "The coffee is ready."

"We can have it later." He threw himself onto the settee and seized her hand, kissing it passionately. "This is a night for great deeds, Katherine, this is a night for great love. My heart is yearning for you."

"Please. Let us have our coffee."

He said incredulously, "You would rather have coffee than make love?"

"Stefan, I'm dying for some coffee."

"It is unbelievable." He sat up. "Very well. If you insist, I will have coffee with you. But I warn you, Katherine, you gain nothing by such delays. My passion for you cannot be switched off like a light." Then, as she began to pour the coffee, he said, "And who is Burford?"

She stopped pouring and looked at him in astonishment. "What did you say?"

"Who is Burford?" He flicked his fingers at the telephone on the end table. "The person who called you a little while ago."

She asked, still astonished, "Did you listen in on the telephone in the bedroom?"

He chuckled. "Of course not. How can you imagine such a thing? No: I heard your voice saying, Burford, Burford; and, naturally, I wondered who he might be."

She resumed pouring the coffee. "A friend."

There was a cheerful note in his voice. "A lover, I presume?"

She looked at him. "You mustn't presume." She put the coffee pot down on the silver tray.

"Of course. I am only a Johnny-come-lately. But I happen to love you. And I happen to be of a very jealous disposition."

"Do you take sugar? Cream?"

"Never mind the sugar or the cream," he said. "Let us now, this minute, establish something that is of paramount importance. I ask you to believe, Katherine, that I am here because my heart brought me here, because you are a woman of greater dimensions than any I have ever known, beautiful and noble, too. I did not come here for an evening's fun, Katherine. I came here out of love and admiration for you." He leaned toward her and demanded, "Do you believe what I am saying?"

She nodded in a vague, frightened way.

He said moodily, "What can I do if this man is actually your lover? Challenge him to a duel? Kill him? No. I must concede that it is the most natural thing in the world for you to have a lover. With your *beauty?* With your *understanding?* My God, you should have a hundred men loving you, banging on your door all night long. But you, for your part, must concede that if I am entitled to love you I am also entitled to be jealous of any man who comes near you."

She said in a faraway voice, challenging his logic, "I don't believe that is right."

"Then you must re-examine your beliefs." He leaped to his feet. "Do you know what effect you have on me? You arouse me so much, you are such a challenge to my manhood, that I cannot keep my hands off you. I want you more than I have ever wanted any woman. It is true, true, true." He beat his fist against his forehead.

"But you have already—"

He cried, "I cannot help myself. I am in agony. What kind of trick is this? Do you play it on all your men?"

"*All* my men?" she asked in some perplexity.

"Yes. Yes. Like this Burford who telephones you constantly. And these others. Have you played the same trick on them?"

She shrugged her shoulders. The game was becoming too complicated. "Let us have our coffee," she said.

He exclaimed, "Wait!"

She looked at him in alarm.

"I have an idea," he said.

Her alarm changed to suspicion.

He said, "Let us go out for supper. I know an excellent little place, only a few blocks from here, where we can have a snack, a sandwich, pastries, anything one's heart desires. There is music, dancing, we can spend an hour or two there enjoyably. What do you say?"

"It's too late, Stefan."

"No, no, it is never too late. Come. Put on a pretty dress and let us go."

"But look at the time! It's a quarter past eleven!"

"So what? The night is just beginning. We will have fun."

"Are you sure you want to go out?"

"Certainly I am sure."

The idea pleased her. She smiled at him and said, "All right."

"Good," he said. "But first, there is some unfinished business we must attend to." She gave a little shriek as he seized her, but he was too quick and too strong. She could not possibly escape.

5.

From the street the restaurant looked dingy. One had to go down three cracked and crumbling stone steps to reach the entrance. A dense growth of clematis hung over the door and almost completely obscured the windows, so that it was impossible to see inside.

She said, "Is this your restaurant?"

"Yes. The Carpathia. It is a jolly little place."

She hesitated. It did not look in the least jolly. She was wearing, at his request, an evening gown, a mink cape, and satin shoes with very high heels, and she had no wish to venture down those crumbling steps, she was reluctant to approach that uninviting doorway.

"I promise that you will like it," Stefan said: "It is your cup of tea." He put his hand on her arm reassuringly, and suddenly she felt close to him, she trusted him, she accepted his word.

He was right. Her eyes brightened as soon as she was inside. It was a great surprise. She was transported from a mean little New York street to a garden café in some unspoiled corner of romantic old Europe. She had an impression of colored lanterns, a ceiling decorated with cupids and lilac blossom, she heard laughter and the glissando of violins, the air was rich with the smoke of cigars and (she thought) the bouquet of crushed grapes. Clustered around the bar near the entrance were about a dozen people, who greeted Stefan, with shouts of pleasure. "'Allo, Stefan!—'Allo, 'allo, Stefan, where have you been all night?—'Allo, Stefan, come and have a drink with us!" The hat-check girl, a plump, bosomy, dark-eyed beauty wearing a dirndl and a peasant blouse, said as she took his coat, "Ah, Stefan! You have just come from the opera? Was it good?" He asked, "Which opera, Marya?" "The Metropolitan opera, of course." He said, "Why do you think I have come from the opera, Marya?" She glanced at him, glanced at Kate, and began to laugh. "Oh, Stefan, you are such a naughty boy. And you are looking so handsome tonight." He whispered in Kate's ear, "You see what you have done to me tonight? You have made me handsome, now." She smiled.

A tall, sinister waiter, with glossy black hair and a thin black mustache, bowed to him and said, "Your table is ready, sair." "Ah, good, Axel," Stefan said, his voice nasal and bored. The waiter led the way around the small crowded dance floor to a large table in a shadowy corner. "Excellent, Axel, excellent," Stefan said through his nose. Another surprise awaited Kate here—a cellophane box containing a hideous yellow orchid covered with brown spots, like something treasured by an obstetrical surgeon. She said, "Good heavens! Look at this! Somebody must have left it behind." Stefan said, in the same bored, nasal voice, "It is for you, dear lady." She blinked. "For me?" "Yes, for you." She said, like a child, "But how did anyone know I was coming here?" He looked up at the ceiling and answered, "I telephoned while you were getting dressed." Axel, the waiter, gave an approving cough. Stefan snarled at him, "Be kind enough to bring us the menu. And also bring us two of my cocktails. Tell Pyotr they are for me, and warn him that if the glasses are not properly chilled I will send them back."

"Yes, sair. Very good, sair," Axel said, bowing as if to Buddha, and turned, and sprinted away.

"Thank you for my orchid," Kate said. "Would you mind terribly if I keep it in its box? Orchids die on me so quickly when I wear them."

"They die of envy. It is only to be expected."

She smiled at him and touched his hand affectionately. She looked around her and said, "It's so gay. From the outside I would never have dreamed it was like this."

He said, "Between ourselves, it is not as good as it used to be. It is going downhill. The service is poor. The waiters are insolent. They expect enormous tips for doing nothing. And, I assure you, they were not always like this. I can remember when a waiter was a waiter, he took pride in his work. Now they are spoiled by too much easy living."

"I thought our waiter was very anxious to be helpful."

"Axel? Only because I treat him like the dog he is."

She was shocked. She opened her mouth to reply, and checked herself. This was not the time or the place to start a sociological argument. Besides, he might well be joking, he had a wry sense of humor. She said, indicating the people on the dance floor, "What are they dancing?"

"It is a kind of folk dance. Would you care to try it?"

"Oh, no. I only wondered what it was." She could not remember when she had last ventured on to a dance floor—ten, twelve, fifteen years ago?—and she found herself suddenly breathless at the thought of dancing with Stefan, being held in his arms, weaving around in time to the music.

He said, "Come. It is easy. You simply follow me."

"No, I'm so clumsy, I'm afraid I would only look like an idiot."

The waiter arrived with two glasses of frothy pink liquid. He set them down and stood looking at Stefan nervously.

"Well?" Stefan growled.

"Sair, are the glasses chilled enough?"

"I will let you know. In the meantime, where is the menu I asked you to bring me? Have you by any chance forgotten?"

Again, Kate was shocked by his brutality. But she had observed in the past that every man had his own style with waiters. Burford always treated them as if they were invisible, her English friend Basil always treated them as if he had known them at Oxford, Giacchino in Dublin treated them as if they were deaf and dumb, Sverre in Rome treated them as if despite all his precautions they would pick his pocket and make off with his stainless-steel watch. She had to admit that Stefan's method worked. Axel bounded away, bounded back a moment later with two folio-sized menus, then retired to lean against a wall, biting his nails. Kate pitied him. His sinister appearance was a fraud, like the reversed bands of color on the harmless little snake that pretends to look like a deadly coral snake.

"Try my cocktail," Stefan said. "Tell me what you think of it."

She sipped the frothy pink liquid and said politely, "It's delicious." As far as she could tell it consisted of vodka and some rather sickly syrup. "What is it called?"

"It has no particular name. But it has the virtue that you can drink it all night and it will make you merry but not drunk. If you ever come in here by yourself, ask Pyotr at the bar for Stefan's special: he will know what you mean." He picked up one of the enormous menus. "Are you starving? Would you care to order something immediately? Or would you rather wait?"

She realized after a moment's reflection that she was virtually starving. She had not eaten anything since her lunch with Mr. Gamage, an eternity ago.

He said, "I suspected you were hungry. Love always gives one a hearty appetite. Now, the chef here is a great friend of mine. You can be sure of delicious food if he knows you are with me. I would like to suggest that you start with one of his famous specialities—sour cherry soup."

"No, Stefan, I don't think I could eat soup so late at night."

"You, of course, are the best judge of that. Allow me to recommend, then, the casserole of partridge."

She thought, *Next it will be nightingales' tongues on toast;* but she was wrong. He offered her blue trout, *truite au bleu Duna,* and when she turned this down he said, "There is no alternative: you must have the oyster omelet done in the Carpathian style." She said, "But, Stefan—" and he took her hand, looked solemnly into her eyes, and said, "Katherine, my love, will you not trust me?" She had to answer, "Yes." He said, "Then it is an oyster omelet for you. And for me, as usual, steak." She asked, "Why as usual?" He said, "Because I am on one of those confounded diets. Steak, steak, steak, day and night, it is driving me out of my mind." She remarked innocently, "Oh, you seem to thrive on it." He glanced at her sharply, and burst out laughing.

He called Axel, gave him the order in a language that sounded like a sword clashing against stone, and then turned to her and said, "My darling, we have to wait at least ten minutes until the food is brought. Come. Dance with me."

"Stefan, I am such a poor dancer—"

"How is it," he said in an icy voice, "that you have such a great reputation for wisdom, when your approach to life is so consistently negative? You are always refusing what is offered to you." He leaned across the table, so that his face was within a few inches of hers. *"Katherine! Dance with me!"*

"All right. But don't say I didn't warn you."

Her heart began to race with excitement as he led her into the boisterous crowd; and as he put his arm around her waist ripples of delight flowed through her body. She whispered, "Hold me tight and tell me what to do." He said, "Follow me, that is all."

There were four musicians: a pockmarked, black-haired violinist; a short, bald cellist; a tall, one-eyed man playing the double bass; and a plump, pretty girl in black lace (the twin sister of the hat-check girl, Kate guessed) who played the piano. " 'Allo, 'allo," Stefan called, as he and Kate reached them; and they called back heartily, " 'Allo, 'allo, Stefan."

Kate said, "Careful!" as he whirled her away, and he said scornfully, "You are an excellent dancer. I knew it as soon as you took your first step." She said, "But I haven't danced for years and years." He said, "So what? Either you can dance, or you cannot dance. It is like being a woman."

It was surprisingly true, although she could not grasp his reasoning. She found herself dancing without any difficulty. He was utterly confident of himself; his confidence reached across to her; and, in addition, all the lovemaking of the evening was now taking effect. It was as if she had been given some fabulous elixir that restored elasticity to all the blood vessels, stimulated the brain, brought roses to the skin, and added a sparkle to each heartbeat. She danced on and on, and every step was delightful; the pressure of his hand on her back was delightful, the hardness of his cheek against hers was delightful, the sense of his physical nearness was delightful. When the music stopped, she stood applauding happily; and he said, in a burst of ardor, "Oh, my Katherine, you look *beautiful!*" "Do I?" she said, pleased beyond words. He said, "Yes. You look ravishing, ravishing." She blushed, so it seemed to her, all over her body. "Thank you," she said. He said, "Let us go back now and finish our drinks. We can dance again later."

Then, as they approached their table, he said loudly, "Well! Look who is here! Mr. Horscht!" A broad-shouldered man in a dark suit stood up, smiling. His hair was unusually bushy, and snow white. His eyebrows were bushy, too, and jet black.

" 'Allo, Stefan," Mr. Horscht said, and shook Stefan's hand with considerable enthusiasm.

"Katherine," Stefan said: "This is Mr. Miklos Horscht. What luck, running into each other! Mr. Horscht, I have the honor to present Miss Katherine Emory. I am sure I need say no more."

"Miss Emory!" Mr. Horscht said with somewhat excessive amazement. "Really! An unexpected pleasure! I am overwhelmed." He kissed her hand.

"How do you do, Mr. Horscht?" she said politely.

"Thank you, thank you, I am fine."

Stefan said, "Is Mrs. Horscht with you, by any lucky chance?"

"Alas, no," Mr. Horscht said. "Not tonight." He twinkled his eyes at Kate. "I have been sitting here watching you dancing with Stefan. It was a charming sight. You are a most graceful dancer, Madame. Permit me to congratulate you."

She was amused by his flattery. "How kind of you to say so. But I'm afraid that I really looked terrible."

"She is instinctively a fine dancer," Stefan said. "As everybody knows, it is either in the blood or it is not in the blood. It happens to be in her blood."

"I could not agree with you more," Mr. Horscht said. He looked at Kate with open admiration. The assault of compliments was too much for her to withstand. She blushed again.

"Why are we standing?" Stefan demanded. "Let us sit down. Mr. Horscht, you will join us for a little snack, I hope?"

"I have already snacked," Mr. Horscht said with a broad smile. "Perhaps I may be allowed to join you for a cup of coffee."

"And cognac?"

"Well, if you insist."

Mr. Horscht, Kate soon discovered, was a man of considerable stature. He was older than Stefan, not as volatile, and not as hypersensitive. He wore a heavy gold wedding ring, and Kate gained the impression that he was a tender and devoted husband and that his wife was a well-satisfied, busy, and cheerful woman. Precisely what he was doing in New York remained unclear. He worked (Kate gathered) at the United Nations, but this was not specifically stated, and Stefan once referred to him as chairman of the Central Regional Cultural Commission, whatever that might be. He referred to himself modestly (only adding to her confusion) as a professional ignoramus, one who could not understand the work of writers, artists, and scientists, yet had the responsibility of passing judgment on their work. This brought a sharp protest from Stefan. "Not true, not true. It is universally agreed that Mr. Horscht is one of our best intellects. He carries a tremendous burden on his shoulders."

"What is this burden?" Kate asked.

"The burden of the future," Stefan said airily. "That is quite a burden for one man to carry, is it not, Mr. Horscht?"

Mr. Horscht made a chuckling noise deep in his massive chest. "Oh, well. If you say so. Perhaps. You may be right."

Kate's oyster omelet was placed in front of her, looking, when Axel removed the silver cover, like a concoction of edible Sèvres porcelain. Stefan's steak was served at the same time, sizzling romantically and emitting the most succulent odors. A half bottle of Badacsony accompanied Kate's dish; a tall glass of dark beer accompanied the steak. "Good appetite," Mr. Horscht murmured. Kate smiled at him, and instantly attacked the omelet as if she had not eaten for a month.

Stefan, she observed after a few moments, was not hungry. Evidently his furnaces did not need to be replenished as hers did, or, possibly, he ran on some different kind of fuel. He ate languidly, he sipped his beer as if it were water, and he appeared to be interested chiefly in keeping up a conversation with Mr. Horscht. After a few general comments he said casually, "By the way, I have been meaning to ask you: are you acquainted with Mr. P. Converse Gamage of the State Department?"

"The name is familiar," Mr. Horscht said, scratching his

snow-white hair thoughtfully. "Let me see, now. I believe he is a colleague of Mr. Edward Smith and Mr. Victor Williamson. Can this be the Mr. P. Converse Gamage you mean?"

"The same."

"He is connected with the cultural exchange program, I seem to recall."

"Correct. And by a strange coincidence he is a friend of Miss Emory."

"Is that so?" Mr. Horscht said politely. "A friend of yours, Miss Emory? How very interesting."

He twinkled his eyes at her. She twinkled her eyes at him. She was unable to reply vocally: her mouth was full of oyster omelet and *pommes de terre à la Hongroise.* At the back of her mind she was aware that Mr. Horscht's accidental advent here was by no means accidental—it had been contrived, and for some definite purpose. She wondered, *What are these two men up to?* but she was too contented to care. The food was delicious beyond words. Her body was glowing. She was happy, lazy, and at peace with the whole world.

Stefan said, "I do not think I am revealing any diplomatic secrets, Mr. Horscht, when I tell you that Mr. P. Converse Gamage has arranged a lecture tour in Japan for Miss Emory. She will be leaving us in a few weeks."

"So soon?" Mr. Horscht said mournfully.

She nodded, sipping a glass of the excellent white wine.

"I am desolated to hear this, when I have only just had the pleasure of making your acquaintance," Mr. Horscht said. "I must nevertheless offer my congratulations again. How nice for you that you are going to Japan, Miss Emory. I hear it is a pretty little country. Cherry blossoms, temple bells, et cetera. Are you happy to be going?"

"Very happy."

"Good, good. That is half the battle, to go in a happy

frame of mind. I assume that Mr. P. Converse Gamage has arranged for you to give lectures at the world-famous University of Tokyo?"

"Yes."

"And you will do the usual tour: Yokohama, Kyoto, Hiroshima, Nagasaki?"

"Yes." Everybody seemed to know her itinerary.

"How long will you be away?"

"Six months. Perhaps a little more."

"And, naturally," Mr. Horscht said, "you will be meeting a great many people from different walks of life? Writers, artists, political personalities, and so on?"

"Perhaps." She sipped her wine.

"H'm," he said. He sat back, looking at her thoughtfully, his bushy black eyebrows compressed in a frown. "I wonder if I should tell you this? On the other hand, in all probability you know about it already, and it will not come as a surprise to you. And besides, as a highly intelligent person you will be able to evaluate it objectively. It concerns the attitude of the Japanese people toward American visitors."

"Oh?" she said, scraping up the last fragments of the omelet.

"I was speaking only the other day to a friend who has just returned from Tokyo. He told me, in strictest confidence, that there is a great deal of hostility toward Americans, more than is generally recognized."

"There is also considerable friendliness shown to Americans, Mr. Horscht."

"Admittedly. But, to a large extent, this comes from the older people. The younger people, particularly the students, are surprisingly hostile. You are aware of this?"

"Students are frequently hostile, period."

"But to be so rabidly hostile is remarkable. They demonstrate against American visitors, shout slogans like 'Go home, Yankee,' and so on. It is a pity that the Japanese, who were once models of politeness, should have become in recent years so rude and hooliganistic."

Kate turned to Stefan. "Please explain what Mr. Horscht is trying to tell me."

"Shall I answer her?" Stefan asked Mr. Horscht.

"By all means."

Stefan said briskly, "Mr. Horscht is only trying to tell you, Katherine, what I tried to tell you earlier this evening. That is, you must come to visit us. You can be sure that nobody will say to you, 'Yankee, go home.' Quite to the contrary, they will take you to their hearts. Especially the students. *They* will go crazy over you. Am I right, Mr. Horscht?"

"Absolutely, my friend. You put it in a nutshell."

"I see," Kate said. "You are both trying to dissuade me from going to Japan."

Mr. Horscht exclaimed, "Oh, no! Nothing could be further from our minds. How could we try to dissuade you from doing something that has been arranged for you by your own Sate Department? It is unthinkable."

"But why do you *want* me to visit your country? What *purpose* would it serve? What *good* would it do *anybody?*"

"The answer is simple," Mr. Horscht said. "As a woman, you will understand immediately. In one word: we need you." He took a silver cigarette case out of his pocket, offered it first to Kate and then to Stefan. Kate declined a cigarette. Stefan took one.

She said, "I am very touched, both as a woman and as an American, to learn that you need me. But I am still not clear *why* you think you need me, and what you think I can do for you."

Mr. Horscht puffed perfumed gray smoke into the air. He said, "I do not like to make speeches, but as you are surely aware, Miss Emory, we are a country that prides itself on a long history of cultural achievement. We have always been painters and sculptors and music-makers and architects and poets. True?"

"Yes," she said. "Very true."

He went on, "But we are conscious that in recent years there has been what one might call a change in our image. We have been cut off from many people with whom we have always had, in the past, a natural relationship. And we now feel a yearning to rejoin our friends, to open a new dialogue with them. Do you understand what I mean?"

"Well," Kate said doubtfully, "I think so."

"I can go into more detail some other time, if you wish," Mr. Horscht continued. "This, at least, will explain in part why I say we need you. We need your sympathy, we need your good will. We want you to come and live with us for a month, six months, a year. We want you to tell *our* people about *your* country; and to tell *your* people about *our* country."

Kate said, "Of course, I would love to visit Hungary. I deeply appreciate your invitation. However, I shall be in Japan until July. There is a chance that instead of coming straight home, I may visit New Delhi and Teheran, in which case I wouldn't get back until September. Then I have to settle down to work on a new book. At the earliest, Mr. Horscht, I wouldn't be free to make a trip to your country until about eighteen months from now."

"Such a long time," Mr. Horscht said with a sigh.

"Yes, I'm afraid it is."

He smiled at her. "What are eighteen months in the history of Europe? We must be patient, that is all." He pushed his chair back. "Please forgive me. I have kept you too long. I have interrupted your dancing." He stood up. "I hope I shall have the pleasure of meeting you again very soon, Madame."

"I hope, too, that we shall meet again."

He kissed her hand, murmured a last compliment, waved genially at Stefan, and walked away through the crowd. He was a very attractive man, she thought. Were all Hungarian men like Mr. Horscht and Stefan Gerhardi? Did they all possess this vigor, this striking vitality, this depth of feeling? A trip to Hungary in the company of one of these warm-blooded human beings might be perfectly wonderful. She thought of little Miss Mitsamushi accompanying her through Japan, day and night for six months, and her heart sank.

Stefan said, "Come, Katherine. Let us dance again."

Unexpectedly, she yawned. She said, "Oh, my dear, I'm so tired, I couldn't possibly dance. Please take me home."

He sprang to his feet. "I am at your service."

She smiled at him. He was so nice, so gallant.

He said, "You have made me the happiest man in the world. I am forever in your debt. Ask anything of me. *Anything.*" His eyes flashed with love.

6.

He insisted on accompanying her right up to the door of her apartment. Standing in the hall, he took her in his arms and kissed her, causing her—to her astonishment and alarm—to become spectacularly excited once more. In order to free herself she had to contend against her own agitation as well as his.

He said fiercely, "Do you think I am going to allow you to slip away from me now? No! I am staying with you, Katherine. *Staying.* Do you hear me?"

"Stefan, everybody in the house can hear you. Another night, perhaps. Not tonight."

"Why not tonight? This is as good as any other night.

Unless—ha-ha!—so *that* is what it is! You have another lover waiting in there for you. Burford! By God, I will kill this Burford. Is that the reason, Katherine?"

"You mustn't shout. No, of course there isn't anybody waiting for me. How can you imagine such a thing? Stefan, I'm tired. I'm exhausted. Please let me go."

He released her reluctantly. He said, "You have broken my heart. And you have inflicted a disaster upon my manhood. I thought you loved me."

She said unhappily, "You have to understand my position here. I have to be discreet."

"*Discreet!*" he said in a bitter voice. "That is just another word for indifferent. You do not give a damn. Look. I offer you one last chance to change your mind. What do you say?"

"Not tonight, Stefan. Please."

"So be it," he said. "I will call you tomorrow." He kissed her hand, inhaled the perfume behind her ear, sighed dramatically, and at last left her. She let herself into the apartment, closed the door and carefully double-locked it, tottered to her bedroom, undressed in a fog of weariness, crawled into the disordered bed, pulled a crumpled petal-pink sheet over her head, and instantly fell asleep. *Stop,* she said to the relentless ghost of Stefan beside her, *stop, stop, I'm so tired, stop.*

7.

The Carpathia closed at half past two. Axel, the waiter, left with the small bald cellist, whose name was Jozsef. They walked slowly to Second Avenue, discussing in detail the charms and the sexual availability of Marya, the hat-check girl. They continued the conversation for a few minutes on the corner of Second Avenue; there they shook hands and parted. Jozsef, lugging his cello, turned south. Axel turned north. He walked two blocks and entered a telephone booth, pulled down the brim of his hat, and dialed a number in Queens.

A voice answered sleepily, "Yes?"

"86," said Axel.

The voice said in Hungarian, "What's new, 86?" and yawned.

"First, when do I get some money for all the work I been doing?"

"Never mind the funny business, 86. I asked you, What's new?"

"Mr. Horscht told me—"

"*Who* told you, 86?"

"Colonel Horscht," Axel said. "My God, I mean, H."

"That's better."

"H told me to report after the Carpathia closed up. He said, let him know what happens with Gerhardi."

"Let him know what happens with *who?*"

"Major Gerhardi."

"*Who,* 86?"

"Oh, Jesus, I did it again. 35."

"So, what happened with 35?"

"He left with this woman, that's all."

"Which woman?"

"By the name of Emory. The Colonel had a long talk with her. Hey, you think that's her real name, Emory? Or could it be short for Emoryi?"

"Never mind what I think. So, 35 left with the woman, and now he's in bed with her doing his usual stuff, eh?"

"Screwing the daylights out of her," Axel said, and gave a short sour laugh.

"That's right, 86, he's screwing the daylights out of her.

And what am I doing? Minding the telephone switchboard all night."

Axel said, "Listen, Imre, we all have our own crosses to bear."

"What did you call me?"

"Imre. I mean, 47."

"You dumb bastard," 47 said. "Won't you ever learn?" He broke the connection.

Axel hung up. He waited a full minute before making any further move. Then he put a coin in the box and dialed a Chelsea number. A voice answered curtly, "Yes?"

"Ragweed here."

"Where are you?"

Axel gave the number on the dial of the telephone.

"Hang up, Ragweed. And wait."

"Yes, sair."

Axel hung up and waited. His name and the telephone number, he knew, would be passed on to an office somewhere in Virginia (or Maryland?); and the return call would come in less than thirty seconds.

The telephone rang. He put it to his ear and said, "Ragweed."

"Go ahead."

"Colonel Horscht was in the restaurant tonight, sair."

"Yes."

"He came in specially to meet Major Gerhardi, number 35."

"Yes."

"The major brought a woman—"

"Name."

"He ordered her an orchid. The name was on a card in the box. I didn't think they'd miss it. Here's the card. It says, *To Katherine M. Emory, fairest of the wise and wisest of the fair. S.G.* Pretty smart, eh?"

"How's that spelled, Emory?"

Axel spelled it out.

"That a Hungarian name, Ragweed?"

"I never heard it before, unless she changed it from Emoryi, which I'm not sure is Hungarian. Seemed to me she was one-hundred-percent pure American."

"Any idea what they talked about?"

Axel took a deep breath. "I heard them say something like about the State Department—"

"State Department?"

"That's right. Someone by the name of Gamage, or maybe it was Damage. Something about she was going to Japan or somewhere for this guy Damage."

"State Department. Gamage or Damage. Japan. Okay, what else?"

"They told her something like she had to go to Budapest."

"Why would she have to go to Budapest?"

"Something about she had to speak to a lot of students there, tell them how to start riots and so on. I didn't get the full hang of it."

"Anything else?"

"That's about the lot, sair. I couldn't get too close to them, they was kind of huddled up close together. She had the oyster omelet, Carpathian style, and he had the steak like always."

"Give me a description of this Emory."

"Gladly. Ladylike, I would say around fortyish, mink cape, nice-looking, if you like that type. Gerhardi, number 35, took her home. I guess he's still with her, right this minute."

"Anything else, Ragweed?"

"That's all."

The line went dead. Axel replaced the receiver. Two hundred and five miles away the voice said, "Katherine M.

Emory. Colonel Horscht. Major Gerhardi. State Department. Gamage or Damage. Looks kind of interesting. Let's check it out, Charlie."

"Okay," said Charlie.

5

THE GOOD habits of a lifetime triumphed in the morning. She woke, as usual, at six-thirty, threw off the bedclothes, and without any hesitation proceeded to climb out of bed, as if this morning were in no way different from any other morning of the year.

Reality caught up with her at once. Her feet became entangled in her evening gown, which was lying on the floor, horribly crumpled. She stared at it, and thought indignantly, *But that is my Balenciaga evening gown. What uncouth person threw it there?*

She looked around her uncomprehendingly. She could hardly believe that this was her bedroom. The debris of love was everywhere: a cashmere bed jacket tossed into a corner, a torn nightgown (where had *that* come from, and why was it torn?), a discarded girdle, cigarette butts (most ominous of all to a non-smoker), wine glasses, stockings like wisps of evil on the white lambswool rug, scattered shoes—not one pair, but several. She was suddenly breathless with shock. A few fragmentary images of Stefan Gerhardi returned to her, and then a too-vivid recollection of the hours she had spent with him. She did not waste another moment. Swiftly and grimly she marched to her shower.

Hot water streaming over her shoulders washed away most of the outward traces of depravity. A piercing needle-spray of ice-cold water hardened her flesh, drove out the lurking demons of lust and licentiousness. It was an ancient ritual, widely practiced at Southcliffe, and it seemed to work. She died briefly, and was reborn.

2.

She made herself a pot of coffee, carried it to her study, and firmly closed the door. Then, sitting at her desk, she found to her surprise that she was feeling remarkably well. Her body ached a little, but it was a good healthy ache, as if she had been climbing in the Dolomites. Her first cup of coffee affected her, after a few minutes, like champagne: she felt extraordinarily gay and lighthearted, and she could not help laughing at everything that had happened to her—not only last night, but all the nights of her life. The whole scheme of things, which normally seemed baffling and tragic, now seemed baffling and amusing; and she switched on her typewriter and recklessly set to work on a private letter to her shadow, Millicent Donothing.

> . . . . So the merry-go-round has started up again? How interesting. And what is your excuse this time? It came out of the blue? I see. You were minding your own business, and it sought you out? Tsk, tsk. And you did not, you could not, turn your back on it because your life has been singularly dull recently; you have a desperate hunger for love, for excitement, for physical satisfaction; they are vital to your well-being; you cannot exist without them. "We live only once," you inform me: "Why shouldn't I be happy?" Let me say at this point that there are times when I can scarcely express my contempt for you. You are a slut, Miss Millicent Donothing, and only too often you speak with the tongue of a slut.
>
> I would not dream, my dear girl, of attempting to dissuade you from clutching at any straw of happiness

in this, your only life. But I cannot help wondering, what is the precise nature of this happiness you prattle about so much? Is it, as Plato might inquire, in itself good? Is it in truth something that deserves to be pursued? Take my hand, Millicent, and let us walk together in our garden for a few minutes.

Consider with me now: what precisely is this hunger for love, for excitement, for physical satisfaction? St. Paul calls it burning. "If they cannot contain," he drones in I Corinthians, vii, 9, "let them marry: for it is better to marry than to burn." We can ask the question, therefore, in different words: What is this burning? And I think we must give praise where praise is due: it is surely one of the most brilliant of Nature's inventions, an uproariously comic device to encourage sexual relationships and thus secure the continuance of the species. You may wonder why Nature should find it necessary to promote an act that is generally considered to be the most enjoyable in the whole repertory of physical experience. The answer is that in most species the female is normally ferociously hostile to sexual intercourse. After all, it is an act that is often painful, that can have highly dangerous consequences, and that is, above everything else, a gross insult to the integrity of the individual. Do you yearn for a dentist to thrust his thumb into your mouth, do you have delicious dreams of an otologist plunging his syringe in your ear, do you sigh for a proctologist to fool around with his gloved and slippery digits in the posterior part of your alimentary canal? Hardly. And what is this act of intercourse? It is no more and no less than the transportation of sperm cells from the male into the female, in the hope (Nature's hope) that one of the sperms will encounter an egg cell which it will fertilize. We cannot very well quarrel with the mechanism of reproduction;

it is too late for that; but let us recognize it for what it is. Some of us find it not at all pretty. Hence, the phenomenon of burning: certain chemical substances are pumped into the blood stream; the female proceeds to experience something called desire; rationality deserts her for a little while; the repugnant act takes place; the bamboozled female thinks she is really living; and Nature goes on her way, laughing her head off.

Occasionally I amuse myself by browsing through the Confessions of St. Augustine; and it is delightful to observe how he foams at the mouth, how he beats his breast, but, ah! how he revels in telling of the fearful wickedness of his youth. "I strayed further from Thee . . . and I was tossed about, and wasted, and dissipated, and I boiled over in my fornications . . . the madness of lust took rule over me . . . the briers of unclean desires grew rank over my head . . . I walked the streets of Babylon and wallowed in the mire thereof, as if in a bed of spices and precious ointments . . . the invisible enemy trod me down and seduced me, for I was easy to be seduced." But, unlike Paul, Augustine was human in his burning. Contritely he begged of the Lord: *Da mihi castitatem et continentiam, sed noli modo*. It is, I think, one of the most charming prayers in history, and I pass it on to you for your own use: *Lord, give me chastity and continency, but not just yet*. And he goes on to explain why. "For I feared lest Thou shouldst hear me soon, and soon cure me of the sin of sexual lust, which I wished to have satisfied rather than extinguished."

So you see, you are in good company, dear Millicent. I regret that you are unable to withstand the sly connivings of old Mother Nature; it is a pity that you cannot help behaving like a biological idiot; yet you can justly claim precedents like St. Augustine, whose holiness is beyond dispute. You can argue that you, too, will arrive at chastity and continency in time, preferably when the fires of Nature have burned themselves out.

Fondly, et cetera
The Party of the First Part

She read the letter carefully, made a few changes in pencil, and put it away in the file labeled *Pressure-Cooker Recipes.* Her spirits were still remarkably high. Looking at her watch she saw that the time was now nearly half past nine and, almost literally, she smacked her lips at the thought of the breakfast that would be awaiting her. She switched off her typewriter, opened the door of her study, and found Giselle and Mrs. Corcoran screaming at each other in the middle of the living room.

"Good heavens!" Kate cried. "What's going on here?"

They continued to scream at each other, as if she were invisible.

She advanced, waving her arms at them. "Be quiet, be *quiet.* I will not have this dreadful behavior. Stop it, at once."

"She—" Mrs. Corcoran shouted.

"She—" Giselle screamed.

Kate pushed between them and said, "Mrs. Corcoran, go to the kitchen and fix my breakfast. Giselle, go to the study and get on with some typing." And when they lingered, unwilling to call a halt to such a rousing engagement, Kate cried, "Now! This very instant! Both of you!"

They separated and slunk away guiltily. These squabbles occurred every few weeks, with such regularity that Kate was inclined to believe that they might well be related to the phases of the moon. It was like having a tough old alley cat and a refined young Persian cat living in the apartment. Normally they would ignore each other, maintaining a sort of cool neutrality; but then (at new moon? or full moon?)

there would be a great deal of hissing, unsheathed claws would flash in the air, fur would fly, and the refined young Persian cat would inevitably suffer a scratched nose, a chewed ear, and hurt feelings.

When Mrs. Corcoran arrived with the breakfast tray, Kate said sternly, "Please listen to me. I want no more scenes in this apartment. Do you understand? I will not have my tranquility disturbed by such outrageous behavior."

"What about my tranquility?" Mrs. Corcoran asked. "Don't that count?"

It was a reasonable question, and it took the wind out of Kate's sails. She decided that the safest way to deal with it was to ignore it. She ate her breakfast quickly and without any pleasure, and then went into the study, where Giselle was typing erratically and weeping. Kate's heart sank at the sight of her, but justice required that she should be admonished as sternly as her enemy had been. "Please get this into your head," Kate said. "You may find Mrs. Corcoran thoroughly objectionable. Nevertheless, I expect you to behave toward her with moderation, with tolerance, with gentleness. Is that clear?"

"Moderation, tolerance, gentleness," Giselle said wildly. "Oh, my God, how can you expect that from me? She—"

"Giselle, I simply don't wish to hear any more. If you and Mrs. Corcoran can't get along, you must both go. I will not have this conflict continuing day after day."

"I will kill myself," Giselle moaned. "I've reached the end of my tether."

"You will not kill yourself," Kate said. "You haven't reached even the beginning of your tether. Now let us get down to some work."

3.

The last three chapters of *The Women of America*—about a hundred and twenty pages—were undergoing a final revision; when this was completed (in two weeks, Kate hoped), the manuscript could go off to Craven Press and Kate's mind would be freed of a prodigious burden. But work this morning was difficult. The telephone rang constantly. Each time she expected to hear Stefan greeting her, and each time she was disappointed.

It rang at ten-thirty. A dry little voice which seemed to come from a thousand miles away said, "Miss Katherine Emory?"

"Yes?"

"Good morning, Miss Emory. I hope I am not disturbing you. I am calling at the request of Mr. Gamage of the Department of State. This is Miss Elsie Mitsamushi."

Kate frowned. Miss Elsie *who?* Then she said, "Oh ! Miss Mitsamushi! How nice of you to call! Yes, I was hoping to hear from you: Mr. Gamage and I made a date on your behalf. For tea, here in my apartment, at four o'clock this afternoon. Can you come?"

"I am honored," Miss Mitsamushi said, as if she were dying. "It is most kind of you."

"Not at all. I was so sorry that we had no opportunity to talk at lunch yesterday. Now we'll be able to have a long chat in comfort. Do you know how to get to Gramercy Park, where I live?"

"Thank you, I have been to Gramercy Park a few times. A dear uncle of mine lived there once."

Kate said, "At four o'clock, then. I look forward to it very much. Good-by, Miss Mitsamushi."

"Good-by, Miss Emory."

A little while later, Rushton Wyle called to say that some magazine wanted, in a great hurry, an article on Our Changing Attitude to Sex. She shuddered and said, "No, Rushton." He asked, "Why not?" She said, "I can't interrupt my work on the book for Norton Goodrich. I *must* get it finished."

Then, within twenty minutes, Norton himself called, to suggest a dinner date for the following week. She repeated what she had told Rushton, and he said, "Sure, sure, I appreciate that, but you have to eat, don't you?" She fobbed him off.

Rushton called a second time to say that a women's club in Kansas City would pay a highly respectable fee if she would fly out and give a brief address on The New Sexual Mores of American Women, and she cried, "My God, what is happening, Rushton? Everyone in this country seems to have gone sex mad." He chuckled and said, "Has that only just dawned on you?" She replied, "No, I will not go out to Kansas City," and hung up.

Ten minutes later, Dean Gilberta Marchmont's secretary, Olive Bartlett, called from Southcliffe and said in a hushed voice, "Miss Emory, the Dean has asked me to say that she would be exceedingly happy if you could come up for the weekend. Is it, at such short notice, possible?"

"Olive, please convey my most sincere regrets to the Dean. I'm afraid my schedule this weekend makes it impossible."

"Could you, perhaps, come the following weekend? The Dean is very anxious to have you speak to the senior class on—"

"On our changing attitude to sex?"

"Yes! Exactly! How did you guess? The Dean feels this is a subject of the greatest importance in these perilous times—"

"Olive, I would be happy to do it, but I simply don't know at the moment how I am placed for the following weekend. Let me call you back early next week."

"Very well, Miss Emory. Dean Gilberta asked me, particularly, not to forget to say that she sends you her love."

"Tell her that I send her my love, too."

4.

At noon, she left Giselle to continue typing and hurried to her bedroom to dress. She was one of the guests of honor at a luncheon at the Waldorf, participating in a panel discussion on the role of American women in world affairs; and suddenly, as she was putting on her shoes, her mind began to cry wildly for Stefan. Why had he not called? He'd promised to call. Why had he not kept his promise? She thought, Perhaps the Department of Commemorative Stamps at the United Nations is in conference all day today; but there was no humor in the quip, and her heart—which had been uplifted until now—became heavy.

She said to Mrs. Corcoran, as she was about to leave, "I have a guest coming for tea. Will you be kind enough to get a small cake and some assorted cookies?"

"For tea today?"

"Yes, for tea today."

"I will try my best to remember," Mrs. Corcoran said, drying her hands on her apron. "And while we're on the subject, do you want me to throw out the steak that's eating its head off in the icebox?"

"Has it spoiled, Mrs. Corcoran?"

"It was meant to be consumed yesterday, you know. It can't lay there forever. And if you want me to throw it out, it would be just as easy for me to wrap it up in a piece of newspaper and take it home for my hubby, that the doctor told him he should go on a steady diet of old meat, he shouldn't eat no new meat at the peril of his life."

"I'll let you know about it later."

"Okay."

Kate walked out of the apartment smiling at Mrs. Corcoran's leprechaun humor. It could be charming occasionally. *The doctor told him he shouldn't eat no new meat at the peril of his life.* How wonderful, she thought.

But as she opened the front door and looked down at the street, the smile froze, her mouth fell open. Stefan Gerhardi was lounging in front of the iron railings that enclosed the little park, looking as if he belonged to some clandestine and dangerous organization. He wore a black suit, a narrow black tie, pointed black shoes, and a sinister little black hat was pulled down to conceal his eyes. His skin was pale, his lips were thin, and as he glanced up at her she was shocked by the expression of hatred and bitterness on his handsome face. She called, "Stefan!" and at the sound of his name he pulled the brim of his hat down another quarter of an inch, turned away from her, and went limping off in a rage. She thought in consternation, *What is the matter, why is he behaving like this?* and she called again, "Stefan! Stefan!" He hunched his shoulders, as if her voice offended him. "Stefan, wait!" she called, and ran down the stone steps, determined to get an explanation, *any* explanation, for this Byronic behavior, but he continued to limp away toward the Gramercy Park Hotel. She realized that she could not possibly overtake him and, since a number of people were now watching the scene with interest, she stopped running and tried to look as if nothing unusual were taking place. For some reason he stopped at the same moment, and turned and glared at her with burning malevolence, as a tiger might turn and glare at a pursuing maharajah. Then, his eyes narrow, he began to walk back to her. When he was within a few feet of her he halted and said, "I warn you. Do not come any nearer."

She said in astonishment, "Why mustn't I come any nearer?"

He gritted his teeth. "Because I shall not be responsible for my actions."

"What have I done, Stefan? What has happened? Why are you so disturbed?"

He grinned like a death's head. "You may be interested to know that I have been here since eight o'clock this morning."

She could not recall having been so bewildered at any time in her life. She exclaimed, "But why? *Why* have you been here since eight o'clock this morning?"

He looked at her with contempt. "Watching the house, naturally."

"Naturally!" That was the end. *Naturally*. "But why were you watching the house?"

"I could not expect you to understand," he said haughtily.

"*Try* me," she said. She was annoyed with him now. "I *might* understand. And wouldn't *that* surprise you."

He hobbled closer. "You could never understand," he said, trembling with emotion, "because it seems that you have no feelings, none at all." His voice became low and choked. "I could not sleep. My love for you kept me awake. All night, I had cramps, I was in agony, it was like being in hell. So I came here just to be near you, Katherine. Just to be near you."

She was deeply upset by his accusation. It was true: she had not been kept awake by love for him. On the contrary, she could not recall a night when she had slept more soundly. A picture suddenly entered her mind, of herself snoring like a contented pig while he, in an adjoining picture, writhed in pain. She was filled with guilt.

He smiled bitterly. "You do not have to tell me what you are thinking. I am being a confounded nuisance, coming here and making a scene in this aristocratic neighborhood. Right?"

"No."

"Why deny it, darling? Last night was simply an episode for you. You were having a little fun at the expense of some bloody foreigner, eh? Hahaha."

"No, Stefan, that isn't so."

"But it *is* so, Katherine. You should see the expression on your face. *This chap Gerhardi is a pain in the neck,* you are saying to yourself. *Why doesn't he get lost?*"

She said desperately, "Stefan, we can't talk here. I have a luncheon date at the Waldorf-Astoria. Come. Ride up there in the taxi with me."

He reacted as if she had stabbed him. "You have a luncheon date at *the Waldorf-Astoria!* Why do you lie to me? You mean, you have an assignation there."

"No, no, of course not."

"Who is this man?" he growled. "I demand to know. You will admit that I have a right to know. Is it the Burford who telephoned when you were in my arms last night?"

She was beginning to feel hysterical. Apparently she would never succeed in convincing him that she was, at heart, a profoundly puritanical woman, not at all inclined to be unfaithful. She said, "Stefan, it's simply a luncheon that is being given by the Mid-Century Club, and I am one of the speakers."

He pulled a handful of invitation cards out of the left pocket of his jacket, more out of the right pocket, still more out of an inside pocket. Her heart sank as she watched the familiar procedure. He flicked through the cards like a Mississippi gambler, and said, "You see? I do not have an invitation to any so-called Mid-Century Club. I suspect it exists only in your imagination. Why can you not be honest with me, Katherine?"

"Stefan, it's a club of women executives, *women*. They do not invite men to these luncheons."

"A very convenient story."

"But it's *true*, it's *true*."

He limped beside her, breathing heavily. Her eyes had filled with tears, partly from frustration, partly because she was so upset by his suffering. She took his arm and whispered, "Stefan, please ride up to the Waldorf with me. I would appreciate it so much."

He shrugged one shoulder in gloomy assent.

But a few minutes later, sitting beside him in the taxi, her openness began to take effect. His truculence ebbed, he acted like a man waking from a dream. In a gesture that filled her with joy he raised her hand to his lips and said, "I beg your pardon, Katherine. I have been horrible to you, horrible, and you have behaved like an angel. Will you ever forgive me?"

"Of course."

He moved closer to her, and his hand touched her breast. She felt as if her breast had been seared by a flash of flame. He said, "I did not believe I could ever love a woman like this. I thought I could always control my passion. But I cannot, I *cannot*. I am mad about you, Katherine. *Mad*."

She shivered. The flash of flame was searing the hollow of her back and spreading up her spine.

He spoke quietly, almost in her ear. "To hell with this damned stupid luncheon, Katherine. Why are you wasting your beauty, your intelligence, your heart's blood, on a bunch of women executives? Tell the driver to turn around. Let us go back to your apartment."

She said desperately, "I have to attend this luncheon. It's an obligation. I *must* go." She attempted to divert his attention. "What about you? Don't you have to go to the United

Nations? The Department of Commemorative Stamps—won't they miss you?"

"They will not miss me, Katherine. And if they do miss me, so what? The hell with them. Even if I went in this afternoon, how could I work? How could I think of perforations, watermarks, when I am obsessed by you? *Tell the driver to turn around.*"

"Stefan, I can't, I can't."

"Let me tell him."

"My dear, it's impossible. I don't want to go to the luncheon, but I must."

"Must?"

"Yes." She was trembling, and she had difficulty breathing. Nothing had really happened; he had scarcely touched her, yet her blood was pounding violently through her body and she wanted desperately to do what he asked—return to the apartment, resume lovemaking, enjoy his kisses and his nearness.

Her New England conscience prevailed. The taxi drove on.

5.

In the foyer of the Waldorf-Astoria he said, "For the last time: you insist on going to lunch with these executive women?"

"I have to, Stefan."

"What time will this luncheon be over?"

"I suppose about two-thirty."

"All right. I will meet you here—right here, on this spot where we are standing—at half past two."

She shook her head.

"Why not?" he asked. "Then we will have the afternoon to ourselves, as well as tonight."

"I can't. I have a date with Miss Mitsamushi at four o'clock."

"Who?"

"Miss Mitsamushi. A Japanese girl who is helping me with the arrangements for my lecture tour."

"Oh, for God's sake. Now a Miss Mitsamushi comes between us. Well, then, suggest a time yourself when we can meet."

"At seven," she said. "Seven-thirty."

"That is too late," he said. "I will call for you at your apartment at six-thirty."

"Very well."

He kissed her hand and, still very agitated, she went on to her luncheon. The honorary secretary of the Mid-Century Club, Mrs. Laurence, greeted her warmly and then, after a few moments of chatter, said hesitantly, "My dear, perhaps I shouldn't say this, but you're looking a little pale, you know. Are you feeling all right?"

"Perfectly," Kate said.

Mrs. Laurence said, "I suppose it's the light in here. It seems to give one a greenish tinge. How thoughtless of the Waldorf-Astoria! One expects better things of them, doesn't one? As if we didn't have enough problems without turning green."

But halfway through lunch, while she was attempting to consume some excellent creamed chicken, Kate was suddenly overcome by nausea. Her imagination had brought Stefan back: he was sitting at her side, whispering passionately in her ear, touching her arms, her breasts, her thighs, trying to arouse her despite the presence of seventy or eighty dignified female executives, and the mental image was so distressing that she mumbled an apology to Mrs. Laurence and crept away to the ladies' lounge, shivering and in physical pain. In a few moments, Mrs. Laurence appeared like a guardian angel, and said in a sympathetic voice, "My dear, I was *right,* it was *not* the lights; you *aren't* up to snuff. I'll wager it's the twenty-four-hour flu; my sister had it last week; she went precisely the same shade of green. You were brave to come, and I appreciate it very much; but, of course, I simply can't allow you to exhaust yourself by taking part in the panel discussion, the only place for you is bed."

The only place for me is *not* bed, Kate thought. She said, "I shall be perfectly all right if you would be kind enough to order me some brandy."

Mrs. Laurence regarded her with horrified suspicion. "*Brandy,* my dear? Are you sure?"

"If I can have some brandy," Kate said, "and sit quietly for a few minutes, I think this spell will pass."

Mrs. Laurence said, "Well, I suppose you know your own insides better than anybody else," a statement that seemed to Kate, even in her wretched condition, questionable; but soon the brandy was brought and, after a brief period of rest, Kate was able to return to her place. When the panel discussion began she was as calm and lucid as ever; her opening remarks brought the appreciative laughter and the applause to which she was accustomed. "You were *so* good," Mrs. Laurence said enthusiastically when she sat down, "and your color is so much better." But Kate did not have, then or later, any recollection of what she had said. Willy-nilly, she had done what was expected of her. It was a principle that Southcliffe had drummed into her brain and engraved on her heart: *You must always fulfil your obligations, no matter what the cost.* Dean Gilberta would have been very proud of her.

6

SHE ARRIVED back at her apartment a few minutes after three o'clock, and once again she found Mrs. Corcoran and Giselle screaming at each other, like two harpies—an ancient one and a youthful one—practicing their art in the middle of the living room.

"*Now* what is going on?" Kate demanded.

Mrs. Corcoran cried, "I caught her trying to throw out my chrysanthemums, that's what's going on."

"She called me a bloodsucking parasite," Giselle cried.

"Mrs. Corcoran," Kate said: "And you, Giselle. I want both of you to leave, now, this very minute. You may return tomorrow *only* if you feel that you can live at peace with each other."

"But—" Mrs. Corcoran said. "But—" Giselle said.

"I am in no mood for your shenanigans. Good afternoon."

She sat on the big settee, ignoring them as they made preparations to leave. This continuing quarrel added to her sense of inadequacy. What right have I, she asked herself bitterly, to be doing a book on the women of America? I really know *nothing* about them, just as I really know *nothing* about sexual relationships. I am a fraud.

Mrs. Corcoran marched over to her and said, "The cake and the cookies you asked me to get, they're in the kitchen."

"Thank you."

"I just want to get it off my chest about that girl of yours—"

"Good afternoon, Mrs. Corcoran."

A moment later Giselle tiptoed over to her. "I typed fifteen pages of the revised manuscript, Miss Emory."

"Thank you."

"I'm sorry I'm so hateful. If you wish, I'll apologize to Mrs. Corcoran and beg her forgiveness."

"That is for you to decide. Good afternoon, Giselle."

When she was alone she thought, Does not St. Matthew counsel firmness? *If thine eye offend thee, pluck it out and cast it from thee.* I shall be equally firm with Stefan when he comes at six-thirty. He is disturbing my equilibrium. I simply won't let him into the apartment. I cannot have my whole life turned upside-down by his pressure upon me, by his abnormal sexual demands, by his Central European dramatics.

The telephone rang, and she stiffened, sure that he was calling her; but it was only Rushton to inform her that one of her books was going to be translated into Swedish, and a chapter of another book was being translated into Hindustani by some obscure offshoot of the United Nations—not the Department of Commemorative Stamps.

The telephone rang again within a couple of minutes. This time she was certain that Stefan was calling: she knew it in her bones. But instead of the sharp, lively, masculine voice she expected, she heard a woman's voice addressing her.

"Miss Emory? Is this Miss Katherine Emory?"

"Yes," she said, withdrawing into her shell like a snail.

"Ah! Miss Emory! It is unforgivable of me to call like this—we have not been introduced—but I could not resist the temptation. I am Emmy Horscht."

"Who?" Kate asked, taken aback.

"Emmy Horscht. Mrs. Miklos Horscht. My husband had the pleasure of meeting you, he told me, last night in the café-restaurant Carpathia. My God! I hope he told me the truth, that he *really* met you! Otherwise I will never be able to hold my head up again."

"Yes, I did indeed meet Mr. Horscht in the Carpathia last night."

"It *was* the truth! Oh, I am so glad. I should not doubt him, he is a very truthful man." The voice was high and tinkly, and it seemed to be on the verge of laughter. She went on, "And Miklos says you were in the company of my dear friend, Stefan Gerhardi."

Again, snail-like, Kate shrank back into her shell. "Yes, I was."

"He is a wonderful, wonderful man," Mrs. Horscht babbled. "A quite outstanding person. I am devoted to him—he is *so* charming, and *so* thoughtful. Don't you agree?"

I can't very well *disagree,* Kate thought. She said vaguely, "Yes."

"Now, let me tell you the reason I am calling, Miss Emory. On Saturday, at the end of next week, we are having a little party at our house, and Miklos and I wondered if you would honor us by coming to it."

"How kind of you."

"Many people from the diplomatic services are coming, from the United Nations, et cetera. I am sure you will know most of them. And I will tell you a secret: it is my birthday party."

"Congratulations, Mrs. Horscht."

"It is a little early for congratulations," she laughed. "But thank you. Do you think you can come?"

"I will have to check my engagement book."

"We would send the official car for you, the Lincoln Continental, with, of course, the chauffeur. At seven o'clock—would that suit you, seven o'clock? Perhaps you will let Stefan know, and he will communicate with us. Not too late, please, because we have to make up our lists. Oh, and another thing," the tinkly voice continued: "Miklos told me that last night you were wearing a gown of indescribable style and beauty—"

Kate laughed. "It wasn't anything special."

"But Miklos has been raving about it, my dear, he has talked about nothing else. Believe me, you have won a great victory for the United States in Miklos' eyes. So, I want to ask you in strict confidence, Miss Emory: where did you purchase it?"

Kate hesitated. Then she said, "Bergdorf's."

"I should have guessed. Well: tomorrow I will pay them a visit and see if they have anything in my size. Would you care to accompany me? We could have lunch at the Four Seasons, of which I have heard excellent reports."

"I would like to," Kate said. "But unfortunately I have a luncheon date tomorrow."

"With Stefan? Oh, you lucky person! He is stupendous, is he not? Phenomenal!"

"No," Kate said, ignoring Mrs. Horscht's girlish outburst. "I have to attend a luncheon given by the Association of American Librarians."

"*Librarians!* But how marvelous! Between ourselves, I am always so impressed by librarians. They know so much! *They have read so many books!* They make me feel so ignorant, I am afraid to meet their eyes. Well, I deeply regret that we cannot meet tomorrow. Perhaps I can telephone you at the beginning of next week. Is that permissible?"

"Please do, Mrs. Horscht."

"You are charming, Miss Emory. I understand perfectly now why Stefan and Miklos think so highly of you. You have won my heart, too." Mrs. Horscht laughed sweetly. "For the present, then, good-by."

"Good-by," Kate said.

She sat back perplexed, wondering why Mrs. Horscht had made this curious telephone call. It was difficult to believe that Mrs. Horscht was as naïve, or unsophisticated, as she pretended. Was she emotionally involved with Stefan Gerhardi? Could she possibly be one of his numerous mistresses? And did she call, Kate asked herself, to check up on me? How many mistresses did Stefan have altogether? Andrea Moscowitz, the dancer whom Kate had met in Marcel Preiss' studio, was alleged by Marcel to be number six or number seven. What number was Mrs. Horscht? *What number,* Kate thought, *am I?*

She became very agitated. Doubts hammered at her mind with disconcerting persistence. She was not only disturbed by her own conduct and by Stefan's conduct; she was also confronted by a crowd of female spectres who, in her imagination, were all young, beautiful, voluptuous, and insanely in love with this volcanic Hungarian. (*He is stupendous, is he not? Phenomenal.*) It must stop, Kate told herself firmly. It *shall* stop.

2.

The security report—marked *Secret and Urgent*—was on Gamage's desk at nine-thirty that morning. He read it with mounting bewilderment, and then checked it against the full security report in his file. The situation appeared to be that up to the time he lunched with Katherine Emory at Charlot's yesterday her reliability (in security terms) was unquestioned. Minutes after he left her on Central Park South her security rating had collapsed and her reliability was extremely dubious. It was almost impossible to believe; nevertheless, he was compelled to believe it. If she had been seen alone with Stefan Gerhardi, or if she had been seen alone with Miklos Horscht, there might have been some simple explanation of her behavior; but to be seen with both Gerhardi and Horscht, to have been overheard discussing with them her trip to Japan and, additionally, to be arranging a trip to Budapest to address the students there, raised the most serious questions. He had no alternative: he was forced to take action at once.

He decided to bypass his colleagues Ed Smith and Victor Williamson. The fewer people who knew about Kate Emory's slipped halo the better. He took the report directly to the Assistant Secretary, Eben Weber, a man with long experience in the muddy waters of state.

Weber read the report and said, "Good grief. Kate Emory? I'd never have believed it. How reliable is Maryland's man on this beat?"

"I checked it out with them before I came up to see you," Gamage said. "They assured me he's one of their best. Never let them down so far. Absolutely reliable."

"What I can't figure out is why she should be going to Budapest to speak to the students and tell them how to start riots. I mean, since when do students need to be *told* how to start riots?"

"I don't buy that," Gamage said.

"It's so stupid," Weber said, "that it's probably true." He pressed a switch on his intercom and said, "Ask Mr. Alvarez to come to my office."

"Yes, sir," said the intercom.

Alvarez arrived within a couple of minutes: a stocky dark-eyed man who had crashed in a jet fighter in Korea. He still bore the scars of the crash and the fire that followed.

He read the report and handed it back to Weber without comment.

"Well?" Weber asked.

"I know Colonel Horscht, of course," Alvarez said. "He's one of their top Public Safety men. Gerhardi's part of their stable of trained stallions."

"Eh?" Weber said. "How come?"

"You haven't heard about that program?" Alvarez said. He never smiled, because the risorius muscle on the right side of his mouth had been damaged. "They have an estate outside Moscow where a number of hand-picked personnel, male and female, undergo special technical training. It's like a small M.I.T., except that instead of taking physics, engineering, and stuff like that, they take courses in sex."

"Sex?" said the Assistant Secretary, as if he had never heard the word before.

"Right. They get instruction from doctors, surgeons, psychologists, whores, madams, queers, lesbians, every kind of pervert you can think of, chemists who've made a study of aphrodisiacs—anyone who can give them a line on sex and on how to improve their performance. By the time they graduate, at the end of eight months, they have the equivalent of a Ph.D. in fornication. They can take on anything, from an ambassador's wife to a two-humped camel."

"You're kidding," Weber said.

"No, sir."

"Do we have anything like that?"

"Unfortunately, we don't," Alvarez said. "Or if we do, I haven't been told about it."

Weber said, "Well, where does this leave Kate Emory?"

Alvarez said contemptuously, "Oh, her. She's guilty as hell, of course."

"Now, wait a minute," Gamage said.

"Wait a minute yourself. This is a question of security. Rule one in security is, they're guilty until they're proven innocent. Rule two is, they're probably *still* guilty. Let me ask you something, Phil: Did you actually ask Miss Emory to carry out certain missions on our behalf?"

"I didn't specify any missions. Everything was left vague and tentative."

"But you spoke to her about Jiro Mitsamushi?"

"Yes, I did."

"You inferred that arrangements might be made for her to meet some of Jiro's contacts on the China mainland?"

"Yes."

Alvarez said, "What's all the argument about, then? She's compromised, beyond a shadow of doubt. She's in possession of classified information of, potentially, the highest importance; and she's sleeping with an agent of a very special kind whose training is such that he can easily extract this information from her. What more do you want?"

"You've made your point," Weber said. "Now, what's our next step? Do we find some excuse and cancel the tour?"

"I'd like to clobber her," Alvarez growled. "But then, I'm old-fashioned. I'd like to clobber all traitors."

Gamage exclaimed, "She's no traitor!"

"God damn it," Alvarez said, "I call it treason, and I'll always call it treason. If she has to sleep with someone, let her sleep with somebody of her own kind."

"I never heard—" Gamage said, stretching himself to his full height.

"Now, now," Weber said. "Let's not fight about who Kate Emory should sleep with." He gave Gamage a lecherous smile. "Phil: who, exactly, was Miss Emory going to meet from the mainland?"

Gamage said, "Wing Tzu Pei, Sin H'sui, and others of that group."

"Group A," Weber said, and grinned.

"I beg your pardon?"

Weber went on, "Well, I now have another group in mind, which we'll call Group B. A younger group. More volatile than Group A. They might be, for example, *defectors* from the Red Guard. Phil, you've heard of a young fellow by the name of Sun Pat Hsueng?"

Gamage was taken aback. "Sure. But—"

Weber turned to Alvarez. "Jim, did you ever hear of this young fellow by the name of Sun Pat Hsueng?"

"No. I haven't."

Weber said, "An idea is beginning to form in this decrepit old brain of mine, and I'd like to give it some encouragement, as the French say, *pour encourager les autres.* Let's kick it around for a while and see what happens, eh?"

About twenty minutes later Gamage said wearily, "Okay. Okay. I'll go along with that. But I just want to observe, for the record, that in my opinion Katherine Emory is a damned fine woman, and I would hate to see her destroyed."

"If she's on the level," Alvarez said, "she won't be destroyed. And if she isn't on the level, she deserves everything she gets."

Gamage said, "You're kind of bloodthirsty, aren't you, Jim? I mean, just a little on the bloodthirsty side?"

Alvarez said, "You bet I am."

The Assistant Secretary interrupted. "Phil, what time is Elsie Mitsamushi having tea with Miss Emory?"

"Four o'clock this afternoon."

"So there's plenty of time to get in touch with her and inform her of the new routine?"

"Yes. She's in her hotel right now, waiting for a call from me to confirm various arrangements."

"Okay," Weber said. "Go to it. And keep me informed."

"While you're about it," Alvarez said, "you might keep me informed, too."

"Sure," Gamage said, and walked out.

3.

Miss Mitsamushi wore the same gray flannel dress she had worn yesterday. She still had difficulty catching her breath, and she was exceedingly nervous, presumably as a result of finding herself alone with her heroine, the renowned Katherine M. Emory. She took tiny sparrowlike sips of the tea that Kate poured for her, she nibbled a few crumbs of the cake that Mrs. Corcoran had bought, and she sat on the edge of the chintz-covered armchair, opposite Kate who sat on the big settee, with an apprehensive look on her face and her knees pressed tightly together.

Kate was filled with despair. She was in no mood to make conversation with this tongue-tied, jittery little woman. Her mind was in a turmoil over Stefan Gerhardi and the woman who had entered her life a little while ago, Emmy Horscht. But an effort had to be made to establish some relationship with Miss Mitsamushi and to put her at her ease; and she broke the ice by saying, as warmly and admiringly as she could, "I think you ought to know that after you left us at Charlot's yesterday, Mr. Gamage said the most flattering things about you."

"No, no," Miss Mitsamushi said shyly, one hand twitching in her lap. "Is that possible?"

"It is not only possible, it actually happened. He sang your praises. I understand that you are an expert on audio-visual devices for education, and that you are writing a thesis on Japanese folk-music."

"*Hogaku.*"

"Yes, *hogaku.* Is this thesis for your doctorate?"

Miss Mitsamushi giggled. "Yes."

"Isn't that *splendid!* Mr. Gamage wasn't exaggerating a bit. Now, tell me about *hogaku.* Is it in any way like our folk-music?"

"Only insofar as it is written by, and for, folks. Otherwise, I am sorry to say, no."

"Is it at all like—let's say—the old Elizabethan music?"

"No, I am afraid, not at all."

"I would love to hear some of it," Kate said. "Is it available on records?"

"I have some tape recordings, but not with me here. They are in Washington."

"Are you living in Washington?"

"Part time," Miss Mitsamushi said.

"And where do you spend the rest of your time?"

"In Tokyo, with my family."

"Ah, yes. Mr. Gamage told me you have just returned from a visit to your family in Tokyo. I hope you found everybody well."

"In excellent health." Miss Mitsamushi's breathing became more labored. She said, "To be truly honest with you, before I came to see you I received a telephone call at my hotel from Mr. Gamage."

"Is he still in New York?" Kate said. "Perhaps I should have invited him to tea, also."

"No. He returned to Washington last night. The reason he called was to let me know what he had discussed with you yesterday, and to advise me that he had mentioned something about the activities of my brother Jiro."

"That's right. He did mention your brother Jiro to me. I hope you don't mind?"

Miss Mitsamushi smiled. "Whatever Mr. Gamage tells you is okay. Mr. Gamage knows best."

"Mr. Gamage told me, in his own words, that your brother is a fervent pacifist and passionately anti-American."

Miss Mitsamushi's smile broadened. It was a cheery, feminine smile that seemed to imply (Kate thought) that boys will be boys. She said, "It is quite true, but you must not be too alarmed about it." She reached down for a black leather dispatch case she had brought with her, and as she snapped it open she said, "I have here some papers on the pacifist, anti-American movement. Mr. Gamage suggested that you would like to read them. They will give you a better idea of what is actually going on among our youth." She extracted three mimeographed documents, each consisting of about six pages, and held them out to Kate.

"Thank you," Kate said. "I shall read them with the greatest interest." She put them on the settee, beside her.

"You must bear in mind," Miss Mitsamushi said, "that

there is much soul-searching going on within our young people. Nobody has come up yet with an answer that is fully satisfying. Leftism is not the answer; rightism is not the answer; the answer must be somewhere in-between, in the center. I think that is why Jiro looks forward so much to talking to you when you come to Japan. Likewise many other people. Mr. Gamage mentioned some contacts on the Chinese mainland, did he not?"

"Yes, he did."

Miss Mitsamushi sat rigidly for a moment, thinking. Her mouth was tight, her eyes were blank. Then, once more, she reached down and opened her dispatch case. This time she took out a single sheet of paper. "I have here," she said, "a memorandum on the subject. I am sure you will treat it as highly confidential, because it relates to my brother's most secret work."

"Are you sure you want me to read it?"

"Mr. Gamage asked me to give it to you." She held the sheet of paper out to Kate. "It is a short account of three meetings held in Shanghai between my brother Jiro and this person we call Brother Hop."

Kate laughed. "Brother Jiro and Brother Hop! Isn't that charming! And who is Brother Hop?"

"He is a young Chinese person. You will learn his real name in due course."

"Now you've really aroused my curiosity. May I glance through the document quickly?"

"Certainly. I apologize for this being only a carbon copy. The top copy was given to Mr. Gamage for transmission to the Assistant Secretary."

"Of course," Kate said.

The carbon copy was smudged; and it smudged a little more when she inadvertently put her fingers on the typed matter. The sheet was headed *Highly Confidential,* and as Kate read it her eyes widened.

For the Attention of:
Asst. Secy.
via: Mr. P. C. Gamage

From:
Hogaku.

Subject: Emory

Three meetings were held between Jiro Mitsamushi and Brother Hop in Shanghai as follows:

September 16, 2 P.M., Six Maidens Restaurant
September 17, 9 A.M., Pine Cone Restaurant
September 19, 6 P.M., Hotel Wei, Bubbling Well Rd.

As relating to visit of Miss K.M.E., following was discussed by Jiro M. and Brother H:

Brother H. knew K.M.E. by reputation. He had also checked through his own sources, confirming that K.M.E. was respected in many countries throughout the world as writer with genuine liberalistic views, also neo-Catholic. Jiro explained to Brother H. that neo-Catholic means updated Catholic, similar to deeply loved, brutally assassinated late President. Brother H. said, late President might have become world-saver, and said he would be glad to hold conversations with Miss K.M.E. To what extent was she backed by U.S. govt.? Jiro explained, private individual, but U.S. govt. would give close attention to anything she reported to them. Meetings to be held earliest possible January. Locality to be decided in next talks.

H.

Kate put the sheet of paper down and murmured, "How interesting. And all this has been going on without anybody mentioning it to me?"

"It is the way things have to be done," Miss Mitsamushi said.

"But I see that these conversations were held about three weeks ago. Yet I only signed the contracts a couple of days ago, and they were given to Mr. Gamage yesterday."

"It was anticipated that you would sign the contracts. All these arrangements for confidential talks must be made well in advance. Now there will be plenty of time for you to be briefed on the various subjects that may be raised by Brother Hop."

"I see," Kate said. She held the sheet of paper out. "Would you like to have this back for safekeeping?"

"You may hold on to it for the present, Miss Emory."

"Very well."

The conversation petered out. Miss Mitsamushi declined more tea, and her breathing became so labored that Kate was alarmed. At five o'clock, with many muffled expressions of gratitude, she left.

4.

For a while, Kate sat listening to a Mozart string quintet, K.516. It was somber and tragic, matching her new mood. When it was over she wanted to hear nothing more. She ran a hot bath and soaked in the steaming, perfumed water, hoping not only to cleanse the outer surface of her body but, at the same time, to clarify the frightful muddle within her mind. She was aware that her behavior (the attack of nausea at lunch, the inability to remember what she had said to the ladies of the Mid-Century Club, her indifference to Miss Mitsamushi, even the act of taking this bath) was irrational; she was also aware that she was caught up in a crisis of considerable proportions, possibly the most serious crisis of her life. But what exactly was this crisis? She could not say. It was vague and imprecise. It had something to do with her age, thirty-nine, with sexual excesses which she could not condone, except in others, with the loss of dignity, and perhaps even the loss of honor. She said to herself, "I will never see Stefan again, never, never, never," and when she stepped out of the bath she went and sat in front of the dressing-table mirror in her bedroom and fretted over her appearance—her complexion, the lines around her mouth, her gray-flecked hair. She wanted to rush out and have her hair tinted—any shade would do—so that he (an unnamed he) would not make the mistake of assuming that she was older than she really was. But then, what did it matter, since she would not be seeing this nameless man tonight, or ever? If he came at six-thirty she would simply not answer the door. If he telephoned she would not pick up the telephone. She put on an Empire gown by Dior, simply because it was the perfect costume for reading, or for typing on an electric typewriter; she dabbed on her most expensive perfume to ward off any germs that might be lying in wait for her in the living room; she checked the supply of ice cubes in the icebox to make sure there was enough in case she suddenly decided to do some heavy solitary drinking; and at a quarter past six she began to grow hysterical because he showed no signs of arriving and thus she would be denied the pleasure of turning him away from her apartment. "I will not be the plaything of any amorous Hungarian," she assured herself and, as the minutes dragged by, she thought, *Why hasn't he come, what is he waiting for?*

He arrived exactly at half past six. She was reclining on the big settee, glancing through Miss Mitsamushi's papers on anti-Americanism in Japan, and the sound of the doorbell paralyzed her momentarily. She said, "*Here he is!*" and found that her throat had closed up—she had completely lost the use of her voice. She croaked in exasperation, "What is the matter with me, why am I afraid of this man?

If he tries any tricks on me tonight I will *kill* him," and she went to the door and opened it.

He said, very softly, "Ah, Katherine! At last!"

Her heart seemed to stop beating. "Hello," she said, as if he were the last person in the world she expected to see there. "Hello, Stefan. How are you?"

He entered, and kissed her hand. Then, looking at her with delight, he said, "My darling. My own Katherine. How lovely you are! How beautiful! That gown is exquisite on you: Dior, is it not? Your hair—how attractive it is! Your perfume—I have never smelled anything so delicious!" He sniffed delicately at her ear. "Is it perfume, or is it you?"

His compliments, she knew, were exaggerated and even preposterous, yet they pleased her, and she laughed at them shyly. She closed the apartment door and said, "You are looking very well, too."

He looked, she thought, overwhelmingly handsome: he wore a dark blue suit and a white and blue striped tie, and carried a dark blue hat and an oyster-white raincoat.

"It is only to be expected that I should look well since I am visiting such a lovely and talented lady."

"Thank you." She had begun to tremble. "Come and sit down," she said.

Tonight he was totally different from the broody, suspicious, and irresponsible man who had caused her such mental distress ever since she saw him at midday. Now he was amusing and lighthearted; and as she watched him she was strangely moved. The boniness of his face, the cut of the mouth, the intelligent blue eyes, the crisp curly hair, reminded her of some of the young priests she had known, and in particular of the one she knew best, Father Justin. I am imagining it, she thought; yet the resemblance was clear in his manner as well as in his appearance—a combination of gaiety and imperiousness, of sensuality and asceticism.

He sat down on the big settee, and for a few moments

there was merely an exchange of commonplace remarks about the weather, about her luncheon with the Mid-Century Club, about a new book on Napoleon. At last she said, "Now. What can I get you to drink?"

He looked up at her mournfully. "Katherine, I would be much happier if you would let me get *you* a drink. Please, sit here. Relax. Put your feet up. I have a burning desire to serve you tonight."

"No. You are my guest. Tell me, what would you like?"

He shrugged his shoulders. "A Manhattan, since I am in Manhattan. Is that sensible?"

She laughed. "A very good idea. I shall have one, too."

She could not recall, as she went to the kitchen, exactly how to fix a Manhattan. She found the information on a calendar sent to her by her liquor store: a dash of Angostura bitters, one part of Italian vermouth, four parts of Bourbon whiskey, poured over ice cubes, stirred until chilled and then strained. But the little bottle of Angostura bitters seemed to have vanished, and she found it eventually at the very back of the cabinet in which Mrs. Corcoran kept herbs and Worcestershire sauce. In addition, her hands seemed to have grown quite ineffectual: glasses and ice cubes slipped away from her. When she returned to the living room she felt it necessary to apologize for taking so long to prepare two simple drinks.

He was sitting back, his knees crossed, smoking a cigarette and flipping through a copy of *The New Yorker*. He smiled at her. "There is absolutely no need to apologize. I kept myself entertained with this magazine. . . . Incidentally, if you are thinking of coming to me for a testimonial to help you in your new career, I am very much afraid that I will not be able to give you one."

She stared at him. "What on earth do you mean?"

"Alas, Katherine, alas. I do not think you will make a good espionage agent."

"I have no intention of becoming an espionage agent. What put that into your mind?"

He patted the settee. "You left, right here, where I could not possibly fail to see them, certain confidential papers dealing with things that are happening in Japan. I presume the Japanese lady, Miss Mitsamushi, passed them on to you this afternoon?"

"Oh, my God!" Kate exclaimed. She was swept by panic for a moment, and she cried to herself, *How could I have been so careless, so stupid?* She asked, "Where are they? What happened to them?"

"Calm yourself," he said. "I saw at once that they were from the State Department, and that they were marked *Highly Confidential.* So, like a true friend, I put them where they would not tempt me. They are on your Steinway piano, Katherine."

She gave a deep sigh. "You're right. I would be a dismal failure as a spy." She collected the papers from the Steinway, and as she prepared to take them to her study she could not help wondering if he had seen the memorandum on Brother Hop.

He laughed. "You know, darling, if you are realistic for a moment you will appreciate that there is not really anything particularly secret about these pacifist groups in Japan. Half of them—as I am sure you will read in those literary masterpieces—are dominated by young people who are devoted to the cause of socialism; and one can assume that the rest have been thoroughly infiltrated. Therefore it is rather absurd to label those documents *Secret,* or *Highly Confidential.* I am willing to make a bet with you that there is nothing in them that is not known to the people in Moscow."

"You may be right," she said. "But I don't make the rules. The State Department makes them."

"True, true," he said. "And one has to obey one's bosses,

no matter how foolish it seems sometimes. However, don't worry. I have not compromised you, Katherine. Your secrets are safe."

She smiled at him gratefully. He was really very nice. She took the papers to her study and locked them away in the bottom drawer of her desk.

5.

They chatted amiably while they had their first drink. But when she went to the kitchen to fix a second round he followed her, saying, "At least, let me get the ice." He opened the icebox and laughed at the nine cubic feet of shiny white emptiness inside. He asked, "Do you never eat, Katherine?" She explained, "I rarely eat in. And I have to confess that I am not a very good cook."

Then he found the porterhouse steak which had been intended for Burford. He prodded it. "But what is this?" She answered with a slight shiver, as if a ghost were walking over her grave, "It's a steak."

He unwrapped it and whistled in admiration. "Ho-ho! And what a steak! It is one of the most interesting steaks I have seen in a blue moon. Katherine, when I was coming here I thought I would take you to dinner in a little restaurant I know, where they make an excellent *kolozsvári rakottkáposzta*—"

"Good gracious, what's that?"

"Darling, it is a famous Hungarian dish with cabbage and sausage and chitterlings and pork and capon and roast goose—"

"You're teasing me."

"No, I am not. Believe me, we will have it one night soon. But tonight I have a better idea: let us dine on this gorgeous steak. What do you say? I will fix it—"

"I'm not *so* dumb," she said. "I can fix a *steak*."

He said, "My dear good woman, this steak is too noble to be entrusted to the hands of an amateur. You have butter, salt, pepper? A potato? Mushrooms? Excellent. Leave the rest to me. What about wine?"

Yes, she had wine: a case of Châteauneuf du Pape had been ordered by Giselle. He scrutinized the label on one of the bottles, wrinkled his nose, shrugged his shoulders, and said, "Well, since you have nothing else, it will have to do."

How funny, Kate thought. *He's like an amoeba. He changes his shape whenever we meet.* She had assumed that almost as soon as he arrived in the apartment he would make a great nuisance of himself until he achieved what seemed to be his primary aim in life—hauling her off to bed. She had also assumed that later in the evening, after he had made love to her six or seven times, he would yawn, stretch, take a shower, and suggest a spot of supper, what, at the Carpathia. Then, rested and refreshed, he would demand to return to the really important business of the night, hauling her off, once again, to bed.

It was a barbarous program. It was revolting to any woman of sensibility. It exemplified, to a frightful degree, sheer animal lust. It was abominable. It was hateful. But emotionally, she was prepared for it to occur; she was, in a sense, *braced* for it to occur. Consequently, she was surprised, even a little put out, when he seemed to find broiling a steak in the kitchen of more immediate interest than taking her by storm, repeatedly, in her bedroom. *It's entirely my own fault,* she thought: *I should have given the damned thing to Mrs. Corcoran when she asked for it.*

With another, more balanced, part of her mind, she had to admire his special skill at preparing a meal. He was obviously an expert. He knew exactly what he was doing. He even seemed to know, by second sight, where Mrs. Corcoran kept spices, vegetables, and her various utensils. If he needed a knife, he flung open a certain drawer and there the knife was. A clove of garlic? Of course: it was in a gaudy little jar that had once contained mustard. Black pepper? He opened a cabinet, and there it was on the second shelf, hiding behind a jar of orange marmalade.

They ate by candlelight in the living room. The steak was delicious. The wine, Kate thought, was excellent, but he found it no more than passable. Most French wines, he explained, were exhausted. They had lost their vitality. Whereas the wines of Hungary were overflowing with life. He described some of them: the Bikavér, or bull's blood wine of Eger; the golden wine of Gyöngyös; the wines of Badacsony that are said to draw their strength from the fires of ancient volcanoes; the great wines of Tokay, the Aszú, and the Szamorodni. She listened to him with pleasure. Wines meant little to her, and thus these names meant little to her, but he spoke so warmly, with such enthusiasm, that she was charmed. All the irrationality of the day, all the confusion, all the fears, all the little angers and despairs and yearnings, left her; she perceived, quite definitely, that here was a man of great talent and also of great sweetness. He said, "Katherine, this is what we will arrange: we will go in the summer to Lake Balaton, and we will swim, and sail a boat, and lie in the sun; and every evening you will put on pretty clothes and we will go to different villages on wine-tasting expeditions. Does this appeal to you?"

"Yes. Oh, yes."

"And we will go to Fertöd, to the mansion of the Esterhazys, and hear the music of Haydn played right there where he composed it."

"Stefan, I would like that very much. But I didn't know that Haydn lived in Hungary."

"Naturally he lived there. I will also take you to Martonvásár, where Beethoven composed the Appassionata Sonata—"

"He composed it in *Hungary,* Stefan?"

"Where else would one compose an appassionata sonata, my darling?" He smiled at her fondly. "You will enjoy Hungary. I can see that clearly. It might have been created for you. And I have a marvelous idea! You must write a book about the women of Hungary. No writer has really done them justice."

She said with a tiny tremor of jealousy, "Why? Are they so special?"

He answered with a laugh, "I have known them all my life, so they are no longer special to me. Let me make this clear: *only you are special to me, Katherine.* You are the most special woman in the whole wide world. I will do anything for you."

6.

At one o'clock in the morning he took her in his arms, gave her a most affectionate kiss, and said, "Now, Katherine, listen. I will have a quick shower, and while I am taking it I want you to put on a nice gown—the one you were wearing earlier this evening will do—and then we will go out to the Carpathia for an hour or two."

She cried, "Oh, no! No! Stefan, I don't want to get dressed again, I'm so comfortable, I'm so happy here. Why do you want to go out? Why?" She was saturated with love, she felt as if it were oozing out of every one of her pores.

He said, "I have a good reason, Katherine. This is the hour when many of my friends will be at the Carpathia."

"And you consider that a good reason? Do I bore you so much that you have to rush out to the Carpathia to see your friends?"

"I am not bored, Katherine."

"What are you, then? Thirsty? Hungry? Restless?"

"I am none of those things."

"Then *what* are you? Tell me, *what?*"

"Proud."

She looked at him suspiciously. "Proud? What do you mean?"

"I am so proud of you, Katherine, I want all my friends to see you. I want them all to know, this is Miss Emory, the woman I love. The men will regard you with envy because you are so beautiful and desirable, and the women will regard you with envy because you are so satisfied."

She said, "Oh, my God, after that eloquent speech I *have* to get dressed. What did you say you want me to wear?"

"Just a pretty dress. A necklace. Earrings. It is not very important. You see, with the expression that you have on your face everyone will bow down to you and pay you homage. Tonight you could go out wearing rags, and you would be treated like a queen."

Tears came to her eyes. "Is that true?"

"Everything I tell you is true. You must remember that I am a Hungarian. We only speak the truth. To what are you referring specifically?"

"To what you said about the expression on my face."

"Well, let us examine the question logically. How do you feel?"

"I feel wonderful."

"There! You have answered yourself! If you *feel* wonderful it is not really surprising that you *look* wonderful, is it?"

She began to cry.

He said in astonishment, "You are *crying!* But why?"

"You don't mean what you say."

"I assure you, I *do* mean what I say."

"You speak like this to all the women you know."

He put his arm around her shoulder. "Come, come. I expect more from a person of your intelligence. Surely, after all that has occurred between us, you realize that I love you?"

She gave a sad little gulp.

"Answer me," he said. "Do you realize that I love you?"

"I don't know."

"Well, let me assure you that I love you with all my heart. And do you love me?"

"Yes, I love you."

"Good. So the matter is settled, and I can go and take a shower." He slid away from her, and she fell outstretched, her face on a pillow. He ran his hand lightly down her spine and said, "You have the back of a girl who rides only on white horses."

She said in a muffled voice, "Stay here."

"Why?"

"Tell me something."

"What else do you want to know, my angel?"

"Do you love me more than Emmy Horscht?"

He sprang away from her as if she had fired a pistol at him. He said incredulously, "What do you mean?"

"You can be honest with me, Stefan."

"*Honest?* Honest about what?"

"Whether you love me more, or less, than Emmy Horscht."

He did not laugh. He did not slap her bottom and brush off the idle question. Unexpectedly he became hoarse with anger. He stamped up and down the bedroom, raging at her. "You are insane, Katherine. How dare you speak like this? Emmy Horscht is the wife of my boss, Mr. Horscht. To be more precise, Mr. Horscht is the boss of my boss, who is at present on temporary leave of absence in Budapest. How could I be in love with the wife of the boss of my boss? It is a vile slander. Where did you hear such a poisonous falsehood? Who is trying to stab me in the back?" He shouted, "I repudiate the allegation utterly! Do you hear me? *Utterly!*"

She pulled the bedclothes up to her chin, stunned by his furious outburst. In one thoughtless moment her world had come to an end. She stammered, "I'm sorry. I didn't mean to upset you. I didn't mean what I said. I was only joking. I'm terribly sorry."

He stopped his pacing and glowered at her. "Is that your excuse? You were only *joking?*"

She was too frightened to speak.

"A fine joke. Oh, yes, a very *fine* and very *funny* joke." He sat down heavily beside her. "You have succeeded in upsetting me considerably with your little joke. Katherine! Let me make this clear! This is no joking matter! In my position, loyalty to my superiors is of paramount importance!" His voice rose querulously. "I cannot understand it, it is a mystery to me: why, in the first place, should you associate me with the wife of Mr. Horscht? What can have put such an evil thought into your head?"

She could not really answer him. She could not explain why, suddenly, she had been swept by the urge to be coquettish. She was supposed to be a mature woman. She was supposed to be an intelligent woman. How could she have been so gauche?

She said with a sigh, "Mrs. Horscht telephoned me this afternoon."

He repeated her words suspiciously. "Mrs. Horscht telephoned you this afternoon? Indeed? Why did she telephone you this afternoon?"

"She invited me to her birthday party next week."

"At her house?"

"Yes."

"I trust you said you would go. It is not everybody who is invited to a party at the home of Mr. and Mrs. Horscht."

"I said I hoped I would be able to go."

"What else did she say?"

"She asked me if I would go shopping with her for a new evening gown."

"And you said—?"

"I said I couldn't."

"What else?"

"Nothing."

"Katherine, it passes my comprehension. How, out of this simple little conversation, consisting of a few simple little questions, could you deduce that Mrs. Horscht is in love with me, or that I am in love with Mrs. Horscht? Please explain."

"She said so many complimentary things about you—"

"But, my darling, she is *Hungarian!* You must get this fact into your head once and for all: Hungarians are not like Anglo-Saxons. Hungarians are warm-blooded! Hungarians are generous! Hungarians are not ashamed of their emotions! Hungarians are always paying each other compliments! But for God's sake, Katherine, when two Hungarians pay each other a compliment it does not signify that they are madly in love with each other, that they are carrying on a sordid intrigue!"

Kate's eyes filled with tears. "Stefan, I apologize. I said the wrong thing. I'm very sorry."

His good humor returned, as if it had been switched off for a few minutes and he had now switched it on again. He kissed her mouth, her throat, her forehead, and said jovially, "The matter is closed." Then he jumped up and said, "Katherine, I have a dreadful confession to make to you. I am starving, absolutely starving. Are you hungry, too?"

She lied: "Yes."

"It is the effect of love."

"Is it?"

"Of course. So, up with you, and get dressed. I will be out of the shower in two minutes, and I will telephone ahead to Pyotr to have a table waiting for us—*our* table. Oh, Katherine, you are beautiful, *beautiful.*"

"Am I?"

"Yes. My darling. I adore you."

7

SHE FELT as if her youth had returned to her, except that her youth had never, for one minute, been so exciting. She remembered herself well: a thin, colorless creature, intellectually aggressive, emotionally blank, given to quoting Plato at the drop of a hat. Now she was bursting with life, and she had a sense that if the love affair continued, in some miraculous way she would be transformed—she would become a truly mature woman, a joyous woman, she would achieve permanent happiness.

It was not only the spectacular sexual aspects of the relationship that gave her the feeling of having been reborn. True, she was intrigued to discover that an immense storehouse of unsuspected sexual energy had been unlocked by Stefan, so that at moments her libido was almost as tempestuous as his. But she had always been a self-sufficient human being, living in a special world of books, of music and painting, of contemplation; and she had always preferred to be alone, she *sought* her solitary state. She knew a vast number of people, but she had no friends. Suddenly she found herself with a man who was a superb lover and who, at the same time, was an utterly devoted friend and an enchanting companion. She could hardly believe her good fortune.

On Thursday, the fourth evening of the affair, he arrived at the apartment bearing a priceless gift: two tickets for a chamber music recital at Carnegie Hall. She was overjoyed.

Chamber music was, for her, the ultimate expression of the spirit, she listened to it constantly on records, but she rarely went to recitals because (an exception to her rules of conduct) it was socially embarrassing to go alone. He said, "I saw in *The Times* this morning that they were performing the Schubert String Quintet; I knew you would like to hear it, so I took a taxi up to Carnegie Hall at lunchtime and managed to get the last two seats in the house. Am I right? Does Schubert's Opus 163 mean a great deal to you?" Tears, literally, came to her eyes. The String Quintet in C Major was, in her opinion, one of the noblest achievements of mankind—it would help to weigh the scales in man's favor when the Day of Judgment arrived. How marvelous that Stefan, her lover, understood this! Later that evening, when the performance began in the hushed hall, and the chilled waves of delight flowed up her spine, she reached for his hand in gratitude and held on to him tightly until the mood of melting tenderness was broken in the third movement. As they left the concert he said, "Ah, wait until you come to Budapest with me! You will hear chamber music played as you have never heard it played anywhere in the world. I am not deceiving you, Katherine. Budapest is your city." She believed him.

The next evening, Friday, he surprised her again. This time he had two tickets for the ballet. And again she was overjoyed by his generosity and his instinctive understanding of what she liked and what she did not like. The bonds between them were growing stronger. She could talk to him without restraint and, indeed, there were occasions when she found herself chattering for minutes on end, passing on to him anything that came to the surface of her mind. He listened to her gravely, indulgently, lovingly; sometimes he laughed at her, but he was never brusque, never indifferent.

That night he stayed in the apartment with her. In the morning, to her embarrassment, he insisted on bringing her breakfast in bed. She cried, "No! No! You are spoiling me! I am not accustomed to being so pampered!"

He said, "Katherine, there is no need to answer this question. But what kind of men have you been going with? Savages?"

"Why do you say that?"

"Katherine, you are a woman. You are a beautiful woman. You are an adorable woman. You *deserve* to be pampered. Any man who could associate with you and not attempt to shower you with attention can only be an ignorant and insensitive cannibal. Let me tell you a secret. I discovered a long time ago that a little pampering, a little worshiping, make a beautiful woman even more beautiful and even more desirable."

It was enjoyable to be paid compliments in the florid style of Budapest half a century ago. He sounded like one of those suave lady-killers in a drawing-room comedy by Ferenc Molnar. As a social critic she deplored his attitude. As a woman she was not displeased. She put on a frilly bed jacket, dabbed herself with perfume, and waited for breakfast to arrive. He brought her fruit juice, bacon and eggs, toast, marmalade, and a pot of coffee. She ate with gusto. When she finished he said, "Now, would you like to sleep a little longer? After all, it is Saturday, there is no reason for you to get up. Sleep! It will do you good." She laughed, and threw her arms around him, and held him tight, and said, "Stay!"

2.

She had to leave him on Sunday afternoon to visit a cousin who was recovering from an operation in New York Hospital. "I *have* to go," she said, almost in tears. "Poor Nancy is *expecting* me, I *promised* I'd drop by and see her today."

"If you have to go, you have to go," he said philosophically. "There is no need to weep about it."

"But I don't want to leave you."

"It is only for a short while, I hope. You are not going to stay with your poor cousin Nancy in New York Hospital for ever, are you?"

"No. At the most, only for a couple of hours."

"Well, then, you will be back in about three hours, correct? That is, allowing half an hour for a taxi each way?"

"Yes," she said. Then, gazing at him despairingly, she cried, "Can't you understand? *I don't want to leave you, I don't want to leave you.*"

He laughed and kissed her. "Go along with you, my darling. I shall be right here when you return. That is, if you have no objection to my staying in your apartment while you are away?"

"Of course I have no objection. I *want* you to stay here."

"There are several of your records I have been hoping to play. Would you mind very much if I make use of your phonograph?"

"Of course not! Why should I mind?"

"Thank you." Then he said, "There is only one little problem, Katherine. I really should take a little walk this afternoon, to shake up my lazy liver. Suppose I go out—how would I get back into the apartment again? Should I leave the door unlatched?"

"No, don't leave the door unlatched. I'll give you my spare set of keys."

"Are you sure you want to do that?"

"Why not?"

"Well, when you return, you might find that I have vamoosed with all your most precious possessions, like your electric typewriter and the fabulous bas relief over the fireplace."

"If you want them," she said, "they are yours. There is no need for you to vamoose with them. I give them to you, with all my heart."

He said, "You know, I have the impression that you are beginning to love me nearly as much as I love you."

She had to turn away from him so that he could not see her face. She was beginning not merely to love him, she was beginning to be obsessed by him. She could hardly bear him to leave her for a few minutes in order to make her a cup of tea. She wanted him constantly in sight.

She was restless in the taxi riding up to New York Hospital; she was restless as she sat with her cousin Nancy who had undergone nothing more serious than a cholecystectomy a few days ago; she silently urged the taxi taking her home to go faster, faster; and she was tense as she let herself into the apartment. He was sitting on the big settee, his eyes closed as if he were asleep. The phonograph was playing the wild and magnificent 32 Variations of Beethoven.

She stood watching him. He suddenly called, "Katherine!" His eyes were still closed.

"Yes?"

"Come here."

She walked across the room and stood silently in front of him. He reached for her hands and drew them to his lips, kissing one and then the other.

He said grimly, "Why should I try to deceive you? Every minute you were away was like a year in Purgatory. I did not know that I could miss any human being so much. I thought I would die."

She was trembling. "Didn't you take a walk?"

"No. I could not go out. I played music all the time. It was terrible, terrible: you had left me, I could not reach you."

She sat down beside him and whispered, "I am back now, Stefan."

"Thank God. I love you so much."

"I love you so much, too, Stefan."

He began to kiss her. She had never experienced such overwhelming desire, she had never imagined that the human organism was capable of such tumultuous passion. He remained in the apartment with her until seven o'clock the next morning, and when he left (to avoid encountering Giselle or Mrs. Corcoran), he said, "I will be back tonight, Katherine. At six-thirty. Make no plans to see anybody else."

"I shall be waiting for you," she said, and when she heard the front door slam she wept for a few seconds and then, smiling, fell asleep.

3.

The morning seemed to be swathed in mist. She was living in a dream, and the sun was shining delicately through the mist, and music was drifting softly through the mist, and she was absurdly happy. Everything made her smile: the sight of Giselle, the sight of Mrs. Corcoran, the headlines of *The New York Times.*

At twelve o'clock Miss Mitsamushi telephoned and asked timidly, "Would it be possible to see you, Miss Emory? I have more information for you, about your tour."

"By all means," Kate said. "Will you come and have tea with me again?"

"You are so kind," Miss Mitsamushi said. "At four o'clock, as in England?"

"At four o'clock, as in Gramercy Park."

Japan, Kate thought, *Japan!* How can I go to Japan? I am in love, I can't go anywhere. But it was too early, she realized, to take any decisive step about the future. This was the time simply to experience love, to accept all the joy and all the happiness, leaving decisions until such time as her mind was capable of *making* sensible decisions.

Miss Mitsamushi brought with her another batch of documents for Kate, all highly confidential. There was a report on new developments in the optical industries, another on the search for markets by the electronics industries, yet another on extreme left-wing student organizations; and one concerned with somebody named Sun Pat Hsueng. Miss Mitsamushi spoke about Sun Pat Hsueng at considerable length, but what she said did not reach Kate's consciousness. She saw Miss Mitsamushi sitting in front of her, she heard Miss Mitsamushi's dry little voice, but she was thinking about Stefan and wondering what she could give him to symbolize her love for him. Japan was a million miles away, and why should she worry about Sun Pat Hsueng, whose code name (*code* name?) was Brother Hop, and who had expressed a wish to meet her in January.

"Perhaps you will put this document with the other one on Brother Hop, which I left with you last week," Miss Mitsamushi said.

"Indeed I will," Kate said. "I shall keep all these documents together."

But after Miss Mitsamushi departed and Kate went to her study and unlocked the bottom drawer of her desk, she discovered that the document which Miss Mitsamushi had mentioned was not there. The other documents, on secret societies, were there, but not the single sheet relating to Katherine Emory and Brother Hop, addressed to the Assistant Secretary, from (code name) Hogaku. "This is very strange," Kate said aloud. "What on earth can have happened to it? Did I take it out to read, is it among the papers here on my desk, or on the end table in the living room?" She began to search for it; but then Giselle diverted her with a question about the revision of *The Women of America,* Mrs. Corcoran suddenly demanded to know where all her spices were going, and for the time being Comrade Hop, otherwise Sun Pat Hsueng, was forgotten.

She expected the doorbell to ring at half past six exactly —not a moment before, not a moment after. That was Stefan's style. She was ready for him, bathed and perfumed and wearing a green silk housecoat; but by a quarter to seven he had not arrived, and she began to feel uneasy. She sauntered around the living room, straightening pictures that did not need to be straightened, shaking cushions that did not need to be shaken, saying to herself, *So he has been delayed. What of it? I'm sure he'll be here as soon as he possibly can.* At seven o'clock the telephone rang and she picked it up hurriedy, but it was only one of her old Southcliffe classmates calling to invite her to dinner next Wednesday. "I'm so sorry," Kate said: "I would love to come, but I already have a dinner date for that night. You have a man you want me to meet? *A banker!* What a pity. Yes, another evening, soon." Ten minutes later the telephone rang again, but this call, too, was from an old acquaintance, not from her new lover. She fretted, *Why doesn't he call, doesn't he know how concerned I am?*

He called at eight o'clock. "Katherine?"

"Stefan! I've been so worried! What happened?"

His voice was strained. "Nothing but trouble. Everything is a mess. I could not even get to a telephone to let you know I am detained. Forgive me, darling."

"Where are you calling from? When will you be here?"

"I am in Queens."

"Queens!"

"Yes. But I am leaving at once, and the trip only takes twenty minutes by subway. Have you eaten yet?"

"No, of course not. I've been waiting for you."

"Then you must be starving."

"I am."

"We are in the same boat. I had no lunch, I have not

eaten a damned thing, I am ravenous. What I suggest is this: let us meet directly at the Carpathia. I will be there as fast as the subway will carry me. On wings of subway, ha-ha."

"All right."

"If I am not there when you arrive, simply ask Axel, the waiter, to give you our usual table, and order one of my special cocktails. Okay?"

"Yes," she said.

She put on a red dress and a necklace of uncut rubies on a heavy gold chain which she had bought in Rio de Janeiro years ago. She made no attempt to hurry. Stefan completely occupied her mind, Stefan completely occupied her heart, but she had no intention of sitting alone at a table in a Hungarian restaurant waiting for him to materialize out of the subway. She did not leave her apartment for nearly three-quarters of an hour after he called her.

Marya, the plump, pretty hat-check girl, beamed with pleasure when Kate entered. "Ah, Madame, how well you look this evening, and how beautiful your dress is—red is so becoming to you. And that necklace! How unusual! Carved cherry stones?"

"Not exactly," Kate said. "Is Mr. Gerhardi here?"

"Stefan Gerhardi? No, I have not seen him come in. Let me ask Pyotr." The girl darted into the noisy crowd, and returned breathlessly in a few moments, followed by the tall, black-haired, black-mustached waiter. "Madame Emoryi?" he said, converting her name into what might have been its original Finno-Ugric form: "Yes, Mr. Gerhardi is not here yet, but he is expected any minute. Will you come with me? Your table is ready."

"Thank you," Kate said to Marya. "Welcome," Marya said, bobbing in a sort of curtsy. Axel led Kate to the familiar table, held her chair as she sat down, and asked politely, "May I get something for Madame?"

"A vermouth cassis."

He looked startled. "Not one of Mr. Gerhardi's special cocktails? Pyotr is already making it for you, in a chilled glass."

She felt the need to impress him with the fact that she was not Stefan's chattel. She said quietly, "A vermouth cassis."

"Yes, Madame," Axel said, duly impressed, and he hurried away to the bar to convey this striking piece of information to Pyotr. Kate sat rigidly in her chair, trying to appear calm and at ease. She had nothing to read, and she felt that she was an intruder in a tightly closed and rather hostile circle.

Axel returned with her drink. He placed it before her carefully, and asked, "Is there anything else Madame would like while she waits?"

"Yes. Would you be kind enough to bring me a newspaper."

He drew back. "*A newspaper?*"

"Yes."

"A *Hungarian* newspaper?"

"No. Not Hungarian. A New York newspaper."

She waited, sipping her vermouth cassis, watching the dancers on the tiny dance floor, recollecting how Stefan had held her in his arms there not so long ago. In about ten minutes, Axel returned with a newspaper neatly folded on a silver tray. She took it and laughed. "But this is a Greek newspaper."

"It is a New York newspaper, and not Hungarian, just as you asked, Madame."

She opened her purse and took out a dollar bill. "Please have somebody go to the nearest newsstand and bring me one of the evening newspapers. In the English language."

"Yes, Madame," he said unhappily.

It was not of great importance. It was like some of the

comic business in an Elizabethan play, a way of bridging time; and as she glanced at her wristwatch to see just how much time had been bridged so far, a tall and extremely handsome young man leaned across her table and said, "Hello."

She looked at him uncertainly. Had she met him here with Stefan? She could not tell: the dark, gypsy-like face was not really familiar. She answered guardedly, "Yes?"

"A beautiful lady should not sit by herself. It is wrong."

"Oh? Do you really think so?"

"Absolutely. Want to dance?"

"I'm sorry. I'm waiting for a friend."

"A beautiful lady should not have to wait so long for a friend. A friend should not keep such a beautiful lady waiting. Try a dance with me. Just one."

She shook her head.

He teased her. "Ah, come on."

She shook her head again.

He said, "Any objection if I sit down?" and before she could reply he had straddled a chair and was seated beside her.

She frowned at him. "Are you a friend of Stefan?"

He smiled sweetly, displaying deep dimples in his cheeks. "Stefan? Stefan who?" And here the conversation abruptly came to an end. A thickset man in a rumpled dinner jacket stepped out of nowhere, reached down, gripped the handsome young man's arm, yanked him up out of his chair, muttered a few words in his ear that caused him to turn pale, and gave him a contemptuous push that carried him within reach of a bigger, heavier man standing a few feet away. There was no real violence, only the threat of it; and the incident was over almost before it had begun.

The thickset man turned to Kate. His face was expressionless. "Madame Emoryi, I will tell the waiter to bring you another drink."

She was breathless. "Thank you, but I haven't drunk this one yet."

"Another drink," he said firmly. "On the house. And do not worry. Stefan Gerhardi asked us to keep an eye on you."

"Thank you," she said again.

"A pleasure, Madame Emoryi."

She might easily become attached to the name, she thought. It provided her with a whole series of appealing new personalities—Madame Katzi Emoryi, the renowned Hungarian mezzo-soprano; Madame Katya Emoryi, the celebrated Hungarian fortune-teller; Madame Kittikit Emoryi, the gorgeous Hungarian courtesan. She asked the thickset man, "Have you heard from Mr. Gerhardi? Do you have any idea when he might get here?"

"He got stuck in the traffic," the thickset man said blandly. "You know how the traffic is these days. Bumper to bumper."

"Yes, it's terrible, isn't it? Well, thank you," she said, for the third time.

"You are welcome, Madame Emoryi."

Axel brought her another drink and a newspaper. But she was restless. She had been sitting here for nearly an hour, the time was dragging, and she was not amused by her surroundings—the gypsy music, the dim lights. Suddenly she decided not to wait any longer. She was sure that Stefan was with another woman, and she experienced a flash of uncontrollable anger. She called the waiter and asked for her check. He blinked at her. "You are leaving us?" She replied, "Yes." He turned the pages of his order pad, hopelessly confused by what was written on them, and said petulantly, "How can I give you a check? It all goes on Mr. Gerhardi's account, Madame." She had no wish to be indebted to the man who had spurned her. She said, "Just tell me what I owe for two vermouth cassis." Axel said, "But it is impossible, Madame." A familiar voice broke in, "What is impossible? Nothing is impossible?" and Kate said, "Oh, Stefan," and sat back, feeling faint.

He kissed her hand, said imperiously to the waiter, "Bring two of my special cocktails, well chilled, at once," and sat down at Kate's side. He murmured, "Ah, my darling, I need a drink, I need a drink very much."

She could not be angry. His face was dark and haggard; his breathing was labored, as if he had run all the way to the Carpathia from wherever he had been, and he seemed to be in pain—he held his right hand to his heart. She said in concern, "Stefan, what happened?"

"Nothing, my dear, nothing. I apologize a thousand times for keeping you waiting."

"You're tired."

He gave her an amused look. "Tired? No, no. Oh, well, perhaps I am, a little. Will you ever forgive me for keeping you waiting so long?"

"Of course I forgive you."

"You have made me happy. Now, tell me about yourself. Did you have a productive day? Is your book marching forward?"

She whispered, "Oh, Stefan."

"What, my dear?"

"I'm worried about you."

He said, "There is no need to worry. It was just one of those days." He smiled at her. "One of the worst days of my life, darling. A perfectly *bloody* day, to be frank."

"Can't you tell me what happened?"

"There is no need to burden you with my troubles."

"They wouldn't be a burden."

"Are you sure?"

"Yes, I'm quite sure."

He seemed to explode inwardly. He said in a low, snarling voice, "How much longer must this go on? How much longer will you continue to persecute us? How much longer will you make our lives miserable? It is becoming intolerable. *Intolerable!* We hold out the hand of friendship, and how do you respond? You spit on it."

She recoiled from him as if he had struck her repeatedly. She could hardly speak. She stammered, "I? I persecute you? I spit on your hand of friendship? Stefan, that isn't so, it just isn't so. You are misrepresenting the truth."

He glared at her. "Not *you. You,* America."

Axel brought the two pink, frothy cocktails, and as he placed them on the table she sat trembling, wondering what she had done to justify such a violent attack on her behavior, and what Stefan's last remark meant. As soon as Axel left, she said, "What do you mean, *You,* America. What does that mean?"

He sneered. "It means, *You,* America. That is what it means." He raised his drink and gave it a little flourish. "Land of the free and home of the brave. To *you,* America."

She was torn by fear and dismay. "Why are you speaking like this?"

He said, "Listen, Katherine. We ask to live at peace with you. Above all, we want peace. But it is impossible. Why? Because we are trapped in a carefully planned program of harassment. We are harassed by your cops on the street corner. We are harassed by traffic cops. We are harassed by patrol cars. We are harassed by state troopers. We are harassed day and night by the FBI. We are harassed by the CIA. Your Congress passes hundreds of laws to harass us. We are harassed by microphones that look like olives in our Martinis, and microphones that listen to our conversations from a mile away. I ask you, how can there be any end to the Cold War, how can there be any rapprochement, when you force us to endure one humiliation after another?"

She said, "Is it so bad?"

"Bad?" he said, and laughed savagely. "It is worse than I can possibly describe it."

"I always understood that there is a certain amount of give and take in international affairs. We harass you here, you harass us there. Isn't that correct?"

His nostrils twitched. "A typical fabrication, spread by so-called American intelligence agents."

She found herself, unexpectedly, matching his rage. She said, "You mustn't talk in clichés. I expect better things from you. And you still haven't told me why you're in this mood, why you're throwing a fit about being harassed by the FBI and the CIA. *What happened?*"

He raised his head and thrust out his chin. He said icily, "There has been a diplomatic incident which may have the most serious consequences for everybody concerned."

"You mean, there has been a diplomatic incident between the United States and Hungary?"

"Precisely."

"But what? *What?* You can't keep me in suspense any longer."

"This afternoon," he said, "at a quarter past two, Mrs. Emmy Horscht was arrested in Great Neck, Long Island, for speeding."

4.

Kate leaned back in her chair. She felt dizzy. Her heart was pounding. She said, "Did I hear you correctly? Mrs. Horscht was arrested this afternoon in Great Neck for *speeding?* You mean, *speeding* in an *automobile?*"

"To be specific, a Lincoln Continental automobile."

"And you think this is going to have the most serious diplomatic consequences for Hungary and the United States?"

"I am afraid so."

"Aren't people arrested for speeding in Hungary?"

"Not the wife of an important official like Mr. Miklos Horscht. It is unheard of. Besides, Mrs. Horscht was not speeding. She was doing no more than thirty-eight miles an hour in a forty-miles-an-hour zone."

"The police say she was doing more?"

"Yes. They claim sixty-five miles an hour. It is, needless to say, a malicious lie."

"Needless to say. But doesn't Mrs. Horscht have diplomatic immunity?"

"Katherine, there is an acid note in your voice I have not heard before. You are very hostile toward Mrs. Horscht."

"I am not hostile," Kate said, "and I don't feel particularly acid. But I really can't believe that peace is imperiled because Mrs. Horscht was arrested for speeding in Great Neck, and I refuse to wring my hands over her predicament because, undoubtedly, as the wife of a diplomat, no action will be taken against her."

"You happen to be wrong. There is every possibility of drastic action. That is why I have been so frantically busy. It is conceivable that she might be expelled from this country and, if so, the repercussions could be disastrous."

"Why should she be expelled?"

"Unfortunately, she had no papers permitting her to drive the car. Furthermore, Mr. Horscht had given strict instructions that she must never drive the car herself. It was to be driven only by the official chauffeur, György. As a result, when Mrs. Horscht telephoned me at the United Nations and begged me to come to her assistance, I was in a quandary."

"Why were you in a quandary?"

"I had to pull wires here, there, and everywhere, in such a way that no hint of the matter reached the ears of Mr. Horscht. There is only one piece of luck in this whole business: Mr. Horscht is at present on a trip to Canada, and he is not due to return until tomorrow night."

"How very fortunate."

"Yes," Stefan said. "Very fortunate indeed."

"But, by pulling wires, you were able to get Mrs. Horscht out of the clutches of the brutal Great Neck police?"

"After hours and hours of telephone calls, Katherine."

"And then what happened, when she was released?"

"Naturally, I had to escort her to her home in Queens."

"I see."

"Then, as soon as everything appeared to be calm and settled, I telephoned you. I told you I would be here in twenty minutes. Do you remember?"

"I remember."

"However, just as I was about to leave the house, Mrs. Horscht began to have a nervous crisis over her terrible experience. She was like a child, Katherine, like a child who has just had a hair-raising nightmare. She wept. She sobbed. She would not let me go. What would you have done in my place? Would you have been so heartless as to leave her alone, with only the chauffeur and the housekeeper and the two silly little maids for company?"

Kate could not trust herself to reply.

"I knew you would understand," he said.

She still could not speak.

He turned and snapped his fingers at the lurking waiter. He said, "I am starving, Katherine, and I am sure you are, too. Will you trust me to choose something delicious for you? Let me suggest the pigs' tails with mushroom sauce."

She said, "I'm sorry. I couldn't eat anything now."

"But my dear girl—"

"It is late," she said, "and I am tired, and I am going home. Good night, Stefan."

"Katherine! What are you doing?"

She pushed her chair back, stood up, and left him.

5.

She was in a state of blind rage as she walked out of the Carpathia. There was not a shadow of doubt in her mind that his story was a mass of lies, that he had been making love to Emmy Horscht all evening and probably all afternoon too, and it was vital (she told herself) to put an end to this despicable and degrading affair, and return to the condition of stability she had enjoyed before he entered her life. She would not tolerate the untruths he spun so glibly. She would not tolerate his blithe infidelity. *Love is love,* she cried to herself. *We are not animals. This must stop, it must stop.*

When she was in her apartment she walked up and down the living room, half hysterical with conflicting emotions. She hated him, she would have nothing more to do with him; and she craved the sharp male odor of his body, the strength of his arms and his thighs, the tight, sunburned skin of his abdomen and the harsh bristly skin of his face. She craved his warm pepperminty mouth and his amused, calculating blue eyes observing her ecstasy. He had access to lines of communication in her nervous system whose existence she had never even suspected, and she knew that no man in the future could possibly match his genius as a lover. *But it cannot go on,* she cried. *I will not permit myself to be turned permanently into what I am this minute, a gibbering idiot.*

Finally, she changed into a robe, made herself a cup of hot cocoa, went to her study, and sought relief by pouring out her bitterness in one of her undeliverable letters.

Dear Father Justin:

I have been absent too long. Now, in humility, I return, and I am instantly rewarded, for simply writing your name on this sheet of paper, tapping the keys that salute you as my dear, gives me the serenity I yearn for. You are—may I say it again?—my dear: dearer to me than any other human being I have known, my spirit's star, the true keeper of my inmost heart. I hope you welcome my love. There have been too many who found it a joke, or a burden.

Let me tell you without any further ado what I have been thinking about recently: pleasure. You should be able to resolve most of my doubts on the subject, for your life has been filled with it in a special form. You derive pleasure from the little weeds that grow between the paving stones in your quiet cloisters, from the *Toccata and Fugue in D Minor* pouring out of the organ in your chapel, from the sight of clouds in the sky, from manuscripts prepared with exquisite care by the scribes of the *quattrocento*. I know pleasure, too, because (apart from the pleasure of conversing with you) it is singularly lacking in my life. I doubt if Bach would give me pleasure tonight, or even my own Mozart. I have no wish to see flowers, or the passing clouds, and I only pity those papal nobodies who wasted their days scribbling flourishes on the skin of a dead goat or, worse still, a slaughtered lamb. Do you recognize this mood? You must be resigned to it: it is the mood that always brings me running back to you.

Let me then continue with the grim subject of this letter: pleasure. I am sure that in your wide-ranging biological inquiries you have encountered the work of Olds, Brady, Lilly, and others, on the sites of the emotions in the brain and, in particular, the discovery of specific loci for what must be called, *faute de mieux*, the sensation of pleasure. Alas! Science has once again brought us low, for what emerges from the investigations of Olds and the rest is that pleasure is the most worthless, the most contemptible of all sensations, and if we trouble ourselves about it from this time on we are fools.

The validity of this conclusion, I am inclined to believe, is beyond dispute. What the scientists did, as you may recall, was to insert (painlessly, we are assured) tiny electrodes in the so-called pleasure centers of the brains of various small experimental animals, principally those martyrs of the biological laboratory, rats. The animals, suitably wired, were then placed in Skinner boxes, where they found only a small lever, in the form of a treadle. One can imagine their dismay at finding nothing to eat, nothing to drink—merely this small and uninviting projection from the side of the box. But joy is frequently hidden from us, and those treadles actually opened the doors of Paradise. They were so constructed that the slightest pressure—as from a rat's paw—completed an electrical circuit. As a result, tiny electrical impulses (scarcely more than a milliampere) passed to the electrodes imbedded in the animal's brain, thus electrically stimulating the pleasure center.

To some uninformed and sentimental observers this might appear to be a cruel, even brutal procedure, a refined form of the torture known as electric shock therapy which is now, I am told, going out of fashion because it was really too vicious even for our most sadistic Dr. Mugwamps. Not so. To the experimental animals nothing could have been more excruciatingly delicious, more piercingly agreeable. Once they had learned how to press the treadle with their paws, the rats were lost to the world; for here in concentrated form were all the satisfactions of the senses—the delights of sex without the effort of sex, the thrill of every conceivable odor and every conceivable taste, the joy of every conceivable kind of excitation of their fleshly being, a thousand times more than would be obtained from LSD or any other juvenile titillant. An insatiable appetite for pleasure inevitably developed, and some of the little creatures became so addicted that they spent every available moment (if one might invent an appropriate technical term) hitting the treadle. A couple of statistics supplied by the scientists who conducted the tests tell the story perhaps as well as it can ever be told. It was commonplace for animals to hit the treadle and stimulate themselves five thousand times an hour, and some rats, we are informed, stimulated their brains more than two thousand times an hour for twenty-four consecutive hours.

These are impressive experiments, and I am sure you will agree that those who originated them deserve our approbation. They are preparing a remarkable new world for us, not at all unlike the new world predicted by Aldous Huxley and George Orwell. In a single hour, comfortably wired to your favorite armchair, you could probably experience a carefully planned program of pleasure that far exceeded everything your grandparents experienced in a lifetime. The reward for twenty-five years of devotion to the super-State might be, not a gold watch, but a pair of gold electrodes and a pretty nurse to insert them when skies are gray.

So I turn to you, revered and reverend Father, and I ask, Whereat have we arrived? We have now established that the phenomenon of pleasure amounts to nothing more than a milliampere of electricity reaching clusters of cells in the hypothalamus or the rhinencephalon. We spend our lives in the pursuit of pleasure in its various aspects: noble, gross, high, low; but the time is approaching when pursuit will be quite unnecessary. Those tiny electrodes, Father, will give you all

> the auditory pleasures of *The Art of the Fugue* for a dollar; for another dollar you could have the declamatory pleasures of *Hamlet;* and for yet another all the visual pleasures of Rembrandt or Titian. How delightful! On the other hand, for me as a woman there might be—

She stopped. Her skin was suddenly icy. She thought she had heard the door of the apartment being opened. She waited, prickling with fear; and then, without any possibility of doubt, she heard the door being closed.

She stood up, quaking, unable to restrain her panic. Now she heard footsteps coming across the living room, toward the study. She wanted to call out, "Who is there?" but the words were trapped in her voice box and all she could utter was a little cry, a little whimper. She had no idea who had entered the apartment—some hunchbacked thief, some tall rapier-thin rapist, the Devil himself—and when Stefan appeared in the open doorway of the study she exclaimed in astonishment, "You! *You!*"

He smiled at her cruelly. "Were you expecting somebody else?"

She was still scarcely able to breathe. "You frightened me," she said.

"Blame that on your conscience, Madame, not on me."

"How did you get in?" she demanded. "How did you open the apartment door?"

He threw a small bunch of keys up in the air dramatically, caught it, and closed his hand over it. "Have you forgotten that you entrusted me with your spare set of keys the other day?" He held them out to her. "Here," he said coldly. "Allow me to return them to you."

She looked at the keys, and turned her head. She asked, "Why did you come here?"

"For the simple reason that I love you, Katherine."

"You don't love me!" she exclaimed. "That is untrue, you absolutely do not love me. You love Emmy Horscht perhaps, but you do not love me—"

He ran toward her and caught her in his arms. He said harshly, "How many times do I have to explain the facts to you? Mrs. Horscht is taboo. She is the wife of the boss of my boss. How can I be in love with her? It would be like committing suicide. You are out of your mind with jealousy, Katherine. I am flattered, but for God's sake, try to be sensible."

She burst into tears. "I am not jealous. I am not."

"What are you then, if you are not jealous?"

"I don't know," she wept. "I just don't know."

Without any further argument he led her off to bed.

6.

She found the missing memorandum on Comrade Hop soon after Stefan left the apartment the next morning. It lay under the big settee in the living room, and except for one corner of the page it was concealed by the fringe of the settee slipcover. She bent down and retrieved it with a sigh of relief, wondering how she had missed it. She thought, *I guess I dropped it the other day,* and there was no need to specify which day, or how she had dropped it without noticing that it had been dropped. She took it to her study, and locked it away in the bottom drawer of her desk with all the other confidential documents Miss Mitsamushi had left with her and with the uncompleted letter on the pleasure centers of the brain. She was a happy woman. She had no tiresome problems, now, to distract her. Love had made her young again, love had filled her heart with delight, and she could face the days ahead with confidence.

8

HER YOUTH, her delight, her sense of confidence, remained with her, in fact, until the afternoon of the following day. At about three o'clock, while she was correcting Giselle's atrocious typing of the penultimate chapter of *The Women of America,* her telephone rang. When she answered it, Stefan's warm voice said, "Darling! Is that you?"

At once her heart leaped with joy. "Yes. Hello."

"How are you?"

"Fine."

"Splendid," he said. "Now, Katherine, listen. You know that I was planning to take you tonight to the private showing of the new movie by Fellini?"

"Were you?"

"Yes. Well, something more interesting has turned up. We have been invited by my dear friend Sir Vivian Wingle, the British ecologist who is here at the United Nations, to take potluck with him. He is giving an intimate little party —twenty or thirty people at the most—for the group of Tibetan puppeteers who have just arrived in New York. I am told they are marvelous. Does the idea appeal to you?"

"Very much indeed."

"I think you will find it a thoroughly enjoyable evening. Sir Vivian is one of my oldest friends—we were in Tunisia together a few years ago—and he always gives excellent parties. You will like his wife Zoë, too. I knew her in Ajaccio even before she met Sir Vivian. She is adorable. Of course, it is a black-tie affair, so I am leaving the office early to change. I hope you have an evening gown suitable for a party in honor of Tibetan puppeteers?"

She laughed. "I think I can find something."

"Darling, your taste is impeccable. Good. I will pick you up, then, at six-thirty. That is not too early, is it?"

"No."

He said, "I can hardly wait to see you again. It has been hours and hours." He whispered, "Extraordinary as it may sound, I love you."

"The sentiment is mutual."

"What? What? Oh, your secretary is in the room?"

"Yes."

"I understand. We must not embarrass her. So good-by, my dearest, until half past six."

"Good-by."

She thought, *Whatever else it is, life is not dull with him. Where does he get all his zest, where does he get all his vigor? And since he mentioned her, was Zoë his mistress in Ajaccio before she became, of all things, Lady Wingle?* But she cut her thoughts short at this point, because what he had done and what he had been in the past was no concern of hers. She had only the right to concern herself with Stefan Gerhardi today.

Work, she found, was impossible after this telephone call. Mrs. Corcoran had already left, and at four o'clock Kate sent Giselle on some meaningless errand so that she would not be disturbed by the girl's mopishness and could concentrate on making preparations for Sir Vivian's intimate little party. Obviously, Stefan felt it was an occasion of a certain importance, and she owed it to him, therefore, to look her best. She went through her wardrobe and, at last, chose a long-sleeved evening gown by Givenchy, in sheer gray wool, very décolleté, with a white collar. It set off her skin and her slim figure, and as she stood in her bedroom musing over it her telephone rang, and she thought happily, *It's Stefan again. I can describe the gown to him and get his approval.* She sat down on her bed, picked up the azure blue Princess telephone, and said, "Hello?"

"Miss Emory? Am I disturbing you? This is Emmy Horscht."

"Oh, hello," Kate said, shaking her fist in the air. "How nice of you to call, Mrs. Horscht."

"I promised to do so last week, do you remember? And how are you? Are you well?"

"Very well, thank you. And how are you? And Mr. Horscht?"

"We could not be better. It is so kind of you to ask. Now, we have been wondering, Miklos and I: shall we have the pleasure of seeing you at my birthday party on Saturday?"

"I hope so."

"Good, good. I am looking forward enormously to meeting you, after all the charming things I have heard. And how is our mutual friend, Stefan Gerhardi? You have seen him? He is keeping busy and well?"

"He seems to be very busy and, I think, well."

"I have a remarkable presentiment," Mrs. Horscht said with a cry of excitement, like a seagull. "Do I hear his voice in the background? Is he there with you?"

"No," Kate said coolly. "I'm afraid he is not here with me. As far as I know he is in his office at the United Nations."

"I telephoned him there already. He went out at noon, and left word that he would not be back. I assumed that perhaps he was having lunch with you."

"No. We did not meet for lunch."

Mrs. Horscht said quickly, "Allow me to explain. I was hoping to see him this afternoon, we had certain things—business matters, very dull—to discuss. But he has not turned up! He has not come at the hour we arranged! He has not even telephoned me! And so I am sitting here, terribly worried, wondering what can have happened to him. Is he sick? An attack of appendicitis, a cerebral hemorrhage? Or has he been in another automobile accident?" Her laughter rang out joyously. "But of course he is not sick, he has not been in an accident, he is simply a little absent-minded. Everyone is running after him, he has a thousand different appointments, the ladies will not leave him alone. Did he tell you about his unfortunate experience yesterday, by any chance?"

"No."

"Poor boy. He was so *angry!* You have never seen anyone so *furious!* I thought he would *explode!* He became absolutely scarlet in the face. I said to him, 'Stefan, Stefan, you must control yourself or you will have a heart attack,' but you know how our dear friend is—it only made him more angry."

"Really?" Kate said, feeling her own anger rising.

"Yes. And do you know why he was in such a rage? It was because he was stopped by the police in Great Neck, Long Island, of all places, for speeding, of all things. Speeding! In the Lincoln Continental, which he was forbidden by Miklos to drive, in any case. How ridiculous it all is! He was doing no more than sixty miles an hour. I will never understand miles. What is that in kilometers? A hundred?"

"I suppose so."

"Well, when you see him, tell him not to brood over it. It is not such a serious crime—after all, he did not kill anybody. A ticket from the Great Neck police—that is not the end of the world. And I am sure we can keep the incident from my husband. That, dear Miss Emory, is really the most important thing."

"Shouldn't you tell him all this?" Kate said acidly. "Wouldn't it mean more, coming from you?"

Mrs. Horscht cried, "You are right! I *should* tell him. And

I will, I will. When you see him, please ask him to telephone me at once. Would you be so kind?"

"Yes," Kate said.

"And also, please mention to him that I waited in for him this afternoon. He is a naughty boy to forget an old friend."

"Yes," Kate repeated. She added abruptly, "Excuse me, I believe my bath is running over. I'm so sorry."

"But of course! That is a catastrophe! I apologize for detaining you so long."

"Not at all. Good-by."

"Good-by," Mrs. Horscht said, taken by surprise.

Thin-lipped, Kate went to her bath. It was, in fact, on the point of overflowing. She believed absolutely in absolute truth. Even if you found yourself on trial for your life it was mandatory to answer every question put to you by the prosecutor without corrupting the truth, because you cannot and you must not lie, you do not know where deviation will end. Plato is dear to me, she could say with Aristotle, but truth is dearer still. Now it appeared certain that somebody had lied to her: Emmy Horscht or Stefan Gerhardi (or perhaps both), and she was shocked and resentful. The reason for the lie was unimportant; the magnitude of the lie was unimportant; the lie itself, with its poisoned tip, was sufficient to cause the death of the soul.

2.

She looked remarkably well, she had to admit to herself, in the décolleté evening gown. She had an interesting pallor, with two flushed patches high up on her cheekbones—a result of her conversation with Emmy Horscht. But, additionally, she seemed to have acquired a certain physical fullness, a softness of outline, an accumulation of flesh in appropriate places, a rather pleasing womanliness. Was this the effect of the rich food she had been consuming recently, the rich food of the Carpathia, the rich food of love? Stefan would no doubt enlighten her about it, as well as about other matters, when he arrived.

But he had not arrived at six-thirty, nor at seven, nor at seven-thirty, and her heart became stony as she sat in the living room, encircled by the dim ghosts of Egypt. Stefan almost lost her then and there because, unexpectedly, there was a call from Burford in Cambridge, inquiring brusquely, but with hidden concern and tenderness, about her health and her well-being, asking when he could see her again. She caught her breath and to her consternation found herself fobbing him off with a half-truth: she was deeply involved at present, she said, with a new project. He accepted her explanation, as any scholar or scientist would, reluctantly but with understanding. A new project, after all, is a new project. It takes precedence. It cannot be dismissed lightly.

But by eight o'clock her new project still had not arrived, nor by eight-thirty. She felt betrayed. It was clear that Stefan was utterly incapable of keeping his word. Last night he had made her wait five hours for him, and he was evidently set on repeating that performance, or even improving on it. She had canceled nearly all her appointments, she had sacrificed her personal life almost totally in order to be with him, and this was how he responded. She thought grimly, *My dear Hungarian friend, you are taking an awful chance. You should not count on my acquiescence. I am not a woman who is accustomed to waiting for a man —any man.*

At nine-thirty, in a towering rage, she strode to the kitchen and fixed herself a substantial Scotch highball, and as she carried it to the living room there were three thunderous bangs on the apartment door and three fierce stabs of sound from the doorbell, like the signal for a great new Massacre of the Innocents. She marched to the door, threw it open furiously, and at once made a move to shut it again, for she did not recognize the man outside. He said in a low, urgent voice, "*Katherine!*" and she stared at him in disbelief. He looked like an Italian movie actor impersonating a Spanish financier. His eyes were completely hidden by a pair of huge and impenetrable sunglasses; a beret appeared to be glued horizontally across the top of his head; he wore a thick, black, belted, cashmere coat, and he carried a large pigskin valise covered with labels—Pan-Am, TWA, Portofino, Barcelona, Beirut. "*Let me in!*" he said in the same low, urgent voice, and as she opened the door wide he slipped through, dropped the valise with a groan, and said fiercely, "Now lock the door. *Lock it!*"

He stood with his back against it, gasping for air. He said with difficulty, "My darling. I am late. I apologize a thousand times."

She did not reply. His dramatics did not impress her. She walked into the living room and sat down in an armchair, the Scotch highball in her hand.

He followed her. He said, "Do not be angry with me, Katherine."

She looked up at him calmly. "Why not?"

"I have an excuse for being late."

"I'm sure you have an excuse for being late."

He came close to her, panting. She could smell peppermint on his breath. He said, "Would it interest you to know that for the past two hours I have been running like a madman all over New York?"

"Really?"

"I had to come here by a roundabout route. The East Side, Broadway, up the West Side, in and out of buses, taxis, subways."

"It must have been great fun."

"Great fun!" he cried, and put his hand over his heart. He was disconcerted by her mood, and he asked with a short, sardonic laugh, "Am I permitted, by any chance, to take my coat off?"

"Yes. Just drop it over a chair."

He unbelted his coat, struggled out of it, and flung it angrily on the settee. He whipped off his beret and tossed it, in the same angry way, onto his coat. Then he took off his sunglasses and said, "You are quite right. I invited you to come to a party at the Sutton Place apartment of my dear old friend Sir Vivian Wingle and his charming wife Zoë; you go to great pains to make yourself look perfectly beautiful—that gown is wonderful on you, *wonderful*—and I arrive nearly three hours late. For the second night I have let you down. You are entitled to hate me, to despise me, to treat me as if I were a social leper."

She did not comment.

He pointed his sunglasses at her. "But I wish to inform you, Katherine, that while you were waiting here in comfort, I was being hunted down by a man who, for all I know, had instructions to kill me on sight."

"Well, imagine that."

He said excitedly, "You do not believe what I am telling you?"

"Do you really expect me to believe it?"

He pounded his hands together. "It is true! It is true!"

Kate said in a voice that was cold and bitter and unforgiving, "Why don't you admit that while I was waiting for you here, you were having a good time with Emmy Horscht?"

He held his hands up in a piteous appeal to Heaven. "*Emmy Horscht*. I have been fleeing in danger of my life, and all that my darling can talk about is Emmy Horscht, *Emmy Horscht*. What is the matter with you, Katherine? What is this insane jealousy that has gripped you?"

She said, "There is nothing wrong with me, except that I am a little put out by your behavior." He began to wave his arms again, but she went on, "And you can tell me if I am really insanely jealous. Mrs. Horscht telephoned me at four o'clock this afternoon. She was very disturbed. She was expecting you, and you hadn't turned up. She asked me to give you a message: would you please call her as soon as you came in."

"Katherine—"

"You may use this telephone, if you wish. I will go into my bedroom. But I assume there is no need, you and Mrs. Horscht have already had your little chat."

He bent down so that his eyes were level with hers. He said harshly, "Surely you realize by now that Emmy Horscht is just a troublemaker."

"Perhaps she is. But I'm sure she also has other talents that make her highly attractive to you. And furthermore, I cannot tolerate this situation."

"Listen—"

"I don't want to listen. I don't want to hear any more glib explanations. I never know whether you are telling me the truth, or inventing some story you think I am fool enough to swallow. I never know whether you are expressing love, or betraying me." She was saying more than she intended, but she was unable to stop or to control the flow of words. "I think we should end this relationship before too much damage is done. I think we should end it right now, at once."

His blue eyes were tragic. There were tiny beads of sweat on his brow. He reached for her hand. "Will you listen to me if I swear to you I am telling you the truth, the whole truth, and nothing but the truth?"

She was trembling. It was a fine, imperceptible tremor that affected every part of her body. She could even hear it in her voice. She said, "Yes. I will listen to you if you will answer one question first."

He straightened himself, as if he were facing a firing squad. "What is your one question?"

"When you telephoned me to invite me to Sir Vivian Wingle's party, were you on your way to see Emmy Horscht?"

He stood looking down at her, his hands clasped behind his back, brooding over the significance of her words. Then he answered in a matter-of-fact voice, "Yes. Your guess is correct. I was on my way to see Mrs. Horscht."

"At her home?"

"At her home."

Kate looked up at him with contempt. "What a busy little fellow you are! Now here is something else you can explain. Who was arrested for speeding in Great Neck, Long Island, yesterday? Was it Mrs. Horscht, *as you told me?* Or was it you, *as Mrs. Horscht told me?*"

He put his hands to his temples. "It was I. Does it matter?"

"Yes!" she exclaimed. "It certainly does matter! Because it seems to have been another occasion when you had a date with me but preferred the company of Mrs. Horscht."

"Not so fast, I beg of you, not so fast. If you will only listen—"

"No," Kate said. "I've had enough. Really, I've had enough, more than I can stomach."

He said, "Katherine, we had an agreement that I would answer one question and then you would listen to my side of the argument. Are you revoking our agreement?"

She turned her head away from him.

"Well?" he asked. "Do I have your permission to speak?"

She had demonstrated that he was a liar, that he was unfaithful, that he was untrustworthy. What could he add to that catalogue? But she had promised him that she would hear him, and she said, "Yes. But please be brief."

"I will be very brief," he said cheerfully. "Then I will leave you in peace. Have no fears, my dear Katherine, I will not impose my company on you against your will."

"Is that what you wish to tell me?"

"Not exactly." He paused to light a cigarette, as if the firing squad had given him this last respite. He blew the smoke in the air, and then said, "You will be happy to learn, my darling, that I am being sent back to Budapest within a few days. That is all. Nothing more. The party is over, and I will now say *adieu.*"

She looked up at him suspiciously. He was smiling, but he was deathly pale. He nodded at her amiably, stubbed out his cigarette, and reached down for his coat and his beret.

She said, "You are being sent back to Budapest? *Sent* back? In a few days? I don't understand. Why?"

He put the coat on and began to fasten the belt. He was still smiling. He said, "I am sorry, but I do not know precisely why. Mr. Miklos Horscht does not take me into his confidence and explain why he does this or why he does that. However, I suspect that I am being sent back to be put on trial before a disciplinary court."

She repeated his words. *"To be put on trial before a disciplinary court!* Why? Why?"

He laughed. "My dear Katherine, to be tried for the same crime that you have accused me of committing."

She jumped up angrily. She said, "I have not accused you of committing *a crime!* I did not mention *a crime!* That isn't true, Stefan! You are putting words into my mouth!"

"Oh, come," he said lightly. "Did you not intimate that I am Emmy Horscht's lover? That I run to her bed at every opportunity? Well, unfortunately it seems that Mr. Horscht has the same impression. That is why he is in Ottawa, to discuss the matter with other high officials. And when he returns I will undoubtedly be put on a plane for Budapest, and the game will be finished. For I have no defense, Katherine, either against you or Mr. Horscht. I *was* Mrs. Horscht's lover; thus I do not have a leg to stand on."

She was too horrified to speak.

"I have only one thing to add," he said. "Please do not imagine that I ever went from your bed to hers. That is quite wrong. We were lovers, we had our little affair, long, long before I met you." He lit a cigarette. "We met yesterday and today for a simple reason: she is in trouble as deeply as I am, and we had to discuss strategy—how to get out of this mess we are in, how we can possibly save our lives. But I am afraid that it is too late for any evasive action. We have to face reality." He held his hand out. "So, Katherine, good-by, for the last time."

She said in a whisper, "Is this true?"

He reacted with a flash of anger. "Frankly, I am not accustomed to being treated as if I am a habitual liar." Then he laughed. "Does it really matter if I am telling the truth, or not telling the truth? This situation, which you find so intolerable, is at an end. I am leaving." He paused. "Well? Do you want me to go without a last handshake, Katherine? Are you so disillusioned with me?"

Her mind seemed to have entered a zone of darkness and fear. She needed him too much. She could not bear the thought of living without him. She must have been out of her mind to attack him so cruelly when he was in physical danger. Her throat was convulsed, and she had difficulty forcing herself to speak. She said, "I am sorry this has happened."

"You are sorry *what* has happened, Katherine?"

"This trouble with Mr. Horscht."

"Oh, it is just one of the hazards of politics," he laughed. "In particular, of Marxist politics."

She said, "Yes. So it seems." Then, after a moment, she added, "I don't want you to go."

"Back to Budapest? That is very sweet of you, but I am afraid there is no alternative."

She said, "No. I mean, I don't want you to go now."

"*Now?*" he said. "I do not follow. Exactly what are you saying?"

"I don't want you to leave me. I want you to stay here."

"*Here!* With you?"

"Yes."

"My darling! My darling Katherine!"

She was afraid she might cry, and she began to walk toward the kitchen, saying in a muffled voice, "I'll fix you a drink. What would you like?"

"Anything," he said. "From now, and forever, I am entirely in your hands. Fix me any kind of drink you wish."

3.

She spoke very little while he drank the Scotch highball she brought him. Too much emotion had been generated inside her; she had temporarily lost control of herself. She was involved in something that was far more important than physical passion and the gratification of the senses, far more important than the discomfort caused by jealousy and betrayal. What was at stake here was literally life, literally death—the life or death of a human being with whom she had become inescapably entangled. It was more terrifying than she could ever have imagined. Somewhere in the dark world outside, a man was seeking Stefan Gerhardi—an assassin, a gunman, with orders to kill on sight, and she shuddered at the mental image of a smoking revolver, a bloody knife.

She asked quietly, "This man you spoke about, did he follow you here? To Gramercy Park?"

"I do not think so. You know, I am an old hand at this kind of chase and, with luck, he is sitting in a movie house on Broadway, watching a thoroughly boring movie and wondering whether I am in one of the front rows or at the back, or possibly up in the balcony."

She was silent for a few moments, gazing at some phantom in the big living room. Then she said, "I think you should stay in the apartment."

"I have already accepted your kind invitation, Katherine. Thank you."

She shook her head. "I don't mean only tonight. I mean for as long as necessary."

"In other words, you are offering me your apartment as a permanent hiding place?"

She nodded, biting her lower lip.

He said, "Darling, you are kind, and wonderful, and generous, and warmhearted beyond words. But there is actually no need for me to go into hiding. In fact, I think the best thing we can do tonight is to go out."

She was dumbfounded by his gay manner. "Go *out?*"

"Why not? You are wearing a beautiful gown. You look marvelous in it. We are unfortunately too late for my friends Sir Vivian and Lady Wingle—you must meet them another night. But I would like to take you to some amusing restaurant for dinner. Then we should drop into one or two nightclubs for a drink. And I think we should end up, as usual, for a spot of supper at the Carpathia. Perhaps you will dance with me again."

"But I thought you were in *danger!* I thought this man was *following* you!"

"That is quite correct."

"And, with this threat to your life, you can still think of going out on the town?"

"Darling, it has now become an exercise in strategy. Surely you understand?"

"No, I don't understand," she cried. "It seems to me that you're just being foolhardy, you're just taking the most terrible risk in order to have a good time for a few hours." She laughed bitterly. "Eat, drink, and be merry, for tomorrow we die—that seems to be your philosophy."

He said patiently, "No, Katherine. Try to consider it in these terms: presumably he has orders from Mr. Horscht to keep me under observation until I return to Budapest. But I have eluded him. Now he has to guess where I am. He does not know that I have come running here to establish communication with you. No. His great fear is that I have given him the slip in order to defect to the enemy. As a result, he is undoubtedly furious, and in a rage to kill. Am I right?"

She cried helplessly, "I don't know. How could I *possibly* know?"

"Take my word for it. I have been in this business for a long time. I think I can read his mind with ninety-nine percent accuracy. If I disappear totally from sight, he will be justified in thinking the worst and I will really be in danger. Therefore, the important thing is to assure him that I am still available to him. Do you follow my reasoning now?"

She shook her head.

"It is perfectly logical. As soon as he discovers that I have been seen in public with you, that we are enjoying ourselves as if we did not have a care in the world, his suspicions will be lessened. He will decide that I am too dumb to realize he is on my tail."

She said, "I suppose you're right."

"I have convinced you!"

"More or less. Do you know who this man is?"

"Certainly. He is the Horscht's chauffeur, György."

"And are you planning to—" She was unable to complete the sentence.

"Am I planning what, my darling?"

"To defect?"

His face darkened. "We will discuss this later. My brain is in a fog. I need your advice, your wisdom, your encouragement. It is a terribly difficult decision to make."

She said, "Yes. Of course it is."
"In the meantime, are you ready to leave?"
"I just have to powder my nose and put on fresh lipstick."
"Hurry, then," he said. "The evening is going fast."

9

THEY WENT, first, to a restaurant on East Forty-ninth Street. In the taxi Stefan maintained his conspiratorial air, wearing his dark glasses, the beret, the black belted cashmere coat with the collar turned up to hide his chin; and when she attempted to make conversation he squeezed her thigh, warning her to keep quiet. Inside the restaurant he explained gently, "You must forgive me for silencing you, but I did not like the look of the driver."

"I happened to notice his name on his registration card," Kate said. "It was O'Connor. Do you think he was one of the Hungarian O'Connors?"

Stefan said, "It is no laughing matter, darling. He could easily have been planted by György."

"But I thought you wanted György to *know* that you and I were together?"

"That is true. However, I want it done my way, not his way. This is a game of wits, Katherine. We must play it with a certain subtlety."

The hat-check girl knew Stefan, so did the barman, so did the captain and the waiters, and Kate was once again impressed by his cosmopolitan connections. A table was free; the captain, with a welcoming smile, led Kate and Stefan to it; and when they were seated, and the first drinks had been ordered, she asked, "Is this one of your haunts?"

He spread the fingers of both hands. "Yes, I come here fairly often. It is, as a matter of fact, a great haunt of racing car drivers. You know, those crazy people who drive Ferrais, Cobras, Lotuses, et cetera." His blue eyes sparkled, a tiny smile curled up on his mouth, as if he were lost in a delightful dream. "I have always had an ambition to own a Ferrari. A Ferrari of one's own! Imagine! I thought that with the triumph of socialism the opportunity would come closer, but, alas, it seems to grow more remote." Then, lowering his voice slightly, he said, "Do not look now, but three tables from you, on your left, there is a man sitting with a pretty blonde. He has only one arm."

"And he is a racing driver?" Kate asked, a little puzzled.

"My darling! Be sensible! Use your beautiful head! How can he drive a racing car if he has only one arm?"

"I'm sorry. I misunderstood you."

"Watch him out of the corner of your eye," Stefan said. "In about three minutes you will notice that he will stand up, excuse himself to the pretty blonde, and go to the telephone."

"Why will he go to the telephone?"

"My darling! My love! What has happened to you? He will go to the telephone to call a certain number, to tell a certain party to pass a message to György that I am here with you."

"I'm terribly sorry to be so stupid," Kate murmured. "I've never been involved in anything like this before. You mean, all that will happen like clockwork?"

"The precise word," Stefan said. "Like clockwork."

Three minutes later the one-armed man stood up, smiled at his pretty companion, and sauntered toward the bar.

"Good heavens!" Kate whispered. Her skin began to tingle. "You were right! Stefan, I'm frightened."

"There is no need to be frightened, my love."

"But I am. Suppose György doesn't react as you think he will? Suppose he decides to come here?" Her voice faltered.

"You do not get the point, Katherine. The point is, the cat is now out of the bag."

"Which cat? Which bag?" Kate asked wretchedly.

"Consider: what will György think when he learns that you and I are sitting in this restaurant? First, that I am not in hiding. Second, that I have not gone over to the Americans. And third, that I am not even aware that he is pursuing me. Isn't this exactly the impression we are trying to convey?"

"I suppose so. I'm sure you're right. You mustn't feel that I don't trust you. But I'm still frightened."

He patted her arm affectionately. "You want to leave right now? Okay. There is no reason why we should not give György a run for his money." He raised his arm, summoning the captain, and then whispered at length in the captain's ear.

"Assuredly!" the captain exclaimed. "But naturally!" He gave Kate a tender glance. "You promise that you will return with Madame Emoryi another night?"

"I promise," Stefan said.

"Be happy," the captain said.

"I promise you that, too."

Stefan stood up. The captain politely held Kate's chair, and at this moment the one-armed man returned.

Stefan looked him up and down with loathing, and said loudly, "Come, Katherine, let us go." The face of the one-armed man, Kate noticed, turned scarlet.

2.

When they were outside, Kate said, "Now what is going to happen?"

"Nothing much," Stefan said. "The man with the one arm will have to make another telephone call, and he will feel like a bloody damn fool, explaining that we were here and that now we are not here."

"But György—"

"Do not worry your head about György. The night is young. He will find us."

"Just as a matter of interest," Kate said, "what did you tell the captain before we left?"

"Merely that I was suddenly overcome with affection for you, and that we had decided to go home and eat scrambled eggs."

"Oh," Kate said.

"He understood."

"Yes. He looked like a very understanding man, he had such nice eyes. Are we really going home to eat scrambled eggs?"

"First let us have a little more fun."

3.

They went roaming from place to place, and it was difficult for Kate to remember that Stefan's life was in danger. Again her youth returned to her. She might have been twenty years old, when there was no greater adventure than prowling around the glittering city all night with some sophisticated Princeton senior. The difference, so many years later, was that a sophisticated Hungarian was incomparably more exciting. She would not have exchanged him for the entire class of '51.

But every now and then she felt a sharp pinprick of terror, reminding her that this was not really a night of carefree pleasure. "The waiter with the thick black eyebrows," Stefan murmured in an elegant Hawaiian bar, where he had ordered a sickly concoction of rum and papaya juice: "Watch him, Katherine. You will observe that he ignores me, as if I do not exist. You would never guess that I once saved his life in the Pyrenees." It was another surprise for Kate: "But he looks like a typical Hawaiian! Do you mean, he's Spanish, or Andorran?" Stefan said indulgently, "He is no more Spanish or Andorran than you are. He is a bloody Bulgarian who is in this country illegally, and who is working here on the strength of forged papers. He will be at the telephone within five minutes."

"Let us go, Stefan."

"In due course, my dear. There is no hurry."

Half an hour later they were in a fashionable bar on Third Avenue, surrounded by the gilded youth of the East Side. Stefan said casually, "The good-looking girl at the table opposite, Katherine."

"The beautiful girl? In the black suit? She's been staring at me. Have you noticed—she has the most extraordinary violet-colored eyes?"

Stefan chuckled. "Be careful what you say. There is a rumor that one of our top men in Athens hanged himself last year because she would not, or could not, return his love. Unfortunately, the poor fellow had not been warned that she is a dyed-in-the-wool Lesbian of the most vicious habits. I would advise you not to *ooh* and *ah* over those extraordinary violet-colored eyes, darling. She is only making an inventory of your charms."

Kate blushed. "I can hardly believe it."

"Well, for God's sake, do not give her any encouragement. She might come over here and break my arm. She is an expert in the art of judo."

"And *she* is going to report that we are here?"

"I am afraid so."

"I don't understand," Kate said vehemently. "I'm not *such* a fool. I'm not *such* an innocent. Is it possible that there are spies, or agents, or whatever you call them, in every bar and restaurant in New York?"

"Another name would be informer."

"Informers, then. Are they all over New York? A hundred thousand of them? It's inconceivable."

"No, Katherine. There are not so many. I have deliberately taken you to places where I know they are operating, so that messages will be transmitted back to those certain people I mentioned earlier. Ah! You see! The gorgeous creature opposite is off to the races. Honestly, I can appreciate why my poor colleague hanged himself."

The violet-eyed girl had risen, tall, magnificent, frozen-faced, like an Aphrodite who has declared war on love. She stood with one hand gripping the edge of her table, gazing speculatively at Kate; then she turned away and strode off to the back of the bar.

"Let's go," Kate whispered urgently. This woman alarmed her.

"There is no hurry," Stefan said. "Now. Let us think. Where would György expect us to appear next? Gatsby's on First Avenue? The Brasserie on East Fifty-third Street? We will fool him, and drop into O. Henry's in the Village."

"Stefan, don't you think we should go back to the apartment?"

"Why? It is only half past eleven. And it is Saturday night. Darling, I may never enjoy another Saturday night in New York."

"I wish you wouldn't say that."

"Dear Katherine. It happens to be true."

4.

They reached the Carpathia at about half past one. Kate still felt the glow of youth: her feet hurt, her legs ached, every now and then her heart seemed to flutter, but she was sustained by the excitement of the chase. The terror of being hunted by an assassin in chauffeur's uniform had gradually been superseded by the intellectual satisfaction of outwitting him, a change of attitude that was made easier by every drink that Stefan urged on her in each new bar they visited. She was not drunk when she entered the Carpathia, but her eyes were bright and her cheeks were rosy, as if she had been skiing all day on some splendid Alp overlooking Manhattan.

"Ah, Madame Emoryi!" said the plump hat-check girl. "I have been hoping you would come to see us, and here you are! Looking so well!" She smiled warmly at Kate, but when she turned to Stefan the smile left her face, she appeared to be anxious as she stood on tiptoe and whispered something in his ear.

He nodded. "Thank you, Marya."

"You are welcome. Go with God, both of you. You make a lovely couple."

Only a few cries, " 'Allo, Stefan," came from the crowd at the bar. A tall man in a dinner jacket clapped him on the shoulder, muttered a few words and then solemnly shook hands with him. The barman, Pyotr, called to him and held a brief, subdued conversation at the far end of the counter; the sinister waiter, Axel, said with a flashing smile, "Your usual table, sair?" and then mumbled to him gloomily, as if Death—two hundred dry and grisly bones, mysteriously clinging together in perfect physiological order—awaited him in the secluded corner near the noisy dance floor.

"Two of your special cocktails, sair?" Axel asked, when they had taken their seats.

"At this time of the night?" Stefan said, raising one eyebrow. "Certainly not. Champagne."

"Of course, sair. Champagne. Dom Perignon?"

"Axel, will you never learn? Dom Perignon is for tourists. I want the special Rothschild Reserve—Pyotr has a few magnums tucked away in the cellar. And while you are about it, bring us some of that good green Caspian caviar—a treat for you, Katherine. It is very rare, and also exceedingly delicious."

Kate said, when Axel galloped away, "Stefan! Champagne *and* caviar! Isn't that overdoing it a little?"

"My darling, like all the best women, you are frugal at heart. But just for once I have the urge to spend money like water, I want to imagine I am a typical American millionaire. Look." He brought out his billfold and held it open so that she could see the money inside. "Do you know how much is there? A hundred-dollar bill if you guess correctly."

"I couldn't possibly guess. It looks like an awful lot."

"About one thousand three hundred and eighty dollars, Katherine. Would you care to have a hundred, or two? Or even three, or four? I am not fooling, I will be overjoyed to give you a little present, a token of appreciation for your great kindness."

"Stefan!"

"You think I am vulgar? Or crazy?" He laughed. "Not at all. Suppose I am sent back to Budapest in the next day or two. What can I do with this money? The bastards will confiscate it. They will take every dollar, every cent, and perhaps the fillings in my teeth as well. I will feel a lot happier if I throw it around on ridiculous luxuries like green caviar, and even happier if you would take it and use it to buy yourself something you want, like a pretty chinchilla cape or a diamond wristwatch."

Tears filled her eyes. "Please keep it. Please don't throw your money around. Suppose, after all, you are not sent back?"

"Sure, sure," he said gaily. "There is always the possibility of a miracle."

She was suddenly seized with an overpowering affection for him. She wanted to kiss him and caress him, she would have done anything within her power to insure his happiness. She murmured, "No. You mustn't go back. I won't let you go back. You must stay here, with me."

"And then what?"

"You will live here. You will become an American citizen."

"It is not as easy as you think. How would I make a living?"

"You would find a way. By teaching, perhaps."

"That is everybody's first thought: teaching. But there are not an infinite number of positions open for teaching the Hungarian language, or Hungarian history, or even how to make a Hungarian goulash."

"You might teach at Southcliffe. I will have a word with Dean Gilberta."

"Impossible. I am not a Catholic, you know."

"I could speak to Mr. Gamage. He might find you something in the State Department."

"Darling, I appreciate your kindness, but I assure you, the State Department is up to its neck in Hungarians. Do you realize how many came here, or were brought here, after the uprising of 1956? Thousands upon thousands. Mr. Gamage could do very little to help, I am afraid."

"There must be *something!*"

He laughed again, but this time with an edge of bitterness. "Oh, undoubtedly, there must be something. And do you know what this something is? To work as a part-time waiter in some depressing restaurant, where you have to hand over half of your tips to the swine of a proprietor. I am sorry, but I would rather kill myself than fall so low. Here comes Axel. Look at his eyes (you are always looking at the eyes of the people you meet) and tell me if you would like to see the same expression in my eyes."

She said, "Never. I couldn't bear it."

"So, there you are. But don't be sad, Katherine. After a few glasses of the Rothschild Reserve everything will look much better, believe me. And the green caviar is guaranteed to restore your faith in mankind. Am I right, Axel?"

"You are always right, Mr. Gerhardi, sair."

5.

Champagne and caviar, Kate thought. How Edwardian! Any moment he will ask for one of my shoes, in order to drink out of it.

He raised his glass and said, "Katherine, I propose a toast. To my guardian angel. May she live forever, and forever be happy."

"Do good socialists admit to having guardian angels?" she asked.

He laughed heartily. "I cannot speak for the millions of good socialists all over the world; I can only speak for myself. Yes! You, my darling, are my guardian angel! As long as I am with you I feel utterly safe! And I believe I am the only man alive who is in love with his guardian angel, and whose guardian angel is in love with him. So drink, Katherine, drink!"

Blushing with pleasure, she sipped the sour and gassy liquid.

He emptied his glass in two gulps, and reached for the magnum to pour more. He paused in astonishment. "But you have scarcely touched yours, my love. Is something wrong?"

"I can never drink champagne fast. It makes me sneeze."

He shook his head. "At times you are so childlike, nobody would suspect you are an eminent social critic." He looked at her sternly. "Hold out your glass, Madame Emoryi. There is a whole bottle to be finished."

"I warn you, I shall be drunk."

"So what? It is good for you to get a little tiddly once in a while. Relax. Enjoy the fleshpots."

The pockmarked man who played the violin, and the pretty plump pianist who was now playing a white and gold concertina, came to the table, and with astonishing squeals, runs, trills and arpeggios, rendered *Play, Gypsy, Play.* Stefan whispered in Kate's ear, "Be good enough to bear with this ghastly noise. They are expressing their friendly feelings for you and me." Kate nodded. Despite the insult to her senses she was stirred by the sentiment of the playing. A lump came to her throat and her eyes were moist. "Bravo! Bravo!" Stefan said when the serenade ended, and he slipped a folded five-dollar bill into the girl's bodice. In an explosion of gratitude and passion she kissed him on both cheeks, and then shook hands with Kate. "God be with you," she said, her eyes flashing, and Kate answered, "God be with you, too." The girl added, "And be sure to treat Stefan good." Kate, taken aback, said, "Yes, I will do my best."

6.

"I want to explain to you, as I promised," Stefan said, spooning more caviar onto her plate, "about Mr. Horscht, and Mrs. Horscht, and how I happen to find myself in such an awkward pickle."

"Stefan—"

"You do not wish to hear about the Horschts?"

"Not now."

"But they exist, unfortunately. One cannot close one's eyes and hope they will disappear into thin air. In particular, Mrs. Horscht exists, and I think if you will listen to what I have to say about her, many suspicions in your mind will be set at rest. May I pour you some champagne first?"

"No, thank you," Kate said. She was already dizzy.

"Just a little."

"Very well. Just a little."

"Years and years ago," Stefan said, twisting the magnum back into the crushed ice, "there lived in Budapest a carefree young journalist named Stefan Gerhardi, who was of the opinion that of all the fine things the good God had created, none was so delectable as that soft little bundle of flesh and temperament known as Woman—"

"I think I am going to be terribly sick," Kate said.

"Be tolerant, darling. I am only trying to recapture the Budapest of my youth. Remember, there had been wars and revolutions, there had been the Nazi invader followed by the Russian bear; and what I am trying to express to you is that despite all these cataclysms, life went on. It was still possible for a young man to lose his heart to a young girl in the old-fashioned way. As I look back on it I can see that it was rather charming. Hollywood could not improve on it. At this time, Emmy was playing small parts at the Studio Theatre, I was writing for the so-called literary magazines, we had no money, and we had a very delightful little love affair that lasted—oh, I would say about six months."

"You never told me that Mrs. Horscht was an actress."

"Probably because we have never discussed her in detail. She was not a good actress, I am sorry to say, and she was even worse as a dancer. Her chief attractions, as far as I was concerned, were that she was pretty; and, even more important, that she was a girl."

"How old a girl?"

"Twenty. Twenty-one. She is now about forty."

"She's older than I thought."

"Nevertheless, she is a couple of years younger than I am."

"Oh, but you look much younger than forty. *Much.*"

"Thank you. The eyes of love see through golden opera glasses. May I continue?"

"No. I am bored with Emmy Horscht."

"Try to be unbored for another minute or two. What I am trying to tell you is important, Katherine. It affects my life, it affects your life, it affects the children we might have had, it affects our entire universe, the universe that you and I, by ourselves, occupy."

She was startled by his vehemence. "I'm sorry."

He touched her arm gently. "There is no need to apologize. I simply want you to know the facts so that you will not feel, later, that I kept you in the dark. Well, then: Emmy and I had our little love affair in Budapest and, in the natural course of events, when it was over we parted. It has been happening to young people since time began. Subsequently I had other little affairs, I was married and divorced, I traveled here and there, and eventually I found myself in New York. There were no clouds on the horizon; everything went like a song. Until one day, a couple of months ago, Mr. Miklos Horscht stepped off an airplane at Kennedy Airport with his elegant wife Emmy." Stefan gazed thoughtfully at the painted cupids in a corner of the ceiling. He said in a sad voice, "It is hardly necessary to tell you that Mr. and Mrs. Horscht are incompatible. He adores her because she is still fairly pretty, she dresses well, she is sophisticated, et cetera. On the other hand, she finds him painfully provincial."

"I thought he was a very attractive man."

"Well, of course, you have a perfect right to think so. But it does not alter the case because, fortunately, you are not married to him, and Emmy is."

"True."

"I can only assure you that when I met Emmy again, after so many years, I saw before me a classic case of marital frustration. You could have put her into one of your books, so to speak, without changing a word. She was dissatisfied. She was restless. She was unhappy. She was forced to receive constant injections of hormones—"

Kate exclaimed, "*Constant* injections of hormones! Are you sure? What do you mean by *constant?*"

"At least twice a week. She told me so herself."

"But that's terribly dangerous! It could have the most serious results! Isn't she aware of that?"

"Katherine, I hate to disagree with you, but you must bear in mind that she has consulted some of the best gynecologists in Budapest. Believe me, in all matters pertaining to sex, Hungarian doctors are the best in the world."

"How can you say that?"

"The reason is simple. They are interested in sex, they really care about it. American and British doctors, I am sorry to say, regard sex as a phenomenon that is best dealt with on the operating table; and French doctors regard it, professionally, as merely an adjunct of the liver." For a moment he smiled gleefully. Then he continued, "Unfortunately, in her weakened state, Emmy fell in love with me all over again and, to be blunt about it, Katherine, I have to confess that she made my life exceedingly difficult."

Kate said crossly, "I'm not the least bit surprised that she made your life exceedingly difficult if she was receiving hormone injections twice a week."

"I see that you appreciate the situation perfectly," Stefan said. "You will also appreciate that I was caught in a cleft stick, for she threatened to reveal to Mr. Horscht our relationship of many years ago if I did not fall in with her wishes. May I give you more champagne, darling?"

"No, thank you."

"Just a drop, to keep your spirits up while I finish this unhappy story."

"All right."

"To be brief," he said, skillfully, brandishing the magnum

first over her glass and then over his own, "about a month ago—before you and I met—I decided that I could not possibly continue with Mrs. Horscht. For one thing, I was definitely not in love with her. For another thing, I was deeply ashamed of deceiving poor Mr. Horscht and placing our diplomatic work in jeopardy. One night I told Emmy of my feelings, and the inevitable happened. She was furious. She blew up. And to strike back at me, she began to fill Mr. Horscht's mind with suspicion of my motives. Up to this time, Mr. Horscht had been most amiable toward me. But from then on, he watched me like a hawk."

Kate listened uneasily. It was all very confusing. She was unfamiliar with these complex rites of betrayal and intrigue that seemed to be a permanent feature of Middle European politics. She felt sorry for Stefan, his happiness was of vital importance to her, and she was shocked to hear of all the trouble he had endured. But she was also sorry for Mr. Horscht. He had been treated rather shabbily. And although Emmy Horscht might well be considered the villainess of the piece, how could one condemn an unfortunate woman whose entire endocrine system must have been wildly unbalanced by excessive doses of steroid hormones? Everybody knows, Kate thought, that the estrogens (like the androgens) exercise a profound effect upon the libido. Thus, Mrs. Horscht was no more to blame for betraying Stefan under these circumstances than if she had betrayed him while she was under the influence of alcohol or marijuana.

Kate said, "When I met Mr. Horscht the other night he was very friendly. I really didn't see any signs of hostility or suspicion."

"Anybody can tell that you are a trained observer!" Stefan cried. "You are absolutely right! And why? Because, when Mr. Horscht saw me dancing with you, and saw how happy we were together, his suspicions flew right out of the window! How could anyone imagine that I was chasing his wife, when here I was so totally in love with you?" Stefan chuckled. "And what was the result? In one word: my fate was sealed."

"I don't follow," Kate said. The endless twists in the story were making her dizzy.

"It is quite simple. When Emmy heard Mr. Horscht describing you in the most glowing terms—your charm, your intelligence, your beauty, your wonderful taste in clothes—she became, literally, blind with jealousy. Without pausing to think, she blurted out to Mr. Horscht the whole story of our relationship, from its innocent beginnings in Budapest so many years ago, to its sordid conclusion in New York just recently. How did Mr. Horscht respond? Bear in mind that, essentially, he *is* provincial. Consequently, he was shocked to the core. Within a few hours, he was on his way to Ottawa for consultations with other officials. So, because of Emmy's insane behavior, not only will I be sent home, but she will probably be sent home, also."

Kate said bitterly, "Isn't that what she wants?"

"Not really," Stefan said with a rueful smile. "It is true that we might stand trial side by side, but it is unlikely that we would be permitted to share the same prison cell. And it is equally unlikely that the authorities will send us to the same labor camp for the next ten or fifteen years."

"I can't bear this," Kate said in sudden despair. "I just can't *bear* it."

"We will not talk about it any more, then," Stefan said. "To hell with Mr. Horscht, to hell with Mrs. Horscht, to hell with everybody except ourselves. Let us eat, drink, and make merry, for tomorrow the rain will fall and the wind will blow." He stood up and held his hands out to her. "Katherine, come and dance with me."

She shrank down in her chair. "I couldn't. I'm simply not in the mood for dancing."

"*Be* in the mood. *Force yourself* into the mood. Dance with me, please."

"Honestly, I couldn't. Besides, the champagne has gone to my head, I'm terribly dizzy."

His blue eyes became grim. "Do you realize that this may be our last dance together? We may never have another opportunity. *Come!*"

Tearfully she stood up and went with him. The champagne had indeed gone to her head; she was so dizzy that she had to cling to him, and the other people on the floor whirled around her like figures on a merry-go-round. *Tomorrow the rain will fall and the wind will blow,* she thought, *and this is our last dance, and my last love.*

7.

They left the Carpathia at about two o'clock, and strolled back to Gramercy Park arm in arm. The air was mild and soft, the sky was velvety. He said in a hushed, deep voice, "Ah, Katherine, I love this city of yours, I love it sometimes even more than my own Budapest. I shall miss it. I shall dream about it." He turned to her, smiling. "May I tell you what hurts me most? More than anything else?"

She could hardly speak. "What?"

"That I could not bring my feelings for you to their proper conclusion."

She said shakily, "You have made me very happy."

"Thank you. But I hoped to accomplish more than making you happy for a few nights. I wanted a permanent relationship with you, Katherine, that would continue for the rest of my life. Not another charming little affair—I have had too many of them, I am thoroughly sick of them. *Mar-*

riage! That is what I wanted. *Marriage,* as firm and solid as a great rock rooted in the ground. *Marriage,* to give both of us security of the spirit as well as security of the body."

She was trembling. "Don't go on, Stefan."

"You wish me to stop?"

"It's very painful."

"For you? I assure you, it is also very painful for me. Because—and do not correct me if I am wrong, let me have my little illusions—if I could have gone on being your lover for another week, another two weeks, I believe I could have won you. You would have had no more mental reservations, you would have been ready to marry me."

She could not see where she was walking. She could not speak. All her strength had drained away.

He laughed at his thoughts. "You know, there is a certain irony about the situation, Katherine. It is actually most amusing. For, if you had agreed to become my wife, do you realize what the result would have been? Mr. Horscht and his friends in Ottawa would have found themselves in something of a fix. What charges could they bring against me? How could they plan to put on trial the husband of the renowned and beautiful Katherine Emory Gerhardi?" He stopped walking and stood facing her. "Even if I still had to return to Budapest, I would return with you at my side; and I would be hailed as some kind of hero! The government would find us a nice apartment, we would have a free pass to the State Opera House, we would have a car, a television set, a refrigerator, anything our little hearts desired. How funny! What a joke!"

She asked tearfully, "What can I do? How can I help you?"

"There is nothing you can do in the present circumstances. After all, darling, you are not ready for marriage. Nobody could expect you to make a martyr of yourself. Why should you ruin your life for a foreigner?"

"You can stay in my apartment until you find a job, a *good* job, a job you will enjoy doing. I'll speak to Mr. Gamage, I'll speak to all my friends—something is sure to turn up. You mustn't think of going back to Budapest to face these false charges."

"No," he said. "I thank you sincerely for your kindness. But I have come to the conclusion that I am bound by my honor to return. Besides, I am not cut out to be a refugee—"

She screamed, "Stefan! *Stefan!* Look out!"

A tall man, with a black hat pulled down over his eyes, was running at top speed toward them. He flung Kate aside with a sweep of one long and powerful arm, and sent Stefan staggering with a tremendous blow that landed somewhere below the ear. Another blow fell on Stefan's shoulder like a great hammer and he crumpled to the sidewalk. The man knelt down on him, pummeling him viciously, and Stefan seemed too dazed to strike back. Then the man hooked his arm around Stefan's neck and pulled back mightily, as if he were trying to remove Stefan's head in one piece, and Stefan, evidently quite helpless, rolled his eyes and made strange agonizing sounds deep down in his throat.

"Don't do that!" Kate cried, "Don't do that!" and she flew at the man like an enraged hen, flailing at him again and again with her pocketbook.

He was forced to stop his efforts to decapitate Stefan in order to shield himself from Kate's furious attack. Growling savagely, he suddenly lashed out at her and sent her spinning into the roadway.

"Coward!" she screamed; and instantly she came flying at him again, in the same disconcerting hen-like way, all her feathers ruffled, swinging her pocketbook up and down and from side to side.

"Go away!" the man bellowed at her. "Leave me alone!"

"I won't go away," she screamed in reply. "I won't leave you alone."

Stefan seemed to have recovered some of his strength. He was thrashing around and making frantic lunges in an attempt to free himself. The man in the black hat appeared to grow alarmed—he had lost the initiative, and he may have felt himself in unexpected danger. He hit Stefan a glancing blow on the chin, pushed Kate away with an out-thrust of a huge hand, and then, pulling his hat more firmly over his eyes, he sprang up, gave Stefan a last kick, and sprinted off into the shadows of Irving Place.

"You bully!" Kate screamed after him. "You gangster! Come back here!" She suddenly caught sight of a thickset, hatless man in a gray suit standing about twenty feet away, watching the scene in utter astonishment, and she called out to him with profound bitterness, "Sir, aren't you going to help us? Are you just going to stand there? Stop that murderer!"

The man in the gray suit looked at her, looked at Stefan, opened his mouth to reply, thought better of it, and hurried off in the opposite direction to the man in the black hat.

"Cowards," Kate said in anguish. "They are all cowards." She crouched down beside Stefan, trying to restrain her sobs, and said wildly, "Oh, my darling, my darling! Are you hurt? What did he do to you?"

"I seem to be alive," Stefan said. "And that is a good sign. I thought the fellow was going to kill me."

"I thought so, too," she cried. "He was *vicious,* just *vicious.*"

"My head," Stefan said. "Look carefully and tell me whether it is still attached to my neck."

She laughed tearfully. "Yes, it is. Who was the man? György? The chauffeur?"

"I had no chance to observe him clearly. Did he have a little black mustache?"

"I think so."

"Waxed at the ends?"

"I'm not sure."

"Long side-whiskers?"

"I really didn't notice."

"Well," Stefan said wearily, "I suppose it was György. Evidently he had received orders to put an end to my activities." He moved his head gingerly and gave an exclamation of pain. "Oh! Oh!"

"You *are* hurt!" she cried. "And there's blood on your face!"

He said, "I will not get better sitting here on the pavement. Help me up, darling," and with her assistance he struggled to his feet. She asked in a frenzy of anxiety, "Are you all right? Can you stand? Does it hurt when you move?" and he replied calmly, trying to reassure her, "I am fine, Katherine. Truly, there is no need to worry about me."

"We are nearly at the apartment," she said. "Do you think you can walk there? Lean on me. Take your time. Don't hurry. We'll be home in a minute."

"Home," he sighed. "What a lovely word."

8.

It was miraculous, she thought, that he had escaped with such light injuries after such a terrible beating. He had widespread bruises, there was a cut on his cheek and another cut on his left temple, and he had bled a little, but no bones were broken and he had suffered no serious harm. "It is all due to you, my guardian angel," he said. "If you had not come to my aid, I would probably be a dead man now. What courage! What ferocity! And what a loyal, wonderful person you are! I think you would tackle the Devil himself, if he were foolish enough to molest the man you love."

His praise embarrassed her. She said, "Anybody would have tried to fight back. György is just a bully, a hoodlum."

When, finally, she crawled into bed, she found that she

was in a state of emotional shock. Even though she lay absolutely still, her head was spinning giddily, and she was afflicted by waves of nausea. All the alcohol she had consumed, all the excitement she had experienced, all the mental distress resulting from Stefan's problems, were now taking their full effect. To her astonishment, Stefan still had enough energy to attempt to make love to her. She said gently, "No, my dear, no. You must rest," but he persisted, and gradually sensation returned to her body. She began to respond to him, and soon her involvement was more overwhelming than anything she had known with him in the past. Her body seemed to be crying out with joy because he had not been seriously harmed, he was safe, he was virile, he was unchanged.

They were still awake when the dawn broke, at six o'clock. The gray-white light crept into the bedroom, giving a ghastly pallor to Stefan's bruised skin. She began to tremble violently. She could not bear the thought of losing him, she could not bear the thought of the terror lurking outside, another day of menace and brutality. She lay holding on to him, crying.

He said, "What is the matter, Katherine?"

"Nothing," she said. "I love you, that's all."

"Is that all, really?"

"Yes."

"And I love you. I have been lying here by your side wondering how I can ever leave you."

"You mustn't leave me, Stefan. You must stay with me."

"Forever?"

"Forever."

He moved away from her slightly, so that he could look down at her face. "Katherine, will you marry me?"

There was only one answer to that question now, and after a moment she said quietly, "Yes. I will."

He gave a great shout. "We must celebrate! We must celebrate! Is there any champagne in the apartment?"

"No more champagne," she said. He celebrated instead by making love to her once again, and a few minutes later she fell asleep in his arms.

9.

After the Carpathia closed at two-thirty, Axel walked to his telephone booth on Second Avenue and dialed the number of his employers in Queens.

"Yes?"

"86."

"What's up, 86?"

"35 was in the restaurant tonight with his woman, Emoryi."

"Listen, 86. Forget you saw 35 tonight. Forget you saw the woman Emoryi tonight. If anyone asks you about tonight, you know nothing. Understand?"

"My God, you mean there's some kind of trouble?"

"Just listen to what I'm telling you and don't worry about trouble or no trouble. As far as 35 is concerned, tonight you were deaf, dumb, blind, and paralyzed. Okay, 86?"

"Okay, Imre."

There was a cry of rage, and the line went dead. Axel waited a full minute, biting his thumbnail savagely; then he pulled the brim of his hat a little lower and dialed the number of his employers in the Chelsea area.

"Yes?"

"Ragweed here."

"Where are you?"

Axel gave the number on the dial of the telephone.

"Hang up and wait, Ragweed."

"Yes, sair."

The telephone duly rang again. He picked up the receiver and said, "Ragweed."

"Go ahead, Ragweed."

"Sair, I have to report that I don't know what the hell is going on around here any more."

"Continue, Ragweed."

"They were in again tonight, Gerhardi and his lady."

"Keep going."

"Well, before they come in, Pyotr had this telephone call from Mrs. Emmy Horscht."

"Pyotr?"

"That's the guy behind the bar, the boss's ex-son-in-law, but the boss don't like to fire him."

"Yes."

"Well, Mrs. Horscht tells Pyotr, if he sees 35—"

"Who?"

"35—I mean, Gerhardi, to warn him that Big György is gunning for him. Big György is the chauffeur and the bodyguard for the Horschts. A very tough fellow."

"Yes."

"Well, it doesn't make sense. First of all, why should György be gunning for Gerhardi who everyone knows is doing a good job here? Second, if Mrs. Emmy Horscht is so worried, why doesn't she just tell György to stay home and wash the Lincoln Continental, or something? I mean, H is in Canada, for God's sake, and she's in charge of the house."

"Who's in Canada?"

"H. I mean, Mr. Horscht. The Colonel, as we call him sometimes."

"How about the woman, Emory?"

"Oh, Gerhardi is giving her the works, you can see that. It's obvious."

"What do you mean, it's obvious?"

"Well, for instance they were dancing on the floor tonight, and she had these big, big tears rolling down her cheeks."

"She was crying? What about?"

"God only knows."

"You don't have any explanation for what is going on?"

"I can't figure it out, sair. You have to remember, I am only half-Hungarian, on my father's side. These sons of bitches are full-blooded Hungarians on *both* sides, and I defy anyone to figure them out."

"What time did Gerhardi and Emory leave the restaurant?"

"Around two o'clock, sair."

"Anything else, Ragweed?"

"No, sair. That's all, sair."

The line went dead.

10

SHE DID not have the heart to waken him in the morning and send him away. There was the possibility that György, or some deputy assassin, might still be lying in wait for him outside in Gramercy Park. He was safe only here, with her. For a while she lay listening to him as he snored gently and contentedly; then she slipped out of bed, taking great care not to disturb him. She went into the kitchen, made a pot of coffee, carried it into the living room, and sat curled up on the big settee.

Question followed question as she thought about the events of last night. Does he really want to marry me? When will we be married? What will happen afterward? Where will we live, what will we do?

He was clearly unwilling to seek refuge in the United States. *I am bound by my honor to return,* he had declared. *I am not cut out to be a refugee.*

She thought, *So I may have to give up my life here, in this old Egyptian sepulcher, and go to live with him in Budapest.*

This, on reflection, was not too disturbing. She was aware that she had been living here too long, she was too settled, she needed the spiritual upheaval that would inevitably follow her marriage to Stefan. Budapest might be an ideal place in which to begin a new life. She discounted its significance as a communist stronghold—Stefan had assured her that it would not continue long as a Soviet satellite. It was virtually the geographic center of Europe, mediating between West and East; it provided easy access to Austria and Germany, to Italy and Greece, to Russia as well as Turkey. France and Spain were only a hop and a skip away. A day's drive would bring one to the Dalmatian coast. Only a couple of hours' flight would leave one, so to speak, at the doors of the British Museum. She became excited as she thought of all the trips she would be able to take hand in hand with Stefan. A marvelous life of adventure and exploration awaited her.

And beside all this, she thought, *I am—after all—not yet forty.* She meant that she would be following a long-established Southcliffe tradition by marrying somewhat late in life (her first marriage didn't really count) and proceeding to raise a healthy, happy, well-rounded little family. Why Southcliffe graduates, more than the graduates of other reputable colleges, should possess the ability to bear numerous offspring with the utmost ease in their fourth decade was a biological curiosity that had long intrigued eugenists, and she thought, *I ought to warn Stefan about it: statistically, he can expect two and three-quarter children within the next five years.* She sat staring into space, simultaneously thrilled and alarmed, seeing herself leading through the misty streets of Budapest a troop of handsome, tow-headed, blue-eyed youngsters, all like her husband Stefan. *Other women have done it,* she thought, *why shouldn't I?*

2.

As soon as Mrs. Corcoran arrived, Kate broke the news to her. She said calmly, "I have a surprise for you, Mrs. Corcoran. Last night I became engaged to marry Mr. Gerhardi."

Mrs. Corcoran's eyes gleamed. "That doesn't come as no

surprise, Miss Em. I knew something was in the wind when I seen that container of paprika in my kitchen. Horrible stuff. I wouldn't give it to a goat."

"Aren't you going to congratulate me, Mrs. Corcoran?"

"Congratulations, Miss Em. I'm sure it's all for the best."

Kate said, "Mr. Gerhardi is having breakfast with me this morning. So would you be kind enough to run out to the delicatessen and get a few things he might like?"

"Such as kippers?" Mrs. Corcoran said. "Such as some good Irish bacon, French bread, and hard rolls? How's that?"

"I leave it entirely to you."

Giselle, on the other hand, was distressed by the news. She congratulated Kate in a choked voice, retired to the study, and came out a few minutes later saying, "Miss Emory, I have a slight sore throat. Would you mind if I go to the drugstore for some troches?"

Kate looked at her with concern. Her face was white and puffy. "If you aren't feeling well, perhaps you'd rather go home?"

"No! No!" Giselle cried. "I only need something for my throat, nothing else. I will be right back."

Kate went to the bedroom, and woke Stefan with a kiss. He opened his eyes, stared at her, and said, "Ah! So, after all, that scoundrel György succeeded in bumping me off. I must have flown straight up to Heaven." She laughed and kissed him again, and said, "I'm sorry, you can't stay in Heaven long, you have to get dressed. Mrs. Corcoran has gone to the delicatessen to buy kippers for your breakfast." He said, "*Kippers!* What barbarity is this?"

But he ate ravenously when breakfast was served. Kate was filled with pleasure watching him. When he had almost finished she said, "Must you go to the United Nations today?"

"Why do you ask in that tone of voice, Katherine?"

"I am still frightened about György. I think you ought to stay here, for the time being."

He said, "H'm. You may be right. In any case, I cannot possibly think about perforations, watermarks, today of all days." He glanced at his impressive gold Rolex watch. "I will call the acting head of my department and make my excuses. May I use your telephone, darling?"

"Of course."

He dialed a number, and as he waited for the connection to be made he put his hand over the mouthpiece and said, "A charming old fellow, Katherine. You will like him." He went on in a firmer, deeper, voice, "Ah, Mr. Hamid! This is Gerhardi speaking. And how are you this beautiful morning? Good, good. Now, Mr. Hamid, brace yourself, my dear friend, I have some startling news. I have just become engaged to be married. Yes. Last night. To whom? The lady's name is Miss Katherine Emory—*Emory*. That is perfectly correct, Mr. Hamid, she is a writer—yes, the author of the books you mention. You have read *which* books?" As Mr. Hamid talked on, Stefan covered the mouthpiece with his hand, and whispered, "Darling, he is simply agog with excitement, and I have a great idea. May I invite him here for cocktails at five o'clock so that he can meet you?"

"By all means," Kate said.

Stefan said, "Mr. Hamid, excuse me for interrupting, but would you do us the honor of dropping in here for cocktails at five o'clock this afternoon? We are having an informal little party, for just a few close friends, to celebrate this great event." He gave Mr. Hamid the address and telephone number, and added, "In the meantime, as I am sure you understand, there are many things to be arranged, and I may be a little late coming to the office. *Do not hurry?* How kind you are! Good-by, Mr. Hamid. Until five o'clock."

Stefan put the receiver down and said, "Katherine, it occurred to me while I was speaking to the old bird, why not invite some other people to share our happiness? What about Norton Goodrich? And Marcel Preiss? Let us have a real party, Katherine, let us have fun. How many times does one get married in a lifetime, after all?"

"Very well," Kate said indulgently. He was like an excited young boy. She was ready to let him have anything he wanted.

In some remarkable manner the news spread like wildfire over Manhattan, and the telephone rang incessantly with calls from his friends offering their congratulations and demanding to be introduced to his future bride. "Darling," he said, after a hilarious conversation in Spanish, "my dearest friend Consuela is on the line, come and say hello to her. She is dying to meet you, and I have invited her to drop by at five." A few minutes later, after a lengthy conversation in Hungarian, he said, "You must speak to my best friend, Imre Lukacs—he is a sort of aide-de-camp to Mr. Horscht—you will adore each other, I am sure of it." Then, "Katherine! Here! Speak to my very dearest friend Pál Zichy and his lovely wife Anna. They cannot be with us tonight, they are coming tomorrow, instead." Kate spoke shyly to them, listened patiently to their eulogies of Stefan, and murmured, "Thank you, thank you, I shall look forward so much to meeting you."

By noon, some forty of Stefan's best and dearest friends had announced their intention of dropping in for cocktails that evening, and Kate began to worry about providing refreshments for such a large number of guests. Giselle had not returned from the drugstore, presumably because of her sore throat; and Mrs. Corcoran was sent out again with a shopping list, prepared in detail by Stefan, that ranged from salted nuts to a cold roast turkey. But a few minutes after Mrs. Corcoran left, Kate had a sudden sense of disaster. She hurried into her study, consulted her diary, and let out a cry of anguish. Stefan, chatting on the telephone to a celebrated Italian journalist in New Jersey, exclaimed, "My God, Katherine! What is the matter?" and she called back, "I have to be at a luncheon of the Larrabee Foundation at one o'clock, and I'm not even dressed." He hung up with an apology to his Italian friend and came into the study saying, "What? What? Where do you have to be at one o'clock?"

"At a luncheon of the Larrabee Foundation, on Fifth Avenue, near Seventy-fifth Street."

"What on earth is the Larrabee Foundation?"

"Darling, I don't have time to explain now. They give grants for research projects on race relationships, and so on, and I am on the awards committee."

He grinned. "You are sure this is not another lover?"

She cried, "Don't, *don't* say such disturbing things. I have to rush. And I want you to stay here, please, it truly isn't safe for you to go out. Mrs. Corcoran will fix lunch for you, and you can play the phonograph all you wish."

He said, "Your word is my command."

3.

She dressed in a whirl. When she was ready to leave she threw her arms around him and kissed him passionately, as if she would not see him again for a year or two, and then went flying out of the house, down the stone steps, and toward Irving Place, where she expected to find a taxi. And at once she became aware, in a way she could not explain, that she was being followed. She *knew,* without turning to look, that as she hurried along the sunny sidewalk another human being was hurrying behind her stride for stride. She thought, *How silly! Hasn't György heard that Stefan and I are getting married? And why, in any case, keep me under surveillance?* She suddenly stopped and swung around, feeling that she ought to put an end to this nonsensical situation by telling whoever was trailing her that he was simply wasting his time (and his country's money). She saw him, or thought she saw him: a rather thickset, hatless man in a gray suit who seemed vaguely familiar and who was now looking intently up at the sky as if he were trying to locate an overdue helicopter. Unfortunately, he had turned away from her, and his face was at such an oblique angle that she could not see his features—she could not even see if he had a mustache, waxed at the ends. She gave a little shrug. It was none of her business if he wanted to behave in this childish fashion, and she continued on her way and caught a taxi outside Pete's Tavern. A minute later she knew, by the same extrasensory process, that he was in a taxi behind her; he presumably intended to follow her wherever she went. It was absurd and incomprehensible. What good would it do him? How would it benefit the Hungarian People's Republic?

She enjoyed the luncheon. She thoroughly relished the good roast beef and the excellent burgundy that accompanied it. Almost anything that was said to her made her laugh joyously, and several of the males present eyed her with appreciative interest. A number of significant matters were discussed and various decisions were made, but she would have had difficulty, ten minutes later, saying exactly what had taken place. She was obsessed by thoughts of Stefan, by the almost incredible change of direction in her life. *I love,* she murmured to herself; *and I am loved.* Who, in this assemblage of dull and decent scholars, would have believed it?

The proceedings ended at three o'clock, and when she stepped out on Fifth Avenue she looked around her with curiosity. Sure enough, she caught another glimpse of the hatless man in the gray suit. But he was very quick, very alert. He turned swiftly, so that she only saw his back. Riding home in a taxi she felt sorry for him. She, at least, had eaten an excellent lunch. He had not eaten anything, and he was probably yearning for his customary midday meal of goulash and noodles, washed down with a bottle of dark beer. It was a shame. He had merely wasted about four dollars on taxi fares. But, probably like the Central Intelligence Agency, the Hungarian Secret Service (or whatever it was called) was lavishly endowed, and it could afford to waste the Hungarian taxpayer's money without turning a hair.

4.

She expected to hear music coming from the living room. Instead, she heard a murmur of conversation and laughter. When she entered she saw a totally unexpected sight, something she could never have anticipated. Stefan sat at one end of the big settee, his knees crossed, smoking a cigarette and looking very animated, while Miss Mitsamushi sat at the other end of the settee, wearing her gray flannel dress her kness pressed tightly together, a shy yet happy expression on her face, her black leather dispatch case on the floor beside her.

"Well, hello," Kate said.

Stefan jumped up. Miss Mitsamushi jumped up.

"Here you are at last!" Stefan said. "I thought we had lost you for sure. Miss Mitsamushi has been waiting at least half an hour, and I have been trying to keep her from being bored. What an interesting conversation we have had! Am I right, Miss Mitsamushi?"

Miss Mitsamushi's expression had changed. She was now looking a little apprehensive, a little breathless. She said, "Miss Emory, I have discovered that Mr. Gerhardi knows friends of mine all over the world."

"Mr. Gerhardi knows *everybody*," Kate said, "*everywhere*. But this is an unexpected pleasure, Miss Mitsamushi. I had no idea you were coming to see me."

Stefan intervened. "I asked Miss Mitsamushi to drop by, darling."

"Oh?" Kate said.

"I was in the neighborhood," Miss Mitsamushi explained, "and I telephoned, wondering if you would be free for a minute to see me—"

"—And I said I was sure you would be free for a minute to see her, although you were not yet home from some luncheon," Stefan chimed in, "and I said, do come over. Was I wrong?"

"Of course not," Kate said. "I am delighted to see you, Miss Mitsamushi. Do you have some new material for me?"

Miss Mitsamushi bobbed down and picked up her dispatch case. She glanced timidly at Stefan, looked appealingly at Kate, and said, "Yes."

"Will you excuse us, Stefan?" Kate said. "We are just going into the study for a minute or two. Is Giselle there?"

"No, I have no idea where Giselle is," Stefan said. He gave the Japanese girl a smile and a courteous little bow; she bowed more deeply in response and Kate, feeling somewhat irritated, led the way into the study.

Miss Mitsamushi looked around her with awe. "What a magnificent room!" she exclaimed. "What books!" She went on quickly, "I hope you will not think I am intruding, coming here like this—"

"No, not at all," Kate said. "Won't you sit down?"

Miss Mitsamushi sat down primly on the edge of the black leather armchair.

Kate, sitting at her desk, waited a moment, composed herself, and said, "I think it is my duty to tell you that circumstances have changed since I last saw you, and I really don't know if I shall be going to Japan, I don't really know *where* I shall be going. You see, Mr. Gerhardi and I became engaged yesterday, and we shall be getting married, I expect, fairly soon."

"Oh! Congratulations!" Miss Mitsamushi exlaimed. "How nice!"

"Thank you," Kate said. She continued, "This raises several rather serious questions. For example, I don't think it would be proper for me to accept any more classified material from you and I wonder, in fact, whether I shouldn't return, here and now, all the material you have so far brought me."

"Is your visit definitely canceled?" Miss Mitsamushi asked.

"Not yet. But I expect to write to Mr. Gamage today or tomorrow, informing him of this new turn of events, and I suspect the lecture tour will then be canceled by mutual consent."

"Perhaps, if you are being married soon, your husband could accompany you, and there will be no need for cancellation?"

Kate smiled. "I'm afraid that isn't very likely."

Miss Mitsamushi said, "The papers I have brought with me are of general interest, and you might like to glance through them." She opened her dispatch case and handed Kate several typed documents. "Here is a most interesting report on the fishing industry and the pollution of coastal waters. Here is one on new methods of training Olympic swimming teams. And here is one I am sure you will enjoy, on Japanese novelists and short-story writers."

Kate said, "Miss Mitsamushi, can you explain to me why this eight-page report on Japanese novelists and short-story writers should be marked *Highly Confidential?*"

Miss Mitsamushi looked embarrassed. "I am afraid that is a policy-making decision of the State Department, far above my humble level." She gave Kate yet another document consisting of three pages stapled together. "Here is a report given to my brother Jiro by Sun Pat Hsueng—you remember? Brother Hop?—on recent tragic events in China. And here is something I thought you would like to see: photograph of Sun Pat Hsueng taken in Shanghai by friends. What do you think of Sun Pat Hsueng? Is he younger or older than you imagined?"

The photograph was a crude enlargement, almost the same size as the sheets of paper on which the various reports were typed. Kate studied it with interest. The man was in his early twenties or late teens, and so skinny that he seemed diseased. His face was bony, sardonic, intelligent, with a shock of untidy black hair. The mouth was sadistic, and he gazed at the camera with a sardonic smile. His clothes were the shabby nondescript clothes of Chairman Mao's China, and he stood outside a crumbling building covered with Chinese scribblings, presumably wall newspapers. Grouped around him were several girls, equally nondescript, equally skinny, equally unlovable.

Kate said, "It is a little difficult to form an opinion about this young man from his photograph. However, he looks very intelligent. Who are the girls with him?"

"Members of his group."

"Which group is that, Miss Mitsamushi?"

She murmured, "The group that is in contact with Jiro, that wishes to meet you and listen to your words of wisdom and encouragement."

"Oh, dear," Kate said. "And now, probably, we shall never meet."

"But who knows what the future holds in store for all of us?" Miss Mitsamushi asked.

"How true," Kate said politely.

"Perhaps you would be kind enough to keep the photograph with the other material until final decisions are made," Miss Mitsamushi said. "Then everything will be together." She snapped the lock on her dispatch case and stood up. "Forgive me for over-staying my visit. And I am so happy to hear of your engagement. I hope you will accept my most sincere wishes." She stood up, smoothing down her gray flannel skirt.

"You must stay and have tea with us," Kate said.

"You are very kind. Another day, another time."

5.

Stefan said cheerfully, when Miss Mitsamushi had gone, "Did you settle all your business with the little Japanese lady?"

"I had to tell her," Kate said, "that you and I are getting married, and consequently it is unlikely that I will be going to Japan."

"And was she upset by this devastating piece of news?"

"Well, it means a change in her plans, too. She was to have been my companion on the lecture tour."

"How deadly dull for you, darling."

"I don't suppose it would have been madly exciting."

"Actually," Stefan said, "we had quite a stimulating chat before you arrived. We were discussing, among other people, her brother Jiro."

"Who?"

"Jiro Mitsamushi. He is a well-known figure in the Japanese anti-war youth movement. Surely she has mentioned him to you?"

Kate hesitated, and then said, "Yes."

Stefan laughed. "Really, Katherine, you must learn that in this game of international politics we all have a shrewd idea what is taking place on the other side. We can guess with about ninety-five percent accuracy what the State Department is up to; and I am willing to admit that they can guess just as accurately what we are up to. It hardly required the brain of a genius to guess that if you were seeing Miss Mitsamushi here, then plans were being made for you to meet her brother Jiro in Japan, and that you might even meet some of brother Jiro's friends. Right?"

"I suppose so."

"Well, it is of no importance now. But I have some other news for you. Do you see something in the room that was not there earlier, when you left to go to your luncheon?"

Puzzled, she looked around her. Then she cried, "Oh! The roses! How lovely! Who sent them?"

"Come and see."

There were two dozen American Beauties in a vase on her piano. Propped against the vase was a small white envelope. She opened it and took out a visiting card. On one side the name *Miklos Horscht* was engraved in copperplate, without any address. On the other side a message was written in purple ink:

> Felicitations on the joyful news which I have just learned, and the wish that you will know much happiness through the years.   M.H.

She turned to Stefan. "I don't understand. How could Mr. Horscht have sent me these roses? Isn't he in Canada?"

Stefan laughed at the mystified expression on her face. "It is not really as strange as it appears. You see, when I spoke to my good friend Imre Lukacs this morning and told him about our forthcoming marriage, he immediately telephoned Mr. Horscht in Ottawa. Mr. Horscht then went into conference with the highly placed officials he was visiting, and an hour later he called back to Imre and gave him instructions to send you, at once, these two dozen roses with a message of felicitation."

"Oh!" Kate cried. "It's just too complicated! Why can't your friends do things simply, in a plain straightforward way? Why must there always be these elaborate maneuvers?"

"I will tell you why," Stefan said. "The reason is that, as I expected, Mr. Horscht and his friends had already made the decision to send me back to Budapest in disgrace." He rubbed his hands together happily. "The news of our engagement changed the situation. Another conference was held, another decision was made, and the roses tell the story."

She felt a surge of excitement. "They are not sending you back to Budapest! Oh, how wonderful!"

"I did not say that, Katherine. I merely said, I am not in disgrace any longer."

"Oh," Kate said. The surge of excitement receded almost as quickly as it had come, like the seventh wave rolling up and down a beach, accomplishing nothing fateful.

He said, "Are you pleased?"

"Of course. Will you excuse me for a little while, Stefan? I want to write to Mr. Gamage; and then I would like to rest for half an hour or so."

"You have not forgotten that we are giving a party for our friends this evening?"

"I haven't forgotten."

"I want you to look your best."

"I promise," she said. "I will look my best."

6.

Mr. Hamid, a plump and elegant man, arrived with a dozen red roses at five o'clock. She was charmed by him, and sat for twenty minutes listening to him expound the neoplatonism of the Arab philosophers Avicenna and Averroës. Then came Imre Lukacs, tall, dark-haired, instantly ravishing her in his mind, giving her the uneasy impression that the moment Stefan showed any signs of flagging he would be happy to take over the burden of providing her with a ceaseless flow of sensual pleasure. A stream of Stefan's friends followed, nearly all of them with an armful of red roses for her. Marcel Preiss made an appearance and said, "You cannot complain, Katterin, that I did not warn you of this fellow's impetuosity. All I ask is, if your firstborn is a boy you will call him Marcel; if a girl, Marcella. Agreed?" She agreed, laughing; and twenty minutes later he departed with an elegant Swedish girl who (Kate thought) would undoubtedly be added to his melancholy collection of females he could not seduce.

The party continued in the apartment until midnight, when Stefan insisted on going over to the Carpathia, where, he announced, there would be music, dancing, and hot roast-beef sandwiches.

There, with a loud scream, the buxom hat-check girl Marya threw her arms around Kate and exclaimed, "Madame Emoryi! Oh, God, what a happy day this has been for all of us! Do you know what Pyotr the barman says? He says, it is the best news he has heard since our team beat the Russians at soccer in Moscow two years ago." She turned to Stefan, boldly pressing her bosom against his chest. "Well! You have sown your last wild oat, eh? You are going to settle down and become a family man now? Ha-ha! You met your match in Madame Emoryi! I knew it the first time I saw you with her! She is not such milk and water as she looks! But there will be many girls staying home tonight, crying into their little lace handkerchiefs." Axel shook Kate's hand warmly, and when he had seated Kate and Stefan and the wide-eyed Mr. Hamid at the corner table he announced that Pyotr was sending them a magnum of the special Rothschild Reserve, as a gift of the management. Soon, half the people in the restaurant were gathered around the table, singing snatches of folk songs, raising their glasses in elaborate toasts. Kate was genuinely moved.

How sweet all these people were! How warm-hearted, how generous, how rich in humanity! She felt a great affection for them, and she was pleased beyond words that they accepted her so readily.

The party continued intermittently for two days. "Do you think you will like your new life?" Stefan asked her at one point, and she answered, "I shall like it as long as you love me." He said, "For ever."

8.

One small problem, only, interrupted her happiness. On Friday morning she decided to gather together all the material that Miss Mitsamushi had left with her, and return it to Mr. Gamage. But, once again, something was missing: the photograph of Sun Pat Hsueng. She tried to recall whether she had actually given it back to Miss Mitsamushi, whether Miss Mitsamushi had taken it or had left it; but her memory was unclear. The matter was resolved the next morning, when she discovered that the photograph had somehow become wedged in the space between the bottom drawer and the drawer above it, and she grumbled to herself, "Really, my mind is going, I'm becoming doddery. I'll have to take care that Stefan doesn't find out, or he'll cast me off like an old shoe."

11

PUNCTUALLY AT seven o'clock on Saturday evening a man in a gray-green chauffeur's uniform rang her doorbell. She opened the door and gazed at him coldly. His eyes were uneasy, his manner was evasive. He had a mustache with waxed, pointed ends, and long side-whiskers, and there was no doubt in her mind that she was face to face with the man who had brutally attacked and almost killed Stefan a few nights ago. He was not a prime mover. He was not in himself pure evil. He merely obeyed orders. Nevertheless, she experienced a flash of fierce physical rage as she looked at him, and she controlled herself with difficulty."

He said meekly, "Madame Emoryi?"

"Emory."

He squinted at a piece of paper which had been concealed in his huge fist. "Correct. *Emoryi.* Madame Emoryi?"

He was obviously an idiot. She shrugged her shoulders, openly expressing her opinion of him. "What do you want?"

"I have been sent by Mr. Horscht to bring you to his house."

She looked at him contemptuously. "Horscht?"

He shuffled his feet, like a peasant. "Mr. Miklos Horscht, of the Hungarian Mission."

"Oh, yes. You have a car?"

"I am the chauffeur, Madame Emoryi."

"That does not mean you have a car."

"Yes, Madame, I have a car, the Lincoln Continental. It is outside. Double-parked, I am sorry to say."

"Very good. I will be out directly."

She was not normally vindictive. Rarely, except in book reviews, was she cruel to her fellow human beings. But whether he could be blamed for the act or not, György had inflicted pain on the man she loved, and he deserved some retribution, even if it was only a ticket for double-parking. She kept him waiting for more than twenty minutes. When, at last, she walked out to the car he was exceedingly respectful: he snapped to attention, held the car door open for her, and as she settled herself on the luxurious back seat he deftly placed a fur robe over her knees. He drove off with utter smoothness, and she sat in solitary state feeling a little like the Queen Mother of an obscure European country, widowed, venerable, and something of a national embarrassment. Stefan was not with her. He was at the Horschts', helping—in an unspecified way—to receive the guests. There was nothing for her to do except contemplate György's thick neck and oily black hair as the limousine rolled majestically into the geographical mysteries of Forest Hills.

The trip took exactly twenty minutes. Suddenly György turned off the main highway, accelerated up a long hill, then slowed down on a quiet, tree-lined street, and stopped outside an undistinguished split-level house which was set back about thirty feet from the road and surrounded by densely packed, unclipped evergreen trees and shrubs. He gave a short blast on his horn, switched off the motor, sprang out of the car and ran around the front to open the door for Kate and to pull the fur robe aside. As she stepped out, Imre Lukacs came hurrying from the house to meet her, very handsome in a well-fitting dark blue suit with a narrow blue tie. He murmured, "Oh, *Miss Emory!*" as if her beauty far exceeded his recollection, and skillfully seized her hand and pressed it to his lips.

She could not possibly match his effusiveness. She said in her bluff New England way, "Hello, how are you?" and without waiting for the conventional reply she went on to ask, "Is Stefan here?"

"Stefan?" he said, examining her critically from head to toe. "Certainly he is here. He is awaiting you, Mr. Horscht is awaiting you, everybody is awaiting you. Permit me," and with the tips of his fingers touching her arm he led her gracefully toward the house.

She heard the prolonged chirping of crickets in the thick undergrowth, and the alarmed cry of a thrush. "How rural it is," she said.

"Rural?" He rolled the word around in his mind for a moment, determining its precise significance, and said with a burst of laughter, "Rural, yes. But agricultural, no."

He meant something quite profound by this remark; he was rebuking, perhaps, the profligacy, the wastefulness of American capitalism, but she would never know exactly what he was trying to express because they reached the front door. He pushed it open, and, like an elegant spider saluting a juicy little fly, he said, "Do enter, please. Do enter. Thank you."

It was a very ordinary suburban house, rather dark inside and furnished in a heavy, overstuffed, Middle European style. There seemed to be too many sideboards, and too many dining-room chairs made of striped fruitwood, and big dull paintings of peasants leading farm horses and fur-swathed hunters, on sleds drawn by foam-flecked horses, thrusting spears into pursuing wolves. As far as Kate could see, the guests were assembled in two large rooms in the front of the house, but Imre led her through a dimly lit hall to a massive paneled door that might have been looted from some Danubian castle. He knocked, waited, and then at a signal only he heard, he threw open the door and said urgently, "Go in, please, go in, Mr. Horscht is ready for you."

The room was a small study. Its chief feature was a large desk, covered with papers and illuminated by an old-fashioned student's lamp with two green shades. Mr. Horscht stood in front of a fireplace in which an electric fire flickered and glowed through translucent chunks of plastic that had been sprayed with fire-red paint. He was dressed in wide, baggy, tan pants and a cocoa-colored sports jacket; otherwise, he looked very much as he had the first time she met him—cheerful, intelligent, and virile. His bushy white hair and bushy black eyebrows were bristling with health.

He greeted her warmly. "How are you, how are you! I am delighted to see you, I am delighted to welcome you to my home. Was your trip comfortable? Did the chauffeur drive carefully? Imre, take Miss Emory's cape. And bring Miss Emory a drink. What would you like to have? Nothing at the moment? A little later? You may go, Imre. Do sit down, Miss Emory. Here: this is the best chair in the house."

It was not customary, in her experience, to go to a party and be led to a shadowy little room where her host awaited her. He was *too* cheerful, *too* welcoming, *too* voluble, and her suspicions were aroused: something, she decided, must have happened to Stefan, and she had been brought here so that Mr. Horscht could break the bad news to her. As soon as the flow of welcoming words ended, she said quietly, "Mr. Lukacs told me that Stefan is here. Did I misunderstand Mr. Lukacs? Has Stefan not arrived yet?"

"*Stefan!*" Mr. Horscht exclaimed jovially. "He has most assuredly arrived yet. We have been having interesting talks all afternoon. Now he is in front, entertaining the guests." He winked at her. "Particularly the pretty young ladies—they find him irresistible. You will be reunited with him speedily." He gave her an admiring smile. "I hope you will forgive me—I could not refrain from the pleasure of greeting you privately like this. I have such happy memories of our meeting at the Carpathia. Your dancing was so graceful. The conversation was on such a dignified level." He meditated on these twin delights for a moment, and then his face became grave. "But, before anything else, I am afraid I have a sad announcement to make."

Her heart fluttered.

He continued in a melancholy voice, "I regret that we shall not see my wife down here tonight. Poor Mrs. Horscht. She is lying upstairs on her bed, in the dark, with the shades drawn over the windows. She has an excruciating headache—migraine."

"A migraine headache on her birthday!" Kate cried. "Oh, what a shame!"

"You speak with deep feeling, Madame. You know how distressing these headaches can be?"

"Yes, indeed, I suffered from them myself when I was in my teens."

"This is a little different. Mrs. Horscht, unfortunately, is no longer in her teens."

The semantic hurdles, Kate thought, were too thick, too high. She said, "Does Mrs. Horscht have some medication for her migraine, like ergotamine, or codeine? They sometimes help."

"She has pills, prescribed for her by Dr. Bánki—you know, the internationally famous nerve surgeon?—but they do little good. Of course, it was the excitement of the party itself that, so to speak, triggered the attack." He added, with a little sigh, "She is so depressed that she hardly recognizes even me, her husband, when I go up to see her."

"I was looking forward to meeting her very much," Kate said. She reached into her handbag and took out a small gift-wrapped bottle of perfume. "I brought her this little present. Perhaps you would give it to her when she feels better."

"You are most kind," Mr. Horscht murmured. "She will appreciate your generosity. I am sure I do not have to tell you how greatly she regrets missing this chance of making your acquaintance." He took up a position with his back to the electric fire. "Let us talk of happier things, now. And first, I must congratulate you officially on your betrothal to Stefan Gerhardi. All of us who know him are overjoyed at this happy event."

"Thank you."

He smiled at her. "Ah! Stefan! Stefan! I have such a warm feeling for him, anybody would think he is my own blood brother. What a scintillating mind he has! And what a big heart! What distinguished presence, what poise! Those good looks! That superb physique! Each time I look at him, I think with admiration, *This* is a man who will go far. *This* is a man who will reach the topmost pinnacles in our government. *This* is a man we *need.* If you will permit me to express a personal opinion, you and he are perfectly matched. With you beside him, I can say, with an overflowing heart, that there are no limits to the heights he will climb. May I ask you a simple question? When are you and Stefan planning to be married?"

"We have not set a date yet."

"In a week, two weeks, a month, two months?"

She refused to yield to his pressure. "I really couldn't say, without consulting Stefan."

"You are already a good wife!" Mr. Horscht exclaimed admiringly. "Well, then, let us talk about something else. When we first met, did we not discuss a trip you were taking at the beginning of next year to Japan? Now I hear from Stefan it is unlikely you will be going. Correct?"

"I have written to Mr. Gamage about it. I expect a reply in a few days."

"I have an idea that when Mr. Gamage learns you intend

to marry Stefan Gerhardi he may decide that you are no longer completely acceptable to the State Department. What do you think?"

"Yes. That is possible."

"After all," Mr. Horscht said, rubbing his hands together, "one cannot blame Mr. Gamage. He will assume that you have been captured by the wicked communists. Therefore you are not a trustworthy person. Isn't that the way his mind will work?"

"Perhaps."

Mr. Horscht looked down at her intently. "The reason I am raising the matter is simple: I wonder if you appreciate that the same principle works in reverse? In other words, are you aware that there is another side to the coin?"

His manner had changed, and she began to feel frightened. "I am not sure that I understand exactly what you mean, Mr. Horscht."

"I mean, just as Mr. Gamage can hardly be blamed for assuming you have defected to the communist world, so we on our side can hardly be blamed if we ask ourselves if Stefan Gerhardi has defected to the capitalist world."

She said quickly and earnestly, "Oh, no! You mustn't think that! *He* hasn't defected. *I* haven't defected. We have fallen in love. Politics doesn't enter into our feelings for each other."

"Politics enters into everything. There are no exceptions." Mr. Horscht's eyes became somber. "You are aware, of course, that I have to give my official approval to your proposed marriage to Stefan Gerhardi?"

"No. I was not aware of it."

"It is true. Furthermore, this is not a simple matter of saying yes or no. I have to submit a full report, with no less than eight copies, to the appropriate departments of the government, explaining the grounds on which (a) I have approved, or (b) I have disapproved of the proposed marriage. That is to say, assuming I have given my official approval, I have to state in full why I believe the marriage will be of benefit to my country and, specifically, how the non-Hungarian partner to the marriage will contribute to my country's struggle for peace and freedom. This is fair and reasonable, is it not? If we are to provide the newcomer with a home, with food, with culture, with the luxuries of life, surely we have a right to expect *something* in return?"

Kate said, "Are you suggesting that I should have an examination, oral or written, to decide whether I am a fit person to marry Stefan?"

"Not at all. Such an idea has not entered my head. But I think we deserve some assurance that when you join us it will be as a true and open-hearted friend." He thrust his hands deep into his trouser pockets. "For example, when we were at the Carpathia the other night I invited you to visit us and talk to our students and workers. Am I right in thinking that you will be prepared to do this of your own free will when you are married?"

She answered brightly, avoiding the trap he had set for her, "Mr. Horscht, I cannot possibly say at this point what I will do when I am married. I may decide to give up all other activities and devote myself to taking care of my husband. Being a wife, as you know, in itself can be a full-time career." She stood up. "It has been so nice having this talk with you. I have enjoyed it enormously. Could we go and join Stefan now?"

"My dear young lady. Permit me one last question."

She stiffened, frightened again.

"Let me return," he said, scratching his left buttock vigorously, "to your proposed visit to Japan."

She cried, "But it is most unlikely that I shall be going!"

"That is a little beside the point. You see, I have had a report from sources which I am not at liberty to name, that one of the principal objects of your trip was to have conversations on behalf of the State Department with certain Japanese youth leaders, among them the well-known pacifist Jiro Mitsamushi,. Is this true?"

"You know that I cannot possibly comment on that."

"I have touched a sensitive nerve?"

"More than that, Mr. Horscht."

"I am abusing my position as a host? I am afraid it cannot be helped, because this is something far more important than social niceties. Let me continue with the second half of the same question. It has also been reported to me that Jiro Mitsamushi had prepared plans for you to meet a certain young Chinese person named Sun Pat Hsueng, and I want to ask you: is this true or false?"

She was silent.

"We have very efficient machinery for gathering information," Mr. Horscht said. "It has been developed over many, many years. Am I correct in saying that this young man Sun Pat Hsueng is one of the leading figures in the Chinese youth organization called the Red Guard, which has been so much in the news lately?"

She shook her head. "I know nothing, virtually nothing, about the Red Guard, except what I have read in *The New York Times* and the *Manchester Guardian*."

"Still," Mr. Horscht said, "we are in possession of the most reliable information to the effect that you were to have secret talks with Sun Pat Hsueng with the purpose of stirring up a pro-American, counter-revolutionary movement inside the Red Guard which might imperil the whole of the Chinese revolution."

She cried in disbelief, "Oh, *no!* This is *absurd!* This is *absurd,* Mr. Horscht, and you *know* it!"

"Then you deny that you were to meet with Sun Pat Hsueng?"

She shrugged her shoulders.

Mr. Horscht said, "I think you will now understand why

my superiors in Budapest are disturbed about your association with Stefan Gerhardi. They have asked me, point-blank, whether your secret purpose is to subvert Stefan as you were to subvert the wretched little traitor Sun Pat Hsueng; to start a wave of counter-revolutionary terror in our country as you were to start such a wave in the People's Republic of China."

"Mr. Horscht! Don't you *know* how ridiculous these accusations are? Don't you *know* I am in love with Stefan, and want nothing more than his happiness?"

He stared at her without speaking for several seconds. Then he stepped away from the flickering electric fire, and held his hand out to her. He spoke in the accents of a Victorian uncle. "Do not fear. All will be well. I believe in your innocence and the purity of your intentions. Now come, I will take you to your man."

2.

There were between forty and fifty people in the front of the house, talking in whispers as if they were at a funeral rather than at a birthday party; and as Kate moved among them she decided that they must be behaving like this to avoid disturbing Emmy Horscht on her bed of pain in the darkened room overhead. Mr. Horscht led Kate from one group to another in a genial fashion, as if nothing at all had happened in the past half hour and, as the shock of that conversation subsided, Kate was touched by the warmth with which she was received. It was as if she had traveled thousands of miles to meet all the members of her fiancé's family, assembled for the occasion in a big old farmhouse on the outskirts of their ancestral village—except that these people, who greeted her so affectionately, came from all over the world. There were Ghanians and Egyptians and Bulgarians, Greeks and Rumanians and Moroccans, Indonesians, Koreans, and Ceylonese, and, inevitably, a couple of magnificent straw-haired Swedish girls busily investigating Life in this obscure little enclave.

At last, near a heavily curtained window, she caught up with Stefan. He was held fast in the talons of two women whom she knew slightly, and he looked pale and exhausted. They were Southcliffe alumnae, unattractively dressed and stupendously aggressive in manner. Kate encountered them at least half a dozen times a year, generally at social functions where, to everyone's embarrassment, they made impassioned speeches about the latest crimes against humanity committed by the United States in Southeast Asia and by Great Britain in Ireland, Wales, and Scotland; and she could not help feeling a pang of dismay at meeting them here.

"Ah, Katherine," Stefan said feebly. He gave her an entreating glance as he kissed her hand. "I believe you know these charming ladies, do you not?"

"*Of course* Katie knows us," they cried, almost literally throwing themselves upon her: "We've known each other for *years!* Katie, this is the most exciting thing that ever happened! *You,* of all people! And *Stefan,* of all people! It's marvelous!"

Very firmly, Kate pried Stefan loose and moved away with him to an unoccupied corner. He said, "Your friends are female vultures. They have been feasting on my liver. Tell me quickly: what happened between you and Mr. Horscht? You were alone with him for such a long time—what did he have to say to you?"

"He bullied me. He threatened me. You talk about *my* friends feasting on your liver, but *your* friends in Budapest are accusing me of plotting to overthrow the Chinese revolution single-handed."

"Oh, God," Stefan said. "I am sorry, I am terribly sorry. They are all so sensitive."

"They aren't *sensitive,*" Kate said. "They're *mad.* They're *paranoid.*"

"Hush, darling. Somebody will hear you."

"I don't care if *everybody* hears me. They're *insane.* And what has been happening between *you* and Mr. Horscht today?"

He laughed bitterly, and shook his head. "Everything has gone wrong, but everything. The same story as yours. But we cannot discuss it here." His voice became unexpectedly urgent. "Darling, do you think you could *smile?* Do you think you could look *happy* and *cheerful?*"

She stared at him in astonishment. "How can I smile and look happy when our entire future is in danger?"

"That is the point," he said in a whisper. "Imre Lukacs and Mr. Horscht are watching us. Please. Try to act as if you are enjoying the party. It is all madly amusing, it is all a great joke." He held her arm and began to saunter toward the bar. Just before they reached the bar he murmured, "We must remain until at least eleven o'clock. We cannot possibly leave earlier than that." He called to a long-haired Englishman in a brass-buttoned, bell-bottomed blue suit, "Tommy!"

"Yass?"

"Would you be kind enough to get Miss Emory a drink?"

"Oh, by all means."

Kate said, "But I don't want a drink."

Stefan said sternly in her ear, "You do not have to drink it. Only, for my sake, try to overcome your hostility to Mr. Horscht. He is my boss, after all. And stay with Tommy—he is the most trustworthy person in the place."

"What do you mean, trustworthy?"

"He is English, darling, and totally disinterested in sex. Talk to him about cricket, if you can think of nothing else. Ah! Mr. Horscht is calling. I will be back soon, my darling."

She watched him as he made his way across the room to

the two grim, unsmiling men, and as he left—one on each side of him, like guards leading him out to execution—she clasped her hands together unhappily. It was all so conspiratorial, and she found herself actually intimidated by the conspirators, and becoming more and more alarmed at their incomprehensible behavior,.

"One Scotch and soda," the young Englishman said; and he handed her the glass with a polite little bow. His hair hung over his shoulders and it had a slightly unpleasant odor.

"Thank you." Like a puppy, she continued to watch the doorway through which Stefan had departed, hoping that he would immediately reappear.

The Englishman said cheerily, "I s'pose they've gone to the kitchen to take care of the goulash."

"The goulash?" She had no idea what he meant.

"Or whatever we're having for supper."

She was still puzzled.

He explained, "Well, you see, since Emmy isn't here tonight, old Stefan is looking after the cooking. He's a first-class cook, as I s'pose you know. But then, so was old Emmy."

"Was she?" Kate said, wondering why he was referring to her in the past tense, as if she had ceased to exist.

He shook his head regretfully. "Rotten luck about poor old Emmy, isn't it?"

"You mean, having a migraine headache on her birthday?"

"Headache?" Tommy said. "A migraine headache?"

"That's what Mr. Horscht told me," Kate said, smiling at him. "Mr. Horscht told me as soon as I arrived that Mrs. Horscht was in her bedroom with the shades drawn, suffering from one of her migraine headaches. What's more," Kate added, suddenly growing very angry, "Mrs. Horscht had taken the pills prescribed for her by Dr. Bánki, the internationally famous nerve surgeon, but they didn't help her in the least."

The Englishman sucked in his cheeks, causing two deep dimples to form. He said, "Well, if that's what Miklos told you, that's where Emmy is, in her bedroom, with the shades drawn. Terrible things, these migraine headaches. I had an aunt in Brighton who used to suffer from them. She still does, for all I know."

"Where is Emmy, really?" Kate asked.

"In her bedroom, with the shades drawn."

"Please. I want to know."

Tommy looked around him. He put his hands in the pockets of his trousers, and jingled some coins. Then he said in a low voice, "I daresay Miklos didn't want to upset you by telling you about his family troubles, but what he told *me* was, Emmy has gone back to the old country."

"To Hungary?"

"That's right. Her father had a stroke, and she had to rush home to take care of him."

"I'm terribly sorry to hear about it," Kate said. "When did it happen?"

"The telegram came last night. She left early this morning." He glanced at his wristwatch. "She's probably there by now. Fancy that! In Budapest! Isn't it amazing how the world has shrunk?"

3.

Before the buffet supper was served, Mr. Horscht stood precariously on a tufted red and yellow hassock and (interrupted frequently by laughter and applause) made a speech congratulating his friend and colleague, Stefan Gerhardi, and the beautiful and renowned social critic and literary personality, Miss Katherine Emory, on their engagement. "And soon," he said, sounding as if he had been trained not for the barricades but for the Church, "they will be united in marriage, and we will have another party to celebrate *that* event. And in due time—Providence willing—we may all assemble for parties to celebrate other happy events, may there be many of them." On behalf of Mrs. Horscht and himself he presented Kate with some exquisite lace from Balatonendréd; on behalf of various of Stefan's friends he presented her with a blouse and apron embroidered by the Mátyos of Mezökövesd; on behalf of the Literary Gazette he presented her with a faience bowl from Hódmezövásárhely; and on behalf of the people of Hungary he presented her with a guidebook to their magnificent country.

In a voice that was barely audible she thanked him. Stefan thanked him in a voice that throbbed with emotion. Everybody applauded. The two female vultures from Southcliffe attempted to make speeches and, at last, the goulash was brought in by two pink-cheeked maids. It was excellent. Kate ate a little and sipped half a glass of wine; she chatted to various guests, and then, at eleven o'clock, she turned to Stefan and said quietly, "Let us go."

He was startled. "But, my darling! The party is only just beginning! It is too early to go."

"You said we had to remain until at least eleven. It is now eleven. Please take me home. I am tired."

"Mr. Horscht will be offended."

"No. Mr. Horscht will understand."

"Katherine, let us stay another half hour. As you can see for yourself, the party is becoming very gay—"

"Stefan."

"Oh, oh," he said. "I hear the voice of the future ruler of my household." He smiled boyishly at her. "Very well. Let us go and say good-by to Mr. Horscht and get out of here." He murmured, "To be truthful, you look so desirable tonight, I can hardly wait to be alone with you. I am *aching* for you."

Mr. Horscht said, "Leaving? But how can you think of leaving? You are the star of the evening. Please stay a little longer."

She said, "I have had a lovely time. But I have had so much excitement these past few days, I am quite worn out. I know you will forgive me."

"I would happily forgive you for anything, Madame, with the sole exception of leaving us. However, if you must, you must." He turned to Stefan. "And you are going with her?"

"I must escort her home, Mr. Horscht. You know how dangerous New York is at night—a lady is not safe alone. I will telephone for a taxi."

Mr. Horscht said, "That is unnecessary. György will drive you in the Lincoln Continental."

Stefan said, "You are sure that is not an inconvenience, Mr. Horscht?"

"I am sure." He kissed Kate's hand, clapped Stefan on the shoulder, and said, "She is now in your care, my friend. See that she gets home safely, and that she is not attacked by any hoodlums."

"Yes, Mr. Horscht."

"See that nobody is lurking in her apartment, and see that she double-locks the front door and puts on the safety chain."

"Yes, Mr. Horscht."

"Then come back here," Mr. Horscht said. "You must stay the night. We have a lot of work to do tomorrow."

Stefan smiled. "Yes, Mr. Horscht."

4.

He gripped Kate's knee as they drove back to the city. She was fuming, and he would not allow her to express herself with György sitting only a few feet away. He chatted about the charming people, the talented people, the remarkable people who had been present at the party; and he only gave expression to his feelings when he held her in his arms outside her apartment door.

Kate said, "I want you to stay with me. I don't want you to go back to that house."

"You do not know Mr. Horscht. He will be keeping an eye on his watch. I will have to account for every minute I have been away from him."

"He cannot do this!" Kate cried. "I won't permit it!"

"Katherine, he can do whatever it pleases him to do, even to the extent of having me removed permanently from this planet. All he has to do is raise a finger, and I will cease to exist."

Kate said in horror, "Did he tell you that?"

"Yes. This afternoon. He expressed himself very clearly. Either I obey his orders to the letter, or I suffer the consequences."

"What orders has he given you?"

"Darling, I cannot talk now. I will tell you when I see you—tomorrow evening. We have to make some important decisions, believe me. I must go, Katherine. György will create the most serious trouble for us if I do not go back to the car immediately."

Kate said, "Is this how our life will be in the future? Shall we always be under the supervision of Mr. Horscht and György?"

"Of course not. It is only now, in this intermediate stage. When we are married, everything will be different."

She said, "Tell me, or I won't be able to sleep a wink tonight: what has happened to Emmy Horscht?"

"She had a terrible migraine headache, Katherine. It was impossible for her to come down to the party."

"Stefan, you must not lie to me. *You must never lie to me.* Now. What has happened to Emmy Horscht? Did her father have a stroke? Has she gone back to Budapest to nurse him?"

He drew away from Kate. "She has been sent to Pécs."

"To *where?*"

"To Pécs. It is the biggest town in Transdanubia. Three thousand years ago it was the burial place of many prehistoric tribes."

"But why has she been sent there? Why not to Budapest?"

"Because in Pécs she will be able to meditate about her future. Budapest is too full of distractions. Now, darling, I must go."

She seized his arm. "One other thing, Stefan."

"But I must go, Katherine, Mr. Horscht is waiting for me."

"You can spare the time to explain this. Mr. Horscht attacked me about a man named Sun Pat Hsueng—"

"Who?"

"One of the leaders of the Red Guards in China. Sun Pat Hsueng."

"Ah! Yes!" Stefan said. "There has been a lot of hullabaloo about this man all day. Budapest was raising quite a fuss over him. Mr. Horscht asked me what I knew, and I had to admit candidly that I knew nothing about him whatever. Evidently you were supposed to have secret talks with this person in the course of your lecture tour in the Far East, right? It was all being arranged by Jiro Mitsamushi?"

Kate said fiercely, "Who *told* Budapest about it? How did this come up?"

"Katherine, if you recall," Stefan said gently, "I pointed out to you weeks ago that there are very few secrets these days in the diplomatic sphere. We have highly efficient people all over the world, including Tokyo; and it is their job to ferret out this kind of information and send it to Budapest. You seem to be surprised! But it happens all the time! *We* have agents, *you* have agents; they have to do *something* to earn their keep, for God's sake. Now, there is no need to be upset. Do not give it another thought. I assure you, Mr. Horscht does not believe in his heart that you are going to start a counter-revolution in China or anywhere else."

The horn of the Lincoln Continental sounded twice.

"There is György, raising the roof," Stefan said. "Good night, my love, good night, my darling. I will come to you as soon as I can tomorrow."

"Stefan!" She clung to him, afraid to let him go.

He kissed her tenderly, and hurried out.

12

SHE WAS unable to sleep. She lay restlessly in her bed, angry and bitter at being alone, and as the hours passed her emotions became more and more inflamed. She craved Stefan as if her life depended absolutely upon his presence. He gave her love, he gave her happiness, he could give her peace, he could give her sleep. She loathed Mr. Horscht, and the murderous György. She fretted over the fate of Emmy Horscht. She fretted over her own fate. She fretted over an emaciated Chinese named Sun Pat Hsueng. At five o'clock in the morning, out of sheer desperation, she took a Nembutal—she had not taken any for more than a year, when she was in the midst of a long and painful spiritual conflict with Father Justin. Now she was so overwrought that the pill failed to have any effect for more than an hour.

She awoke shortly after midday, her head thick and woolly, and she frittered away the afternoon and most of the evening, unable to concentrate on anything worthwhile, waiting to hear from Stefan. When he called, at last, at about nine o'clock, her first words were, "I haven't seen you for two days. Where are you? When are you coming here?"

"My darling, I have been working like a dog. I am exhausted. And I am still not finished."

"What do you mean, you still are not finished?"

"There was an avalanche of work to be done, Katherine. I cannot see myself digging out of it until tomorrow morning."

She wailed, "You aren't coming here tonight?"

"My love, it is utterly out of the question."

"I can't understand why you are working for Mr. Horscht," she cried. "I thought you worked at the United Nations, in the Department of Commemorative Stamps."

"Of course. You are perfectly right. But on this occasion I was, as we say, seconded to Mr. Horscht because he was short of staff. Do not take it so hard, my darling."

She was on the point of tears. "I miss you. That's all."

He said gaily, "Let us here and now make a date for lunch tomorrow. How do you feel about that? I promise you on my word of honor that I will pick you up at twelve o'clock sharp."

"All right," she said. "That is, unless some other man turns up before you do, and sweeps me off my feet."

"You are not frightening me. You are the loyal type, the faithful type. I have complete confidence in you."

She went to bed at eleven o'clock, and the pattern of the previous night was repeated. She tossed and turned, she craved Stefan, she loathed Mr. Horscht, she fretted over Emmy's fate, and her own fate, she was haunted by the bony face of a sadistic Chinese youth; and at five o'clock she crawled out of bed and took a Nembutal. It worked instantly.

2.

She was awakened by her bedside telephone. It rang on and on, like the two clawed feet of a black crow stamping repeatedly on her head, and all at once she sat up with a startled cry, realizing that Stefan might be calling. She picked up the receiver and said, "Hello? Hello?"

"Miss Katherine M. Emory?" It was a man's voice, brusque and unfamiliar. Not Stefan's voice, musical, affectionate.

"This is Miss Emory," she said. "Who are you?"
"Hartman of the *Daily Gazette*."
The name meant nothing to her. *Hartman of the Daily Gazette*. Her eyes closed. Go away, Hartman of the *Daily Gazette:* I have nothing more to say about the Pope and non-celibate priests, or about the Catholic Church and the population explosion. Let me sleep, Hartman of the *Daily Gazette*. But she said with a sigh, "Yes?"
He spoke in a curiously clipped way. "I have a dispatch on my desk from a usually reliable source to the effect that, quote, Katherine M. Emory, American author and critic, will shortly marry Stefan Gerhardi, stated to be an official of the Hungarian Communist Party, currently employed at the United Nations, unquote. Do you have any comments on this report, Miss Emory? Is it true that you and Mr. Gerhardi are getting married?"
The sharp voice, momentarily, stunned her. She sat up in bed, trying to collect her senses. She whispered, "I'm sorry—I didn't catch your name. Mr. Partman of the *what?*"
"Hartman. *Daily Gazette*."
"Mr. Hartman—I'm sure you'll understand—I didn't get to bed until very late—I can't answer any questions now. If you would call back a little later—"
"Just a minute," he said. "The report goes on, quote, Miss Emory, hitherto noted as a neo-Catholic apologist—"
She couldn't help laughing. "Oh, no!"
"Miss Emory, hitherto noted as a neo-Catholic apologist," he repeated stonily, "is expected to leave New York in about two weeks to take up residence in Budapest with her husband. According to a highly placed spokesman, she will act as a special advisor to the Ministry of Culture in the Hungarian Government—"
She cried, "Wait! Wait! Who told you that I would act as a special advisor to the Hungarian Ministry of Culture?"
"You wish to deny that statement?"

"I most certainly deny it. It's absolutely untrue."

He sounded unmoved. "I've made a notation of your denial. Now, how about your engagement to Mr. Gerhardi? Do you wish to deny that, too?"

"No."

"You're aware that he's a ranking member of the Hungarian Communist Party? That comes as no surprise to you?"

"To be perfectly frank, I know very little about his political affiliations. We haven't discussed them."

"Miss Emory, when you go to live in Budapest, do you intend to apply for membership in the Hungarian Communist Party?"

"What a ridiculous question! Certainly not!"

"I can't see why you consider that a ridiculous question—"

"Well, it is."

"If Mr. Gerhardi came to live in the United States with you, would you consider it ridiculous if he applied to join the Democratic party, or even the Republican party?"

It was a point she herself might have made, in other circumstances. She remained silent.

He went on, "Have you ever been a member of the American Communist Party? Or a sympathizer?"

"No."

"Could you describe, in broad terms, the kind of work you will be doing for the Ministry of Culture in Budapest?"

"Mr. Hartman, I'm sure you heard me the first time. In case you did not, I'll repeat what I said: *I will not be working for the Hungarian Ministry of Culture in any capacity whatever*. Is that clear now?"

He said testily, "The story came to us from Transatlantic Press. It was checked and rechecked."

"You asked me to confirm or deny this story, and I've denied it. You can't expect me to answer for your sources, can you? Good-by, Mr. Hartman."

"Miss Emory—"

She replaced the receiver, and sat holding the bedclothes to her bosom. What kind of subterranean creatures, she asked herself indignantly, invented these falsehoods? How could people like Hartman of the *Daily Gazette* live with themselves?

There was no hope of falling asleep again. She put on a robe and plodded into the kitchen, where Mrs. Corcoran was hard at work scrubbing the perfectly clean kitchen table.

"Heaven protect us," Mrs. Corcoran said, staring at her in awe and admiration. "And what misfortunes befell *you* during the weekend?"

"I haven't been sleeping well, Mrs. Corcoran. Would you fix me a pot of coffee, please?"

"It's fixed already, Miss Em. How about some nice buttered toast to go with it?"

"No, thank you."

"Please yourself. Incidentally, look at the time. A quarter past ten, and your Grizzle isn't in yet. Late, isn't she?"

"She had a sore throat last week. She may not be feeling too well."

"That's what I hoped," Mrs. Corcoran said. "The poor thing."

Kate went into the living room and sat curled up on the big settee, thinking about Hartman of the *Daily Gazette*. Something would have to be done about him and his brethren; she could not fight off the press single-handed; she needed expert assistance; and as soon as Mrs. Corcoran brought in her coffee she telephoned Rushton Wyle. He was the perfect ally. He knew all the rules, and there was nothing he enjoyed more than the noise of battle. She was disconcerted to find that he was in a tremendous rage, not, as usual, with the world at large, but with her. His first words, snarled into the telephone, were, "Well, thanks for calling. Thanks a lot. It's nice to know you remember I'm alive."

"Rushton—"

"I've been trying to reach you for days. Where the hell have you been hiding yourself?"

She answered in a sweet voice, "Please don't be cross with me. Everything has been chaotic. Rushton, I have a surprise for you."

"*Surprise?* What surprise? You mean, you're getting married?"

"Oh! You've heard!"

"God Almighty, *everyone's* heard. It's all over town. You're going to marry this character by the name of Gerhardi, right? The communist playboy. Kate, what the hell *happened* to you?"

She laughed shakily. "Oh, Rushton, he's awfully nice, you'll like him a lot. He works at the United Nations, and he isn't at all wild-eyed." She went on quickly, "The reason I'm calling is that I've just had a telephone call—"

He listened without interrupting her as she told him of the conversation with Hartman. When she finished he was silent for a moment; then he asked coldly, "Well? What do you expect me to do about it?"

"I'd like you to make sure that Hartman doesn't print any untruths about my forthcoming marriage. Particularly, I want you to scotch this silly rumor that I'm going to work for the Ministry of Culture in Budapest."

He asked in a faraway voice, "*Are* you going to work for the Ministry of Culture in Budapest, Kate?"

"Rushton! It's a pure invention! There isn't a shred of truth in it!"

"Okay. I'll see what I can do. Now, let me have a few hard facts. What's the full name of this man? Where did you meet him? What's his background? Exactly what does he do at the United Nations? What does he do when he's at home?"

She said, "Rushton, I don't see why he has to be dragged into this. And I really don't want any invasion of our privacy, his or mine—"

Rushton almost exploded with fury. "Now, you listen to me, Kate. Just get it into your head that Hartman of the *Daily Gazette* didn't dream up this story. *You*, the pin-up girl of the avant-garde Catholics, *you* dreamed it all up by yourself and handed it to him on a silver platter. So cut out this damned nonsense about invasion of privacy, and give me the information I want."

Reluctantly, she did so.

"Now," he said, "when are you getting married?"

"We haven't fixed a date yet, Rushton."

"When do you *think* you'll be getting married? A month? Six months? A year? Two years?"

"I would say, at a guess, within three months."

"And where will the happy event take place? In the Budapest General Post Office, or wherever it is they hold their grubby little ceremonies?"

"Rushton, I cannot understand why you are trying to hurt me."

He answered snappishly, "I'm not trying to hurt you. These questions will come up a hundred times, and I have to know the answers."

"We haven't decided yet where the wedding will be."

"Was Hartman right about your going to live in Budapest with Gerhardi?"

"If Stefan goes back to Budapest, naturally I will live there with him."

"May I remind you that you have a commitment, in the form of a signed contract with the Department of State, to go to Japan at the end of December for a period of six months? What do you propose to do about that?"

"I've written to Mr. Gamage, Rushton, explaining that I'm getting married. I'm sure he'll agree that it is impossible for me to continue with any plans for the lecture tour."

"You think so?"

"Of course. He's a sensible person. He wouldn't expect me to go to Japan in these circumstances."

Rushton gave a noncommittal grunt. Then his voice became hard and businesslike. "All right. This is what I suggest you do. Instruct your telephone answering service to take all messages from now on. Any calls from the press, wire services, or television networks should be referred to me. I don't want you to speak to any reporters, and I'd advise you not to go out more than is necessary. Lie low for the time being."

"You mean, the reporters might come here, to my apartment?"

"Why not? You're news. Kate, do you know what I'd do if I were you, and wanted to avoid a lot of unpleasant publicity?"

"What?"

"I'd leave town for a few days."

"Leave town?" The suggestion took her by surprise.

"Yes. Go somewhere and relax, and *think*. Think this whole thing over."

"It's impossible for me to leave town just now, Rushton."

"It isn't impossible. Pack a bag and go."

"No, I'm afraid it's out of the question. May I call you later to check on what is happening?"

"Sure. I'll be here until five o'clock." He said good-by curtly, and hung up.

3.

Stefan arrived promptly at noon. He strode in looking even more handsome than usual, wearing a dark blue suit, carrying a narrow-brimmed Borsolino hat and pigskin gloves. He threw his hat onto an armchair, flung the gloves into the hat, advanced on Kate, kissed her hand, and said, "My darling, here I am, as promised."

She restrained her laughter. "I am very glad to see you."

He looked at her critically. "There are dark circles under your eyes. Not too noticeable—only I could see they are there. You had difficulty sleeping last night?"

"Some difficulty."

"Because I was not with you?"

She nodded.

He hugged her. "You are really a loving woman, not sleeping on my account. I have to admit, Katherine, that I slept very well, but I dreamed all the time that I was in bed with you, making love, so I woke with dark circles under my eyes, too."

"They don't show."

"They disappeared as soon as I came into your presence, because of my extreme happiness." He smiled at her fondly, and then became serious. "Now. What about lunch? Where would you like to go?"

"Stefan, I can't leave the apartment."

He drew away from her. "Why not? Are you sick?"

"No. I'm being pursued by the press."

He screwed his eyes up in bewilderment. "My dear Katherine: you are being pursued by the press, you mustn't go out—what on earth do you mean?"

"Sit down, and I'll tell you all about it."

He sat on the settee beside her, and listened attentively as she told him about Hartman of the *Daily Gazette*, and the advice Rushton had given her. The puzzled look was still on his face when she finished, as if she had been speaking in a language with which he was not completely familiar. He reached for her hand, held it gently, and said, "And this is why you will not go out to lunch with me?"

"Yes. Rushton advised me to lie low."

"Really? It was my impression that rabbits lie low, not human beings." He stood up and walked away from her. "Frankly, I fail to follow your reasoning. As for this Rushton of yours, he strikes me as being a fool. Katherine, you and I are in love and we are getting married. Is this statement true or untrue?"

"It's true."

"In that case I cannot see why you must hide, or lie low, as this fellow Rushton has advised you. Why try to keep the truth from the press? You say it is none of their business whom you are marrying. But you are wrong. It *is* their business. They make their living providing the public with such information. Do you know what I would say to them if they should question me? I would say, Gentlemen of the press! Come with me to the nearest bar, and I will buy each of you a drink so that you can toast the happiest man in the world! For I am delighted to inform you that one of the most remarkable women of our generation, who also happens to be one of the most beautiful, has consented to be my wife! I am not kidding, Katherine. That is what I would say to them, and I think they would respect me for being frank with them and telling them the absolute truth."

Her eyes filled with tears.

He asked, "Honestly, is there anything in our feelings for each other of which we should be ashamed?"

She shook her head.

"Very well, then. Put on a pretty dress and come out to lunch with me. I do not think you will be bothered by reporters, but even if you are, I will be with you, so what do you have to fear?"

She stood up, and walked over to him, and gave him a long and heartfelt kiss.

"Ah!" he said. "And how did I earn that?"

"By being more sensible than I am," she said. "And more honest. And more courageous. And for wanting me to be your wife." She turned, overwhelmed by her emotions, and began to walk away from him.

He called, "Where are you going now?"

"To change into another dress for lunch."

He ran after her. "Wait a minute, Katherine, wait a minute. You have put other ideas into my head. To hell with lunch—"

"Later," she said. "We have all day."

"All day is not long enough. I need all year. I need the rest of this century."

She loved him with a tenderness that seemed to fill her mouth with sweetness, and a passion that made her body tremble. She said, "You shall have everything you ask."

"Hurry, then," he said. "The sooner we eat lunch and get back here, the better. Hurry."

4.

He took her to a French restaurant on Second Avenue where he insisted that she order lobster cooked in absinthe. She hesitated. Somehow it aroused memories of Baudelaire, a poet for whom she had no special affection. But, as usual, Stefan was right. It was delicious. Her eyes gleamed with pleasure as she consumed it, and she said, "My dear, you're spoiling me with all this wonderful food. I'm going to gain an awful lot of weight, and then you'll be sorry."

He was toying with some gigantic shrimp cooked in beer. He said, "Pooh, you have a perfect figure, and you are simply not the type to put on weight. May I tell you something? You look quite adorable eating that lobster, like one of the naughtier women of Toulouse-Lautrec. Avril—but much lovelier."

She laughed. "Thank you."

"It is true. Every time I see you, you captivate me more and more. Katherine, let us get married soon."

"How soon?"

"Soon, soon, soon. Tomorrow. The day after tomorrow."

"Why are you in such a hurry?"

"Because I want to take no chance of losing you. Seriously, now: we must get married within the next two weeks."

"Why within two weeks?"

He pushed the plate of giant shrimp aside as if they offended him. He leaned forward, over the red-checked tablecloth, and said earnestly, "I had several talks with Mr. Horscht yesterday. He made it clear that he wants me to return to Budapest—with you, of course—at the earliest possible date. There is a splendid job awaiting me in one of the cultural agencies, really splendid: we can expect to travel all over the world, on the most important cultural missions. From the Congo to Ceylon! From Brazil to Bombay! Can you imagine anything more exciting?"

"It sounds wonderful."

"Mr. Horscht recommended that we should get married in Budapest. I disagree. I have a secret idea that such a ceremony might be used for very extensive propaganda—you know: there would be diplomats from Russia, Czechoslovakia, Bulgaria, Poland, East Germany, possibly even China, together with groups of intellectuals and scientists, an honor guard of factory workers who have exceeded their quota of tractor carburetors, and movie cameras everywhere. This is not the way you and I should get married, Katherine. It is revolting."

"What do you suggest?"

"My feeling is that we should be married before we leave, here in New York, and preferably in a church."

She was surprised. "In a church?"

"Yes. Anyone has to admit, a church ceremony inspires respect. It has an air of importance, of dignity, of spirituality. Do you feel the same?"

"Yes, I do."

"So: a wedding in a church it shall be. And since you know so much more about these matters than I do, I leave it to you to decide which church it should be."

"Isn't there a Hungarian church in New York?"

"No!" he cried. "Not that! But if I may make a suggestion, I have heard many charming things said about a church called The Little Church Around the Corner. Have you heard of it? It is quite famous. I understand that many celebrities choose to get married there."

She tried not to smile. "Yes, they do. But I'm afraid it's an Episcopal church."

"Not a Catholic church? Very well. Let us go the whole hog and be married in St. Patrick's Cathedral. We will get the Bishop, or the Archbishop, or whoever is the top man there, to perform the ceremony, and I will wear a cutaway jacket and striped trousers. Does that appeal to you?"

"But, darling, you aren't a Roman Catholic."

He said indignantly, "Both my father and my mother were devout Catholics. You must not forget that Hungary is a strongly Catholic country. Sixty-five percent of our people are Catholics. Until a hundred years ago, Latin was our official language."

She stroked his hand tenderly. "Dear Stefan, we couldn't possibly be married in St. Patrick's. I'm so sorry."

He looked at her in disbelief. "Even with your influence?"

"Yes, even with my influence."

"At least, Katherine, you could try. You could speak to somebody there."

"Stefan, I could not speak to somebody there. For a number of reasons, which I will be happy to explain to you in detail when you have an hour to spare, it is impossible for us to be married in St. Patrick's."

He said gloomily, "It is a great pity. The publicity might be very valuable for your books. There would be pictures in *Life, The New York Times,* and so on."

"I thought you were opposed to publicity."

"To propaganda, Katherine, which is a very different kettle of fish. You are absolutely sure it cannot be arranged? Even if we were prepared to slip a suitable amount of money to the Bishop or the Archbishop?"

"Quite sure."

"Well, then, I leave it to you to think of some other place that would be appropriate. Or perhaps it would be wise to follow Mr. Horscht's advice and get married in Budapest, after all."

They returned to Gramercy Park at half past two. Mrs. Corcoran had finished her work and had gone for the day. The apartment was quiet and welcoming. Horus, Anubis, Sekhmet, and the various other deities and semi-deities appeared to be awaiting them with interest. "Come with me," Stefan said as they entered the living room, and he led her by the hand directly to her bedroom. He said, "We have wasted too much time, Katherine. I have such a fire for you, I cannot contain myself. Oh my God, I love you, I love you, I am burning for you." His lovemaking was furious, as if only now, for the first time, he had been granted the opportunity to enjoy the many pleasures of her body. And she, burning equally for him, responded with the same violence. She had never imagined that so much energy was locked up in her, seething to break out, or that she could give herself so freely and take from him with such greed. It was as if her nature as a woman had undergone a total metamorphosis: there were no hesitations, no hindrances, only this great new openness of feeling and expression.

An hour later he looked at her in astonishment and whispered, "*Mon Dieu,* Katherine, I could never have expected this to happen. You are leaving me far behind. I cannot keep up with you." She laughed at him, as if he were making an absolutely hilarious joke. He said, "It's true, it's true," and rolled over with a sigh and went to sleep.

She was glowing, much too alive to waste the rest of the afternoon sleeping, and she left him and went to the kitchen to make herself the indispensable pot of coffee. On the kitchen table she found one of Mrs. Corcoran's notes. It was briefer than usual.

Your ansring servic says
call them urgent. 2 o'clock.
P. (Pearly) Corcoran

"What can they want?" she said aloud, and while the coffee was brewing she called her answering service and asked the operator, "Do you have an urgent message for me?"

"Oh, Miss Emory, yes. Mr. Gamage of the State Department wants to get in touch with you. He telephoned at 12:55."

"Did Mr. Gamage say it was urgent?"

"He said he would appreciate it if you would call him back as soon as possible."

"But did he say it was urgent?"

"Miss Emory, I thought, the State Department is the State Department, and you would like to be informed right away that they are trying to reach you."

"Thank you. Have there been any other calls?"

"The following," the girl said, and she read off about a dozen. Four were from newspapers. Hartman of the *Daily Gazette* had called again; so had Rushton Wyle; and so had Olive Bartlett, Dean Gilberta Marchmont's secretary in Southcliffe.

Being reuinited with Stefan after two long days, the pleasure of *homard à l'absinthe,* and the joys of love had driven a number of important matters out of Kate's mind. But only briefly. They still had to be resolved. She wanted to know more about the fate of Emmy Horscht (and the reason, indeed, that such a term could be used at all). She wanted to know more about the domination of Stefan's life (and presumably her own, in the near future) by Miklos Horscht. She wanted to know more about the ridiculous rumor that she would act as a special advisor to the Hungarian Ministry of Culture. There was also the matter of her trip to Japan—the loose ends still had to be tied up, and she assumed that Mr. Gamage had called to tell her he had taken the necessary steps to negate the contract.

She reached him without difficulty. After the preliminary greetings he cleared his throat and said, "Ah, we received your letter informing us of your engagement to Mr. Stefan Gerhardi. May I offer my congratulations?"

"Thank you."

"At the same time—I need hardly tell you this—all of us here are extremely sorry that you think you will be unable to undertake the lecture tour we had set up for you in Japan, Taipei, and the rest." He sounded disapproving. "We all had the highest hopes that this would prove to be an outstanding venture, from every point of view."

"Mr. Gamage, I'm just as sorry as you are—perhaps even more—that the tour has had to be canceled. I was looking forward to it enormously."

"What must be, must be, I suppose," he said, and paused, as if he were unsure how to go on. Then he cleared his throat again and said, "There are a few outstanding details I would like to discuss with you. I shall be in New York tomorrow with a colleague, and I wonder if it would be convenient for us to meet you for a little chat?"

"By all means."

"At your apartment?"

"That would be very nice."

"What time would suit you best? Around three o'clock?"

"Yes, that would be perfect. Incidentally, Mr. Gamage, all the material Miss Mitsamushi left with me is in an envelope, ready to be mailed back to you. Would you prefer to pick it up tomorrow?"

He said, "Ah—the material Miss Mitsamushi left with you? Yes. Yes, I think we might perhaps pick it up and save you the trouble of mailing it. In fact, Miss Mitsamushi will be with us tomorrow, and she might herself pick up the material and give you an official receipt for it."

"She's such a delightful person. I shall look forward to seeing her again."

"Three o'clock, then," Gamage said. "Good-by, Miss Emory."

"Good-by, Mr. Gamage."

The conversation left her feeling vaguely disturbed. She could hardly expect Gamage to bubble with enthusiasm over her engagement to Stefan; but she had not anticipated such coolness. And what did he mean by saying he would be in New York with a colleague? What kind of colleague? She thought about it for a few minutes, and she was suddenly siezed with panic. She hurried into the bedroom and woke Stefan.

13

HE OPENED his eyes and looked at her in a puzzled way (as if, she thought, he had been dreaming of somebody else) and said, "Ah, Katherine! I have missed you. Where have you been?"

"In the kitchen. I made a pot of coffee. Would you like a cup?"

"Yes. But give me a cigarette first."

She gave him one of his cigarettes, and as she lit it for him she said, "Stefan, something has happened that is rather disturbing."

"In the kitchen? What on earth can have happened to disturb you in the kitchen? You saw a mouse?"

"I had a message from my answering service to call Mr. Gamage in Washington."

The smile left Stefan's face. "Oh? Really? And you did so?"

"Yes."

"Well, do not stop there. Go on. What did you say to Mr. Gamage, what did Mr. Gamage say to you? I am all agog."

"He's coming to see me tomorrow afternoon at three o'clock."

Stefan puckered up his mouth thoughtfully. "How interesting."

"He told me there were some outstanding details about my lecture tour to be discussed. I don't know what that means. He also said he was coming with a colleague, and I believe he is bringing Miss Mitsamushi."

"Quite a party, Katherine. Who is this colleague you mention?"

"Mr. Gamage didn't explain. He just said it in an off-hand way: *a colleague.*"

"No name?"

"No."

"And no indication of what this colleague does?"

"No."

Stefan lay perfectly still, holding the cigarette in the air, watching the thin line of smoke ascending. He said quietly, "And why are you disturbed by this, darling? Is it so terribly sinister for Mr. Gamage to visit you with a colleague?"

"I don't know. Perhaps I'm being stupid and jittery." She sat down at the foot of the bed and said, "I wrote to him the other day to inform him of our engagement. It's perfectly obvious that in the circumstances I can't go on any lecture tour for him. Why should he tell me he has some outstanding details to discuss? And why should he tell me he's bringing a colleague with him?"

"Keep talking, Katherine," Stefan said. "I think you are beginning to answer your own questions."

"Do you think he is attempting to intimidate me?"

"That is a possibility."

"Could this colleague be someone from the legal staff of the State Department?"

"That, too, is a possibility. But have you any theory to explain why Mr. Gamage should be dropping in to see you with a colleague from the legal staff of the State Department?"

"I suppose it's related to the contract I signed to go to Japan."

"I am inclined to agree. I think you have hit the nail on the head."

She cried, "What am I going to do?"

He shrugged his shoulders.

She said passionately, "I don't trust Rushton Wyle. My own lawyer is hopeless. You're the only person I trust, you're the only person I can turn to for help."

He said, "I would be happy to help you, darling. But my ideas may appear to be very radical."

"Please don't split hairs, Stefan. I'm frightened. I need your advice."

He said, "Very well. Let us start from the beginning. Let us assume you had announced to Mr. Gamage that you had fallen in love with somebody named Rockefeller, or Du Pont, or Cabot Lodge; you were going to marry him in a couple of weeks, and therefore your lecture tour would have to be canceled. Do you think Mr. Gamage, or the State Department, would put any obstacles in your way?"

She did not answer him. She sat watching him intently.

He said, "Of course no obstacles would be put in your way. On the contrary, all the bigwigs in the State Department would shower you with congratulations. Right?"

She continued to watch him.

He lit another cigarette. "Unfortunately, you are not marrying one of the pillars of American society. You are proposing to marry a Hungarian named Gerhardi, and you intend to go to live with him in Budapest. Be honest with yourself. How do you expect the State Department to respond? Surely I do not have to tell you. They will try to prevent this calamity by every means at their disposal. Their prestige is at stake. And, in my opinion, they will insist that you go to Japan come hell or high water. They might keep you there for six months without allowing you to address a single meeting, but they will keep you there, just to prevent you from going to Budapest with me."

She looked at him in horror. "Is that possible?"

"Of course it is possible. The State Department will not

sit quietly and suffer what it considers a stinging diplomatic defeat. It will strike back. My darling, I have been expecting some move of this kind for days."

"But this is terrible!" she exclaimed. "They can't force me to go against my will! They *can't!*"

"You signed a contract to go, did you not?"

"Yes."

"Is there any clause in the contract to the effect that if you get married you have the right to terminate the agreement?"

"I can't remember any clause to that effect."

"Then I am sorry to inform you that you are completely in Mr. Gamage's power. I predict that when he comes here tomorrow you will be told that you must postpone your marriage and fulfill your contract, otherwise you will be in the most serious trouble."

She said in despair, "But what can I *do?*"

"Well," he said, "let us now examine the various possibilities. The first and the most obvious is, of course, to fall in with their wishes. That is, to go to Japan and fulfill your contract, postponing your marriage until you return, next June, or July."

She cried, "No! I wouldn't dream of postponing our marriage."

"Then we come to possibility number two, which is to give Mr. Gamage the slip, and defect to my country."

She said in astonishment, "*Defect!*"

"Certainly. Nothing could be simpler. When you see Mr. Gamage tomorrow you ask for a little time in which to think matters over. During that time you take the precaution of transfering out of the country whatever money you possess, together with stocks, bonds, jewelry, paintings, objets d'art et cetera. You have them conveyed to Switzerland or, if you like, to our State Bank, where they would be, of course, one hundred percent safe."

"No. I couldn't do that, Stefan."

"You think it might appear to be a little dishonest?"

"Yes."

"That is how I guessed you would react. So we come to the final choice: to fight Mr. Gamage and the State Department to the bitter end."

"My God! How can I fight the State Department to the bitter end?"

"Katherine, can you suggest any other course? You must obey their edict, and go to Japan. Or you must leave the United States for ever. Or you must fight the State Department—literally, to the death—for your rights as a human being."

She asked incredulously, "Do you think I should fight?"

"It is up to you. But you must be realistic about it. If the State Department takes you to court for breach of contract, any monetary verdict they may win against you—and it may amount to every penny you possess, or more—will be trifling in comparison to the damage that will be done to your name and your career. You will be blackballed by every magazine, by every women's club, by every publisher. Do you think Norton Goodrich will be prepared to antagonize the all-powerful State Department by publishing your new book? I am afraid Norton is not the type to make a martyr of himself. He will draw in his horns."

It had never occurred to her that she faced such total disaster. She felt as if she were drowning, hopelessly out of her depth and miles from any sight of land. Only he could save her, because only he loved her. The rest of the world had joined forces to encompass her destruction. She said, "Now you have really frightened me. Is there anything I can do?"

He said, "You can bring me the cup of coffee you so nicely offered me a little while ago. And in the meantime, I will get dressed. And then we will put our heads together, and think."

2.

He drank the coffee in the living room, walking up and down, talking rapidly, and looking very Byronic in his flapping white shirt, his well-cut trousers, and bare feet. His hair was tightly curled all over his head; his eyes were bluer than usual, bright and alert. This was a situation, she realized, for which he was perfectly fitted. He had been trained for it.

He said, "One thing is absolutely certain: we shall require a complete word-for-word transcript of everything that Mr. Gamage says to you tomorrow, everything that Mr. Gamage's colleague says to you, and everything that you say in reply."

"Why, Stefan?"

He laughed. "Sometimes you are like a character in Dostoevski: utterly simple, utterly pure at heart."

"I wouldn't go as far as that, although I'm quite ready to admit that I'm completely out of my depth. Just explain to me why we need a word-for-word transcript of the conversation tomorrow."

"Listen, darling, I know these people, I know how they operate. They will argue with you, they will threaten you, they will try everything in the book to beat down your defenses; and it is vital, for your personal protection, to have a full record of what they say, a record that will stand up, if necessary, in a court of law."

"Do you want me to keep notes? While we're talking? I'm afraid that might be rather difficult."

"Difficult!" he said. "It would be virtually impossible. Fortunately, science has provided us with a much better way. Tell me, my love, where is the valise I brought here the other night?"

"The valise?"

"Yes," he said impatiently. "The valise, the pigskin valise I brought here when I was being chased by that damned György."

"Oh, yes, I remember. It's in my study. Mrs. Corcoran brought it in from the foyer."

"Good. Let us go to your study and see what is in the valise that will help to insure our future happiness."

Hand in hand they went to the study, and he dragged the heavy valise into the middle of the room and pulled the zipper open. He brought out a black rectangular object, about the size of the dictionary she had intended to give Burford.

"Here," he said. "The answer to our prayers."

"What is it?" she asked. She had no idea. It might have been a miniature atom bomb, and what he termed the answer to their prayers, for all she knew, might be to blow Gramercy Park sky-high.

He said with pride, "A tape recorder." He raised the shallow lid and showed her the deck of the instrument, with its knobs and dials and sockets and spools. "It happens to be the best of its kind in the world: the famous Cosmo Mark 2. Have you heard of it?"

"I'm sorry, I haven't," she said. Then she asked, "What are you going to do with it, Stefan?"

He said dramatically, "I am going to record you, and Mr. P. Converse Gamage, and Mr. Gamage's colleague, and the lady from Japan, if she is in the act, too."

She became pale. "Oh, no."

"Yes. Here is your witness, Katherine, a witness whose testimony cannot be disputed. When Mr. P. Converse Gamage or his colleague threatens you with ruin, when you plead for your life and happiness, this little machine will preserve the scene for posterity. How do you like that?"

She said, "It would not be admissible in any lawsuit, Stefan. It would be considered wiretap evidence."

"You are wrong," he said triumphantly. "*They* could not install a recording instrument, and produce the tape as evidence. That is illegal. But this is your home, and the law does not say you may not record the voices of those who come to visit you. *You* have the right to do as you please, particularly in self-defense."

She said in a worried voice, "I don't believe that is so."

He patted her arm reassuringly. "You can trust me. I would not lead you astray. Besides, the tape can be used in other ways, if necessary. It is indispensable."

3.

He stood very still, his blue eyes narrow and calculating, looking around the study. He knelt beside her desk and rapped on the wall; then he went into the living room and, after a few moments, into her bedroom. When he returned he searched through the valise, dragging out several shirts, a pair of striped pajamas, several pairs of socks, a leather camera case, and a tangle of gray plastic-covered wire. He examined the wire carefully, peered at a white tag attached to one end, gave a deep sigh, and threw it back into the valise.

He said, "Darling, I assume you will have your meeting with Mr. Gamage here in the study?"

"Here. Or in the living room. Does it matter?"

"I recommend that you have it here. You see, here you can arrange the seating so that everybody will be approximately the same distance from your desk. In that way we will be able to pick up all the voices at equal strength."

"Is the tape recorder going to be on my desk?" she asked unhappily. "Won't they see it? Won't they hear it running?"

He chuckled. "I can tell that you have not been trained in the science of electronics, Katherine. No. The tape recorder will not be on your desk. *This* will be on your desk." He opened a little trapdoor on the side of the tape recorder case, and extracted a small black and gold cylinder.

She was inexplicably alarmed by its innocent appearance. "It looks like a fountain pen."

"True. However, it happens to be an exceptionally sensitive microphone. That, you might say, is the point: hardly anybody would recognize what it really is."

"But where will the tape recorder itself be?"

"In your bedroom, where I will monitor it during your talk with Mr. Gamage and his friends."

"*You* will monitor it?"

"Who else? *Somebody* has to monitor it. It cannot perform that function by itself. The sound level has to be controlled, the tape has to be changed, and so on. Who else would you elect to take care of these things?"

She said unhappily, "I see." She was profoundly worried. What he proposed to do offended her concept of morality. It was unethical, it was unworthy of a human being.

"Now," he said, "I am trying to figure out the length of cable I will require. Let me measure it for the last time." He paced off the distance to the door of her study, and continued across the living room to her bedroom. He returned, shaking his head. "Unfortunately I do not have enough wire. I will have to run up to my electronics store on Forty-sixth Street and buy some more." He glanced at his watch. "Thank God, there is still time. Will you forgive me if I rush away, Katherine? I will be back in about an hour."

"Yes," she said sadly. "I will forgive you."

He went to the bedroom, finished dressing, came back to the study, kissed her affectionately, and hurried out. She sat down at her desk and surveyed the disorder that had come to the quiet, familiar room: the open pigskin valise, the sinister little tape recorder, the leather camera case, the tangled wires, the shirts and the socks and the pajamas. What was not revealed was the spiritual disorder that had overtaken her entire life. She seemed to have lost the ability to appraise her problems rationally. She could only assure herself, *I love him, he loves me, I must trust him, he is doing what is right for both of us.*

She remembered suddenly that she had promised to call Rushton before five o'clock, and it was now nearly half past five. She dialed his number, and to her pleasure he was still there. He said frostily, "I've been waiting for you, Kate. You must have been pretty busy all afternoon, eh?"

"Yes, Rushton. I'm sorry." She was gentle, submissive. She had no wish to quarrel with him.

"All right. Let me tell you how things stand, after a day spent in defense of your fair name. I spoke to Hartman of the *Daily Gazette*. He maintains that according to his sources of information, which are chiefly Transatlantic Press, you and Gerhardi will be married in New York within the next two weeks, that you will then go to Budapest with your husband, and that you will then act as a special advisor to the Hungarian Ministry of Culture."

She said in a puzzled voice, "But, Rushton, how can *any* source of information give out these alleged facts? Please believe me: *I* don't know exactly when we're getting married, or where; it's *possible* that I will go to Budapest with Stefan, but it is simply untrue that I'll act as a special advisor to the Hungarian Ministry of Culture. I assure you, nobody from the Ministry of Culture has even *asked* me to be a special advisor! Hartman invented the story."

"He didn't invent it."

"Well, somebody invented it."

"I told you: his source was Transatlantic Press."

"Then Transatlantic Press invented it."

"No, they did not. They picked it up from a perfectly reliable source: the Swiss Legation in Budapest."

Kate laughed. "Now I've heard everything! Rushton, I'm in love with, and I'm going to marry, a man of Hungarian nationality named Stefan Gerhardi. How can this be of any concern to the Swiss Legation in Budapest? Stefan isn't Swiss, I'm not Swiss, so how do they get into the act? And why should anyone take the least bit of notice of what they say?"

"It happens to be true, Kate. I checked it out. The story was given to the Swiss Legation by the Hungarian press bureau. I don't profess to understand the motives of your Hungarian friends; I guess they decided to play it cool, and instead of issuing the story themselves, they issued it through one of the neutral countries, figuring it would have more impact that way."

"Fiddlesticks," Kate said.

"Furthermore, they've been hinting that there's an even bigger story in the works, one with international ramifications—"

"Rushton, don't let them pull the wool over your eyes."

"Ask your communist Casanova if it's true or not, Kate."

She said quietly, "Rushton, I'm sorry, I hate this conversation, I hate every minute of it. I'll call you tomorrow."

"Please yourself," Rushton said, and hung up.

4.

The sound of Rushton's voice remained in her ears: angry, out of patience with her, disgusted with her, as if she had been physically defiled by her relationship with Stefan. She thought, *I might have expected it from him. He is a bigoted, stupid man.* But a few minutes later she felt grief and remorse. She knew that she could not afford to lose his friendship.

Stefan returned within an hour, carrying a brown paper package and looking thoroughly pleased with himself. He said, "I have to admit that American capitalism has its virtues. Look at this! One simply walks into a store and buys what one needs—a spool of microphone cable, one hundred feet for a mere six dollars, plus connectors, staples, et cetera. And now we are all ready to go!" He opened the package and showed her the spool of gray vinyl-covered wire. "No forms to fill out in triplicate, no need to wait a month for the order to be filled! It is all there in the store." He kissed her cheek. "I had better get right to work, or I will be all night on our little project. And I have plans to go to the Carpathia for dinner."

"Must you really do it?"

"Must I really do what, darling?"

"Set up the tape recorder?"

"I thought we had settled that question. Katherine, it is purely for your benefit. Look. If you made notes of your conversation with Mr. Gamage, would you be worried? Of course not. What you will have on the tape is simply a complete *aide-mémoire,* one that is accurate to the last syllable."

"I am still disturbed about it."

"My dear girl, allow me to point out to you that if Mr. Gamage has any suspicions concerning your motives, you can be sure that he, or his mysterious colleague, or his exotic Japanese lady, will be carrying a concealed tape recorder. Had this possibility occurred to you? You must realize that the tape recorder is as common as an umbrella in present-day diplomacy. So, let me get on with my work."

"Stefan, I'm sorry. There's one other matter I would like to discuss."

He threw his hands up in despair. "My God! I will never get finished tonight! I will never even get started!"

"It's very important."

"Well? What is it?"

She stood facing him. "I have just heard from Rushton Wyle that the Swiss Legation in Budapest has been informed by the Hungarian news bureau that when you and I are married I will act as a special advisor to the Ministry of Culture."

He frowned, as if he could not quite comprehend her heated and complex statement. Then he said, "Oh? And what is troubling you about that?"

She exclaimed incredulously, "You ask, what is *troubling* me? What is troubling me is that we have never discussed such a possibility; and I would not, in any case, agree to act as a special advisor to your government."

"Really! Do you know what you are saying?"

"I'm saying that this story should not have been put out without my approval; and I am saying, further, that I would not have *given* it my approval."

"Oh, Katherine, you are being childish."

"I don't think I'm being in any way childish."

"Yes. As they say in England, you are going off half-cocked."

She said irritably, "For goodness' sake, it isn't only the British who say it. We say it, too."

"Well, I will try to smooth your ruffled feelings. You are shocked at the Swiss Legation getting this story? But why? I assume what happened was simply that in the course of his official duties Mr. Horscht sent Budapest a notification that you and I are getting married. This is what we call standard operating procedure, SOP. In his report, he would naturally include a brief account of your distinguished career, with a list of your many books; he would also undoubtedly refer to the fact that you have a well-deserved reputation for your lectures to women's clubs, university students, et cetera. Surely you are not distressed by *this?*"

"No."

"It is not hard to imagine the next step. Eight copies of Mr. Horscht's memorandum have gone to Budapest. One copy goes to the press bureau. It is read by one of the officials there, and he is filled with enthusiasm by the news, which, after all, is somewhat sensational. As he goes out to lunch, he happens to bump into Mr. X of the Swiss Legation. Surely you can guess what happens next! Our excited little man from the press bureau blurts out the story; Mr. X hurries back to his office, and *he* blurts out the story; and so it gets started on its journey around the world. Of course, it is distressing for you to hear about it from a source like your Rushton Wyle, who seems to be nothing but a gossipmonger; but when you think about it, has such great damage been done? We *are* getting married, are we not? You *are* the author of certain books, you *do* give lectures. So what is so terribly disastrous?"

"What is disastrous is the statement that I will act as a special advisor to the Ministry of Culture. It isn't true."

He sighed. "Katherine, tell me: do you happen to know in detail how a hydrogen bomb is constructed?"

"No, of course I don't."

"How familiar are you with the mechanism of atomic submarines? Could you describe how I might build one?"

"No."

"What about the latest research on nerve gases? Or on the microbes that might be used in bacteriological warfare?"

"That is not my field."

"Then what vital information can you pass on to my country? The deadly secret that American women prefer to cook by gas rather than by electricity, or vice versa?"

"I am not talking about passing on vital information."

He said gravely, "*I* am talking about it, Katherine, and I tell you, with my hand on my heart, that I *expect* you to pass on vital information. If you are resolutely determined not to do so, then I think—before it is too late—we should reconsider whether it would be wise for us to go ahead with plans for our marriage."

She stared at him in bewilderment. A few hours ago he had been pressing her to marry him at once. Now he was ready to abandon the marriage. She said, "Why do you say that? What do you mean?"

His voice remained grave. "I had great hopes for our future, Katherine. We have a great love for each other, and that is a fine way to begin. But do you honestly intend to stay aloof from everything else? I would be in despair if you did." He came close to her. "Let me ask you this: what were you intending to talk about at the University of Tokyo?"

"Only about contemporary American writers."

"I see. But if the Ministry of Culture in Budapest asked you to address some of our students on the same subject, you would refuse? You would feel that you would be acting disloyally to the United States? Is that right?"

"No, that isn't right, Stefan."

"Let us suppose that the Minister of Culture himself came to you, and proposed that you give a series of lectures dealing with the true nature of the United States—its accomplishments, its problems, its intellectual climate—would you consider *that* an invitation to betray your country? Or would you consider it a glorious opportunity to help our people understand your people? For God's sake, Katherine, what do you fear? What terrible consequences would follow if you *were* to advise our Ministry of Culture on how friendship between our countries might be established, and enmity ended?"

She said helplessly, "I don't know."

"I am going to install the microphone cable," he said. He put his hand gently on her arm. "Come and help me."

5.

He experimented for a considerable time with the microphone, trying to find a suitable place for it on her desk. Finally he stood it upright in a small, heavy, Swedish glass bowl which he brought in from the living room; and he surrounded it with pens and pencils of different sizes and colors. An exceedingly thin, translucent cord came from the bottom of the microphone, curved over the top of the bowl, and was fastened behind it with tiny strips of Scotch tape. Kate had to look closely to perceive the wire—it was to all intents and purposes invisible. It continued down to a small plastic box, rather like the case of a hearing aid, which Stefan attached with electrical tape to the back of the desk. The gray vinyl cable was connected inside this box and was then carried on an intricate path across the back of the desk, through a very small hole drilled in the skirting board at the side of the desk, out into the living room, and then to Kate's bedroom, where the tape recorder stood on her bedside table, looking thoroughly sinister, with a miniature pair of headphones like a doctor's stethoscope already attached. By ten o'clock, when Stefan completed his work, there was scarcely any evidence of what he had been doing. Every tiny speck of plaster had been carefully swept up, the gray vinyl cable was effectively concealed, the slim black and gold microphone was lost in the array of pens and pencils in the heavy Swedish bowl.

"Now," Stefan said, panting a little after his exertions, "we will do a level test, Katherine."

"Must you? Now?"

"It will only take a minute." He dragged a chair into position about four feet from the desk. "I want you to sit here, please, where Mr. Gamage might be expected to sit. Just talk naturally, anything that comes into your mind; and we will see what we pick up. I will give you a signal when I am ready to roll."

She sat down. He pressed a kiss on the top of her head, then he strode off to the bedroom, and a minute later he called, "Go ahead, darling. I am ready for you."

She began,

Arma virumque cano, Troiae qui primus ab oris
Italiam fato profugus Lavinaque venit
Litora—multum ille et terris iactatus et alto
Vi superum, saevae memorem Iunonis—

He came tearing into the study. "Virgil! Virgil! Why must we have Virgil? You are supposed to be Mr. Gamage, Katherine. Kindly talk like Mr. Gamage."

"I always expect him to recite from the *Aeneid*."

"No, no. Be sensible. Just talk."

Back he trotted to the bedroom, and again, a few moments later, he called, "Go ahead, go ahead."

She said, "And the grasshopper shall be a burden, and desire shall fail: because man goeth to his long home, and the mourners go about the streets; or ever the silver cord be loosed, or the golden bowl be broken, or the pitcher be broken at the fountain, or the wheel broken at the cistern—"

He stood looking down at her. He said gently, "You surprise me, darling. You are just a ham when you get in front of a microphone. I would never have thought it of you."

"I can't stop," she said. "Then shall the dust return to the earth as it was: and the spirit shall return to God who gave it." There was suddenly no happiness in her, no joy; she jumped up and threw her arms around him, and pressed her face against his shoulder. She wailed, "Oh, *Stefan.* Oh, *Stefan.*"

"What is the matter with you?"

"I'm afraid."

"Silly girl. Afraid of what?"

"I don't know."

He said, "There is nothing to be afraid of. Come with me. I want you to hear how you sound on the Cosmo."

She went into the bedroom with him and waited as he turned a switch here, a switch there. The spools of tape spun back, reversed themselves, and a hollow voice declaimed, "*Arma virumque cano.*"

"There!" Stefan said. "It is excellent, don't you agree?"

"It's remarkable."

His eyes shone at this triumph of the machine over the human larynx. He listened proudly until all the mumbling came to an end; then he turned to her and said, "So. Everything is ready for tomorrow. Now, what about tonight? Shall we go over to the Carpathia and have fun?"

She had no wish to have fun. She wanted to crawl into bed and pull the sheets over her face and shut out the world. But she had a presentiment that something terrible and unexpected might happen to him if she let him out of her sight, and it was therefore necessary for her to stay close to him. She said, "Yes, let's go."

14

HE SEEMED to be tired in the morning, heavy-eyed and irritable; and he astonished her by muttering that she was making excessive demands on him, she was insatiable, he was no longer as young as he had been. But it was only a pre-breakfast mood. He became quite cheerful after his second cup of coffee and said, "You know, I have been worrying about Mr. Hamid, my superior at the United Nations. Poor little fellow. He is so good-natured! He has not protested once about my continual absence. I think I might go and spend an hour or two with him before lunch, and take care of such vital matters as picking up my paycheck."

When he was ready to leave he put his hands on her shoulders and said, "Katherine, shall I tell you something? In these past two weeks you have blossomed before my very eyes. You are quite a woman."

"Am I? Well, thank you."

"It is gratifying to me to feel I have played some trifling part in bringing those roses to your cheeks, even though, as a result, I feel a hundred years old."

"You don't look a hundred years old."

"Good. I will return at two o'clock, before your Mr. Gamage arrives here. In the meantime, I beg of you, stay away from my equipment. Do not breathe on the little microphone; do not disturb any of the wires—they are very delicate; and, above all, do not let your crazy Mrs. Corcoran go anywhere near my tape recorder in the bedroom."

"Yes, Stefan."

He kissed her affectionately. "*Au revoir.*"

"*Au revoir,* Stefan."

At ten o'clock she telephoned Olive Bartlett in the Dean's office at Southcliffe. "Ah, Miss Emory!" Olive said. "I'm so glad to hear from you. I tried several times to reach you yesterday, without success."

"I'm sorry you had so much trouble," Kate said. "And I'm sorry I was unable to visit you last weekend, as I hoped to do. I've been extremely busy here. Everything has been chaotic."

"Perhaps you can come next weekend?"

"I don't think I can. But let me see how I stand on Thursday, or Friday."

"Good, good," Olive said. She coughed delicately, and went on, "As a matter of fact, when I tried to reach you yesterday there was another matter which I felt I ought to discuss with you."

"And what was that, Olive?"

"Your secretary is here."

"My *secretary?*"

"Yes. Giselle Bonney."

"I don't understand, Olive. What is she doing at Southcliffe?"

Olive's voice became solemn. "She arrived here yesterday in a most alarming state. She seemed to be sick—"

Kate interrupted, "When I last saw her she complained of a sore throat."

"Yes, she had a sore throat, and a fever—not dangerously high, just over a hundred. But it was not her *physical* condition that was so distressing: it was her *mental* condition. The poor girl was positively distraught."

Kate said, "Distraught? But why?"

Olive's voice dropped to a whisper. "It was one of the most embarrassing things I have ever witnessed. The unhappy creature fell to her knees, right here in my office, and asked for sanctuary."

"*Sanctuary!*"

"Yes. Imagine how I felt! I was scared out of my wits. I thought she must, at the very least, have committed a murder. Miss Emory, in all the years I have been here, *nobody* has ever come into my office with such a request. I don't know if we're legally *entitled* to grant anybody sanctuary—we aren't a cathedral, or a church, or even a convent. I think I ought to speak to Mr. Auchincloss and get a ruling from him on our status."

"But why was Giselle *asking* for sanctuary?"

"That was my first question to her, as you can imagine. And she replied—I have her exact words written down on a piece of paper here in front of me—*Because I have betrayed the person I respect most in this world, Miss Emory.*"

"How could she possibly betray me?" Kate said. "Olive, the child is sick. Has Dean Gilberta seen her?"

"No, Dean Gilberta has been tied up with some visitors from Nigeria and I didn't wish to add to her problems. I called Sister Clementine when I saw how disturbed Giselle was, and Sister Clementine took her to the infirmary."

"And how is she this morning?"

"Sister Clementine advised me that she had a few screaming fits during the night, but she is now much calmer, and her temperature is almost down to normal."

Kate said earnestly, "Olive, please assure her that I have complete faith in her, that I am sure she has never betrayed me in any way. Some trivial thing has become magnified in her mind as a result of her sore throat, and she must stop worrying about it at once."

"I will give her your message when I go to the infirmary to see her at lunchtime," Olive said. "I'm certain it will encourage her greatly."

2.

Stefan returned at two o'clock in a remarkably good humor, and Kate noticed, without really wishing to notice, that there was a smear of lipstick around one corner of his mouth. She tried to persuade herself that it was a trace left over from last night, or a remnant of her good-by kiss this morning; but the attempt failed, and she had to admit to herself that the lipstick must have been acquired from another woman in the course of the past few hours. From his secretary, perhaps, or Mr. Hamid's secretary, or the secretary of some other worker for world peace, happy to see him back where he belonged. She thought, *I suppose I will have to learn to live with it: he likes women, and women enjoy being liked, and there is no way that situation can be changed.*

"You have made a tremendous impression on my Mr. Hamid," he said cheerfully. "So much so, the dear fellow informed me that he intends to issue a special stamp to commemorate our wedding. A joke, of course; you must not take it seriously. Now, before your good friend Mr. P. Converse Gamage rings the doorbell, I would like to give my little tape recorder a final check. Will you go into your study, and when I give you the go-ahead, just say a word or two in the direction of the microphone? You remember where it is: in the glass bowl. Nothing dramatic this time, darling. Just recite for me the days of the week—Monday, Tuesday, Wednesday, et cetera."

She went into her study, and when he called out to her from her bedroom she began to recite the days of the week, unwillingly, like a child resenting the pressures of an overzealous teacher, holding her voice back so that it would not reach the disguised black and gold microphone. But he was right: it was highly sensitive; and he bustled into the study looking pleased with himself. "Splendid, my darling, splendid. You might be Sarah Bernhardt—your voice is so plangent. And the Cosmo seems to be working even better than last night, for some reason. Perhaps the humidity in the air is helping it."

"How could the humidity help it?"

"Ah, electronics is a mysterious science: we never know exactly what is going to happen at any given moment. The uncertainty adds to the excitement." He burst out laughing. "Oh, my dear, dear Katherine! You have such a long face! But, believe me, nothing catastrophic is going to occur."

"I'm sorry if I have a long face. I'm very unhappy about this recording."

"Then you should make an effort to be adult, and not allow yourself to be unhappy. I am not going to all this trouble in order to harm you. This is merely a form of insurance, entirely for your protection." He glanced in annoyance at his large gold wristwatch. "Your friends will be here any minute. I think I will go and shut myself in the bedroom." He kissed her, and just as he was about to leave he tried to win her back to him. "Trust me, darling. All will be well. And when you are finished with Mr. P. Converse Gamage, I will be there on that big comfortable bed of yours, waiting for you impatiently. My God, what an attractive woman you are! I have been yearning for you all morning!"

"I thought I was making too-excessive demands on you."

"Never. Never."

She said vaguely, "You have lipstick on the side of your face."

He wiped it off with his breast-pocket handkerchief, glanced at it, and said with a knowing smile, "A souvenir of last night. Delicious." He drifted away from her, and out of the room, as if he were a little afraid of what she might say next.

She stood staring at the microphone in the heavy Swedish glass bowl. It had taken on the aspect of a small black and gold snake, innocent, hidden, potentially deadly. She thought, No: I cannot allow this to happen, it is ugly and unpleasant; Mr. Gamage and the others are coming here as my guests, and I must treat them honorably.

She had no idea how to go about neutralizing Stefan's equipment. She was afraid to touch the microphone itself; it was undoubtedly a very delicate and expensive instrument and she did not wish to damage it in any way. All she could do, she decided, was cut a wire; but which one, and at what point? A large pair of scissors lay on Giselle's desk, used normally for clipping newspapers and magazines, and with this in her hand she examined, first, the fine translucent wire which emerged from the microphone and was taped to the back of the glass bowl. She was reluctant to touch it. It looked—perhaps because it was so fragile—as if it might be irreplaceable. She knelt at the side of her desk, and noticed where the gray vinyl-covered cable came out of the small plastic box which resembled a hearing-aid; and she remembered Stefan telling her that this cable had cost only six dollars for a hundred-foot spool. It was a useful clue. She decided that if this were cut, no great harm would be done. But since she knew nothing whatever about electronics, she could not tell whether there was a possibility of getting a shock, or even of being electrocuted; and the only way to safeguard herself, on the spur of the moment, was to wrap Kleenex tissues around the handles of the scissors, hold them with the very tips of her fingers, and keep her head well averted and her eyes tightly closed. As she snipped the wire she expected a flash of light, or a crackling spark, but nothing at all happened, and she wondered if she had actually accomplished what she had set out to do. She stood up, breathing heavily, and as she replaced the scissors on Giselle's desk she heard the door of the bedroom open, and Stefan called, "Katherine! Katherine!" Her heart stopped beating. But at this moment the doorbell rang, announcing Mr. Gamage's arrival, and the bedroom door closed quickly. It was like a French farce, Kate thought, except that it was not in any way funny. She had betrayed Stefan in order not to betray herself, and she wondered if he would understand it when she explained it to him later.

3.

Mr. Gamage gave the impression that he had grown at least two inches since she lunched with him at Charlot's. She asked, "And how is your daughter, Babette? I think of her often." He answered shyly, "Oh, Babette is fine, fine. Thank you." He was uneasy, and obviously reluctant to engage in small talk.

Miss Mitsamushi was unchanged in her gray flannel dress. She carried with her, as usual, her black leather dispatch case, and she seemed to have more difficulty than before with her breathing. Kate felt deeply sorry for her.

More interesting to Kate was the man who accompanied Gamage, the colleague who, in her mind, had acquired an almost Satanic personality. He was short and broad, his face was unnaturally white, and Kate was puzzled and repelled by it until she realized that he must have been in an accident of some kind. The skin was mostly scar tissue, and completely hairless. He wore an ingenious toupee with ragged ends at the sides and back, as if he, or the toupee, needed a haircut. His name was Alvarez.

The conversational preliminaries were brief. Gamage, unable to look at her, said, "Miss Emory, I'm sure you'll agree that the sooner we get down to the business in hand, the better. The news of your forthcoming marriage has raised a number of serious problems. Unfortunately, I am not really qualified to deal with them. If you don't mind, therefore, I will ask Mr. Alvarez to discuss them with you. Mr. Alvarez?"

Kate said, "Could you explain, first, what Mr. Alvarez' special qualifications are?"

Gamage glanced at her and quickly looked away. "Certainly. Mr. Alvarez is one of our security officers."

"*Security!*" Kate said. "Do you mean *legal?*"

Gamage shook his head.

"This is very curious," Kate said. Her voice was sharp. "May I know what security regulations I have broken by getting engaged to be married?"

Alvarez said, "We'll deal with that question fully in a few moments. However, I would like to start by saying that we all appreciate that you are a person of considerable standing in our community—my wife is a great admirer of your books, incidentally—and we wouldn't wish to cause you any unnecessary embarrassment. On the other hand, we have the gravest reasons for being here today, and I ask you, as a loyal American, to cooperate with us as fully as possible."

She replied curtly, "Mr. Alvarez, before we go any further, I suggest that you forget about the pointless flattery and make up your mind to treat me as a fairly intelligent person. You tell me you are here today for the gravest reasons, presumably because I am under some sort of security cloud; and in the next breath you tell me you expect my cooperation as a loyal American. Which is it to be? Am I being interrogated as a loyal or a disloyal American?"

His white skin seemed to become even whiter. He said, "Miss Emory, I hoped we could keep this on a high level—"

She swung round to Gamage. "Mr. Alvarez insists on double talk. Please tell me, Mr. Gamage: am I under suspicion of disloyalty?"

He answered unhappily, "Questions of loyalty may possibly be involved."

"Oh, indeed. What are these questions? I think I have a right to know."

"Mr. Alvarez will discuss them."

She turned back to Alvarez and said icily, "Yes?"

"I will be perfectly frank with you, Miss Emory. There is no need, in my opinion, to conceal or to pretend we do not have in our possession certain key facts. I will begin by reminding you that on Monday, October 14, you had lunch with Mr. Gamage at Charlot's restaurant, here in New York. Also present were Miss Mitsamushi and your representative, Mr. Rushton Wyle. Is that correct?"

"Yes."

"When the luncheon was over, Miss Mitsamushi and Mr. Wyle left. You and Mr. Gamage stayed on for some time and continued your conversation. Right?"

"Yes."

"In the course of this part of the conversation, Mr. Gamage referred to a certain Jiro Mitsamushi, and raised the possibility of your meeting some unnamed persons from the Chinese mainland. Is that correct?"

"Yes."

"I also want to ask you whether you recall that Mr. Gamage specifically stated that the matters he discussed were confidential, and you agreed to treat them as confidential?"

"Yes, yes."

"Miss Emory, that very night, only a few hours after your confidential talk with Mr. Gamage, you visited a restaurant called the Carpathia. You were in the company of Stefan Gerhardi, whom you now say you are going to marry, and after a little while you were joined by another man, named Miklos Horscht. Both of these men are high-ranking members of the Hungarian Communist Party, as you undoubtedly were aware. You had a lengthy conversation with them and, among other things, you discussed with them very fully your forthcoming visit to Japan under the auspices of the State Department."

"Now, Mr. Alvarez, please, just wait one minute—"

"Miss Emory, this isn't part of our case. You are a commentator on current affairs, and you are entitled to sit down and talk with anyone you please. What I am trying to explain to you is this: your association with Mr. Gerhardi and Mr. Horscht, which we had not known about before, caused us a lot of anxiety. We were worried not so much about your involvement with these men as about the possibility of compromising certain people, certain friends of ours, in Japan and elsewhere. After the most careful consideration, it was decided that simple precautions must be taken to protect these people; and I think it is only fair to inform you that, since that night, you have been under surveillance. Consequently, we have a pretty clear picture of what has been going on here recently."

Unexpectedly, Kate's hands began to tremble. She exclaimed, "*You* have been spying on me! The man in the gray suit was *your* man! How strange! And I thought he belonged to the other side!"

Alvarez asked innocently, "The other side?"

"Never mind. But I'd like you to know, Mr. Alvarez, that he wasn't very efficient. I hate to say this, since it might reflect on him, but he stuck out like a sore thumb."

"I'll see that your criticism is passed on to the right quarter," Alvarez said. He shifted position and crossed his thick legs. "Let's get down, now, to some of the fundamental aspects of the case. You and Mr. Gerhardi are getting married in New York some time within the next two weeks—"

She cried, "Who told you we're getting married within the next two weeks?"

He looked surprised. "It was announced a couple of days ago by the Hungarian news bureau."

She said bitterly, "Go on."

He continued, "You therefore expect us to release you from the contract you signed with us, in which you undertook to lecture in Japan and sundry other places on our behalf for a period of six months beginning next January."

"Yes. I ask and expect to be released from that contract."

"Miss Emory, ignoring anything I've said up to this point, suppose the State Department decides that it isn't in the national interest to release you from your contract. What then?"

"I will still go ahead and marry Mr. Gerhardi."

"And afterwards you will go to Japan, as arranged? Alone?"

"I believe it is a wife's duty to be with her husband."

"And, if he returned to Budapest, you'd go with him?"

"Yes."

"Have you considered the possibility that the United States government might take steps to implement the contract?"

This is what Stefan predicted, she thought. *Threats. Pressure.* She said, "Mr. Alvarez, what possible good would it do anybody to send me to Japan against my will? Do you think, when I got there, I would be an eloquent spokesman for the American way of life?"

"The contract was freely arrived at. Nobody twisted your arm to sign it. Therefore it wouldn't come as a shock to you if the government asked for substantial penalties for breach of contract?"

Exactly what Stefan foretold, she thought. She said, "How substantial, Mr. Alvarez?"

"To the extent of stripping you of your American citizenship."

She cried in outrage, "You couldn't do that! Really, Mr. Alvarez, I'm not a child! Don't try to frighten me with silly threats."

He looked slightly pleased at provoking an outburst from her. He said, "It isn't as silly a threat as you seem to think. Our laws permit a woman who marries a foreign national to retain her American citizenship in normal circumstances. But the law isn't so tolerant of a woman who marries a foreign national and then goes to work for her husband's government, particularly—"

She interrupted vehemently, "Mr. Alvarez!"

"Let me finish. Particularly when that government is hostile to the United States. Furthermore—"

She cried again, "Mr. Alvarez!"

"I would really appreciate it if you would let me finish. Furthermore, you must surely be aware that before you go to work for a foreign government, *they* will require from you an unequivocal renunciation of your American citizenship. So it's a little unfair of you to accuse me of trying to frighten you with silly threats, isn't it?"

She said, "I know there's a rumor to the effect that I shall be working for the Hungarian Ministry of Culture, but I ask you to believe that it's absolutely unfounded."

He smiled at her. "Are you suggesting that the Hungarian press bureau issued an unfounded *rumor*?"

"I'm saying that the story isn't true, Mr. Alvarez. It simply isn't *true*."

He said, "What about the statement they issued this morning? Do you claim that isn't true, either?"

"I don't know anything about a statement issued this morning." She leaned forward, appealing to him. "What was in that statement?"

"We'll come to it in due course, I assure you." He uncrossed his knees and said to Gamage, "Do you want me to go on?"

"Yes," Gamage said unhappily.

4.

Alvarez took a deep breath and said, "Miss Emory, since that luncheon at Charlot's, you have had several meetings with Miss Mitsamushi, haven't you, and you've received from her a number of documents?"

"Yes."

"You're aware that all of these documents were of a highly confidential nature?"

"They were marked highly confidential."

"Sometimes, you know, what seems to be a harmless little document, like a survey of Japanese novelists, can turn out to be positively explosive if it finds its way into the hands of those who seek to embarrass us. I don't have to tell *you* that. Now, what has happened to those documents?"

"I have them here," Kate said. "They're locked in the bottom drawer of my desk, in a large sealed envelope, ready to be returned to Miss Mitsamushi."

"They haven't been out of your possession?"

"Certainly not," Kate said angrily.

"Let me put that question in another way. You didn't pass them on to Mr. Gerhardi?"

"No. Of course not."

"From information we have received, it appears that Mr. Gerhardi not only read this classified material, but he made photographic copies which were then forwarded to Budapest and other centers of communist culture."

"Who gave you this obviously false information?" Kate demanded, and before Alvarez could reply she had found the answer herself. "Was it my secretary, Giselle Bonney?"

He said, "As a matter of fact, Miss Bonney has been in touch with us. With Mr. Gamage, to be exact."

So she did betray me, Kate thought. *I never suspected that she was so disturbed.* She said, "You may not have heard, Mr. Alvarez, that Giselle is in the infirmary at Southcliffe, suffering from some sort of nervous collapse. I think you'd be awfully unwise to rely on any information which she supplied."

Miss Mitsamushi stood up, tiptoed across to Alvarez, and whispered in his ear for a moment. He said quietly, "Thank you, I was just coming to that." She tiptoed back to her seat and resumed her position, knees pressed together, eyes downcast.

Alvarez said, "Miss Emory, last Tuesday night Mr. Gerhardi arrived here carrying a large leather valise. Do you know what was in that valise?"

"What is usually in a man's valise? Shirts. Pajamas. Socks. Various other odds and ends, I suppose."

"Did you know that among these various odds and ends was a camera that could be used for copying documents? What kind of camera was it, Miss Mitsamushi?"

"From the description I received," Miss Mitsamushi said, "it is probably a camera called a Zenit, made in Russia."

"I know nothing about this camera," Kate said.

"Were you aware," Alvarez said, "that among these odds and ends, as you call them, there was—beside the Zenit camera—a tape recording machine?"

Kate did not answer.

Alvarez said, "Miss Mitsamushi, can you describe the machine to us?"

"Again from the description I received," Miss Mitsamushi said, "it appears to be a type known as a Cosmo Mark 2. It is manufactured in Czechoslovakia, and it is considered to be of fairly high quality for such a compact piece of equipment."

"Do you see it in this room?" Alvarez asked.

"No, sir."

"Miss Emory, can you tell us where this tape recorder is at the present moment?"

Kate shook her head.

Alvarez said, "I would like to bring these facts to your attention. Last evening, at about five o'clock, Mr. Gerhardi went by taxi to an electronics store on West Forty-sixth Street." He took a sheet of paper from his pocket, and read from it as he spoke. "Mr. Gerhardi made the following purchases: a spool of one hundred feet of Belden microphone cable, type 8420; one male, one female Amphenol type 80 microphone connectors; and three dozen insulated wall staples. Can you tell me why Mr. Gerhardi needed these various articles?"

"You know as well as I do," Kate said, "that I can't answer for my fiancé. If you have any questions about his activities, you will have to ask him, not me."

Alvarez said sourly, "Just for the record, Miss Emory, you may not have a high opinion of the men who have been keeping tabs on you, but you'd be making a big mistake if you underestimated their abilities. Now, come. You must be able to offer *some* explanation of why your fiancé needed all that microphone cable and those insulated wall staples. Can't you even guess?"

Again she shook her head.

He said, "Do you think it's possible that your fiancé used that microphone cable to hook up his Cosmo Mark 2 tape recorder so that he could make a recording of our conversation here today?"

She remained silent.

"Of course," he said, "if you and Mr. Gerhardi conspired to record, secretly, and without authorization, and to the detriment of the United States, a confidential conversation between yourself and certain officials of the government of the United States, then I don't have to tell you that you're in trouble right up to your neck." He reached into his pocket and brought out another sheet of paper, and held it up so that she could clearly see the markings on it. He said,

"I hold here a floor plan of your apartment which one of our so-called dumb agents obtained a little while ago from your housekeeper, Mrs. Pearl, or Pearly, Corcoran."

Mrs. Corcoran, Kate thought. *First my secretary betrays me. Then my housekeeper.*

Alvarez pointed to a roughly drawn rectangle on the right side of the page. "At the present moment we are here, in your study. I figure that a run of eighty to a hundred feet of microphone cable might bring us *here.*" His finger moved up to another roughly drawn rectangle at the top left-hand corner of the page. "Isn't this your bedroom, Miss Emory? And isn't this where Mr. Gerhardi is hiding with his Cosmo Mark 2 tape recorder? And hasn't he been recording our conversation since we arrived?"

She said desperately, "No, Mr. Alvarez, our conversation hasn't been recorded."

Alvarez said to Miss Mitsamushi, "Can you put that thing out of commission?"

Miss Matsamushi, without a word, leaned across Kate's desk, took the little black and gold microphone out of the heavy Swedish glass bowl, and detached a tiny plug in the base. Kate thought enviously, *It's as simple as that. There was no need to cut the wire.*

Alvarez said, "Is the door of the bedroom locked, Miss Emory?"

"I have no idea."

He said to Gamage, "Like to come along?"

"Sure," Gamage said.

The two men went quietly out of the study, and made their way across the living room to the bedroom. Kate followed, her eyes unaccountably filled with tears; and behind her came Miss Mitsamushi, her sallow cheeks flushed.

Alvarez slowly turned the brass doorknob, and flung the door open as if he expected to be greeted with a salvo of machine-gun fire. But there was no need for caution. Stefan was stretched out comfortably on Kate's bed, his eyes closed, his hands clasped in contentment over his abdomen. At the sudden noise he opened his eyes, frowned momentarily at Alvarez and Gamage, and then smiled. He said, "Ah! The conference is over! Excellent! Now we can all have tea." He slid off the bed, stood up perfectly straight and gave the two men a stiff little bow. "Gentlemen: permit me to introduce myself. Stefan Gerhardi."

Alveraz said, "Major Gerhardi, you are under arrest."

"Under arrest?" Stefan said in a high, joyous voice. "Nonsense, my dear fellow. I am unarrestable."

15

IS THAT why I love him, Kate thought, or loved him? For his bravado; for his prodigious masculinity (now a little diminished) and his finesse with the female form divine; for his brilliance in so many different aspects; for exactly *what?* And exactly what is the condition of my love at this moment? And for that matter, exactly what is the condition of my life? He is under arrest, according to that faceless man, that man without a smile, Security Officer Alvarez. Am I under arrest, too? He, in his amusing way, can claim that he is unarrestable. But what, in my unamusing way, can I claim? And *Major Gerhardi:* that is new. I did not know my fabulous Hungarian was a major—he kept that from me, and I wonder why.

Alvarez looked down at the Cosmo Mark 2 standing on Kate's bedside table. The stethoscopic headset was still plugged in, the take-up spool was half filled with tape. He asked, "Is this your property, Major Gerhardi?"

"This machine?" Stefan echoed, as if he had never seen anything less likely to be his property. "The little tape recorder? No, my dear sir, I am afraid it is not my property." He turned away from Alvarez, and then cried, "Good heavens! The tall gentleman! I cannot possibly be mistaken! You, sir, can only be the famous Mr. P. Converse Gamage, of the State Department. Am I right, sir?"

"Yes," Gamage said, taken aback.

"Mr. Gamage, I know your colleagues. Mr. Edward

Smith and Mr. Victor Williamson. They have spoken most warmly about you. Imagine my pleasure, sir, meeting you at last in the flesh!"

Alvarez said loudly, "Major Gerhardi, let's keep to the point for one minute. Do I understand you to say that this machine is not your property?"

"My dear sir, it was my property *once*. But no longer. What use would I have for a machine of this kind? So I presented it to my fiancée, Miss Emory, who *does* have some use for it. That is why it is here in her bedroom, where she can dictate into it whenever the mood seizes her. Isn't that so, darling? Mr. Gamage, I have so many things to discuss with you, I hope you can spare me a little of your valuable time. Shall we adjourn to the living room, where it is not quite so crowded?"

"You can adjourn," Alvarez said, "when we've settled exactly who owns this tape recorder, and exactly what has been recorded on it this afternoon."

Stefan scowled at him. "You keep interrupting me, sir, and you have not even had the courtesy to tell me your name."

"Alvarez."

"Alvarez? Alvarez? Are you by any chance related to the sculptor, José Alvarez de Pereira y Cubero?"

"Not to my knowledge."

"Oh. Well, Mr. Gamage, as I was saying—"

"You were saying," Alvarez cut in savagely, "that you don't own this tape recorder. Just tell me, Major Gerhardi: wasn't it issued to you by the Hungarian Secret Service?"

"Oh, my God," Stefan said, groaning. "You seem to be hipped on this machine. You have an obsession about it. If you are so crazy about it, borrow it, Mr. Alvarez, play with it, have a good time with it, take it to bed with you, if you wish."

"Just answer my question, sir. Is this a Cosmo Mark 2?"

Stefan rolled his eyes, as if he would never comprehend what motivated men like Alvarez. "Perhaps. Who knows? Frankly, I do not bother my head with such technical trivialities."

"Issued to you by the organization for which you work?"

"I can't recall who issued it to me. A chap with brown hair, as far as I remember."

"*The Hungarian Secret Service,* Major."

"No, no. I almost certain it was a tall thin chap with brown hair."

Alvarez, trembling with rage, said, "Miss Mitsamushi."

"Yes, sir?"

"You know about these machines. Please take charge of it. Don't try to carry it yourself. Get one of my men to carry it for you."

"Yes, sir."

Still in a rage, Alvarez said, "Major Gerhardi, and you too, Miss Emory: I must ask you to accompany me to the office of the United States Attorney. Let's not waste too much time, if you don't mind. Miss Emory: your coat? Your hat? Believe me, it will be best for everyone concerned if we get to his office before he leaves for the day."

2

She could not move. She stood in the doorway of the bedroom as if her body had turned to stone.

"Mr. Alvarez," Stefan said, drawing himself up to his full height and speaking through his nose, "I beg to inform you for the second time that I am not subject to arrest by you. As your Mr. Gamage will confirm, I am fully protected by the rules of diplomatic immunity. Furthermore, I wish to express as forcibly as I can that I consider your behavior to be a prime example of American police brutality. If you are serious about taking Miss Emory and me before your

United States Attorney, surely we are entitled to know why we are being treated as criminals? In other words, what have we done wrong, what crime have we committed, what is your accusation against us? As far as I am concerned, I was lying peacefully in this bed when you burst in—without even knocking—and announced that I was under arrest. Is lying on the bed of one's fiancée now a capital crime in your country?"

"If you want a charge I'll give you a charge," Alvarez said; and he went on in a loud sing-song, "Stefan Gerhardi, I am in possession of substantial evidence that you and Katherine Millicent Emory, jointly, have conspired to record on magnetic tape, secretly, and without due authorization, and to the detriment of the United States, a conversation of a confidential nature held between said Katherine Millicent Emory and certain officials of the government of the United States. In my considered opinion, this is an offense which must be brought to the attention of the United States Attorney, and I now formally request you and Miss Emory to accompany me to his office. Let's go, Mr. Gerhardi, let's go."

Stefan cried passionately, "Mr. Gamage! I ask you, as a representative of the State Department, to restrain this man from the mad abuse of his powers! It could result in irreparable damage to the friendly relations between our two countries."

"I'm sorry, Mr. Gerhardi; but I believe Mr. Alvarez is right. The act he describes has been committed. He is therefore fully justified in asking you to accompany him for further questioning."

Stefan's eyes flashed. His nostrils flared. He pointed a scornful finger at the tape recorder, and said in a voice burning with indignation, "God knows what false evidence you have already manufactured in order to incriminate me, and the woman I love, Katherine M. Emory. The whole world has learned from bitter experience that certain elements in the United States will go to any lengths to inflame passions against my country and its allies, and to pave the way for war."

"Oh, rubbish," Gamage said.

"*Rubbish!*" Stefan exclaimed: "Let us see who in this room is speaking rubbish. Mr. Gamage! I demand that you play the tape on this tape recorder here and now, in the presence of all concerned, and before any of your electronics experts can falsify it, so that we can establish exactly what is on it. Thus we will prove beyond any shadow of doubt that this person's accusations are despicable, untruthful, and fraudulent."

Gamage looked puzzled. Alvarez was glowering, and the scar tissue on his face had become chalk-white.

Stefan strode up to the tape recorder crying, "If *you* will not play it, *I* will play it. Let us decide once and for all who is lying and who is telling the truth. Let us see whether this is a vile conspiracy, or not."

Alvarez leaped in front of him. "Don't touch that machine!"

"You're scared, Mr. Alvarez," Stefan jeered. "Your bluff has been called. You are afraid your carefully laid plans are about to be exposed."

Alvarez said emphatically, "No, sir. That is not so." But the needle had pierced the skin. He was clearly worried.

"Then *play* it!" Stefan insisted. "Why don't you *play* it?"

Alvarez glanced at Gamage. Gamage shrugged his shoulders. Kate watched them as if she were in the front row of a theater, observing the action of a meaningless play that became more incomprehensible as every moment passed.

She heard Alvarez say angrily, "How do I know he hasn't rigged it so that everything on the tape is erased the moment we switch it on? Phil, I don't want anyone to lay a finger on this machine until it's safely in our own laboratory, under the supervision of our own technicians."

She heard Gamage reply, "But it's a reasonable request. We can't refuse him. Suppose he's right?"

Then, to her surprise, she heard Gamage say, "Miss Emory," and it was as if one of the actors in this super-ashcan play had leaned down from the stage to address a stranger in the audience.

"Yes?" she said.

"How do you feel about this?"

"How do I fell about *what?*"

"Playing the tape. After all, you're involved. Do you agree with Mr. Gerhardi?"

She answered scornfully, "Do you honestly think Mr. Gerhardi would stick his neck out if there were anything incriminating on the tape? Be sensible, Mr. Gamage."

He winced. He turned to Alvarez and said unhappily, "I think you should play it, as Major Gerhardi requests."

"I'm damned if I'll play it here," Alvarez said vehemently, as if he suspected that Kate's bedroom was packed with hostile spirits: "I'll play it in the study."

"May I help you to set it up there?" Stefan asked with a gentle smile.

Alvarez snapped, "Miss Mitsamushi and I will take care of it."

"Ah, Miss Mitsamushi," Stefan said. "Are you familiar with this equipment? You know how to set it up and operate it?"

"Yes," Miss Mitsamushi replied, her eyes lowered.

Kate saw the look he gave her: amused, interested, brimming over with sexual curiosity. "Good," he said: "But if you have any questions, do not hesitate to ask me."

Miss Mitsamushi's tiny bosom appeared to flutter.

3

"*Arma virumque cano,*" the Cosmo Mark 2 began, causing Gamage to blink and Alvarez to lean forward as if he could not believe his ears: "*Troiae qui primus ab oris—*"

"Well, well," Gamage said under his breath. "Just listen to that."

"What the hell is it?" Alvarez whispered.

"Virgil."

"Dante's Virgil?"

"Not exactly," Gamage said. He glanced across at Kate in admiration.

The voice stopped, and for a few seconds there was silence. Then the Cosmo Mark 2 began to declaim again from its place on Kate's desk. "And the grasshopper shall be a burden, and desire shall fail: because man goeth to his long home, and the mourners go about the streets—"

"It must be a code," Alvarez said hoarsely.

"Hush," Gamage said.

Kate sat on the black leather sofa, her hands in her lap, her ankles crossed. She was in no way related to what was happening, or to what was being said, or to any of the figures grouped around the small black succubus of a tape recorder. She was alone, isolated, dishonored, ashamed. Alvarez wants to send me to jail, she thought, he wants to put me in jail now, this afternoon, as soon as possible. What should I take with me? What will I need? Should I call Rushton Wyle? What can I do?

The Cosmo was silent again. Then, in a strange, faraway voice it said, "Monday. Tuesday. Wednesday. Thursday. Friday. Saturday. Sunday."

Again it was silent; and Gamage and Alvarez stood waiting for the next verbal outpouring. None came. The silence was broken by a curious rustling sound, followed by a click and then a deep rumbling hum. The hum continued for a minute; stopped; returned; stopped; and then continued without any interruption.

Alvarez said sharply to Miss Mitsamushi, "What's happening?"

She was distressed. "Something seems to be wrong with the machine, sir."

Alvarez stormed at Gamage, "I told you he had it rigged. I knew he'd pull some trick on us." His face appeared to have acquired new scars, new plaques of scar tissue.

Stefan, sitting on the edge of Giselle's desk, called blandly, "Well, gentlemen?"

"Well, what?" Alvarez replied with a growl.

"Surely you have heard enough of this awful humming noise. Do you find it full of top secret information? Or do you think you owe Miss Emory and me an apology?"

The tape recorder was suddenly silent. Alvarez cried, "Now what has happened, Miss Mitsamushi?"

She was bent over the machine, inspecting it. "I am trying to locate the fault, sir."

Alvarez raged, "Keep it running! I want to hear the rest of the tape!"

"Yes, sir."

The spools began to revolve slowly. The hum pulsed through the study again.

"Now, now," Stefan said: "You should not lose your temper with the young lady, Mr. Alvarez. She is doing her best, like the celebrated piano player. But between ourselves, you can take my word for it, there is nothing incriminating on the tape. Nothing whatsoever. Just this bloody hum." He smiled, bubbling with good humor. "An apology, gentlemen? And then we can part like good friends."

Gamage cleared his throat. He said ponderously, "Mr. Gerhardi, in view of the—ah—rather negative nature of this demonstration, I believe it would not be in keeping with our—ah—traditions of fair play to charge you with illegally recording any conversation held here today. I think Mr. Alvarez will be willing to drop the charge against you. Is that right, Mr. Alvarez? The charge is dropped?"

"Yes," Alvarez said bitterly.

"You disappoint me, Mr. Gamage," Stefan said. "Withdrawing the charge is hardly enough. The situation clearly demands an official apology."

"I haven't quite finished," Gamage said. "As you know, we still have to settle the matter of Brother Hop."

"Who?"

"Brother Hop. Sun Pat Hsueng."

Stefan said, "Katherine! Do you hear? Another big lie is coming up! They are determined to catch us, one way or another."

She scarcely heard him.

16

GAMAGE SAID, "Major Gerhardi, just over a week ago you were arrested for speeding in Great Neck, Long Island—"

Stefan exclaimed indignantly, "What! You are bringing that up as a crime! You have failed to substantiate the despicable charge of recording your conversation with Miss Emory on this tape recorder, and now you are trying to frame me on an equally false speeding charge?"

"No, sir. What I am trying to establish will become clear in a moment, I hope, if you will allow me to go on. In this Great Neck affair you claimed, as usual, that you were entitled to diplomatic immunity and your arrest was therefore illegal. Your claim could not be substantiated immediately for the simple reason that you have succeeded in getting the records about your work and your status here into such confusion that nobody can say for certain what your position is. In fact there are several experts who state flatly that you aren't in this country at all, and at least one expert who asserts that you don't even exist, you are a figment of the Hungarian imagination."

"Ha ha," Stefan said coldly. "How amusing."

"As a result of this confusion," Gamage went on, "you were released from custody by the Great Neck police. However, you were given a summons to appear in court last Thursday, when the arguments relating to your diplomatic immunity could be heard in full. Rather unwisely, if you will excuse me for saying so, you failed to make an appearance."

Stefan smiled knowingly. "You have to admit, Mr. Gamage, that the incident smacked of a typical American frame-up."

"Really?"

"It did, sir, it did, most emphatically."

"Unfortunately," Gamage proceeded, "since you failed to answer the summons, the court had no alternative but to order an investigation to determine whether you were actually entitled to diplomatic immunity or whether an order for your arrest should be issued—"

"Arrest!" Stefan cried. "My *arrest!* Incredible! What next?"

"Well, in pursuance of the court's instructions, two police officers visited your apartment on Eighty-fifth Street yesterday and were told by the superintendent of the building that you had not been seen for several days and your mail had not been collected. So, on the basis of evidence that you had lied to the court and that you might now be a fugitive, a search order was obtained. At nine o'clock this morning your apartment was entered."

"This is monstrous!" Stefan said furiously. "Believe me, there will be international repercussions."

"I hope not. Everything possible was done to avoid any chance of a diplomatic incident, and you may like to know that I was assigned to accompany the police officers and to remain with them while they carried out their duties."

Stefan called out in a high-pitched voice, "Do you hear all this, Katherine? Do you remember how I told you of all the indignities we suffer from your people? Now do you believe what I said?"

She was incapable of replying to him. Her body was frozen. Her life seemed to have ended.

Gamage continued, "I'm sure I am not telling you anything that you don't already know. For example, the police found a quite extraordinary collection of whips, corsets, high-heeled boots, and other objects which surprised us a little—"

"Mr. Gamage, this is insufferable! Insufferable, sir. I demand to be allowed to call our delegation's legal expert—"

"He wouldn't be able to help you, Major," Gamage said. "We also found considerable evidence that strongly suggests you were engaged in espionage. For example, there were photographic copies of a number of classified State Department documents dealing with pacifist groups in Japanese universities—"

"I know nothing about such documents, absolutely nothing. They must have been planted in my apartment in my absence."

"These documents can readily be identified by special markings as having been issued to Miss Emory, and I am not willing to believe that Miss Emory entered your locked apartment during your absence and planted them there. Among them, of course, were several documents relating to Brother Hop, including a rare photograph of him taken recently in Shanghai."

"Brother Hop? And what, sir, is a Brother Hop?"

"Major, for the record, it's the code name of Sun Pat Hsueng, one of the organizers of the Red Guards in Communist China."

"How interesting."

"The information we have about Hop indicates that he has been responsible, at least partially, for the Red Guards' policy of unrelenting terror against liberal elements both inside and outside the Chinese government. He has been described as far to the left of the most extreme Maoist factions, and some Sinologists have called him one of the most dangerous men in the world today."

"Mr. Gamage," Stefan said, closing his eyes wearily, "why

this long speech? I am not really such an idiot. Why must you take such pains to hoodwink me?"

Gamage waited.

Stefan made an airy gesture with one hand. "I am not completely in the dark about this fellow Sun Pat Hsueng, you know. For example, I seem to have heard somewhere that agents of the Central Intelligence Agency based in Japan have been in touch with him. He is not quite such a dangerous extremist as you make out, after all. And if I am not mistaken, it was part of Miss Emory's mission when she went to the Far East to meet secretly with Sun Pat Hsueng for conversations. Not to urge him to go on terrorizing liberal elements in China, but precisely the opposite—to encourage him to step up his counter-revolutionary activities. In other words, Sun Pat Hsueng is nothing but an American stooge. Right, Mr. Gamage?"

Gamage shook his head.

"Come, come," Stefan said gaily. "We have reached the moment of truth. Admit it, Mr. Gamage. Sun Pat Hsueng is being paid off in good American dollars. Or does he prefer gold?"

"Your people in Budapest seem to have the same idea," Gamage said. He turned to Miss Mitsamushi. "Would you let me have the statement issued this morning by the Hungarian press bureau?"

"Yes, sir." She opened her heavy dispatch case, took out some papers, and handed them solemnly to him.

He put on his glasses and read: "A stunning blow to the war-making policy of American imperialism can now be revealed. The world-famous writer and social critic, Katherine M. Emory, has openly condemned the interventionist activities of the State Department and Central Intelligence Agency, and exposed plans to infiltrate the Chinese Red Guard. Confidential documents, supplied by Katherine M.

Emory, show that she was to meet with Sun Pat Hsueng, a high-ranking official of the Red Guard, for private talks designed to lay the groundwork for future uprisings and revolt against Communist Party leadership." Gamage took off his glasses and looked across at Kate. "Accompanying this statement were photostatic copies of various documents which had been entrusted to you, together with a photograph of Sun Pat Hsueng with various members of his group taken in Shanghai."

"It is not true," Kate said.

"What isn't true, Miss Emory?"

"I did not make that statement. I did not supply anybody with documents."

"We can *prove,*" Alvarez said heavily, "that these documents were given to you by Miss Mitsamushi."

"All the same, I did not make that statement, Mr. Alvarez."

Gamage turned again to Stefan. "You will be happy to learn," he said in a strangely detached, dreamy voice, "that following your announcements in Budapest, Peking Radio has announced the arrest of the traitor Sun Pat Hsueng and about thirty of his followers. Documents supplied by certain Western sources, as well as documents supplied by certain Japanese sources, proved beyond a shadow of a doubt that Sun Pat Hsueng had been plotting all sorts of dreadful things. A speedy trial is promised, though with so much evidence available I doubt whether a speedy trial will be necessary. A speedy execution is much more likely. In fact, I wouldn't be a bit surprised to hear that this vicious person has already been disposed of, together with his friends. What is your opinion, Major Gerhardi?"

Stefan did not answer. He had turned deathly pale and he was staring at Gamage in horror.

Gamage said, "I suppose I ought to express our gratitude for your help in disposing of Brother Hop. I suggest, though, that when you get back to Budapest it might be unwise to boast about it too much. Some of your people might be just a little upset to hear that you fell for such a simple little ruse."

Kate said, "Oh, my God," and sat down, her hands over her eyes.

Stefan said, "Very neat, Mr. Gamage."

Gamage smiled modestly.

2

After a few moments Stefan said, "Mr. Gamage, with your permission, I have a request to make of you."

"Yes?"

Stefan pulled himself erect, drew in his chin, marched over to him, and said in a loud, firm voice, "Mr. Gamage: I wish to ask for political asylum in the United States of America."

"Really? Why?"

"You have just made it absolutely clear why, sir. Because your brilliant ruse has made my position vis-à-vis my government completely untenable."

Gamage said, "Major Gerhardi, I'm afraid you're a little late. In order to meet your request we would have to get Congress to pass a special act, and they might be reluctant to do so. You see, just about thirty minutes ago a note, signed by the Under Secretary of State, was delivered to your delegation. This note requests that you be recalled from the United States and sets a time limit of thirty-six hours in which you must leave this country."

Stefan opened his mouth to protest, and then merely shrugged one shoulder, as if he had decided not to waste his breath.

"You mustn't feel too badly about it," Gamage said. "A

similar note was delivered to your delegation at the same time, asking for the recall of Colonel Horscht."

"That only adds to my problems," Stefan said. "And what about my fiancée, Miss Emory?"

Alvarez spoke up. "She remains under arrest."

Kate suppressed a cry of pain.

3

Stefan said, "Mr. Alvarez, there is one last thing I want to say. I want to assure you, on my word of honor, that Miss Emory is absolutely innocent of any wrongdoing."

"That," Alvarez said sourly, "is something we shall have to establish for ourselves. In the meantime, please come with me, Major Gerhardi."

"Just a moment," Stefan said. "Before I leave I would like to make a brief statement on the subject of Miss Emory's innocence." He smiled at Gamage. "What do I stand to lose? You can only expel me once. Mr. Gamage, Mr. Alvarez, I admit that it was actually my intention to record your conversation today. Everything was set up. However, one minute before you arrived, Miss Emory—inspired, I am sure, by the loftiest of motives—contrived to put my tape recorder out of action. May I show you how?" He stepped briskly over to the little black and gold microphone in the heavy Swedish glass bowl, and held it up in the air so that it could be seen by everybody. "There! Note what Miss Emory did! She very cleverly disconnected the wire. Consequently I could not hear or record a single word that was said in this room."

Alvarez said, "As it happens, you're wrong. The wire was disconnected by Miss Mitsamushi."

Stefan looked thunderstruck. He cried, *"What!"* and bobbed down beside Kate's desk and fumbled around wildly. Then, in triumph, he sprang up, holding the cut end of the gray vinyl microphone cable. "Here it is! Here it is! *She cut the wire!*—Isn't that correct, darling: *you cut the wire!*—Let me point out, Mr. Gamage, that *cutting* the wire is a much more decisive act of patriotism than merely pulling out a little plug. I hope you will give credit where credit is due."

"Let me see that," Gamage said, striding toward him.

"Could you ask for anything more convincing?" Stefan said proudly. He handed the wire to Gamage and, before Alvarez could stop him, he walked over to Kate and said, "Ah, Katherine, Katherine, I am afraid you would not really make a good Hungarian wife, even if the authorities allowed us to get married. You were rebellious. You disobeyed my instructions." He chucked her lightly under the chin and whispered, "And in any case, you were becoming too much for me in bed. Fantastic, eh? I never for one minute imagined such a thing could happen, but it did."

"Oh, Stefan," she said helplessly. He was so handsome and so utterly impossible.

"Let's go, Major Gerhardi," Alvarez said. He put his hand on Stefan's arm and, before Stefan could say another word, led him swiftly out of the room.

4

The act of cutting the microphone cable, which had been (in Kate's mind) an act of simple decency, affected Gamage profoundly. He was convinced that she had sacrificed herself, that she had resolutely turned her back on love and happiness in order to keep her country from being harmed. He stayed with her for more than an hour after Alvarez had departed with Stefan, and Miss Mitsamushi had departed with the sinister black leather dispatch case; he sat beside her patiently while she wept, making rather ineffectual comforting sounds; and when at last she was able to listen to him he said in his gentle way, "You mustn't worry. This whole business will be hushed up. The trip to Japan—how do you feel about that now, Miss Emory? Would you be prepared to go on with it?"

"I don't know, I really can't say at the moment."

"You have been most unfairly treated, in my opinion. You have been the victim of circumstances."

"Stefan Gerhardi was the victim of circumstances, too," she pointed out weakly.

"Philosophically, perhaps, you may be right. Speaking for the State Department I'm afraid I must differ. We must all take full responsibility for what we are. I'm sure you realize that there is not the slightest possibility of your joining Major Gerhardi in Budapest?"

"Why do you say that?"

"The Hungarian government will never allow you into the country in view of your part in the Sun Pat Hsueng affair."

"But I truly had nothing to do with the Sun Pat Hsueng affair."

"I doubt if they would listen to any explanation. They'll assume that you played the part of *agent provocateuse*, leading Gerhardi to his political destruction, as well as causing an awful lot of trouble with the Chinese."

"And Stefan can't return here?"

"I'm afraid he can't."

"So I may never see him again?"

"Oh, I wouldn't go so far as to say that. He's a very ingenious man. And nobody can foretell what may happen in Hungary tomorrow."

He left her, at last, with a reassuring handshake, and she sat in the dark living room brooding over the events of the past three weeks. She was numb with despair. *Did Stefan ever love me?* she asked herself. *Ever? Ever?* She would never know. She only knew that she had been living in a bizarre dream, a dream that was quite inappropriate to her personality, a dream that was rather bawdy and distasteful when seen in retrospect. Now she had to go on with the life that was really hers, the life of the spirit, the life of the mind, the life of awareness and perception. She had to resume being who she was, Katherine Millicent Emory, a writer whose principal topic was the problems of women.

For the time being, she felt, she needed peace more than anything else, she needed to escape; and she decided that she would go to Southcliffe for a week or two and stay in one of the guest cottages—the one she always stayed in, near the Library. She would read, and meditate, and talk to wise old Dean Gilberta, and try to recover from this overwhelming disaster.

She picked up the telephone and called Southcliffe. Olive Bartlett gave a cry of pleasure. "Oh, Miss Emory, how nice to hear that you are coming! The Dean will be overjoyed. And you will be able to address the senior class on the subject we discussed earlier?"

"What subject was that, Olive?"

"Our changing attitude to sex."

One has to face up to one's obligations, Kate thought, one cannot use one's misery as a cloak. "Yes," she said. "I will be happy to address the senior class on our changing attitude to sex. But I'm sure all the girls know far more about it than I do."

Olive laughed. "You say such amusing things, Miss Emory."

Kate put the receiver down and sat thinking. *I have been used,* she thought. *I have been, literally, betrayed. I am really very glad that I shall never see Stefan again.*

At once his image appeared in front of her, bright-eyed, mischievous, beckoning, and she burst into tears.